HER FIRST AMERICAN

ALSO BY LORE SEGAL

Other People's Houses (1964)

Lucinella (1978)

★　　★　　★　　★　　★

HER FIRST AMERICAN

a novel by

Lore Segal

THE NEW PRESS

NEW YORK
LONDON

Requests for permission to reproduce selections from this book should
be made through our website: https://thenewpress.com/contact.

This revised edition published by The New Press, 2004
First published in paperback by The New Press, New York 1994
First published by Alfred A. Knopf, Inc., New York, 1985.
Portions of this work originally appeared in *The New Yorker*.
Distributed by Two Rivers Distribution

ISBN 978-1-56584-949-5 (pbk.)

LIBRARY OF CONGRESS CATALOGING-IN-PUBLICATION DATA

Segal, Lore Groszmann. Her first American.
I. Title.
PS3569.E425I4 1985   813'.54   84-43067
ISBN 978-1-56584-145-1 (pbk.)

Book design by Cecily Dunham

The New Press publishes books that promote and enrich public
discussion and understanding of the issues vital to our democracy
and to a more equitable world. These books are made possible by
the enthusiasm of our readers; the support of a committed group
of donors, large and small; the collaboration of our many partners
in the independent media and the not-for-profit sector;
booksellers, who often hand-sell New Press books;
librarians; and above all by our authors.

www.thenewpress.com

To Beatrice
To Jacob

And for David

. . . the man replied that there was no
need of testing the load, he said that once
we put it on our head either it was heavier
than what we could carry or not, anyhow
we should carry it . . .

AMOS TUTUOLA
(from *The Palm-Wine Drinkard*)

prints, contrasting, metaphorically, the uniquely American nature of the color prejudice brought to life in the memories and stories of the daugher's black friends. When the mother is taken back to Europe to find the place where her husband was shot in the street by the Nazis, she is unable to do so. In other words, there is only memory, accurate or false, and the sometimes unbearable truth of our humanity is how we feel about those memories or the myths that they engender over time and *against* time.

Lore Segal describes her book as an "upside down Henry James novel because Henry James believed that the innocent American would expand his knowledge, or her knowledge, by coming in contact with the sophisticated European. Here the European is the innocent and the black man is endlessly sophisticated. She does not teach him anything, but he teaches her everything." The wonder of the novel is that all of his sophistication comes through with authority, so much so that he becomes one of the most perfectly detailed and believable characters in the entire sweep of our fiction. On one side he is the nearly helpless drunk, on another the droll world traveler, on another an expert on American behavior and misbehavior. He is greatly respected by his friends, black and white alike, for his formidable intellect, his charm, and his broad range of human comedy, which steps back and forth from the dirty details of the alley to the twinkling wit of the palace. His appetite for life is revealed by the range of people he has come to know and accept for all their strengths, weaknesses, and peculiarities. He is capable of charming a representative of an adoption agency because he can tell by her accent exactly where she hails from in England, which is no more difficult for him than cajoling sleeping pills from his doctors or blithely holding together a fascinating group of racially mixed friends, with whom he and the young immigrant girl spend a summer in the Connecticut countryside. Though his alcoholism brings him many troubles and a number of visits to the nuthouse, his stature is never reduced and he remains an expansive soul whose vitality rises above the sorrowful fate foreshadowed by the bottles of bourbon that he consumes and avoids in the running battle that is his life.

Nearly overstuffed with memorable characters, the novel so adroitly draws distinctions in manners from the worlds of the black and the white, the Christian and the Jew, that stereotypes have no hope of prevailing in the face of such convincing variety within each group. No single character is *just* white or black, Christian or Jew, an achievement that comes through Lore Segal's fearless evocation of points of view, beliefs, and animosities. Whatever their backgrounds, not one of these men or women escapes the irresistible literary net with which Segal captures the differently hued butterflies of human personality. The sustained mastery and the quality of the writer's ear, revealed in the long scenes, might therefore be insipidly misunderstood if thought of as no more than "set pieces"—the wedding parties and the lengthy dinner parties, the scenes at the United Nations, a seder dinner, an Alcoholics Anonymous meeting, and an Episcopalian funeral, are equal in their intimacy to the moments when the young woman is alone with her lover, be she happy or struggling with the complex of despair and frustration she has chosen by embracing him as her man.

I still cannot say whether this is or is not a masterpiece, but I know that it is close enough to maintain a lasting place not only in American literature but in that of the world. As we move planetwide into more and more complicated versions of integration and the hostilities wrought by memory and myth, this novel maintains the kind of welcoming humanity that lifts up the tragic optimism we forever need in order to better recognize our strengths and our weaknesses. That is the level of accomplishment that only the best of our writers ever achieve. See that woman out there, confidently circling the bases in the wake of a home run that rose and rose until it left the bleachers behind and landed in the parking lot? That's Lore Segal.

—Stanley Crouch

Acknowledgments

This book has been long in the making. The author was simultaneously engaged in bringing up the children and bringing home that bacon. Sincere thanks are due for the incomparable gift of time to: The National Council on the Arts and Humanities, the Creative Artists Public Service Program of New York State, the National Endowment for the Arts, and the Illinois Arts Council.

I want to thank the Villa Serbelloni for a splendid three weeks' residency on Lake Como, and the Corporation of Yaddo for many invitations to paradise.

I am particularly grateful to the Department of English of the University of Illinois at Chicago for permitting a teaching schedule that lets the writer write.

Thanks are due to several friends who made the time to read the ms., to Barry Schechter, who helped me with my Americana; to Herbert Hill, who always knows more stories; to Alan Friedman, who says "Put this here and that there, and move that over" to make it work; to Bernard Hallote, for the invention of Fishgoppel's name.

I thank my mother and my two children for their humorous kindness when they talk to me while I'm listening to the story inside my head.

HER FIRST AMERICAN

PART ONE

ILKA HAD BEEN three months in this country when she went West and discovered her first American sitting on a stool in a bar in the desert, across from the railroad. He was a big man. He bought her a whiskey and asked her what in the name of the blessed Jehoshaphat she was doing in Cowtown, Nevada.

"Nevada?" Ilka had said. "I have believed I am being in Utah, isn't it?"

"Utah!" The big American turned a sick color. "Where the hell am I?" he asked the barman.

"Hagen, ass end of Noplace, Nevada," replied the barman and swiped his dish towel at a glass mug.

"Aha! So!" Ilka sipped her whiskey and, hiding her smiling teeth inside her glass, said, "I do not believe."

"What don't you believe?" asked the American.

"That I sit in Utah."

"Nevada," said the American.

"I do not believe Nevada, Utah, America."

It had taken Ilka Weissnix more than a decade to get to the United States, of which she knew next to nothing and came prepared to think ill: Ilka was twenty-one. The Viennese Weissnixes had known so little of their relations, the Litvak Fishgoppels, that Ilka was not aware that she had an American cousin until some time after the war was over. It was early in the fifties when the cousin traced Ilka to Lisbon and sent her an affidavit and a ticket.

Fishgoppel came into New York to fetch the refugee from Idlewild. *"Ich muss nemen ein examen. Ich muss gein back to school,*" shouted Fishgoppel across the roar of the subway that carried them uptown. *"Ihr will stay in mein apartment in New York, O.K.?"*

"Excuse please?" Ilka shouted back.

"My horrible Yiddish!" yelled Fishgoppel and hit herself in the head.

"Yiddish!" shouted Ilka, lighting on a word she understood. "By us in Vienna has nobody speaken Yiddish outside the *Polischen!*"

"What?" hollered Fishgoppel, and they laughed and turned out both palms of their hands, perfectly understanding each other to mean "Too noisy. One can't hear oneself talk!"

Fishgoppel's small Upper West Side apartment had the simple layout of a dumbbell. The front door opened into the middle of a narrow foyer with a room at each end.

"One for you," said Fishgoppel, "and one for your mother, when we get her to America."

"I do not know where is my mother living. My father was found after the war on the list of dead but not my mother. I do not know if she is living," said Ilka. She was looking around at Fishgoppel's possessions. Each object was out of harmony with every other in a way for which the laws of probability did not account. Ilka looked at Fishgoppel. Only a persevering spirit could have parlayed such skin, such wonderful black hair and sweet, clever eyes into this dowdiness. Ilka stared at the crosswork of faint scars, like a deformation on Fishgoppel's fair young forehead; the hallucination as suddenly passed: it was only Fishgoppel frowning. "Look at the time!" Fishgoppel spread the subway map in front of Ilka. "Here is where you get off for the employment agency. This is where they give English classes. Are you going to manage?"

"Thanks!" said Ilka.

"The butcher on the corner of Broadway speaks German. This is my number. Call me. I'll call you. I'll come in for a day as soon as my exams are over. Will you be all right?"

. . .

Minutes after Fishgoppel had run to catch the train back to New Haven, Ilka took the elevator down and burst into the streets of New York, which looked like the streets she remembered from her childhood Vienna—the same flat, staid, gray façades except that here, in front of her, walked a real American couple, having an American conversation. Ilka accelerated and walked close behind them and perfectly understood the old man saying, "Because I wear proper shoes in which a person can walk." The old woman said, "Because you don't have bunions." The man said, "Because I wear proper shoes," and Ilka recognized that it was German they were speaking, with the round Viennese vowels cushioned between relaxed Viennese consonants.

When she got back, the telephone was ringing: Would Fishgoppel collect for the United Negro College Fund?

"I will collect. I am the cousin from Fishgoppel," said Ilka: Ilka wanted to see the inside of an American home.

The nameplate outside apartment 6-A said "Wolfgang Placzek." He handed her fifty cents through the cracked door. While 6-B went to look for change, Ilka put her head inside the foyer and saw the little green marble boy extracting the same splinter from his foot, on the same tree stump, on the same round lace doily on which he had sat in Ilka's mother's foyer in Vienna. The woman came back. "Nix! Nothing," she said. It did her grief but her man was not to house. Six-C was Fishgoppel, and 6-D would not open; the voice through the peephole came from Berlin. It did her grief but her sister had a stroke had and was to bed.

"*How?*" Ilka asked the woman at the employment agency, who told Ilka to come back when she had practiced her English. "With *whom* shall I praxis? *You* are the only American I met in New York? The onlies others I met are in my English class, which are yet other outlanders, which know always only other outlanders, which know yet lesser English as I!"

The woman on the other side of the desk drew her head back from Ilka's complaining. She was a stout woman with a lot of useless bosom and looked as if there was some complaining *she* might do, give her a chance. "New York," she said to Ilka, "is not America, like all you people always think."

When Fishgoppel came to town to see how Ilka was getting on, Ilka complained that New York was not America. Fishgoppel frowned, did some mental arithmetic, and offered Ilka a week's trip West.

Ilka practiced her English on the train conductor. He leaned over the back of the seat in front of the girl and asked her to guess how long he had been on this Denver–Los Angeles run.

"Excuse please?" Ilka smiled the self-conscious smile she knew from her mirror, and regretted. It exposed her two long front teeth with the little gap between that made her look, she believed, like a friendly village simpleton. Ilka was a thin girl. In certain lights her hair matched the color of her eyes. After she acquired the word Ilka thought herself khaki, but interesting. Ilka thought she was interesting. She smiled sweetly, apologetically at the round, pink-faced conductor; he looked like a healthy old baby. He held up three left and two right fingers. "Thirty-two years on this same run!"

"*Aha!*" said Ilka.

"Know it like"—he pointed into his pocket, "like the"—he held up the palm of his hand and pointed at it. "I'll be back," he promised.

Ilka looked out. The land was level as the primordial waters before the creation of breath disturbed its surface, uninterrupted by objects, man-made or natural, as far as the ruler-straight horizon west and north and east, except outside the window, on the left, where a grid of apartment buildings formed a small, perfectly square city. Its near perimeter coincided with the platform of the railroad. The train stopped when it had aligned Ilka with Main Street, at the far end of which a mountain, like a giant purple ice-cream cone, stood upside down on the perfectly flat world. Ilka wanted somebody to turn to and say, "I don't believe this!" She might have imagined that she had imagined this Atlantis onto the desert floor but for the details, which were not in her experience to engender: bars, bowling alleys, barber shops, eating places with neon signs that ran and jumped and stopped, and switched from pastel greens to pastel yellows to pinks leached out by the tail end of daylight.

Ilka's conductor returned: a ninety-minute stopover. He handed her down the steps. And that was how Ilka Weissnix from Vienna came to stand in the middle of the New World, she thought. Ilka thought she was in Utah, and she thought Utah was dead in the heart of America.

Ilka was intensely excited. She ran up the platform until it stopped across from the long, low building which formed the northwest corner of the tiny city. The low building was made of a rosy, luminescent brick and quivered in the blue haze of the oncoming night—it levitated. The classic windows and square white letters, saying AMERICAN GLUE INC., moved Ilka with a sense of beauty so out of proportion to the object, Ilka recognized euphoria. It knocked out her common sense of time. Afraid of being left behind, but more afraid of missing what more there might be to be seen, Ilka turned and ran close alongside the train until the platform stopped across from the shack that held this northeast end of town down upon the desert the way one of those little gummed corners fixes your snapshot in its place on the page of your album. A neon sign read LARR 'S B R ND EATS.

With the reluctance of one who puts a foot out into an alien element, Ilka stepped off the platform, crossed the dirt road, and, with a palpitating heart, depressed the handle of the door.

The barman went on wiping his glass mug with an agitated white dishcloth, but the huge American on the stool swiveled to see who had walked in. Ilka, feeling looked at, ducked into the booth nearest the door. By the time she had settled and raised her self-conscious village smile, the American on the bar stool had returned to his conversation with the barman. Ilka felt ever so faintly hurt. There were women—Ilka knew this—who got looked at longer. Anyway, this was an older man, a very large, stout man, with a look of density, as if he were heavier, pound by pound, than other men of equal bulk. His grizzled hair was cut peculiarly short. It was flattened against the large skull in a way the girl did not understand. His skin had a yellow hue, the nose was flat and the mouth wide—like a frog's, Ilka would have thought, if it had not been for a look about him of weight, of weightiness, like a Roman senator, thought Ilka.

Anyway, what Ilka had come West for was American conversation and she listened and thought the barman said, "Coming down cats and dogs." Thinking she hadn't listened properly, Ilka listened harder. The barman said, "This kid I knew in high school's dad is in this cab coming down Lex I think it was."

The man on the bar stool said, "This is in New York?" which Ilka understood. Encouraged, she leaned forward to really listen, and the barman said, "Where else is there? Guess the brakes quit on the guy. This kid's dad. He lost his thumb, busted both legs, left side of his face is all chewed up, and this pip of a shyster out of nowhere is running alongside the stretcher, says he can get him a lump sum in compensation, which is what I'm telling you is what you have to have, once in your lifetime, give you an opportunity."

Ilka was trying to connect "shyster" (the English cognate, presumably, of the German *scheissen* with the "er" suffix meaning "one who shits," a "shitter") and "lump" (as in a mattress) plus "sum" (the mathematical result of totting up), and missed everything the barman said after that. Ilka gave up. She stud-

ied the red plastic booth in which she sat. Ilka thought that
the back seats out of two automobiles had been placed face to
face. Three booths times two back seats—that was six red automobiles!

The barman said, "Got the wife to sue for deprivation of sex-
ual excess, is it?"

"Access?" suggested the older man on the stool.

"You name it, he sued for it." The barman walked around
the bar and was coming toward Ilka. "Physicaltormentalan-
guishdiminishedreproductivity what'll it be?" he asked her.

"Excuse please?" Ilka said and smiled at him with her apologetic teeth and shook her head and said, "I can not yet so
well English."

The barman, who seemed worn to bone and nerve by a
chronic high of exasperation, raised his chin like a dog about
to howl and said, "You want a drink?"

"Please, coffee," said Ilka.

"Coffee!" howled the barman in a voice outside the human
range of sound, walked back around the bar and disappeared
through a door into a region beyond Ilka's sight and outside
the range of her imagination. She pictured a blackness out of
which the barman's voice went on with what he was saying to
the man on the bar stool: "This kid's dad I was telling you
comes out the hospital, lost his hearing in one ear—or *wishes*
he lost it, is what he used to tell us kids, so he wouldn't hear
this noise all the time like someone was pissing inside his ear,
loud like Niagara."

"Jesus!" the man on the stool said. "That could drive a man
to drink."

"Only thing would drown it out was trumpets turned with
the volume all the way up. See," said the barman, "this is hi-fi
coming in. This guy. He buys every damn book, reads up in
all the magazines and goes into audio with his lump sum in
compensation, makes a mint with his own home in Bayshead,

but you don't get a lump sum," said the barman, coming out with Ilka's coffee, "you don't got a opportunity I don't care what anybody is going to tell you."

"Isn't that the truth," said the stout older man. And raising his voice to the tenor pitch that best carried into the booth by the door, where the young blonde sat watching him, he said, "The problem, as I see it, is how you're going to put your idea over."

"My idea?" said the barman.

"I can introduce it for you in the next session of the United Nations, or were you thinking in terms of an amendment to the Bill of Rights?"

Ilka was surprised at the high, hilarious note coming from such a heavy, older man.

"Was I thinking . . . ?" said the barman.

"We hold these truths to be self-evident, that all men, blah blah blah, have the unalienable right to a lump sum?"

"Once in your lifetime," said the barman, "is all I'm saying to you."

"See if I understand you, now, this is for white only, or for colored as well?"

"Listen! I ain't prejudiced. I'm New York!" said the barman. "Ain't I standing here? Ain't I talking with you like you are a person? You want me, I'll make you a sandwich."

"Jesus God!" the man on the stool said gaily. "Imagine every one of us black sons of a gun going to have an equal opportunity, same as any white man in the land, to get our thumbs, legs, and eardrums busted! Let me check *this* out with you now: everybody has to first get pretty much chewed up, is what you're saying?"

"That's what it's compensation *for!* The way I figure you don't get something for nothing, but how it is now you get nothing period."

"It's an idea will revolutionize the economy!"

"It is? It will?" The barman looked nervous.

"Sure!" the man on the stool said. He crossed one ankle over the other, effecting a quarter-turn in Ilka's direction. "Say you take the Social Security money for the year X and, instead of pissing it away on the poor, the old, and the sick, you divvy it up—let's say three thousand bucks apiece, to every baby born in that same year, black *and* white, and—stick with me here—the government invests each baby's three thousand at, say, five percent, till the baby gets to be twenty-nine—or would you say thirty-five?"

"Thirty-five has more horse sense," said the barman.

"O.K. Now," said the man on the stool, "when the baby is thirty-five they cut off its thumbs, break its legs, pierce its eardrums, and hand it the lump sum of . . ." he patted his breast pocket, took out an envelope, and said, "You got a pencil there? Thank you. Three thousand at five percent times thirty-five compounded"—the man on the stool did arithmetic for a while—"dollars fifteen thousand seven hundred and sixty!" he said triumphantly.

The barman looked agitated. "And the poor, old, sick folks?"

"*What* poor, old, sick folks!" cried the man on the stool. "*They* got *their* lumps when *they* were thirty-five and made a mint! They own their own homes, colored, whites, everybody! In Bayshead!"

"I guess," said the barman.

Ilka was studying the expanse of the older man's tweed back—an autumnal mix of heather flecked with rust, with mauves and greens. . . . Ilka had observed the same easy angle of the wrist of the hand which held the cigarette in other men, and in women, too. She thought it connoted the carnal know-how of which she despaired for herself. Ilka could see the man's tongue laughing. She had never seen a grown person laugh so loudly for such a long time, with the mouth so wide open. Now he raised his right hand. He was beckoning. Ilka turned to see who might have come in the door to claim the gesture, but there was no one behind her; she turned back with her conscious smile, trusting it to double for an acknowledgment, if he meant her, or for a general complaisance, in case he did not.

"You ever get yours?" the man was asking the barman.

"Worse luck," said the barman. "I was in construction, damn near killed in this cave-in. Man, it was a mess! See, here's what I'm telling you, now. When they used to hand me my thirty bucks Saturday nights, by Monday morning—like you said—I pissed it away, what else is there? But you put five thousand smackeroos *into* my hand, I'm a capitalist! I'm going to hang on to every last lousy buck! I'm going to *make* something out of myself, right?"

"What did you do?"

"I read where they were building this four-lane highway, and I come out here, I see the surveyors with my own eyes! Outside this window! I figure I buy cheap—the big money wants to be *on* Main—do it up nice, like New York. You can't tell now, but ten years back this was a real sharp place. I figured every one of the fellers be coming in here for his breakfast, lunch, a home away from home and booze it up nights for the three or whatever years it's going to take them to build me a highway up to my front door, I sell out at a price, go back— open myself a classy joint on Third Avenue, how can I lose?"

"So what happened?" asked the man on the stool.

"They built the highway four miles the other side of town, is what happened."

"You going to sell out, then?"

"To who? Are you going to be fool enough to take my monkey and put it on your back? Are you? No, you are not!"

"You got the custom from the railroad," the man said.

"Oh, right!" the barman said. "There's the ten-forty-five a.m. Denver–L.A. and the twelve-fifteen L.A.–Denver, and the five-forty you got off of, and the eight p.m. the lady came on"—he indicated Ilka watching in her booth—"that connects

with the dinky at nine-forty. Maybe a couple rednecks drop
in for a beer and put two nickels in the juke. You want another
bourbon?"

"Maybe the lady will join me?"

He meant me, thought Ilka, gratified. It was me he beckoned.

"Will you have a drink?"

"Thanks, no," she said. "I must soon again back into my
train. Thanks!"

But the man had risen and was standing with a nice formality
next to his bar stool. It took Ilka a moment of time to extricate
her feet from under the table and walk across the floor. The
man waited until she had seated herself before resuming his
place. He offered her a cigarette. "Thanks, no." Ilka did not
smoke. Ilka did not drink.

"Yes, you do," said the American.

"Likör makes me—how do you say that in English?" Ilka
did him a charade and he said, "Liquor makes you throw up?
No, it doesn't." To the barman he said, "The lady will have
a Black and White diluted with a little water, start her off nice
and easy. I'll teach you how to drink," he told Ilka.

"You are living here?" Ilka asked him.

"Christ no!" the man said. He told Ilka that he was en route
from California to New York for a brand-new start and had
stopped off for one last, big bender.

"Speak, please, slower," said Ilka.

"I'm going to tie one on," explained the man. It was here
that he asked Ilka what in the name of the blessed Jehoshaphat
she was doing in Cowtown, Nevada, which Ilka had mistaken,
and was, for years to come, to persist in mistaking, for Utah.
Ilka told him she was looking for the real America. "New
York," she explained, "is not the real."

"Well, this is," the man on the stool said. His left hand,
which held an easy cigarette between fore and middle fingers,
performed a baroque motion that seemed to take in the air

around them, the bar they sat in, the drink on the bar top, around which his other hand lay loosely curled, and ended in a downward direction, pointing to his own person, at his considerable stomach, including the genitals—or maybe not?

Ilka said, "Except the woman from the employment agency you are my first real American."

"Of the second class," said the big man.

Ilka shook her head and smiled. "I am understanding always lesser and lesser."

It was here Carter Bayoux introduced himself. He said, "I'm a wonderful teacher."

"I am Ilonka Weissnix," said Ilka. "And I want to learn"— and Ilka, too, made an inclusive gesture—"this all."

They shook hands. He said, "Let me buy you a sandwich. What do you like?"

Ilka smiled inside her glass and said, "I ken not yet the names of the American sandwich."

"You make Reubens?" the man asked the barman.

"Do fish swim?" is what Ilka thought the barman replied before he disappeared back into his private darkness.

"I'll teach you the New York sandwich," the man said.

"You are a teacher? You don't look like," Ilka said and blushed; she thought she was flirting.

The American regarded her with his bright brown stare and asked, "Like what do I look?"

"That," said Ilka, "is what I am not understanding. When I walk on Broadway and see an old Viennese pair I understand even from behind . . ." Ilka stopped, appalled at the number and the complication of the English sentences ahead.

"Go on," the man said.

Ilka shook her head. She meant that she recognized the proportions, height by width, of the old man's back, which fit and failed to fit, in the same places, into the same suit Ilka's father used to wear to the shop Monday through Saturday. The fabric that upholstered the old man's fat wife was the navy cotton,

patterned with the same cabbage roses, bows, and violins on
Great-Aunt Mali's Sunday dress. Those German prewar cottons
wore like iron and had outlasted Great-Aunt Mali, as well as
Ilka's father, three aunts, four uncles, and two of the cousins
who used to gather for Aunt Mali's afternoons of *Kaffee und
Gugelhupf.* Aunt Mali's oversize table had stood square in the
middle of the room; the blue tile stove in the left corner gave
off too much heat. The walls were dark and striped, the curtains
lace, and the drapes flowered and fringed with black wooden
beads, which little Ilka, lying on the Turkey carpet—cozy, too
hot, bored, more than half asleep—used to pull off one after
the other. Aunt Mali had sat at the table drinking coffee and
watched Ilka.

Ilka shook her head and said, "It is too complicate to tell
it. But when I look at you . . ."

"Ye-es?"

Ilka shook her head. She meant that she did not recognize
his hair, and that the size of his mouth and his laughter did
not go with the urbane way he bent his wrist and crossed his
ankles; that the luxurious tweed of his jacket contradicted his
flattened nose with its small outgrowth of wild flesh at the
bridge, which intimated to the girl disastrous chances, moving
accidents his youth had suffered.

Ilka said, "Take for an example these two Americans which
are there coming in by the door." She swiveled and watched
the newcomers settle into the booth she had recently vacated.
"Larry!" they shouted. "Couple beers, Larry!" One was a little
shorter, with a barrel chest, the other a few years younger, perhaps. Both were in their thirties, of middling height, and wore,
it seemed to Ilka, their undershirts. They had ruddy arms and
round heads and looked underdone, as if they had been taken
prematurely out and put down in the world.

Ilka said, "I look: I am seeing two men, but I cannot imagine
what are they working for a living, how dress themselves their
wives, how is it looking inside their rooms . . ."

The one who was perhaps younger stuck his head out of the booth and called for Larry. "What's with Larry?" He looked slowly around the room, and the American on the stool said, "Keep talking," in a high, different voice that made Ilka look at him to see what had happened: Nothing had happened. There was nothing different in the way his ankles crossed, his right hand surrounded the glass on the bar. He had not moved so much as his eyes to take in the newcomers. He sat like a cartoon of a smoker drawn by the lazy new breed of animators: head, neck and trunk remained fixed; only the left arm, pivoting at the shoulder, brought the cigarette to his mouth and took it away again. In this new voice, pitched in the high, thin register of the castrato, he said, "I'll buy you dinner over on Main Street."

Ilka said, "But Larry is making already our sandwich, isn't it?" And here came Larry with two foaming mugs, which he carried around the bar and across the floor. He set them down on the table between the two men and slid into the booth, next to the one with the chest. (The aborted and unexplained sandwich Ilka laid away in the patient back part of the mind where a child keeps the things it doesn't know what to make of, and other things it doesn't know it doesn't understand. There they lie unattended, but available to join with future information that will elucidate some but not all.)

The man on the stool had smoked his cigarette down to a nubbin. He said, "We leave separately."

"Excuse me?"

"Get up. Go out the door, walk to Main Street, and wait for me."

"But," said Ilka, "I can wait in here."

The man was patting his two trouser pockets, his right and left jacket pocket; he located his wallet. Was it that his neck had thickened, or shortened? Or withdrawn into his shoulders? Had the ears retracted? The head and shoulders had streamlined as if an outside pressure, failing to eliminate his person, had compacted it and reduced the size without affecting the bulk. He looked like a high-caliber torpedo.

Ilka saw what she saw and stored it away in the back of her mind. She said, "Yes, so, then, I wait corner Main Street," and rose. He did not raise his head; he was busy with the wallet.

"We are not all white" was what Ilka thought one of the men inside the booth had said and she stopped, and looked. The man with the big chest was looking at her. It was Ilka to whom he was talking.

Ilka said, "Excuse, please?" and smiled apologetically and leaned to listen more closely. The other, younger man, and the barman, too, were looking at Ilka. She said, "I am new in America. I cannot yet so well understand." The man looked her straight in the eye and, enunciating very clearly, said it again: "We are not all white." Ilka smiled. She shook her head. She didn't understand. As she went out the door, the barman was asking the two men, "Either of you fellows ever once in your lifetime got a lump sum? Did *you* have a opportunity?"

This end of town was deserted and dark, the way the blacked-out wartime cities of Europe had been dark, except for that same curious pink glow Ilka had observed in the night sky over Manhattan. She imagined that it emanated from the noisy neon lights of every Times Square or Main Street, floated upward and spread like a comforter of rosy, possibly noxious haze over America.

Ilka waited at the curb and presently the big American from the bar stood beside her. He kept a slice of the night air between them. The purple mountain had been assumed into the blackness that pepped up the colored lights. Over the restaurant across the street a blue cow blinked glamorous Disney lashes once, twice, and went out. THE BLUE COW spelled itself in capitals. Ilka felt excited and hilarious: on both thronging sidewalks everyone was male and young.

"I believe *you* have conjured this all, isn't it?"

"I have conjured," said the big American, looking at her. Then he looked deliberately across the street and back at Ilka, and said, "You and I stand here, side by side, but I don't know what the hell you're seeing."

"That *is* it, which I have been meaning," said Ilka with a sensation of bliss. She came, afterward, to identify this as the moment in which she had fallen in love; it coincided with a break in the traffic and the man's first, slightest touch, under her elbow. He withdrew his hand as soon as he had assisted her across the street and up the other sidewalk.

"Where would you like to eat?"

"I would like it that you are choosing."

"Right," he said. He walked her past The Blue Cow, past the Bar and Beef, past the Steak and Swill, and Harry's Hash, but at The Versailles—no better, it seemed to Ilka, and no worse—he opened and held the door for her, walked her past the empty window table, past a second empty table, and made a U-turn around a table from which three men raised simultaneous eyes. The three men watched a very large middle-aged, light-skinned Negro marching out the door with a thin blonde following behind him.

Back in the street he asked her, "Are you hungry?"

"Not very," said Ilka.

They passed Harry's Hash and the Steak and Swill. Ilka said, "I don't understand what for men are all these . . ."

"Men," said the man. They passed the Bar and Beef. "Good enough fellows, as fellows go—care for their kids, satisfy their wives some of the time, do their work as well as can be expected, and pay their taxes, mostly, go to church, or not, and will string me up as soon as look at me."

"String you?" Ilka did not understand him. She said, "I think I must soon again instep back in my train, isn't it?"

"I will wait with you," said the American. They walked past The Blue Cow. He supported her elbow across the dirt road and up onto the platform. They walked alongside the empty, darkened train. "You're not afraid of me?" he asked her.

It was this moment that brought to the forefront of Ilka's attention the series of violent occurrences that had been unfolding parallel with, and on a level below, the actual events: those two men in the bar had been the law, drinking unwitting beers in the same room with the object of their manhunt—Ilka's big American on the bar stool. In the dark, under the sinister pink sky, he had jumped her. Over The Versailles was a sleazy room in which Ilka lay naked and strangled across an open bed. Ilka looked at these imaginings, looked at the man who walked beside her and understood that she did not believe, and had at no point believed, any part of them. Ilka said, "No."

They sat down on a bench underneath one of the half-dozen lamps, weak and unsteady as gaslight, that made no inroads upon the darkness.

"I would have liked to make love to you," said the American gloomily.

Ilka, who had not been in the habit of receiving propositions, understood this one as a courtesy, intended as a compliment. The American said, "When a man hasn't managed to buy a woman dinner, it is not conducive."

"I'm not so hungry," said Ilka.

"Well well well well well," said the big American. "I owe you."

They exchanged addresses. He wrote Fishgoppel's telephone number into a well-worn leather-bound address book. On the corner of an envelope he wrote down for Ilka the name of the hotel in New York where, he said, he used to live and might take a room, if they had one, until he figured out what the hell he was doing.

"There is my conductor," said Ilka.

"When do you get back to town?"

"Sunday," said Ilka. "Monday I must go again to—I call it the agency of unemployment."

"Ah, yes, indeed," the man said. He handed her up the steps.

She found her seat and let down the window. When had the platform filled with all these people saying good-bye, getting on the train? It took Ilka a moment to identify the back of the American from the bar stool, already walking away.

★   ★   ★

ILKA CONTINUED her westward trek. At the Grand Canyon she opened her eyes wide, wider, but it was too large to look at. And she never got to see Big Sur. A single, massive cloud hid everything from Malibu to San Francisco. There the mists rent. As through a ragged window Ilka beheld bridges, bays, islets, skies, mists. Something on a distant hill glimmered. Turner has taught nature these vistas! Charmed, exhilarated, euphoric, Ilka got back on the New York train a day ahead of schedule, which was silly of her: Why would he call on Saturday when she had told him she would not be back till Sunday? Sunday he might have decided to give the traveler a day of rest. If he called Monday, Ilka was not at home.

The early-Monday-morning commuters sat sleep-tranced, like veiled people. The woman next to Ilka sighed, "Ai Mamita!" out loud, which startled her awake. She was embarrassed and smiled apologetically at the people who turned their faces, without interest; they had already forgotten why they were looking, and relapsed into a shallower half-sleep, a step closer to the day.

The woman at the employment office sent Ilka across town, where an elegant brownstone housed the Council for Eretz Israel. A Mrs. Apfel interviewed Ilka tilting her head as if Ilka were a brand-new puppy. Ilka tried to explain to Mrs. Apfel the sort of American job she was looking for. (It was some time before Ilka's English was up to reading the novels of Henry James, which Fishgoppel kept bringing her. There Ilka was going to meet those refined grandeurs of places, persons, passions, virtues that she had in mind for herself, an intimation of which the girl thought that she had caught in the luxurious tweed jacket, the eloquent and witty hands, and the Roman head of the big American on the bar stool.)

Mrs. Apfel said, "We'll start you filing."

In the elevator like a rococo bird cage, Ilka said, "Can you, please, help searching my mother? I don't know if she is living." Mrs. Apfel's eyes glazed over with a film of tears.

She introduced Ilka to a roomful of elderly young women, who tilted their heads at Ilka. The one in a baby-blue hand-knit sweater set brought Ilka a chair and a stack of file cards, which Ilka was to file alphabetically, in chronological order. The pink cards, which listed what quantity of spare parts had been shipped to which kibbutz on what date, went into the top file. The orange cards cross-listed the dates on which each kibbutz had received what quantity of which spare parts, and when, and they went into the middle drawer. The yellow cards listing the names of the suppliers, and the dates on which they had shipped what quantity of spare parts to which kibbutz, went in the bottom. When Ilka loused up, the woman in the sweaters came and sorted her out.

On the subway platform, going home, Ilka stood next to a group of little round women in black coats, black hats, black shoes, gloves and purses. They talked excitedly in what Ilka recognized as Russian. Sure, said her friend in the sweater set, when Ilka questioned her next morning. The Russian consulate was two blocks east.

Fishgoppel came on Sunday and brought Ilka an oversized dictionary. Fishgoppel said there was a man living in her land-

lady's kosher household. He was from Vilna. He had lost a
pregnant wife. The child would have been eight years. Fishgoppel's forehead looked riddled. She said, "He speaks the pure,
classic Yiddish. He is teaching me. When your mother comes
she will tell me everything that happened."

"But my mother does not speak Yiddish," said Ilka. Ilka
was wanting to tell Fishgoppel about the man on the bar stool
in Utah.

"A bar? In Utah? I think Utah is dry."

"Maybe Nevada," said Ilka.

Fishgoppel brought out the map of America. Ilka looked in
the middle and there was Kansas.

Ilka showed Fishgoppel the envelope on which the American
had written the name of his hotel, and Fishgoppel was excited
and said, "The Bloomsbury Arms is where a lot of poets live.
What does your friend do?"

"I *think* he said a teacher. He will teach me about America."

Fishgoppel beamed at Ilka: A job at the Council for Eretz
Israel! A friend who was a teacher! Fishgoppel returned to New
Haven with a perfectly new notion that everything might be
going to be all right.

But the American never called. The pain was slight—a
chance acquaintance, in an improbable place. Ilka tossed away
the envelope, or lost it.

In the Council elevator she met Harvey Blum from Youth Aliyah on the fifth floor. Harvey was taking Russian at the New
School. Ilka told him about the contingent from the Russian
consulate, who might be talking God-only-knew what state se-
crets. Harvey walked Ilka to the subway. They stood near the
chattering women and Harvey translated what they were saying
into Ilka's ear: "I wish the train would hurry up and come!"
"Yesterday I waited eleven minutes for a train to come." "In
the rush hour trains are supposed to come every three or four

minutes." "So! Where is the train? Why doesn't it come?" "Yesterday I waited eleven minutes." "Hurry up, train!"

That evening Ilka came upon the envelope with the name of the American's hotel stuck into the outside pocket of her other handbag. Ilka threw the envelope away, but next morning it was under the sugar bowl on the kitchen table. In the evening it was holding her place in *Daniel Deronda*, which Fishgoppel had brought her.

Ilka looked up the Hotel Bloomsbury Arms in the directory. Ilka was not a girl who could call a man on the telephone—but anyone can call a hotel. . . .

A woman's voice said, "Bloomsbury Arms can I help you?" and Ilka said, "Lives there, please, Mr. Carter Bayoux?"

"Mr. Carter Bayoux is not living here at the present," said the woman's voice.

"Where, please, lives Mr. Bayoux?"

"Hold the line," said the voice. A pause and a man's voice, polite and unpleasant, said, "What can I do for you?"

"Is this the Bloomsbury Arms Hotel?"

"Yes, ma'am."

"Please, is there living Mr. Carter Bayoux?"

"Mr. Bayoux is registered at the hotel," said the hateful voice, "but he is not living here."

"Where is Mr. Bayoux?"

"In the bughouse" was what Ilka thought the man said. "Where, please?"

"In the bughouse," the man said.

Ilka looked up "bug" in her new dictionary:

> bug (bug), *n.*, *v.*, bugged, bugging.—*n.* 1. Also called true
> bug. a hemipterous insect. 2. (not used scientifically) any
> insect or insectlike invertebrate. 3. *Chiefly Brit.* a bedbug.
> 4. *Informal.* any microorganism, esp. a virus: *He was laid
> up for a week by an intestinal bug.* 5. . . .

It was the end of May. Fishgoppel's exams were over. Her thesis was entitled "Anti-Semitic Paraphrasis in Poetry in the English Language: The Jew from Beowulf to Pound." Fishgoppel brought Ilka *Oliver Twist* to read.

Fishgoppel discovered the free "Baroque Series" in the Village.

"A village?" Ilka asked.

They brought a blanket and Fishgoppel read Ilka the program notes. Fishgoppel happened to know that the date of Pergolesi's birth coincided with the anti-Jewish edict of Cita on Flumen, which had incited a decade of pogroms. The concertmaster lifted his arms. Fishgoppel sat taut with listening: she happened to have a passion for Pergolesi.

Ilka watched an overly tall, thin young Negro with a pretty face and neat mustache. He wore a light suit with a waistcoat and sat on the grass, snapping his fingers to a music inside his own head. An elderly couple, who looked like more of Ilka's aunts and uncles, turned on their folding chairs, frowned, and shook their heads at the young man, who leaned toward them and said, "It ain't got that swing!"

"Tz, tz," the elderly couple turned to say to each other.

"Psst," everyone on the grass said. The slow movement had begun and all the young man could do in the way of nodding his head and pumping his pelvis did not urge on Pergolesi's deliberate speed.

The applause was decorous. The Negro rose. He might have been a little high—there was a looseness of limb and tongue. He was sincerely baffled. "Where," he asked the elderly Viennese, "is the goddamn beat?"

"*Polizei,*" they murmured to each other.

The young man saw Ilka looking at him and came and squatted beside her. "Where's that swing?" he asked her. "Where," he asked Fishgoppel, "is the goddamn sex?"

★   ★   ★

ILKA WAS SURPRISED and gratified when the American called, early in October, to remind her of the dinner he owed her. Would she excuse him if he didn't come and pick her up? Could she find—let's see—did she know where Fifth Avenue was?

Yes, Ilka knew Fifth Avenue. Of course, she knew the Forty-second Street library, and the lions!

The only other person waiting on the windy stair was a big elderly Frenchman. He wore his beret pulled down over one ear. His black trenchcoat was unbuttoned and flared behind him like a great, single, black wing. He, too, looked up and down the avenue. He turned. He was looking directly at Ilka standing by the lion, so he couldn't—or could he?—be the American from Utah? It had begun to spatter rain. Ilka watched him cup his match trying to light a cigarette. Now he had it. Now he was walking toward her, and it was the man from the bar stool.

They had a decision to make, Carter Bayoux said to Ilka. He'd plumb forgot, when he invited her to dinner, that he had this damn wedding he was supposed to go to.

"Slower, please!"

"Daughter of a very old friend is getting married," he said. He'd leave it up to her: a wedding or a dinner?

"I was never yet at an American wedding."

"Wedding it is. *Afterwards* I'll take you to dinner. You won't mind if we give church the go-by?"

"Go buy? The church?"

"Let's go straight to the party," Carter Bayoux said.

"I was never yet in an American church."

"You go someday, then," Carter Bayoux said, "and tell me

all about it." He offered Ilka the courtesy of his hand under her arm down the great steps and hailed a cab.

A black maid received their coats.

"Where are you taking those?" Carter Bayoux called after her. "Can't stand it when they hide your coat. Cuts off the line of retreat."

Ilka was impressed with her new friend for bringing her into—with herself for being in—these immense blond rooms; every edge was sharp and new, every object large, expensive and excellent. The silence rustled with half a dozen early guests changing positions, trying to remember how one stands at ease. No one seemed acquainted. Almost the girl exclaimed. Again she had a sense that the man had conjured up what was in front of her eyes: Beyond the great plate window, twenty floors below, lay the city like a modern cosmology spreading outward from the square of Central Park to the retaining waters.

Ilka whispered, "Where am I? Which is north? Where is the Fifth Avenue?" But the man was gone. Ilka looked around. Everybody was looking in the direction of a small commotion at the bar, set up at the far end of the enormous room, where Carter Bayoux lofted a squat, short-necked bottle as if to toast the astonished bartender, saying loudly, "Save you the trouble of serving me is the way for you to think about it."

The bartender, a black man about Carter's age, watched his bottle walking off. Carter Bayoux was coming back to where Ilka stood. "Chivas Regal! Trust my old friend Harris! Come," he said, "I'll teach you to drink good Scotch." He walked away across the room and out the door.

Ilka did not follow. She stood and she looked around the room for him whom her soul would immediately recognize. It was Ilka's fear that *she* might not be recognizable—might be invisible. She kept her eye on a narrow-chested young man with an intelligent nose, who looked like someone Ilka knew and did not much care for. It irked Ilka that she could and could not remember of whom the man reminded her. He stood with his head at an excruciating angle, pretending to be reading the names on the spines of the books on the thick glass shelving. Ilka smiled at him and said, "Are you a friend from the bride or from the bridegroom?" The young man righted his head and pulled it back, as if he suspected himself of being propositioned. He adjusted his glasses and told Ilka the dates from and until which he and Philip had written speeches for which Washington congressman.

"Who is Philip?" asked Ilka.

"The bridegroom. Philip. You're a friend of Fanny's?"

"Who is Fanny?"

The young man showed his two front teeth in a self-conscious and apologetic smile, and Ilka thought, I don't have to put up with him, and said, "I must search my friend."

The foyer was filling up with guests arriving from the church, taking their coats off and greeting one another. It sounded like a railroad terminal. Where had Carter Bayoux gone? Now Ilka was glad of the presence of the narrow young man, who kept at her side: She had rescued him from his conspicuous singleness; he was not going to be lost again. He told her his name, which, with the simultaneous ringing of the doorbell and an influx of noisy newcomers, Ilka did not catch, or immediately forgot. She heard Carter Bayoux's voice saying, "The best Jew of you all is nothing but a first-generation drunk." Ilka and the young man turned as if a gun had gone off.

"It's Professor Bayoux!" a shrill, childish voice called out. A plump girl with blue-framed glasses and sweet, moist skin pressed around Ilka through an open door into the kitchen, where Carter Bayoux sat on the edge of the sink. He said, "Susan Goldshine, as I live and breathe!"

"That's Carter Bayoux!" the young man said to Ilka.

"Who is Carter Bayoux?" Ilka asked him.

The young man said, "Didn't you come with him?"

"Yes," said Ilka. "Who is he?"

But the young man was advancing his eager nose into the doorway. By bobbing her head, Ilka could see over and between the heads of the small crowd that had collected around the big man on the kitchen sink. He lifted his bottle by its short neck as if to toast the plump girl and said, "I'll teach you how to drink good Scotch."

The girl, whose back was to Ilka, raised her forefinger and said, "Maybe some people don't like to drink! Is that a sin?"

"No, my girl, a bore," Carter Bayoux said and he impaled her on his bright, brown stare entirely surrounded by the whites of his wide-open eyes; Ilka was jealous of the absolute attention with which the big man on the sink was teasing silly Susan Goldshine.

"Friend of mine at the UN once took me home to a seder," Carter Bayoux said, raising his voice to a tenor pitch, so that people in the foyer stopped and bobbed their heads to look over and around Ilka and the young man in the doorway. The colored maid had to carry the plates of canapés, like so many great flat posies, high above the heads of people pressing into the kitchen. "They served the wine in liqueur glasses," said Carter Bayoux, and between his two forefingers he described a glass the size of a midget's thimble. "Every time the damn bottle passed, the woman across from me put her hand over her glass"—he laid his right palm over the rim of the imaginary glass, which his left forefinger and thumb held by its imaginary stem—"and she'd say, 'That's enough for me, and that's enough for my husband.' " With his flat palm Carter covered the imaginary husband's infinitesimal thimble.

"Carter holding court in the kitchen," a man behind Ilka said.

"It's Harris!" cried Carter, abandoning the plump girl. He climbed off the sink and came, carrying his bottle, his arms wide. He embraced the elderly man, and seeing Ilka in the doorway, introduced the father of the bride to her. "Dr. Harris

Wharton. My friend Ilka Weissnix. So," he said, "our little
Fanny has done well for herself!"

"Fanny has done for herself," said the father of the bride.
His small, handsome features, chiseled out of some hard wood,
allowed minimal mouth action. The lips described a permanent
line associated with a sneer. "Come down to my office, Carter,
and sit. Let's get out of this."

"With all my heart," Carter Bayoux said.

The father of the bride swiveled and moved away as if wheels
propelled him. But now the young man breathing beside Ilka
adjusted his glasses and said, "You're Carter Bayoux."

"True," said Carter.

"I'm interested," the young man said, "in what you were
saying about Jews and drinking."

"Aha?" Carter Bayoux said.

"I mean the implications," the young man said, "of the dif-
ferences between Jews and . . . the other races."

"The other races. Ah," Carter Bayoux said. Ilka was looking
anxiously in the direction of the door through which the father
of the bride had gone out. She imagined him sitting in—what
sort of an "office"?—waiting for Carter, who had promised to
come—down where?—to sit with him.

"What races are those, now?" Carter Bayoux was asking the
young man.

"What I mean . . ." the young man said, "I mean that the
Jew tends to abstain from the use of alcohol. . . ."

Carter Bayoux's ear was inclined to the young man, but his
straying eyes caught sight of the bride moving in their general
direction. The bride looked like Ilka's notion of the American
girl—wide mouth, neat nose, good jaw, a fine color and long,
straight, blond hair. She came in her pale, elegant silks with
a boy's athletic stride, laughing her way through the good
wishes and bad jokes. When she saw Carter Bayoux she stood
still. He stepped forward, took her hand with his free hand and
said, "Give me your cheek."

Ilka watched Carter Bayoux kiss the bride on the cheek. He said, "You're looking very handsome."

The bride shrugged, dipped and shook her head and said, "I'm glad you could come."

"I could and I did," Carter Bayoux said.

Ilka watched the bride look down at her hand, which Carter Bayoux continued to hold. She said, "You haven't met Philip."

"That is correct," Carter Bayoux said.

"He's really nice. Really, Carter, I mean," the bride said.

"I never doubted it."

"I'm going to find him and bring him here. Wait, will you, Carter? Promise you'll wait right where you are?"

"*Ab*solutely," Carter Bayoux said. He watched the bride walk away and turning to Ilka said, "Let's go have dinner. *Where* did they put our bloody coats?"

"But," said Ilka, frowning, "you promised to sit in the father's office. . . ."

"Right," Carter said. "Let's go sit in the father's office."

"Then will the bride know where you are?" said Ilka in a small despair.

"I shouldn't think so," Carter Bayoux said.

"But you promised . . ." said Ilka and was shocked by his eyes bulging at her at such close quarters.

"Why," Carter Bayoux said in a high, complaining tone, "do all the little Jewish girls at this damn party keep on telling me what I am and what I'm not supposed to be doing!"

"Excuse me?" Ilka said.

"Doesn't occur to Miss Goddamn Goldshine I might be *choosing* to get drunk! It doesn't occur to *you* I might want *not* to meet Miss Fanny's brand-new husband, eh? Come." He opened the door to a carpeted stair, and Ilka learned a new English word: duplex. Here was a whole other apartment, including a doctor's fully furnished office, in which the father of the bride was sitting at his stiff ease behind a massive black desk.

Carter and Ilka took the two patients' chairs, facing him. "So?" Carter said, and there was a silence for some long moments, while Carter had difficulty lighting his cigarette. He reached for the ashtray, which stood by Dr. Harris Wharton's elbow. Ilka watched Dr. Wharton make no move to push it toward him.

"You don't like Fanny's man? What, as you doctors are supposed to ask, seems to be the trouble? He's rich, you tell me; nice, says Fanny; young, it's true, but that'll pass; and white— he *is* white, isn't he? Or is he Jewish, which will never pass."

Dr. Harris Wharton cracked his mouth to say, "Stick around, Carter. That young man is going to need some back-up screwing."

"Well well well well well," said Carter Bayoux. "Superb though your daughter indubitably is, you know the saying, 'Old farmers never die, only their tools wear out,' except yours, my dear Harris!" Carter cried. "Damn it, congratulations! I almost forgot! You are getting married, too! Harris, here," Carter Bayoux cried in his highest, gayest tones, "is getting married for the sixth time. The bride is seventeen, isn't that right, Harris?"

"No," said the father of the bride. "The fourth time. Nell is twenty-seven."

"Twenty-seven!" Carter Bayoux cried. "Goddamn! I mean God *help* you! Me is what I mean! You manage without Him. Harris, here, is sixty-one," Carter Bayoux turned to explain to Ilka, "aren't you, Harris? Starting a new family, a new career! Harris has given up doctoring and taken up—what have you taken up, Harris?"

"Oceanography."

"Oceanography! Amazing!"

"The human mechanism," said the bride's father, "unlike other machinery, increases its capacity with use. The more you work the more you work, the more you study the more you study. . . ."

"The more you screw the more you screw," Carter Bayoux said cheerfully, "the more you drink the more you drink, and the less, as it turns out, you screw or work or sleep. Talking of sleeping, Harris, I've got the granddaddy of insomnias. Prescribe me some of those little pills, will you?"

Someone knocked. The cake was about to be cut. The bride's father was waited for. He rose, swiveled, and rolled out the door.

"Now," Carter Bayoux said, "I'm going to liberate, as they used to say in the war, a couple of Harris's little pills. Then you and I will go have dinner." He walked around a partition of frosted glass. Ilka could see him moving about, could hear drawers and doors of metal cabinets being opened and closed. Ilka wished she were at home.

Carter Bayoux reappeared. He threw a couple of small capsules into his mouth, upended what remained in the Chivas bottle and said, "Let's go."

"I think I must home," Ilka said, "not too late."

Carter Bayoux stopped, turned and faced Ilka. He opened and dropped his arms in an outsize gesture to demonstrate the breadth of her freedom, his powerlessness to hold her. "Any time at all," he said.

Upstairs, at the bar, a damp, very young man with a flying tie and glistening black hair that looped into his eye thrust a hand at Carter. Carter was big, but the young man was bigger. Champagne and excitement were keeping him in perpetual motion. "I'm Philip," he said with a large, loose smile. "I'm glad to meet you, really."

"Not at all," Carter said, shaking his hand ceremoniously. "This is my friend Ilka Weissnix," he said, "and we are going to dine, after we have drunk your health." He filled a glass and emptied it into his mouth.

The large young bridegroom continued to smile affectionately at Carter Bayoux and said, "Fanny's told me all about you."

"All about me! Knows the heart of my mystery, eh! Smart girl, Fanny. We'll drink her health as well." He poured and emptied.

"I mean," the bridegroom said, "about your sleeping with her, in California, and it's all *right.*"

"No it's not, young man!" said Carter Bayoux and brought the bottle down onto the bar so that the glasses jumped. Heads turned. Into the sudden silence Carter Bayoux's high, outraged voice said, "That is not a thing one man says to another! Have you no sense of protocol?" And leaving the large young bridegroom standing flushed and loose-lipped in the center of the public eye, Carter set off in the direction of the foyer. Once he staggered a little to his right, but ignoring a dozen instinctive hands offering support, he overcompensated to the left, straightened out, lowered his head and bulled himself a path through the crowd. He stopped when he saw the bride's father and said, "Had a run-in with your callow son-in-law."

"Good," said Dr. Wharton.

"And now I am rather drunk, and I'm going home to sleep. Nice wedding." Carter Bayoux threw out an expansive arm to include Dr. Wharton's rooms, daughter, view, booze, and guests, and plowed on in the direction of the door, where Ilka's young man stood in wait. "What I was going to say . . ." he began.

Carter Bayoux looked at him, completely at sea.

"In respect," the young man said, "to the use of alcohol."

Carter Bayoux stared at the nervous young man, who said, "I mean that the Jew tends to abstain because of a subliminal perception, at all times, of a danger, don't you think?"

Ilka was struck. It was a notion that had not come her way before. They were waiting, Ilka and the young man, for the older man to say something, but he inclined his head at an angle of attention that excited the young man to greater exertions of clarity. "It is fascinating to me how differently the Negro responds under conditions of identical psychological stress." Here Carter Bayoux actually cupped his hand behind his ear. The young man adjusted his glasses. "Whereas the Jew will not allow himself any relaxation of control vis-à-vis the world's chronic hostility, the Negro wants to obliterate it."

"Drown the hell out of it, eh?" Carter Bayoux said.

"Precisely!" the young man cried. "I mean, you see what I mean?"

"Oh *dear*, yes!" Carter Bayoux said and resumed his interrupted march out through the door into the foyer, where he demolished plump Susan Goldshine, who stood in his path saying, "Professor Bayoux! You're not leaving!"

Carter stopped. "I'm not?" He looked so ill the girl asked, "Are you all right?"

"*Hell*, no!" Carter Bayoux said, and it was Ilka's recollection, afterward, that he had walked straight on and over the young woman, leaving her, in some final way, floored.

"Where," asked Carter, "are our bloody coats?"

Ilka found the bedroom and she found Carter's black trenchcoat among the crowd of outer garments on the temporary rack. What Ilka wanted was to get him out the door and to go back to the clever, bespectacled young man her own size and age, whose ideas were just new enough to be familiar. "You go home to sleep, isn't it? I stay a little longer here," she said, but Carter strode away and the great wing of his black coat flew out behind him. So Ilka snatched up her own coat and ran slap into the man's back. He had come to a full stop and was draining a glass of flat champagne someone had left on the dressing table, in the mirror of which Ilka saw, with a shock, that they were not alone: a man stood flattened against the opposite wall, his face hidden in the crook of his elbow on the mantel. His shoulders shook. It was the bridegroom silently weeping! He sobbed out loud in one last appeal, perhaps, but Carter was already marching out the door into the foyer, where he upended a stray glass on a console before passing into the silent corridor.

Inside the elevator Carter Bayoux put on his beret, turning himself back into Ilka's Frenchman. Ilka was working on an English sentence. She meant to say, Why did I come away with you when I wanted to stay at the party with that interesting young man? But the weight of the flesh of Carter Bayoux's face had gone all to jaw and jowl; the lids drooped; the corners of the mouth tucked down and back. Ilka recognized, with a thrill of interest, the look of a face alone with itself.

It drizzled. They strode side by side along the east-west block and had passed a French restaurant and an Italian restaurant before they rounded the corner into the avenue where Carter marched her into the nearest lighted door of a luncheonette—a sad, brown little place. They sat down in their wet coats. Ilka said, "Can I ask you a thing?"

"Not before I've ordered. Waiters all gone home? Tell you a story," he said.

"Slowly," said Ilka.

"Time I took Percival Jones to lunch—you've heard of Percival Jones?"

"No," said Ilka.

"I'll get you a copy of *Black Sons*. There's a real American novel."

"Ah, please!" Ilka said, and this was not Ilka's first jolt of suspicion that Carter Bayoux was telling her he was a Negro. She peered surreptitiously into his face; it was not black. Ilka studied his head, averted to survey the back of the luncheonette. If Carter Bayoux could be said to be a color it was a dangerous purple red, as if the blood had risen into his head, close to the surface of the skin. His short, flattened hair looked suddenly white.

"Waiter!" he shouted over his left shoulder, so that he did

not see the one standing behind his right. "Ah," he said. "Waiter. I will take a cup of coffee. The lady will have . . . what'll you have?"

"Coffee?" Ilka said.

"Make that two coffees, and, waiter, bring me a glass of water, right away, will you?"

"Tell the story," said Ilka.

"I took Percy Jones to this restaurant across from the UN," said Carter. "Asked him where would he like to sit—I'm the host. He says anywhere is fine. Both of us make a line like the crow flies to the table next the kitchen door—like a saloon door in a Western. I'll take you to see a Western," Carter promised Ilka. "This door swings both ways and bops Percy on the elbow. It's the waiter coming in with a stack of plates, smacks them down on the service table. I say, 'The menu, please.' The waiter is walking out into the kitchen. The door bops Percy's elbow. 'You want to get another table?' I ask him. He says this is fine, this is O.K. He is the guest. Damn door bops him on his elbow: *another* waiter is coming in with the biggest batch of knives, and starts pitching them—he's tossing the damn things into a metal basket—sounds like the demolition derby. . . ."

"Slower," said Ilka.

" 'Could we have the menu?' I ask this waiter. 'We can try another place,' I tell Percy. Percy says, 'They're busy. It's lunch hour'—Percival and I used to wait tables."

"You!" Ilka said.

"Sure! In a dining car. When you come and have dinner at my hotel I'll teach you how to carry six plates on your left arm. Damn door slams Percy's elbow: it's the first waiter bringing in the second batch of plates I don't *believe* he's going to stack on top of the stack that is already listing! The other waiter keeps throwing knives so we can't hear each other talk. I can hear Percy thinking, Bastards are doing it on purpose. I see he's watching this stack of plates like a fakir *knows* once he takes his eyes off the damn snake for one second all hell will break . . . 'We'll go some other place! Hey!' I tell him. I see his arm is lifting. His fist is coming straight toward this leaning tower of dishes. Ah!" Carter Bayoux said. "Here is my water."

Ilka watched him tease two pills out of a little vial and toss them in his mouth and pour the entire glass of water after them. Ilka, a small sipper, marveled at his capacity. Carter raised the glass to the waiter, who was coming back with their coffees: "Another water, please." He downed that also, in one long single swallow, and said, "What is your question?"

Ilka said, "What has the bridegroom said so wrong?"

"I'll buy you *The Sun Also Rises*—you've heard of Hemingway?"

"I read it, I read it!" cried Ilka. "Fishgoppel brought it."

"Remember the Jew—rich, good-looking, a good athlete —but he bumbles through the plot because he's got no sense of protocol."

"Are you anti-Semitish?" Ilka surprised herself by asking.

"Of course," said Carter Bayoux. "Aren't you?"

"I am a Jew," said Ilka.

"Then you know more Jews you cannot stand, no? Just as I'm anti more Negroes. A matter of one's opportunity."

He *is* a Negro! Ilka thought. Or does that mean he isn't . . . ?

"You think *I* am anti-Negroes?" Ilka marveled.

"Of course. Give you a test. You're at the wedding and the skinny fellow with the nose asks you, 'Who's that out in the kitchen?' Are you going to tell him, 'It's the Negro guzzling Chivas Regal'?"

"No! Of course not!" said Ilka, and thought, So he *is* a Negro.

"Of course not!" Carter said. "Or would you say, 'It's the Jew in the kitchen'?"

He's *Jewish?* Ilka thought. "No, I don't say that!" she said.

"No," Carter said, "you don't say that. You say, 'It's that guy in the tweed jacket drinking himself into a coma.' But, say,

I'm an Englishman drinking myself into a coma—you'd say, 'It's that English chap in the kitchen,' wouldn't you?"

"But that is different," said Ilka.

"Yes?" said Carter, and Ilka laughed and blushed, embarrassed and bedazzled in the full light of his brown stare on which he held her impaled.

"But about the bridegroom," said Ilka. "Protocol" (Ilka pronounced it *Protokoll*) "does not have to do with human feeling."

"Damn tootin'," Carter Bayoux said.

"I think," said Ilka, "the bridegroom meant it friendly. I think he said it humanly, no? He was meaning, 'You and I loved the same woman. We have this together.' "

"Oh?" said Carter. "Is that what he was meaning? *I* will tell you what the bridegroom was saying. He was saying, 'I am a white liberal and you're a black son of a bitch.' "

He is definitely Negro, thought Ilka with relief.

"He was saying, 'You laid my woman, but not only am I not going to kick your ass, I'm going to kiss it, because it's more fun to forgive than to need forgiveness!' Where did you say you lived?" Carter asked Ilka.

"Washington Heights. Finish the story." Carter was already on his feet. "Why," Ilka asked quickly, to stop the evening from running out, "are you angry with me?"

"I'm angry because your Mr. Bridegroom, who is half my age, is six inches taller. O.K.? Also I haven't slept in a week. I've got to race Harris's little pills to bed before I fall on my face, so you won't mind if I grab you a cab?"

"I can grab myself," she said. "Finish about the plates." But Carter Bayoux was turning her through the revolving door. Ilka stood confused in the black buffeting cold. It was raining hard. Carter Bayoux leaped across the sidewalk, stopped a taxi and held the door for her to get in, raising his left hand in a loose salute. By the time Ilka had settled and raised her answering hand, he was stepping back onto the curb.

From inside the idling taxi Ilka could see him at the corner, thrusting his hand into his right coat pocket and his left; he beat his left trouser pocket, put in his hand and drew out the beret. Ilka watched him trying to pull it down over both ears. The light had changed. Ilka's rattling, ancient taxi started up so slowly it crossed the street abreast with Carter. Ilka could tell that he had forgotten about her, and she saw what she had no business knowing: how a man looks when he is alone with himself at a moment without hope, unless it might be for the relief of the crash of crockery, before the consequence.

★　　　★　　　★

THE BOY HANDED Ilka the telegram through the door at 7:45 a.m. She clawed it open and read:

PROTOCOL IS THE ART OF NOT REPEAT NOT LIVING BY NATURAL
HUMAN FEELING . . .

and understood that this did not say that her mother was dead. It was not from—it was not about—her mother. Ilka started over:

PROTOCOL IS THE ART OF NOT REPEAT NOT LIVING BY NATURAL
HUMAN FEELING STOP BUMP INTO A LONDONER AND HE BEGS
YOUR PARDON SO YOU BEG HIS PARDON STOP LONDON RUNS ON
PROTOCOL BUT A NEW YORKER BUMPS INTO YOU AND KNOCKS
YOU DOWN AND TELLS YOU TO WATCH WHERE YOURE GOING SO
YOU KNOCK HIM DOWN AND HE KILLS YOU AND YOU KILL HIM
BACK STOP NEW YORK RUNS ON NATURAL HUMAN FEELING STOP
WILL CALL AND BUY YOU THAT ETERNALLY JINXED DINNER CAR-
TER BAYOUX 2:25 AM

"An eighty-eight-words telegram! That is normal?" Ilka asked Fishgoppel, who had arrived late the night before, and now came into the kitchen, fully dressed, to catch the early train back to school.

"He must like you," said Fishgoppel radiantly.

"He is older," said Ilka. Ilka did not wish to boast to Fishgoppel in such a matter. It was always after Fishgoppel had left that Ilka remembered that she had been going to look if her cousin had a waist, breasts, legs. But next time Fishgoppel came, she had on another one of her blouses that deflected the eye and the speculation as to there being any body inside. And each time Fishgoppel brought Ilka the Thackeray or Hawthorne or Melville she had put in her dissertation; each time Ilka found her cousin more interesting and delightful, and liked her more.

Ilka studied her telegram. "Five 'ands'!" she boasted.

"Bayoux," pondered Fishgoppel. "Did his family came via France?"

"Africa. He says he is Negro." Ilka watched Fishgoppel's face.

Fishgoppel said, "How do you mean Negro?" and she blanched. "He's not Jewish!" Fishgoppel wailed.

Ilka called the hotel and asked for Carter Bayoux.

"Here speaks Ilka," said Ilka. "I got your telegram. Hello?" Ilka listened to the dial tone, hung up, redialed and said, "Mr. Carter Bayoux, please. We were disconnect."

"Okey-dokey," said the switchboard. Ilka heard the phone ringing. It rang and it rang. The switchboard said, "They don't answer."

"I call Mr. Carter Bayoux," said Ilka.

"They don't answer," said the switchboard.

"You have the right room, yes?" asked Ilka.

"*Yes*, miss." The switchboard was annoyed.

Ilka had an idea. "Was it, maybe, before the wrong room, do you think?"

The switchboard girl did not think, or did not choose to dis-
cuss with Ilka what she thought. "Miss," she said. "There is
no answer."

Ilka hung up: Carter Bayoux must have gone out between
her first and second rings.

Ilka went to lunch with Harvey from Youth Aliyah. She studied the menu, which covered both sides. When she raised her
eyes and saw Harvey from Youth Aliyah sitting across the
table, she was surprised. Ilka had forgotten him.

Back at the office Ilka called Carter Bayoux but he was still
out and he continued out all week.

*   *   *

Monday night he called and said, "Hop in a cab. I'm
taking you to dinner. I've had a windfall! Goddamn royalty
check!"

"Excuse me?"

"I'm sitting here, going through my mail I haven't looked
at in a week and here's this check: forty-seven dollars
fifty-seven cents! A book I wrote in the forties. I called it *Pan-
African Power: The Hope of the American Negro question mark*.
I'll give you a copy." He gave her the name of a restaurant in the East Sixties and said, "We're going to put on the
dog."

Ilka found "windfall" in her dictionary but no definition of
a dog that could be put on. She stowed the animal away in the
back of her head along with the barman's dogs and cats who
had "come down," and with the bug whose house Carter had
lived in the first time Ilka telephoned.

The polished mahogany door had a glass inset with a little
white curtain. Putting behind her the temptation to turn around

and go home, Ilka depressed the brass handle. A frock-coated gentleman the size and shape of General de Gaulle advanced his massive black-and-white stomach to bounce her back into the street; Ilka said, "Carter Bayoux!" and the man inverted into a bow. Ilka followed the measured motion of his back into a soft interior darkness. White rounds of cloth glowed. There was silver, a lot of glass. Carter Bayoux rose to his feet. General de Gaulle held the back of Ilka's chair.

The waiter looked like Ilka's grandfather in a tuxedo. He brought menus. Lesser waiters hovered, bending at their waists, fetching rolls, butter; one poured water, one unfolded Ilka's napkin and laid it across her lap. One was dispatched into the kitchen for the chef's explication of the herbs in the *paupiettes* so that Carter and the sommelier might determine the wine. Carter Bayoux put on his bifocals, studied the label and said, "That is correct." Ilka thought this was the life.

When the last servitor had withdrawn to a watchful distance, Ilka said, "I have thought maybe it is the wrong place, maybe the wrong day. Both, and you might not be here."

"Introphobia," said Carter. "The fear of entering doors. I always wonder, how will I know to turn right or left?"

"You!" said Ilka. "But you know how to do all this! I have brought you a question." Ilka unfolded a front newspaper page and said, "Can you explain me what means 'NJ COPS QUIZ JINGLE BRA GALS'?"

"New Jersey police question the young women who tried to get away with stolen money hidden in their underwear," said Carter.

"How do you know?" cried Ilka.

"So! Have you found America?" asked Carter.

"I found you," said Ilka and blushed. "I live in—Fishgoppel calls it Washingstein Heights. In my building live only other Austrian, German and Czech. The Polish butcher corner Broadway used to live, before Hitler, on our street in Vienna. My English teacher is a pedicure from Budapest. I work for the

Council for Israel. Fishgoppel and I go to hear Italian baroque."

"I'll take you to hear jazz," said Carter. "I'll introduce you to—who d'you want to meet?"

"Everybody!" said Ilka.

"I know everybody," said Carter Bayoux, and here, walking between the tables toward them, came a small, fresh-faced older man, who said,

"It is! It's Carter Bayoux!" His white hair was cut square, like a country lad's.

"William Rauschenquist, you old villain!" cried Carter and rose with his arms outspread.

"You in New York and you don't call me?" said the small man inside Carter's embrace. "How are you? What have you been doing?"

"Going to the dogs, William, going to the dogs! But you, man!" Carter cried. "You went and got famous! You hit the big time! I hate you!" boomed Carter and embraced the small man again and again and said, "Remember the hole in the wall, Rue St. Sulpice, where you and I used to get drunk? *I* used to get drunk!"

"And you used to say a man who would not get drunk could not be a proper painter!"

"And you went and became famous, and I went to the dogs!" (Ilka added the dogs that Carter said that he had gone to to the menagerie awaiting elucidation in the back of her mind.) "Remember the sketch you gave me? On a brown paper bag? Brought it to New York. I have it up on the wall in my hotel."

"You gave me your book!" said the other.

"Which nets me an annual forty-seven dollars fifty-seven cents, and you became rich and famous, god*damn!*"

"Come up! Come and see me and I'll give you another sketch. I'll give you a canvas."

"I'll come, I'll come. I'll come."

"Come tomorrow."

"I absolutely will."

The small, shy-voiced man and the huge, expansive Carter kept patting each other on the arm. Carter now introduced his friend Ilka.

"I've got Kate over there. Come and join us!"

"Let me come and kiss Kate," said Carter.

An emaciated older woman in a minimal black dress that exposed her thin breasts had been watching with a long smile. Her black stick legs were crossed at the knee; her right hand, bent at the wrist, held a cigarette in a long silver and black holder, between fore and middle finger: That was what Ilka wanted to look like. Ilka watched the woman receive Carter Bayoux's kiss on her mouth.

Carter returned between the tables.

"Will we join them?" Ilka asked hopefully.

"Eat your dinner," said Carter. "Drink up your wine."

When they stood on the sidewalk Carter asked Ilka if she would like to come up for a nightcap.

"Excuse me?"

"Would you like to come up and see my room and have a drink?"

"Yes," said Ilka.

("Just to see where he lived," explained Ilka to the court that leaped into session inside her head to question her motive.)

"Just for only a minute," Ilka said to Carter.

Carter hailed a cab. "Yessir?" the cabby asked.

Carter gave the address. He said, "Joe Dillard—you know who Joe Dillard is?"

"No," said Ilka.

"Joe Dillard! Heavyweight champion of the world! Joe used to *love* taking taxis. Said cabbies are the only white folks are color-blind. They *know* colored don't *take* cabs, so you get *in* their cab they say, "Yessir. Where, sir?"

Ilka said, "You know the heavyweight champion of the world?"

"Screwed my wife one time, when he was staying over."

Ilka laughed. "Am I color-blind?" she asked.

"You," said Carter, "are a foreigner, but we're going to get you naturalized. We'll open up your eyes."

★　　　　★　　　　★

THE LOBBY of the Bloomsbury Arms—designed by a teacher, later, briefly, a partner, of Stanford White—had been wired for electricity some years after its opening. Today, three lights burned in the gilded five-armed bracket on the right side of the baronial fireplace, one in the left. (The hireling whose duty it had been to replace the bulbs had himself burned out in a nursing facility in Far Rockaway half a decade earlier.) Successive owners had come in with a will to spruce up the great, lavish gloom, but costs being what they are, what with workmanship these days, the dry linoleum was cracked and curled away from the marble flags in the grubby corners. Last year they had faced the massive scrolled and scarred mahogany of the front desk with the clean modern lines of wood-grain Formica. Behind this desk a snub-nosed, underslung desk clerk in a silver-gray suit picked up a pile of mail, turned his back on Mr. Carter Bayoux and his visitor waiting for the elevator, and began to sort letters into pigeonholes.

Ilka was afraid. She wanted to make the man standing beside her say something and she said, "What is it your hand is doing inside your pocket?"

"Counting my fingers," said Carter.

They rode up in silence. The tiny black operator stood with her back to Carter and Ilka. Ilka wished she would turn around.

Ilka studied the stitching that pulled and blistered the fabric of her black little dress, woven of a fiber like imitation glass. Her neat black shoes stood side by side. The ankles were so thin Ilka was startled and looked again and they were thinner.

The doors opened. Ilka stepped out onto a shaggy carpet the color of blood with a pattern of chevrons like white teeth flecked with black. If the thing reared and chewed the stranger nobody would know the difference. The corridor was empty. Ilka walked beside the large, elderly Negro from the bar in Utah. They turned a corner and another corner and another corner. When they arrived back at the elevator doors Ilka knew the man was trying to mislead her, unless this was a different elevator. . . .

They stopped. The door said 1306. "Keys," Carter Bayoux said. "Keys, keys, keys, keys." He slapped his coat pockets, both jacket pockets; he searched through the pockets of his trousers. "Show me the man who knows which pocket he keeps his keys in, I'll show you a man who is the master of his fate, who is the captain of his soul. Aha! Keys. Come in. Take your coat off and sit down," said Carter Bayoux, and without taking off his own coat walked through a door and closed it behind him.

Ilka listened tenderly to the man peeing behind the door. She looked around the good-sized, well-proportioned room for some place to put her coat down, but there was no such place. There was a big square club chair. Ilka could imagine the big man sitting in it. Ilka heard the water running behind the door. There was a wooden, kitchen-type chair that had been pulled up to the bed to act as a night table. There were things on the seat—an ashtray, a water glass, a small plastic radio. (If someone had said to Ilka, "So, why don't you put your coat on the bed?" she would have answered, "Because one can't put one's coat on the bed." It would not have occurred to her to remember her father coming into her room, on a day when she was home from school with a cozy earache, and her mother saying "Not on the open bed, Maxl, not in your street coat.")

Carter's bed was not open. It was a large bed neatly covered with a plaid counterpane.

Ilka held her coat and walked around the room. The excessively pink female hand, severed at the wrist, that lay on the top of Carter Bayoux's dresser, turned out to be rubber. Ilka smelled it. Framed on the wall was a brown paper bag on which a fast and furious brush had sketched a female face with silly eyes and appalled nostrils and smiling teeth turning into a line of demonic calligraphy. Next hung an antique print of a ship diagramming the utilization of deck space: Two parallel rows of black stick figures were arranged down each side, with a short additional row where the ship was widest. Inside the triangle formed by the prow, the bodies were necessarily child-size. Ilka moved on. She looked and looked and tried to admire the meticulous etching of a male Negro with his mouth open in a heroic scream, the eyes raised toward a source of light outside the frame.

When Carter Bayoux came out of the bathroom, Ilka was studying the illumination of a saint, prone, with a halo. Out of his belly sprouted a tree of many branches bearing a harvest of lesser saints' heads with smaller haloes.

"*This* I like," said Ilka.

"So do I," said Carter Bayoux. "It tickles me. Let me have your coat."

"I must soon again home," said Ilka.

"Then I will give it back to you." Ilka watched him hang her coat away in his closet, next to his coat. "All I have in the house is bourbon," he said.

"Thanks. No. I look around your room to learn about you!" said poor Ilka with helpless archness, and blushed.

"What do you want to know about me? Sit here." He meant the big club chair and he brought a fat leather-bound album, put it on Ilka's lap and walked back into the bathroom and closed the door.

Ilka deduced a pious female hand that had cut out, pasted and dated all these many newspaper columns. Ilka did not feel like reading them. She studied the face in the photo inset, under the byline. It was too small to really see. Ilka brought it closer and closer to her eye until it disintegrated into its constituent dots of printer's ink. She removed it to the distance at which it reassembled into an image too small to really see: Ilka could tell it was the face of a man in the arrogant health of mid-life with his mouth wide open in laughter—the face, presumably, of the man peeing—again!—behind the bathroom door. Ilka turned the page: the same face, caught in the identical degree of laughter, across the debris of an elaborately appointed table. The pious hand had written, "Carter Bayoux, Special Adviser on Race Relations to the U.S. Ambassador to the United Nations." Ilka made a mental note to boast to Fishgoppel.

Ilka turned the page and looked with greedy interest at the snapshot of a slender woman in white—it looked like a white linen suit. The face was deeply shaded by the wide brim of her white hat. *This* was what Ilka wanted to look like. The woman in the photo had one long foot hooked into the rung of the ship's railing behind her. The Carter Bayoux who leaned at her side was well-fleshed, wore a white suit and hat, and tossed his shout of robust, public laughter past Ilka's left ear. Ilka felt snubbed: the man in the picture would not have given her, Ilka, a second look. If he had, Ilka would have looked away.

It was silent inside the bathroom.

Ilka turned the page. The faithful female hand had printed, "Carter, Yale, 1920" under the photograph of a laughing young man in a scholar's cap and gown.

This history unraveled backward: "Carter and Jonas, Xmas '09." Two little boys in knickerbockers, holding bicycles. The cruel photographer had made them squint into the sun.

("And it did not occur to you that he might be ill?" asked the prosecutor of a future court, convening inside Ilka's head, to try her in the death of Carter Bayoux on the bathroom floor of his suite in the Hotel Bloomsbury Arms while she, Ilonka Weissnix, had sat in his bedroom and done nothing to prevent it.

"I worried about it," Ilka was going to reply.

Prosecutor: "Did you knock on the door? Did you call to ask him if he needed help?"

Ilka: "One doesn't call a man one hardly knows inside his bathroom."

"Did you call down to the desk?"

"I kept thinking how embarrassing if he turned out to be all right."

Prosecutor: "Are you telling this court that you chose to risk a man's life rather than embarrass yourself?"

Ilka: "Yes.")

The toilet flushed. He was perfectly all right. Ilka heard the opening and closing of bathroom cabinets.

She turned the page. The old sepia family group. Ilka had just such a photograph of her father's family, mounted on the same thick cardboard, across the bottom right-hand corner of which was printed "Photo Wien, Kärntnerstrasse 112." She kept it in the box underneath Fishgoppel's studio couch. The mother in Carter's family picture sat three-quarter face, looking left. She had a baby on her lap. The father stood behind her with his right hand resting on her right shoulder. She wore the same modified leg-of-mutton sleeves with lace at the wrist, and a lace dickey, which Ilka's father's mother wore, except that *she* faced right, and both the father's hands rested on the chair back. In each picture a bevy of young ladies faced front unsmiling, out of an era before one had oneself immortalized saying cheese. Some of the young ladies stood, one sat, to form a pleasing skyline, with the little brothers placed according to the requisites of composition. Ilka didn't know which one of the little Jewish Austro-Hungarian boys in her trunk was her father. All had had their heads shaved for the photographer and wore oversize polka-dotted bowties. The two little American boys in Carter's album had on knickerbockers, and their faces, as well as the faces of the young ladies, of the father, the mother, and even the baby, were Negro. Across the bottom corner of the cardboard it said, "Studio Elite, Washington, D.C."

The bathroom door opened. Carter came out and said, "When there's a crisis at the UN . . ."

"Slowly," said Ilka.

"I used to be in the United Nations. When there was a critical debate in the General Assembly, we stationed the junior people in the bathrooms to keep track—who was getting nervous. Now, how about that bourbon?"

"I must go home," said Ilka and was hurt by the promptness with which he got her coat out of his closet. He held it for her. He got his own coat.

"I can go alone," said Ilka.

"Very fine," said Carter Bayoux. "I'll see you down into the subway. Protocol," he said.

They waited at the elevator doors. Ilka could tell his hand was counting its fingers inside his pocket.

"Is that your wife, on the ship, in the white hat? Very elegant."

"My ex-wife, Georgia. She was a looker!" said Carter. "When we hit England I divorced her."

"Because of the heavyweight champion?"

"That was my wife Olga. Georgia was a bitch."

Ilka said, "A bitch is a dog, yes?"

Carter explained the concept. Ilka thought *that's* what she wanted to be—a bitch and a looker. Think of the opportunities! The elevator came. Ilka had meant to remember to turn around and take a look at the tiny operator's face, but when the doors opened into the lobby the bantam desk clerk was haranguing the black bellboy and Ilka wanted to listen. The desk clerk was saying, "So, why *didn't* you?" and the bellboy said, "I did! I told her, but she said you told her . . ." "What did I tell *you?*" the desk clerk asked the bellboy. "I know, but she said you said . . ."

Carter held Ilka's arm across the street and down the stairs into the subway. At the turnstile he would have kissed her, but Ilka laughed and turned her head to look up and down the drafty platform. It smelled of cold and urine. "Here?" said Ilka.

"Why not here?" said Carter in a voice of strong surprise and displeasure and this, too, made Ilka laugh. The blast of air from the tunnel announced the approaching train. "Josephine Baker kissed me in the Paris Métro," said Carter in ringing tones. "Do you know who Josephine Baker is?" he asked her.

"No," said Ilka and laughed, and threading herself through the turnstile, ran into the train and turned to wave to Carter, but he was already walking up the stairs.

It must be midnight: the liquor-store man was closing the iron concertina across the glass front. He wished Carter a good night with unsmiling courtesy and an expression incorruptibly mild and earnest. Carter Bayoux privately thought of him as the Liquor Store Christian.

Carter wished him a good night.

★   ★   ★

CARTER BAYOUX returned to his room, did not take his coat off, but sat down on the edge of his bed and gave the switchboard his brother's number. When his brother picked up, Carter put the phone down, lit a cigarette, picked the phone up again, and gave his brother's number. His brother picked up and Carter said, "This is big brother calling."

"Was that you just now?" asked his brother. "The phone rang . . ."

"And you thought, 'There goes Carter.' "

"Carter, come off it."

"What *did* you think?"

"Come on . . ."

"I told you, I'm doing great," said Carter. "I got a news desk at the UN. Don't you read the Negro press? Don't you see my column in the *Harlem Herald*, Tuesdays, on the button? I was doing great until this insomnia thing hit. I need to talk, Jonas. Can I come up and just sit, just to talk for half an hour, Jonas?"

"Now, you mean? Jesus, Carter, it's ten o'clock. We were on our way to bed. We're going to turn in pretty soon. Ellen is tired."

"Not as tired as I am tired!" said Carter. " 'A thousand years in God's sight are as a watch in the night.' It says so in Ellen's Bible. Jonas! I can't sit another thousand years in this bloody hotel room! I could snap out of this, I think, if you and I could just sit for half an hour and talk. . . . Send Ellen to bed, and you come over, eh, brother?"

"Maybe not tonight, Cart. Ellen is in some kind of a state."

"Ah, well! If Ellen is in a state . . . What's the laughing back there?"

"Just some people dropped over. They'll be leaving soon, I *hope.*"

"Why don't you have me up next time you have people over? I don't get around much any more. I know people galore, Jonas, you know that. I need to get back into the swing. . . ."

"Whatever you may think," said Jonas, "Ellen and I hardly see anyone except her family."

"Christ! Ellen's family! Well," Carter said.

"New York . . ." Jonas said. "We're both bushed all the

time. These people just dropped over and anyway you wouldn't like them."

"Why wouldn't I like them?"

"When did you ever like any of my friends!" shouted Jonas, "or my wife, or my wife's family! When did you ever like anything of mine?"

"Well well well well well! That's my little brother," Carter said. "And so, good night, and I hope that you sleep well."

"Hold it a moment," said Jonas and must have covered the mouthpiece. After a moment's mumbling his voice returned full strength. "Ellen says to come over for a bit."

"For a bit! Ah!" said Carter. "I get the message!"

"What do you want from me, Carter!"

"Nothing. Not one bloody thing," said Carter, and replacing the receiver with his left hand, he turned on the radio with his right, stood up and marched out into the little kitchen, where he opened the refrigerator. It was empty. Carter stood looking into the empty refrigerator until the Mantovani strings came on the radio, then he went inside and turned the dial till he found a speaking voice.

It was a male voice saying, "Dear, that's what I've been trying to tell you. The date for Thanksgiving is set every year by a presidential proclamation. . . . ."

"Every year," said a woman's voice, "he has to set it over, which he wouldn't have to if they had it like they have Christmas or Washington's birthday, which they always have it on the same day, every year."

"Dear," said the pleasant professional male voice, "Christmas and Washington's birthday are celebrated on the birth-*dates* of Jesus Christ and Washington respectively."

"*Right!*" said the woman's eager voice. "And Thanksgiving is just as respective, just like any regular American holiday!"

"Except Thanksgiving has no *ipso facto* date," said the male voice.

"Which is what I'm saying," said the woman. "They could

have it on November twenty-fifth, like they always have Christmas in December, is all I'm saying to you."

"O.K., dear," said the man's voice.

"Or like they have the Fourth of July every year," the woman said.

"O.K.," said the man's voice.

"Or New Year's is always on January first," the woman said.

"Right you are. I'll be moving along to the next call, then. Nice talking to you."

"Nice talking to you, Bucky. I always listen to your program, every night."

"Okay, dear. Thank you. This is station WXYZ. If you have a beef, or a bone to pick, call Bucky Bailey. Our number is WX 9-1100. This is *Your Time to Talk* with Bucky Bailey at the telephone, every night, all night from eleven p.m. till six in the morning. Hello, hello. Bucky Bailey here . . ."

Carter had been emptying out his pockets onto the dresser top. Now he took his coat off and drew the curtains. He put on a fresh pair of pajamas, sat down on the edge of the bed, turned the radio down, and gave the switchboard Harris Wharton's number.

"Harris!" Carter said. "So! The kids off on their honeymoon?"

"Kids are back from their honeymoon."

"Back! Christ!" said Carter. "Did I lose a week in there someplace? Where did the kids go on their honeymoon?"

"Paris. No imagination."

"Forget it, Harris! It's no go! Even you can't knock Paris! What are you people doing Thanksgiving?"

"Come have it with us and meet Nell," said Harris.

"I have to meet Nell! Darn you, Harris, you're going to outmarry me, you old villain!"

"Catch up," Harris said. "Bring your young Viennese friend to Thanksgiving dinner."

"I will. I will certainly do that." Carter replaced the receiver, picked it up again and gave the switchboard Ilka's number, but Ilka was not at home.

Carter sat with his address book and paged through the A's he knew in Paris, Stockholm, Chicago, New Haven, Jackson, Mississippi, and Washington, D.C. Carter looked through the B's. Ebony Baumgarden and what's his name—Stanley—must be in New York, but that meant explanations. . . . Carter kept turning pages and there were dozens—there were hundreds of people Carter Bayoux knew in New York, black and white, each one of whom, it seemed to Carter, was the one he felt least like talking with tonight, fools and bores the lot. Carter picked the phone up and tried Ilka's number, so that the phone was ringing for her when she unlocked Fishgoppel's front door.

Carter asked her what she was doing Thanksgiving. Ilka was not doing anything. Carter said, "You're having Thanksgiving dinner with me at Harris Wharton's. Holidays are a bitch."

When Carter put the phone down, he turned the radio up and Bucky Bailey had another caller.

"Can I speak with Bucky Bailey?" said a younger woman's voice.

"This is Bucky Bailey."

"Is that Bucky Bailey?"

"Yes. And what can I do for you?"

"Bucky?"

"Yes."

"How are you, Bucky?"

"Just fine," Bucky Bailey said. "What can I do for you?"

"How is your wife?" the young woman's voice said.

"Fine, thank you. What would you like to talk about?"

"And the kids?"

"Kids are great. Is there something you would like to talk about?"

"What the lady said about Thanksgiving," said the young woman.

"Aha?" Bucky Bailey said.

"Lincoln's birthday . . ." the young woman said.

"Aha?" Bucky Bailey said.

"In Arizona they celebrate Lincoln's birthday the second Monday in February," the young woman said.

Bucky Bailey said, "Are you from Arizona?"

"My husband," the young woman said.

"Aha?" Bucky Bailey said.

Carter turned the radio down, picked the phone up, gave the girl Harris Wharton's number and said, "Did I wake you up?"

"No," said Harris Wharton.

"I have got to sleep. Harris, could you let me have a couple of those little pills?"

"No," said Dr. Wharton.

Carter said, "I don't want to start in again! Harris, you said yourself a judicious pill can turn this thing around."

"A judicious pill, judiciously taken," said Dr. Wharton.

Carter said, "So what do you suggest?"

"I'm out of suggestions," said Dr. Wharton.

"You're saying you're through treating me?"

"I'm out of suggestions," said Dr. Wharton.

"Because you're through doctoring! I forgot. Oceanography indeed! So then," said Carter, "good-bye."

Dr. Wharton said, "See you Thanksgiving."

"Absolutely," Carter said, put down the receiver, picked it up again and said, "What is the name of the hotel doctor?"

"Dr. MacSamuels," said the switchboard.

"Get me Dr. MacSamuels."

"His office hours are two to six Monday through Friday," said the switchboard.

"What day is this?" asked Carter.

"Sunday," said the switchboard.

Carter sat on the edge of his bed and smoked. Presently the line of light that surrounded and divided his curtains turned blue. A breezy baritone on the radio sang, "Happy in the morning, happy in the evening, happy the whole day long," to the accompaniment of a nice jazz piano. "The time is six a.m. on the nose," he said. "Eighteen brrr degrees! The program is *Barry in the Morning* with your host Barry Johnson, happy to report that all major arteries into New York are flowing freely at this time, and the time is six-o-four. See what the almanac has got for us today. In the year eighteen-seventy the U.S. government issued its first weather bulletin. Didn't know that, did you? First auto show opened in New York on this day in nineteen-hundred." Barry had some handy hints for the ladies: "Mrs. F. Fletcher of Union City, New Jersey, formerly of Whipsnade, near London, England, writes, 'Dear Barry, I wonder if your listeners know what to do with those little pieces of leftover soap. During the war, in England we collected all the little pieces and tied them in a cheesecloth, which you can keep on your draining board and just swirl around in the washing-up water.' " The arteries were still free and flowing at eight-fifteen. Outside the Bloomsbury Arms, too, the rush hour peaked. Buses sighed to a stop and started up with a sigh and a puff.

Barry Johnson went off the air at nine, and Carter walked to the window and looked out between the curtains. At ten o'clock, the Liquor Store Christian drew back the iron concertina and Carter put on his pants over his pajamas. He went across the street and brought back a quart of house bourbon, poured a water glass brimful, set the glass on the bedside chair and sat down on the edge of the bed.

The maid had turned the key and put her vacuum and her pail inside the door before she saw the man in his pajamas, sitting on the edge of the bed. She asked, "You want I could clean now or come back?" She was a new girl, very big, black, very young, in a skimpy pink cotton dress.

Carter raised his heavy head out of his supporting hand and looked at her. He said, "You could clean now or come back," and he shook his head slowly from side to side and said, "it do not matter."

The girl looked at her feet. She said, "You want I could clean now or come back?" and she seemed about to cry.

Carter said, "Clean now," and lowered his head into his hands and raised it again and said, "I can't sleep." Carter watched the girl plug the vacuum into the wall and then he put his chin back in his hands. The maid vacuumed. She vacuumed a ring around Carter's bare feet on the carpet. She dusted around the money and things on the dresser top.

Later she was outside in the kitchen singing five reedy notes that climbed two tones, fell three, climbed and fell again with no alteration in the volume and no expression and no possibility of any resolution.

The maid was gone. The phone rang.

"They're not picking up," the switchboard told Ilka.

Carter sat with his chin cupped in his right hand, smoked and drank. When the level of the bourbon in the glass fell to the halfway point he refilled it from the bourbon in the bottle. He kept his eye on the level of the bourbon in the bottle. Once in a while he checked the line of light around the curtain. Presently it turned gray. Carter gave the switchboard his brother's number. Jonas picked up and Carter said,

"What time is this?"

Jonas said, "Five of four. What happened to your watch you had from dad?"

"Hocked it when I first hit town," said Carter. "I keep forgetting to go and get it out."

"Oh," said Jonas. "You O.K.?"

"I'm O.K.," said Carter.

"O.K.," said Jonas.

"Carry on," said Carter.

Once Carter looked and the air outside the curtains had turned a profound electric-blue color. Carter called down for Wallace to go across the street and get him a quart of house bourbon. He let the bellboy in, gave him money for one bottle of bourbon and a quarter tip.

★ ★ ★

I L K A C A L L E D Carter before she left for work next morning and heard the phone picked up. The man at the other end said, "Eight-fifteen on the nose."

"Did I wake you?" asked Ilka.

"Wake up, Jacob! Jacob's our engineer, and I'm a poet and I didn't know it. If you have just joined us, this is your host Barry Johnson. . . ."

"Can I speak, please, with Mr. Carter Bayoux?"

"This is Carter," said Carter.

"On this day in nineteen-o-eight Toscanini conducted his first *Aida* at the Metropolitan Opera," the man said.

"Excuse me?" said Ilka.

"First Mickey Mouse was drawn in nineteen-twenty-eight."

"Is this, please, room thirteen-hundred-six?"

"Yes," said Carter.

"How are you?" asked Ilka.

"Sick," said Carter.

"Your voice is different," said Ilka.

"I have a bad throat," said Carter.

"I let you go back to sleep," said Ilka.

"I have to sleep," said Carter.

"Mrs. Burdick from Glen Head on Long Island has a handy hint for the ladies. She writes, 'I wonder if your listeners know a dandy way to remove old, dried blood. . . .' " Ilka heard the click, at the other end, of the receiver being returned into its cradle.

"Leave it," said Carter, making the maid jump. She had been going to open the curtains. Carter watched the girl vacuum. The phone rang. The maid looked at the instrument, which the man on the bed made no move to answer. After a while the ringing stopped. The maid dusted. When she was singing outside in the kitchen the phone rang again and Carter took it off the hook.

"He's got his phone off the hook," the switchboard told Ilka.

The phone was ringing when Ilka got home. It was Carl.

"Carl . . ." said Ilka.

"From Fanny and Philip's wedding."

"Aha," said Ilka.

Would Ilka like to see a movie?

Ilka would like very much to see a movie, sometime. But she had her English class. Thursday she was having her first American Thanksgiving with Carter Bayoux. Ilka said, "He has a bad throat."

"So how are you doing?" asked Carl.

Ilka was funny about filing at the Council for Eretz Israel. Carl told Ilka about his law firm that handled mostly civil liberties cases.

"What are they?" asked Ilka.

Carl explained civil liberties. Fascinating! They talked a long time.

Ilka hung up and called Carter but his phone was still off the hook.

("What if he was dying? Did you go down to see?" the prosecutor was going to ask Ilka.

"I hardly knew him," Ilka was going to answer. "I mean

he was a man. . . . What if I got down there and he wasn't
dying at all? Also, I didn't feel like getting dressed again and
going back on the subway.")

"You think maybe he is really ill?" Ilka asked the switchboard girl.

"Miss," the girl said, "I'm the switchboard."

Bucky Bailey had a young fellow on, talking ball.

"It's their defense faltered," said the fellow.

"Just about fell apart," agreed Bucky Bailey.

"Look at their shot selection, I mean," said the fellow, "from
twenty feet out! Two airballs and a brick."

Carter felt his eyelids drooping, shut them and lay down on
his side, thinking he might sleep, but Bucky Bailey said,
"Picked up a three pointer and hit the jumper with one-forty-
three to go and tied it!"

"Forced the first overtime," the fellow said.

Carter knew that lifting his arm to turn the radio off would
wake him right up, so he lay very still and kept his eyes shut.

"When you're carrying a seven-game scoring slump and
miss the lay-ups," said Bucky Bailey, "you got to do something—regroup—something, before you find yourself down
and out the bottom of the division."

Carter sat up, put his feet on the floor, lifted the receiver
and gave his brother's number. Jonas picked up, and Carter
said, "I'm in a scoring slump. I've got to regroup."

"What?" said Jonas.

"I've got to regroup," said Carter.

"Carter? Where are you?"

"Down and out the bottom of the division," said Carter.

"Are you home?"

"No, I'm in a bloody hotel room."

"O.K., Carter," said Jonas.

"Carry on," said Carter.

.   .   .

When Barry Johnson went off the air Carter called down and said, "Send Wallace across the street."

The switchboard said, "They don't open till ten."

Carter said, "Send Wallace at ten."

"What time is this?" Carter asked the maid, but she didn't know.

"He's not picking up," the switchboard said. Ilka hung up. Ilka had wanted to tell Carter that her mother had been traced to Israel and was alive, though ailing, in a kibbutz in the Negev.

Ilka went in and told the women in the office and they surrounded and embraced her. Ilka kept saying, because she kept feeling she had not got it properly said, that all this while she had been filing this kibbutz where her mother had, all this while, been alive!

Mr. Bayoux opened the door for Wallace and went and sat back down on his bed. Mr. Bayoux said, "Will you bring me the money from the dresser over there? D'you see my glasses someplace?" Wallace found Mr. Bayoux's glasses on the bedside chair. Mr. Bayoux put them on. He withdrew a bill out of Wallace's hand and stared at it for a long time and gave it to the boy and withdrew another bill and gave it to him and said, "You can keep the change."

"*What* change!" Wallace complained to the obese blond switchboard girl. He had been stewing over the transaction all the way down the elevator. "Bottle bourbon is two-thirty-five and he give me two bucks is thirty-five cent! *He* owes *me!*"

"You want I'll tell Mr. Boyd for you," the switchboard girl said. "He can get it from him."

"*I'll* get it," said Wallace. "He got money all over up there. I'm going to get it from him."

.   .   .

All day Ilka filed, and in the spaces between the putting of one card into its correct place in the file and reaching her hand for the next card, Ilka glimpsed her fear about her mother that had grown so normal for so many years that Ilka became acquainted with it only now, by its having been taken away and replaced by a new fear: they hadn't said what ailed her mother.

Harvey treated Ilka to lunch. Fishgoppel came to town to get started on arrangements for bringing Ilka's mother to America. All night Ilka and Fishgoppel sat and talked. Ilka asked Fishgoppel if she had heard of Jane Austen. Carter had given her *Emma*.

"Carter? Jane Austen? I thought," Fishgoppel said, "you said he was a Negro."

"Two bucks and a quarter is ten cent he owes me plus thirty-five today. . . . He owes me forty-five cent!"

"Let me tell Mr. Boyd for you," said the switchboard blonde.

"I'm going to tell him!"

"I can get it," said the bellboy.

But the switchboard told Mr. Boyd anyway. The next time Mr. Bayoux called down, Mr. Boyd said, "I'll take it over here. . . . I'm sending Wallace up for his money, *if* you don't mind."

"I don't mind," said Carter.

Wallace went up. Mr. Bayoux was sitting on the edge of the bed and said, "Help yourself," and pointed to the dresser. Wallace went and stood at the dresser with his back to Mr. Bayoux and picked up two singles and thirty-five cents for the bottle and a dollar for himself. Mr. Bayoux said, "Take a tip." Wallace looked up and saw Mr. Bayoux looking at him in the mirror, in his pajamas. He dropped the dollar and picked up a quarter and kicked himself all the way down because he hadn't even helped himself to the forty-five cents Mr. Bayoux *owed* him.

. . .

At 6 a.m. on the nose Barry Johnson signed on with "Happy in the morning." There was a dilly of a seven-car pile-up on the Major Deegan. Motorists traveling south were advised to stay clear of the two left lanes. In 1651 Boston had set a ten-shilling fine for chimney fires. Andrew Carnegie, industrialist, was born this day in 1835. At 7:15 motorists planning to drive into the city on the Major Deegan were advised to choose alternate routes; traffic was backed up as far as Fordham Road with motorists slowing down to rubberneck. At 7:50 traffic was at a virtual standstill on the Major Deegan. Carter's bottle was down to three fingers and he rang for Wallace.

"They don't open till ten," said the switchboard.

"I know that," said Carter.

The maid unlocked the door and was putting her vacuum in the door when she saw the man on the bed and backed out and locked the door.

When Wallace took up Mr. Bayoux's bottle, Mr. Bayoux was lying down on the bed and said, "Take a tip." Wallace swiped a fiver and got out of there in a hurry.

Ilka thought, If his phone is off the hook I will go down in my lunch hour, but when she called Carter picked up.

Ilka said, "You are better?"

"I'm the best," said Carter.

"I mean is your throat good again?"

"My throat is the best," said Carter. "How is your throat?"

"Excuse me?"

Carter said, "What are you doing?"

"Filing," said Ilka. "I thought you may be really ill?"

"I'm fine," said Carter.

"Because you didn't answer your telephone," said Ilka.

"I was at the UN," said Carter.

"Yesterday?" said Ilka.

"African meeting at the UN, yesterday," said Carter.

"I called you in the morning and the evening."

"Meetings in the morning, meetings in the evening, meetings the whole day long," said Carter.

Ilka understood that she should leave this alone but she said, "All day yesterday your telephone was off the hook."

Carter said, "African meetings. Tuesday."

Ilka experienced an emptying out of the gut as when an elevator drops a floor and leaves your stomach and heart to catch up. Ilka said, "Tuesday you said your throat was very bad."

"A wicked, wicked throat," said Carter.

And so Ilka did not tell Carter about her mother. She decided never to speak to Carter Bayoux again. "Good-bye," she said.

"Good-bye," said Carter.

"It's that I must get on filing," added Ilka.

"Carry on," said Carter.

In the lobby, Mrs. Rinkler, the housekeeper, was saying, "The girl says she's not going in there any more."

Mr. Boyd wore a fresh carnation in his buttonhole and may have been smiling: a white row of baby teeth showed between his parted lips. "Did he do you something?" he asked the big black girl, who was trying to hide behind the smaller housekeeper.

"He didn't do nothing," said the girl and began to cry.

Wallace said, "He's got some almighty mess up there with the bottles and papers and butts and his clothes all over."

The switchboard buzzed. The girl interlocked her eyes with the eyes of Mr. Boyd and said, "Eleven minutes past eleven." She hung up. The switchboard buzzed. The girl raised her eyes to the heavens.

Mr. Carter Bayoux at the other end said, *"Which* eleven is this?"

"Hold on," said the switchboard.

When Carter understood that he had been disconnected, he put the phone down, turned up the radio and set his chin back in his hands.

Bucky Bailey had two advertising experts in the studio with him, who would be delighted to answer listeners' questions. The program was *Your Time to Talk,* with Bucky Bailey at the telephone. What, Bucky Bailey asked the two experts, was the hardest problem they had to deal with?

"Clients," said one of the two experts in an exasperated voice.

Carter studied the level of the bourbon. He picked up the phone and said, "If it's Bucky Bailey, how is it all the way to the top?"

The switchboard said, "Would you like to speak to Mr. Boyd at the desk?"

"I would not," said Mr. Bayoux and hung up and rose and walked, not without difficulty, to the window. It was *dark* outside. Carter could see the Liquor Store Christian moving inside the lighted liquor store. It was *nighttime.*

Carter went and sat back down and looked at the bourbon. It was all the way to the top, which it could not be: Wallace had brought him up a bourbon after Barry Johnson went off the air. That was in the morning. Carter looked at the bourbon and it was so full he had to bend and sip the hump off the liquid before he could raise it to his lips.

The expert with the exasperated voice was saying, "Our creative people *tell* the client; they say, 'This girl is talent.' The client says, 'She doesn't sparkle!' I mean. What is he talking *about!* Sparkle! This is a Mary Martin type! She invented the word!"

"You have to understand the client's problem," the other advertising expert said in a reasonable voice.

"Don't," said the exasperated expert, "talk to me about the client's problems. They don't know what they're talking *about!*"

Carter turned the radio down, picked the phone up and gave the switchboard Ilka's number.

Ilka picked up and Carter said, "Is this the same night?"

"Excuse me?"

"Is this the same *day?*"

"Which day?" said Ilka.

"Is this nighttime? What time is this?" asked Carter.

"Five minutes to twelve," said Ilka.

"Carry on," said Carter, replaced the receiver into the cradle and his chin into his right hand.

The reasonable expert was saying, "Let me give you an actual for-instance. These breakfast-food people come to us. They have a new-improved product with extra nutlike flavor. We hire this Marilyn Monroe type and the survey shows nobody paid attention to 'extra nutlike,' so the client tells us, 'Try a spot with a more girl-next-door type.' "

"Don't you understand," the exasperated expert said, "we're not talking spots! This could go network! I mean, God!"

"But suppose we'd gone ahead," said the reasonable expert, "and flooded the market and *no* one paid attention to 'extra nutlike'!"

"Listen," said the exasperated expert, "clients wouldn't know sparkle if it bit them! It's frightening!"

Carter put out his hand to pick up the glass and it was empty. He picked up the bottle in order to refill the glass and the bottle was empty. Carter picked the phone up and said, "Is this a different night?"

There was a pause.

Carter said, "Send Wallace for a fifth of house bourbon."

The switchboard said, "They close at twelve."

Carter gave the switchboard his brother's number. There was nobody home . . . yes, there was: the receiver at the other end was lifted and dropped with a clatter, a fumbling, and Jonas said, "Yes?"

"Is this a different day?" asked Carter.

"What?" said Jonas. "Carter? What time is it?"

"I don't know what time it is," said Carter slowly, "and I don't know what day it is. That's why I'm calling. Is this the same night as it was this morning?"

"*What?*" said Jonas.

"What day is this?" asked Carter.

A pause, and Jonas said, "You're calling me at—Christ, Carter, it's twenty after twelve and you're asking me what day this is? Have you lost your mind!"

"I think so!" said Carter with a sob. "That's why I'm calling you."

"Shit, Carter!" said Jonas and hung up.

Carter hung up. He returned his chin into his hand.

At 8 a.m., on the nose, Barry Johnson announced his intention of losing ten pounds before Christmas. He invited the guys and gals, out there, who had a weight problem, to step up on their home scales while Barry stepped onto the scale in the studio, weighing in at 233 pounds 2 ounces! Well, what can you expect after a day of guzzling! He encouraged the ladies to send in their skinniest recipes, which he would pass on to the guys and gals, with whom he made a date for the next weigh-in one week from today, eight o'clock on the nose. In 1777 Congress approved the confiscation of Loyalists' estates. A hoard of Roman silver was discovered in Suffolk on this day in 1896.

★   ★   ★

I LKA!" they said. "Telephone for you!"

Carter said, "Can you have lunch?"

"Today?" asked Ilka joyfully.

"Yes," said Carter.

"Where do we meet?" asked Ilka.

"Where?" said Carter.

"We can meet again by our lions."

"Yes," said Carter.

Ilka supported Carter's violently trembling arm down the steps. They stood on the sidewalk. The Fifth Avenue lunch crowd revolved around them. Ilka was frightened by the gray pallor about his mouth and chin and said, "Should you go home?"

Carter said, "I have to go home."

"I will grab you a cab," said Ilka.

Carter called Ilka in the evening and said, "Could you come down and see me?"

In the subway Ilka sat across from a small brown man who wore no coat over his skimpy summer suit; he was going to be cold when he got back into the street. His straw hat tilted at a snazzy angle. His wide face smiled an archaic smile, meaningless and profound, built into the bone. Ilka had learned she didn't know a Negro when she saw one—or was this a Chinese?

The desk clerk had the telephone trapped between his ear and shoulder and did not look up, but Ilka caught the blue left eye in the half of the obese blond face that appeared and disappeared so rapidly behind the switchboard Ilka wondered if she had seen what she had seen. Ilka stepped into the elevator and stepped out on Carter's floor, forgetting, once again, to turn around and get a look at the elevator woman's face. Ilka walked along the corridor and wondered how people got from sitting in chairs, talking, maybe drinking coffee, to lying together in a bed. How did the bed cover—how did their clothes—get to have been taken off?

Ilka knocked. She heard the man inside. He was coming.

Carter Bayoux was barefoot and had on a pair of elephantine, green-striped pajamas. The curtains were closed. The bed was open. Carter went and sat down on the edge, braced his elbow on his thigh, and lowered his chin into the cup of his hand, but raised his head again to say, "I drink."

"I know," said Ilka and found that she did know, and had known this all along.

"What do you know?" Carter asked with a slow tongue and looked Ilka in the face.

Ilka smiled, blushed, raised a shoulder and shook her head.

"Have you ever known a drunk?"

"No," said Ilka, "and that is why for me it is very interesting."

Carter continued, for a couple of moments, to look into Ilka's face, then he said "Christ!" and let his head drop into his hand like a piece of luggage he had carried a moment past his strength. His left hand brought his cigarette slowly to his lips. He raised his head and said, "Would you like a drink?" forming his words laboriously, as if his tongue were too big to fit inside his mouth but he was nevertheless committed to finish saying what he was going to say: "I have only house bourbon." During the pauses between one word and the next Ilka was aware of a tiny sizzling sound; it came from the small radio whispering to itself on the seat of Carter's bedside chair. Ilka wondered if it would be all right to ask him to turn it off and thought not. Carter stubbed out his cigarette on the rim of the burgeoning ashtray. Ilka thought it would be overly familiar to offer to empty it. He said, "Will you sit down?"

The black trenchcoat lay over the back of the club chair. There was a pair of trousers, one leg turned inside out, on the seat. Ilka sat on them. Ilka watched Carter Bayoux reach his hand in the direction of the glass. He appeared to experience a difficulty identifying its exact position. It took another moment for the inner surface of his hand to become aware that contact had been made with the outer surface of the glass and a longer moment for the fingers to bend and take hold. Carter raised the glass and sipped like a cat, his tongue preceding his lips into the liquid. "What time is it?" he asked, and added, "My watch is in hock."

"Excuse me?"

"What day is this?" asked Carter.

"Friday," said Ilka.

"Friday!" Carter's head snapped up, his eyes very wide and very round. He looked at Ilka in a sort of horror. "Which Friday is this? When is Thursday!" he cried. "When is it Thanksgiving?"

Ilka said, "Thanksgiving has been."

Carter shot straight up from the edge of his bed. "I missed Harris's Thanksgiving dinner?" He looked at Ilka with a look of such tragic consternation she said, "It doesn't *so* much matter."

"It matters!" cried Carter. "It matters!" He struck both fists downward and stretched his neck and lifted his chin.

"You were sick," suggested Ilka.

"I did not call!" cried Carter. He walked up and down in his green pajamas, on the carpet in front of Ilka, repeatedly pounding the air. "That's not a thing one does! One does not miss a dinner engagement! One doesn't not call!" He put the heels of his hands to his temples. "I have broken protocol. It matters!" Carter sat down on the bed and gave the switchboard Harris Wharton's number, waited with the receiver to his ear, and lifting his head, covered his eyes with his other hand. Ilka thought he might be crying and looked to see if he was. "Harris," said Carter, his tongue released by his agitation, "I am, as the French put it, desolated. I lost a couple of days in there someplace. I missed your Thanksgiving dinner. I've been under the weather, which is no excuse for bad manners. Will you allow me to compensate by taking you and your bride to dinner? When is the wedding? Neither wind nor storm . . . *And* my Viennese friend. You bet. Absolutely! But first I'm going to buy you dinner. We'll put on the dog. Again, *je suis désolé.* Carry on," said Carter, replaced the receiver not without difficulty into its cradle and returned his chin into his hand.

Now Ilka said, "We have news from my mother. She is in Israel, ill, but alive."

Carter turned his slow head and looked at Ilka and said, "That is news! That is news indeed."

"Fishgoppel is sending an affidavit."

"That is news," said Carter.

"All this time she has been in a kibbutz, which I have been all this time filing!"

"Did you leave Vienna with your mother?" asked Carter.

"And my father, across the border into—how do you say in English 'Czechoslovakei'?"

"Czechoslovakia," said Carter, and because he continued to look at her, Ilka said, "I think that everybody has heard already so many such stories. Fishgoppel would like that I would tell her all the things that happened. I think Fishgoppel thinks I don't tell her because it is too terrible, but it is because it needs so many, many sentences."

Carter's hand reached in the direction of, found and lifted his glass. He sipped and said, "What year did you go to Czechoslovakia?"

"The year I am not sure. I was still small."

"Was it before or after Munich?"

"I will write to ask my mother."

"Were you trying to come to America?"

"That is complicate to tell," said Ilka. "I went with my father to the American consulate. He put our names on the list. But there was a quota. Our number took eleven years to come up and by this time my parents were already long ago taken away. My father has been found on the list of dead."

"How did you get separated from your parents?" asked Carter.

"When the Germans came to Grenoble . . ." said Ilka.

"You went to France! Christ!" said Carter.

Recollection produced recollection and now nothing could stop Ilka. Carter sat, smoked, and sipped and had to be made to comprehend the words missing from Ilka's vocabulary in order to supply them. Once in a while he interrupted Ilka: "That was the same spring?" he asked. Or, "After that did you hear from your mother?" and, "You came back via occupied Hungary!" Carter Bayoux was trying to understand the history and geography of the route by which Ilka had crossed and recrossed Europe to Lisbon, thence to New York into his room in the Hotel Bloomsbury Arms. "So you see," concluded Ilka, "you need not take me over the street into the subway."

"I believe I will beg off for today," said Carter, but he got up and walked her to the door, where he took her in his arms.

Like someone who has been approaching a terrain—a mountain perhaps—across the intervening landscape and presently finds the slope underfoot, Ilka felt the astonishment of his actual chest, the feel of the stuff of the green pajamas against her cheek, the thrust of his stomach, and the heat that radiated from his flesh, its breathing, and, way in the center of his bulk, a faint but perceptible trembling.

He said, "I'm going to snap out of this and I'll call you."

"You're not Wallace," Carter said to the bellboy. He was no boy. He was a yellow man with deep yellow freckles and doll-size ears set high on his long head. He wore pointed, fox-colored shoes. Carter thought he said, "Bones," and said, "What is your name?"

"Bones," said the bellboy.

"Well, then, Bones," said Carter with his slow tongue, "take money, on the dresser, and walk across the street and get me a quart of house bourbon. What time is it?"

"Five of twelve," said Bones.

"Twelve!" Carter's head snapped up. "Run, Bones! What day is this?"

"Saturday," the bellboy said.

"Run, Bones, run!" cried Carter. "Run, run, run, Bones!"

*   *   *

I N T H E M O R N I N G Carter called down and said, "Get me Dr. MacSamuels."

The switchboard said, "Doctor's office hours are two to six Monday through Friday."

"I am ill now," Carter said. "Get him now."

"Hold on," said the switchboard.

Carter held the phone in his right hand while his left counted thumb two three four five four three two thumb two three four . . .

On the sixteenth floor of the Bloomsbury Arms lived and practiced Dr. J. C. MacSamuels, whose nature, appearance and manner had predestined him to be one of the lovable characters in a novel Charles Dickens did not get around to writing. Dr. MacSamuels was a tall, thin, straight-backed old man with a jawful of dead-white false teeth, which clicked out of sync with the ordinary motions of his mouth.

Carter let the doctor in, and said, "I can't sleep," and turned cumbersomely on his bare heel. Picking his way over empty bottles and balls of crumpled paper bags, he laid himself back down on the bed.

"Pugh!" said the doctor. He marched fiercely to the window, drew the curtains and threw up the sash, exposing the shambles of Carter's room to the light of a cold Sunday morning.

"Grrghk!" commented the doctor's teeth.

"I frightened the hotel maid," said Carter from his prone position on the bed. "She doesn't come in any more."

"Do you blame her?" snorted the doctor.

"Blame? Blame? Blame! I'm not in the blaming business," said Carter.

"Gshstrrts!" sputtered the doctor's teeth.

"I've got to get my column in the mail," Carter said.

"You've got to wash up," shouted the doctor. "I'll tell you what I'm going to do! I'm going to give you an injection to make you feel better, and I'm going to prescribe some medicine to help you sleep, if *you* will go put on a fresh pair of pajamas. And wash your face! Make you feel like a new man."

"I will go put on a fresh pair of pajamas. And I will wash my face," Carter said.

"Grbblwhts!" said the doctor's teeth. He tossed Carter's trousers off the chair and sat down, wrote out a prescription and said, "Hand me that phone. Send Wallace up to thirteen-o-six!" the doctor barked into the receiver. "And send the maid with some clean sheets. Yes. Yes. Well, yes. I can see that with my own eyes! So, then, send up some sheets with Wallace. Tz-rmpts!" added the doctor's teeth. He snatched Carter's trousers off the floor, picked the coat up and went and pitched them into Carter's closet, stuffed Carter's socks into the toes of his shoes and tossed them in too. He went and opened the door for Wallace and put down on a piece of paper which drugstores might be open on a Sunday morning. "You got money?" he shouted at Carter.

Carter pointed to the top of the dresser. Wallace looked under the handkerchiefs; he turned over book matches, keys. Standing with his back to Mr. Bayoux and the doctor, Wallace put his hand in his own pocket and said, "He got a fiver here."

"Go!" Dr. MacSamuels said. "Where d'you keep your clean pajamas?" he asked Carter.

While Carter was in the bathroom showering and putting clean pajamas on, Dr. MacSamuels, grumphing and ruckling his teeth, tore the dirty sheets off Carter's bed and stuffed them into the closet, slammed the closet door to, and kicking bottles every which way, made up a fresh bed.

"Next time!" he shouted when he left the sick man sitting on the edge of the bed, "I'm going to send you to the hospital, you hear me!"

"No hospital!" said Carter.

"You behave, then!" shouted the doctor and with his fist he patted Carter five or six times on the shoulder.

When the doctor had closed the door, Carter turned the radio up. An elderly male voice said, "Mrs. Fenimore, honey, why don't you read us one of our listeners' letters?"

"Here is one," said an elderly woman's voice, "from a long-time friend of Jesus in Pasadena. She writes, 'Dear Dr. Fenimore, I want to tell you what a blessing the *Hour with Jesus* was to my dear mother. She was a shut-in for the last twelve years of her life. When she passed on I didn't have anybody I knew and I didn't want to live. Then I turned on the *Hour with Jesus* and it was as if we were all together again, my dear mother and I, and you, dear Dr. Fenimore, and dear Mrs. Fenimore, visiting with our Saviour.' "

"Isn't that a beautiful letter, friends?" said the elderly man's voice. "Now, Miss Beverly, will you step up to the microphone and give us the blessing of a song?"

Chords and arpeggios, and Miss Beverly sang,

> *Lord, I trust in you*
> *Always, always,*
> *With a faith that's true*
> *Always. . . .*
> *When my days are drear,*
> *And no friends are near,*
> *Jesus, you are here*
> *Always. . . .*

Carter put out his hand and turned the knob. Tunes from the
Vienna Woods. He turned. A *Sunday Morning Opera* was presenting *Götterdämmerung*. Carter turned and a woman's huge
voice sang,

> *I got shoes. You got shoes.*
> *All God's chillan got shoes,*
> *My Lord,*
> *When I get to heaven*
> *goin' put on my shoes*
> *goin' walk*
> *goin' talk*
> *all over God's heaven.* . . .

Carter turned her off. The alternative was silence. Carter turned
the radio on, and Miss Beverly was singing,

> . . . *Jesus is my bow'r*
> *Through the passing show'r*
> *Till the world's in flow'r*
> *Always.* . . .

Carter turned the knob. There was a voice crying, "And will
He who has numbered the hairs of your head suffer your head
to ache you?"

Carter widened his eyes.

"If one of your little ones comes to you, says, 'Pa, I got this
pain here,' are *you* going to tell him, 'Don't come bothering
me; I got my business to attend to'? No! You're going to tell
him, 'Come here, son, and tell me, where does it hurt you?'
And aren't you, every least one of you, like unto one of these
little ones?"

Carter put his chin back into his hand.

"Is he going to tell you, 'Sorry! But I'm about my business:
I have to keep the world going round, I have the spheres to

stay on their courses, I got the oceans to hold in my hands, don't you come bothering on at me with your bitty aches and pains'? No, sir! *You* know what he's going to say to you because your Bible tells you! He's going to say, 'Come unto me, all ye who are heavy laden, and ye shall find rest unto your souls.' So what are you waiting for? You come right on up here and tell the Lord Jesus, 'Here is my pain. Heal me, Lord.' "

Carter lay down on his side.

"Step up here, brother! Stand right beside me and speak into this microphone so Jesus can hear you. Tell the Lord your name. Don't you be shy."

"John Manley," the child of God said too loudly.

Carter meant to turn the radio off but the intention operated like a thought in a dream, exerting no influence on the weight of his hand on his thigh.

The preacher said, "Tell the Lord Jesus what burden of pain you have come to lay upon Him."

"Yes, sir. It's not so much a pain, sir . . ."

"Don't be shy, Brother Manley. Jesus is not ashamed of your pain! Don't you be ashamed."

"No, sir. But it's not a pain—more like a noise, right *inside* my ear."

"It's his ear, Lord," the preacher told Jesus.

"Sometimes there is just this real little noise, like someone is"—here the radio bit a word out of Brother Manley's speech—"right inside my ear . . ."

Carter's eyes had closed. The air he blew through his nose encountered a blockage and sought outlet through his closed lips in a series of small explosions.

". . . Other times it's loud, like Niagara. Onliest thing can drown it out is the hi-fi with the volume turned all the way up that drove my wife right out the house! After thirty-one years. Said she couldn't take it another minute." The child of God was weeping very bitterly.

"In the name of our blessed Lord," said the preacher, "I put my hand on—which ear did you say this is?"

"The left, sir."

"On the left ear of your child, Lord, and I say to the evil one, 'Cease from passing your water inside the ear of this beloved one of Jesus, and come out of him! Come out! Come OUT, in the name of the blessed Trinity, COME OUT!' Lord! I felt a rushing out of this brother's ear up my arm and out of my fingers! *Now* you can't hear him!"

"Only just this real *little* noise, right *inside* my ear," said Brother Manley.

"Arise, everybody! Stand and sing praise unto the Lord for his miracle, which your eyes have witnessed upon this brother!"

An avalanche of sound; thousands of believers scraped back their chairs. They sang,

> *Come, ye disconsolate,*
> *Here tell your anguish.*
> *Earth has no sorrow*
> *That heaven cannot heal. . . .*

And Brother Manley cried, "*Now* with everybody singing real loud, I don't hear the noise inside my ear! Oh, sir, thank you!"

"Don't thank me, brother!" cried the preacher. "Thank the blessed Lord Jesus! He has taken your pain away."

Going up in the elevator and along the empty corridor Wallace continued the computation that had occupied his bus ride—10 cents there, 10 cents back, way the hell to the other side of Fifth Avenue, to find an open drugstore—was 20 plus $3.55 for the medicine was $3.75 plus 35 plus 10 was 45 Mr. Bayoux owed him was $4.20 or was it take *away* 45 from $3.75 was $3.30 out of the fiver, which he pinched off of Mr. Bayoux, which he put back, was $1.70, or take away $4.20 was 80 cents. Wallace knocked and knocked again. He pushed the door open.

Mr. Bayoux slept on his back. Put put put put, like a motor-bike.

The boy put the package from the drugstore on the chair next to the bed and he put ninety cents back on the dresser and helped himself to a quarter tip; that left sixty-five cent on the top of the dresser. Wallace put his hand in his pocket and he put a dollar back.

"Dearly beloved," said Carter's radio, "know this, that Almighty God is the Lord of life and death, and of all the things to them pertaining, as youth, strength, health, age, weakness, and sickness, wherefore whatsoever your sickness is, know you certainly it is God's visitation." Carter turned with a moan. ". . . For what cause soever this sickness is sent unto you: whether it be to try your patience for the example of others, or that your faith may be found in the day of the Lord laudable, glorious, and honorable, to the increase of glory and endless felicity. . . . "

Carter's sleeping breath forced an opening between his lips and popped out like a necklace of little farts.

*　　　　*　　　　*

MONDAY MORNING. Carter filled his glass and was going to pick it up and drink it; however, he did not. Like the series of points that make a line, the moments in which Carter did not pick up the glass made half a minute, a minute, five minutes, half an hour—became the morning Carter Bayoux stopped drinking. He sat on the edge of the bed and waited for his hand to stop shaking and his heart to calm so he could pick up the phone and speak to the switchboard. There was a moment when Carter understood that the shaking was not going to stop. The commotion in his chest was increasing. He picked the phone up. "Get me room service. . . . Room service, send me up a quart of milk."

"A quart of milk?" Room service did not recognize quarts. Milk came by the glass.

"Send a glass of milk, send cheese, send good black bread."

Room service had cheese danish, English muffins, doughnuts; room service had white toast.

"Send two—send three glasses of milk. Put it on my bill."

There was another moment when Carter understood that room service was not going to send anything. He picked the phone up and gave the switchboard the name of the Council for Eretz Israel. The switchboard, responding to a sign from the desk, said, "Mr. Boyd wants to talk with you, can you hold on?"

"I can hold on." Carter watched his hand shake.

Mr. Boyd in Carter's ear said, "Mr. Bayoux, will you be coming down any time at all?"

"I shall be going out to lunch."

"Then, Mr. Bayoux, would you stop by the desk. We're having a little trouble here."

"I will stop by the desk," said Carter, "if you will send somebody up to clean my room."

"That's one of the things," said Mr. Boyd, "we're having a little trouble with. Also, Mr. Bayoux, we are having trouble with your bill here, which you owe us a month's rent."

"I'll stop by," said Carter. "Give me the switchboard." Carter called Ilka and asked her to have lunch.

It took Carter time to get dressed. He was easily winded and discouraged. When the bottom dresser drawer would not open, Carter kicked it and sobbed and hooking both hands into the handles sat hard on the floor when the thing slid smoothly out of its moorings. Carter sat on the floor and looked into the drawer. There were no socks. He wept, the whole project of getting dressed put in question. Men have died and worms have eaten them with or without socks, but in the fifties none had gone with naked ankles to a mid-Manhattan lunch.

But recovery, once it is under way, is as inexorable as a collapse. Carter found the pair of socks Dr. MacSamuels had stuffed into the toes of his shoes and wept, as at a sign of grace—a warranty of good to come. That the $1.65 on the dresser was not going to pay for two lunches was a fact too drastic to think about. Carter did not think about it, and he did not think about the rent. He wished he knew what day of the month this was. He shoveled the things on the dresser into his pockets and walked out of that room and walked down the corridor and rang for the elevator. Carter Bayoux stepped out into the lobby, and putting one foot before the other, crossed to where Mr. Boyd waited behind the desk. Wallace draped across the desk top; the switchboard girl's left ear projected from behind the switchboard. He said, "Do I have mail?"

Mr. Bayoux went through the accumulation of his letters, extracted one, took out of it his check from the *Harlem Herald* and said, "Give me a pen." He braced his uncontrollably shaking arm, signed, and said to Wallace, "Run this over to the bank. First get me a *Times,* will you? I'll be sitting on the couch over there."

(Many years later, when he was a man—a superintendent on Riverside Drive, married, with three boys, one in the service—Wallace would wake sometimes, in the pre-dawn, adding or subtracting the dollar tip Mr. Bayoux had given him when he brought him his money from the bank, to, alternatively from, the sum that Wallace never could figure out if he had made off of Mr. Bayoux or which Mr. Bayoux still owed him.)

★   ★   ★

THEY STOOD on the Fifth Avenue sidewalk. Ilka looked at him and said, "Should you go home?"

"I have to eat," said Carter.

Ilka said, "On Madison Avenue is a luncheonette." They walked east on Forty-second Street.

"Is in here all right?"

They waited in the noisy, inadequate space just inside the door, which kept opening to let patrons out and let patrons in. "Do you want to go to another restaurant?" Ilka asked him, but the four women at the corner table were collecting their four separate checks, four handbags, four coats, three hats, two scarves, and several paper bags and packages.

Carter sat in his coat at the tiny table. "Are you all right?" Ilka asked him.

Carter snapped his head around and said, "Is this self-service?" but a waitress walked toward them. She said, "Lunch kraut!" in a German accent. "Animals."

"Bring me milk," said Carter. "You have something you like," he said to Ilka.

Ilka said, "I have a question."

"Shoot," said Carter.

"About the bridegroom," said Ilka.

"Ye-es?" said Carter and he did not look so ill. He looked suddenly charming and formidable.

Ilka said, "You said he has no protocol?"

"Ye-es?"

Ilka laughed. She said, "Did I understood that, that the father of the bride has asked you to screw his daughter, yes?"

"Yes." Carter regarded Ilka with the most cheerful satisfaction. "You are something else! You act so prim and can talk so dirty!" Carter did not understand that the German words Ilka would not have taken in her mouth lost their taboo in the translation.

"And this is protocol!"

"Ah! Well. Harris. He's a queer fish. Race and sex—it's a queer business."

"I have another question?"

"What is your other question?"

Ilka said, "Because I don't say the Negro is in the kitchen means I am anti?"

"What does it mean?"

Ilka said, "That I wish to be polite."

"You mean it's impolite to be a Negro?"

"It means," said Ilka, "one is nervous. You must allow being nervous."

"Must I?" said Carter.

At the checkout counter Carter stood looking into his stuffed wallet.

"Mister," the girl at the cashier's desk said. The lunch queue was forming behind Carter. Carter stared at the bills. Somebody said, "Get with it," and Carter put the wallet on the counter in front of the girl and said, "Help yourself."

"Tz tz," the girl said.

They stood on the sidewalk and Carter said, "What are you doing tonight? I'll buy you dinner and teach you to listen to good jazz."

★   ★   ★

Move," Carter told Ilka. "Tap your foot."

Ilka smiled inside her glass. She averted her eyes from the large, stout Carter, who was nodding his head, tapping his foot. He looked silly. Ilka would have liked the music without this insistent beat. She said, "I have still a question about the bride-groom."

"Oh, Jesus!" said Carter.

Ilka said, "Do *you* think he needs forgiving?"

"He is unforgivable." Carter was waving to the guitarist on the bandstand. The guitarist spoke to the trombonist on his left, who went on playing. The guitarist put down his instrument, rose and seemed to be sleepwalking across the dance floor toward them.

"Chrissake, Carter!" said the guitarist. His eyelids were descending; just before they closed he opened them very wide. They began, once more, to descend.

"Eddie! A long time!" Carter said. "This is my friend Ilka Weissnix, from Vienna. I'm teaching her to drink whiskey and listen to good jazz. Sit down, man." Carter reached his hand toward the guitarist, who radically slanted. Gravity was about to get him, but he twisted his shoulders in a complex maneuver that restored his body to the upright, and opened his eyes very wide. The two men talked over old acquaintances.

"Did you know Ebony Baumgarden was in town?"

"*Is* she!" said Carter. "Going to give old Ebony a call. She still married to that bitty Jewish fellow—what's his name?—Stanley."

"Sure is! Jonas came in and jammed some."

"You see Jonas! I don't see Jonas. Jonas is my kid brother," Carter explained to Ilka. "Played one hell of a piano before he married my sister-in-law, the pill. Getting so I can't stand churchgoing black folk. Eddie, play 'Doing the New Low Down' for my friend from Vienna. . . . I want you to meet my brother, Jonas," Carter said as they watched Eddie somnambulate toward the bandstand. "Jonas is a charming man. You'll like Jonas. I'll call them and maybe we'll drop over."

Ilka watched Carter Bayoux's massive back; she observed how the fold of the back of his neck bulged over the collar of his sport jacket and decided she must start to go out and see other people. Carl from the wedding came promptly into, and went as promptly out of, Ilka's mind. Harvey Blum never so much as occurred to her. It did occur to Ilka that she precisely *was* "out": the room was full *of* other people, men—young men. What was she supposed to do about it?

Ilka watched Carter Bayoux, large, stately, sad, coming toward her. He sat down. He said, "They were on their way to bed." His great head loomed over the table. "Ellen can't abide me."

"Excuse me?"

"My sister-in-law. She doesn't like me."

"Not like you!" marveled Ilka.

"She has reasons," said Carter, "but I'm snapping out of it. I'm going to start going out and seeing people."

"Are you going to see that painter?"

"I'm going to call William. Have you had dinner?"

"No."

At the door they waved to Eddie, the guitarist, asleep on his chair on the bandstand and he waved back.

Outside, Carter put on his beret. They walked, and he said, "There used to be a good Spanish restaurant right someplace around here. Do you like Spanish food?"

"Yes."

"Maybe it was Eighth Street? Do you like Italian food?"

"Yes," said Ilka.

They walked past one Italian, one Chinese, and two French restaurants. They walked past a luncheonette.

"I think you are not feeling so well?" said Ilka. "I can grab the subway here. You need not to come down really."

"Protocol," said Carter gloomily. At the turnstile he stood and said, "Damnedest thing! One day I take you to dinner at the Coq d'Or and put on the dog, next day I can't walk into a lousy luncheonette."

Ilka raised her eyes to the heavy droop of Carter Bayoux's

face and the sad expanse of his cheek grew larger, larger—it filled her vision; her lips touched and depressed the surprising softness of male flesh while her mind went scampering after something funny, quickly, in English, with which to unsay what she was doing here. Ilka laughed and said, "This is not protocol!" and removed her face to the distance at which his face recollected its surface and outlines, with a difference: his wide-open, unblinking eyes looked without a hint of irony, shameless with emotion, full into Ilka's face.

★   ★   ★

CARTER DID NOT CALL the next day or the next day. All day Saturday and Sunday Ilka's telephone kept not ringing, but on Monday he called her at the Council and said, "We're going Uptown. What's Uptown?" Carter quizzed Ilka.

"Fishgoppel's apartment is uptown from the Bloomsbury Arms," replied Ilka.

"Fishgoppel's apartment is two blocks west of Uptown," said Carter. "In ten years Uptown will catch up with Fishgoppel, and you and Fishgoppel will move down—or out of—town. A friend of mine is doing a benefit."

"What is a benefit?" asked Ilka.

And that is how Ilka Weissnix from Vienna arrived in Harlem, by taxi. Carter Bayoux walked her into a group of Negroes chatting on the sidewalk.

"Carter, good to see you back!"

"Jack." Carter shook hands with a man in the brownest suit Ilka had ever seen. "Ilka, Jack Davis. My friend Ilka. Ilka is from Vienna. Ilka, Susan. Dave, how are you? My friend Ilka Weissnix. Ginny, goddamn!" Carter kissed a brown woman with red hair. "This is my friend Ilka."

Ilka shook a lot of people by the hand and was so preoccupied with being afraid that she might not remember their names she couldn't hear what their names were. Chatting, asking after each other's health, work, children, the group moved through the door of a town house and up the stairs into a room full of more Negroes than Ilka had imagined there could ever be in one place. The men wore sober three-piece suits, the women had on hats and gloves. They stood around a very black woman in a black dress. Something gauzy covered her bare arms; something cinched and spangled her waist, which was improbably narrow for such a width of hip and fullness of bosom. The woman's hair had been pulled back to fit like a black cap close to the small skull. Her face was so neatly featured it was in danger of prettiness except for the eyes, which shone with an uncommon luster, rather like a glare. She saw Carter and raised a hand. Carter walked over and kissed her. She said, "I heard that you were back in town."

"Back," said Carter, "and getting into the swing. Why don't you and Stanley have me over? Where *is* Stanley?"

"Just got out of the hospital. Winter's a bad, bad time for Stanley."

"Damn," said Carter. "I didn't know that."

"Yes, indeed," said the woman and compressed her lips and nodded her head with a big up-and-down motion. "Come and have dinner Sunday."

"Sunday I can't! A raincheck!" said Carter. "Sunday I'm taking Ilka to the Jet Fashion Ball."

"The Jet Fashion Ball, aha!" Ebony nodded up and down. "Taking Ilka."

"Is that Uptown?" asked Ilka, who had been trying to think of something to say so as not to keep standing there saying nothing.

"Uptown! The Jet Fashion Ball! No *way!*"

"Not on your tintype," said Ebony.

Here Carter excused himself and left the room. Ilka said to the woman, "I have never yet been to any ball."

"No more have I," said the incandescent Ebony.

Ilka could think of nothing else to say and was glad when the man in the brown three-piece suit, whose name she had been told and had forgotten, approached to claim Ebony's attention.

Ilka had all this while been keeping a corner of an eye on the two other white people in the room—a pair of pleasant-looking women with short, graying hair. They wore blue knit suits and many strings of beads and were taking their places at the far end of the rows of chairs arranged like seats in a theater. Everybody was sitting down. Carter came in and sat down beside Ilka. The red-haired black woman introduced Ebony Baumgarden to the roomful of her well-wishers and friends and then she came and sat on the seat Carter had kept for her on his other side.

It was a one-woman show—a skit. Ilka had no difficulty following the switch from one character to another because the changes in Ebony's voice and accent were accompanied by alterations in her aspect. Like the portraitist and the caricaturist, this Ebony was privy to the mysteries of likeness. By tightening her back, narrowing the brow and recessing the lip, she metamorphosed herself into an excruciatingly fine white lady, "Because a fine white lady," she said in her ordinary voice, "is what every man, woman and child would really like to *be.*" This sank a hook and ripped from her audience a simultaneous howl of laughter. Ilka, who didn't know why they were laughing, smiled. Ilka thought she must be misunderstanding the development of the plot. If the fine white lady were climbing into the bed of a big black boy, would the black boy be climbing out the other side, striking from the roomful of sober middle-aged Negroes a second communal scream of laughter? If, went Ilka's theory, this *was* what was happening in Ebony's skit, Ebony would not be acting it out here, with Ilka and the two other white ladies sitting right in front of her. Ilka looked past the laughing Carter, past the laughing red-haired woman, past the whole roaring row to where the two pleasant-faced white women sat smiling, and Ilka kept smiling.

By loosening her wrists, rounding her shoulders and letting her arms hang with inturned hands, Ebony turned herself into the caricature of a scared black boy, who hollered, "Rape! Police!" and leaped out of the window.

During the protracted volley, discharge after discharge, of black laughter that seemed not to know how to come to any end, Ilka's smile grew embarrassed. She stopped smiling, but finding that her facial muscles did not know how to produce the likeness of an absence of expression, returned the corners of her mouth to the "smile" position and looked along the row. The corners of the white women's two smiling mouths looked as if four invisible clothespins were holding them up.

Afterward Carter walked Ilka into the nearest bar, asked the waiter for a glass of water, and swallowed a palmful of pills.

"From Dr. Wharton?" asked Ilka.

"From the bathroom, at the benefit," Carter said.

"What are they for?"

Carter put on his glasses, studied the label on the little vial and said, "Damned if I know."

Ilka said, "Ebony is beautiful, no?"

"Ebony," said Carter, "is something else."

"She didn't look at me. She didn't notice me," said Ilka.

"She looked. She noticed. Ebony is a quick study."

Ilka said, "A question."

Carter braced his elbows on the table and cupped his hand behind his ear in token of the absoluteness of his attention.

Ilka laughed. She said, "You said when Uptown moves to 'Washingstein Heights' Fishgoppel and I will move. I think not."

"You will move," said Carter.

"I will not move," said Ilka.

"You will be the last to move," said Carter, "but you will move."

★　　　★　　　★

CARTER CALLED and asked if Ilka knew what a gospel singer was. Ilka did not know. Carter said, "You are going to meet the world's greatest."

They walked down a sunny street. In unevennesses of the ground lay pillows of snow. Little Negro children, booted, mittened, scarved, and stuffed into padded suits that made their arms stick out sideways, ran and fell over and had to be picked up and stood back on their feet, like knights incapacitated inside their armor.

Carter rang a bell. A mustachioed black man showed them into a parlor with a green velvet sofa, and Ilka saw her first television. The soundless image kept rolling, like a Cyclops's giant eye, continually disappearing into a nonexistent forehead.

The mustachioed man introduced himself. He was Ulalia's manager. He went upstairs to fetch the world's greatest gospel singer. Carter muddled with the tape recorder, the size of a suitcase, lent him by the *Harlem Herald.* The thing kept shutting itself off.

Ulalia Dixon was a moving black mountain of woman with a lovely face. She lowered herself onto the other end of the little green sofa on which Ilka had seated herself. Carter sat in the wing chair and kept an eye on the tape machine. The manager perched on the piano stool.

Carter seemed nervous. He had prepared an opening gambit:

He asked Ulalia if there was a time in her life when she was so shy or scared that she couldn't sing.

"No," said Ulalia.

Carter said, "Was there that moment when someone, or something, maybe inside yourself, told you you were going to be the world's greatest gospel singer?"

"I always sang," said Ulalia.

The tape recorder whirred softly. All through the interview Ilka kept thinking that somebody must be about to get up and turn off the television. And all the time Ilka kept trying to think of something that she could say or ask with which to inject herself into the proceedings.

The manager said, "Ulalia used to sing in the church where her daddy was preacher, didn't you, Ulalia?"

"No," said Ulalia. "I never sang in Medgarsville church. I lived with my grandmamma in Connersville. I used to sing in the Connersville choir."

The whirring rose half a pitch. Carter and the manager looked at the machine. The manager seemed about to leap up but the tape relaxed. It whirred softly.

The manager said, "Ulalia's grandmamma was so poor, Ulalia told the man from *Jet* magazine she never had a dolly when she was a little girl."

"I didn't tell him," said Ulalia. "You told him that I didn't have a dolly. I told you we used to tie two sticks together and my grandmamma gave me a kerchief and made a baby doll. We used to play all the time."

"Anyway," said the manager, "the people in Connersville saw this spread—did you see the spread *Jet* magazine did on Ulalia March sixteenth?—so when Ulalia went on tour down in Alabama they had a reception for Ulalia in Connersville church, didn't they, Ulalia?"

"They got a new church down there now can seat two thousand," said Ulalia.

"Anyway, two cute girls—all dressed up—presented Ulalia

with a life-size baby doll, which Ulalia never had when she was a little girl. I got the pictures here you can use for your spread. Here: Ulalia accepting the dolly. It was the happiest day of Ulalia's life, wasn't it, Ulalia?"

There was a pause. Ilka asked, "Alabama—is that Southern?" and each of the three Negro faces underwent an alteration: Carter looked up from his anxious watch over the tape recorder; Ulalia looked suddenly not absent and turned her face in Ilka's direction; the manager stopped trying to look sly and in a different, normal voice said, "Man, is Alabama Southern!"

"Southerner they don't make 'em," said Carter and the tape recorder stopped turning and started to whistle.

"I'll fix it. You go on," said the manager.

Carter said, "What I want to talk with you about: As a Negro artist, have you been able to make what Richard Wright has called 'an honorable adjustment to the American scene'? Have you found such an adjustment within the church?"

" 'Thou art Peter, and upon this rock I will build my church.' Matthew sixteen, eighteen," said Ulalia.

Carter said, "I'm talking about what I have called the fear-hate-fear complex which inevitably, I believe, afflicts the Negro in a racist society."

Ulalia looked at the manager's back bending over the recorder and said, " 'Fear God, keep His commandments; for this is the whole duty of man.' Ecclesiastes twelve, thirteen."

Carter said, "I'll send you a column I did for the *Herald.* I'm talking about the vicious circle that turns our fear of the white man into hate of the white man into fear of retribution into more hate."

" 'Serve the Lord with fear,' " said Ulalia, " 'and rejoice with trembling.' Psalm two, verse eleven. 'I know that my redeemer liveth,' " she added. "Job nineteen, twenty-five. 'Though after my skin worms destroy this body, yet in my flesh shall I see God.' Ibid., twenty-six."

"I read where you refused to ride in a limousine, is that right?"

"All God's children walking, I ain't riding in *nooo* car the white folks be sending round for me," said Ulalia, and the tape recorder began spewing loops of tape like a calligraphic extravaganza. Carter knelt down on the floor next the manager. Behind their busy backs Ilka asked the immense black woman, "Do *you* hate white people?" Ulalia turned toward, without looking at, Ilka, and in the tone one might use to somebody else's tiresome little girl, said, "Oh, *honey!*"

Carter asked if he might use the bathroom and the manager leaped up. "I'll show you."

Ulalia watched the men out and said, "Close the door. You tell me when you hear them." She lifted her gigantic skirt to the level of her waist, revealing an expanse of pink corset, and forcing her hands between the flesh and the rubber constriction began to roll it downward. "Another minute and I was like to die. . . . They coming?"

"No!" said Ilka with her ear to the door.

"You tell me when they on the stairs." Ulalia heaved and labored against the laws of mass and elastic and time.

"They're on the stairs!" whispered Ilka.

"Hold that door!" said Ulalia, stepping out of the huge rubber doughnut.

The two men found the two women where they had left them sitting, one at each end of the green sofa, Ulalia heaving her breath, Ilka's heart pounding with the near squeak of scooting the evidence behind a green cushion in the nick of the moment in which the door had opened.

★   ★   ★

C ARTER CALLED and said, "Can you come quickly?"
Ilka ran all the way to the subway: she sat and tried not to
worry. She hurried to the hotel and was turning into the door
when Carter came out of it in the act of putting his coat on.
His right hand emerged from the sleeve to hail a passing taxi.
"Come!" he said to Ilka. "Carnegie Hall," he told the cabby.

The lobby of Carnegie Hall is lit with a stingy brown light,
drafty with the continual opening of doors, and too narrow to
accommodate the pre-concert traffic. An unnaturally tall black
man tapped Carter on the shoulder and said, "Carter."
Carter said, "Paul! I'll be damned! You're back! Are we letting you sing?"
"Going back to Moscow in the morning," said the tall man,
and turned to greet someone, tapping his shoulder from be-
hind.
"Duke, for Chrissake!" said Carter to the man walking into
the auditorium ahead of him.
"Eh! Carter!" said the duke, turning a wonderfully desic-
cated face. "How're you doing?"
"This way and that," said Carter. "Strange Fruit in Carnegie
Hall!"
"Say that again" is what Ilka thought the duke replied.
"Excuse me. Excuse me," said a woman, pushing a very old
black man in a wheelchair up the aisle. She stopped and said,
"Carter! How are you?" and bent down and said, "Dad, it's
Carter Bayoux."
Carter took both of the old man's hands. The old man smiled
faintly and sadly into the air. Ilka could see that he was blind
and wishing he was at home in his bed.

．．．

On the great, bare stage was a grand piano; a brown woman in a white strapless gown, with a white gardenia in her hair, stood in a round of light. Ilka sat beside Carter and wondered if this was wonderful, or if she couldn't bear the childish voice squeezing through emotions outside Ilka's range. (Long after she had become familiar with that predictable proscenium where small men in tuxedos and occasional women sit in curving rows of chairs and bring forth Bach, Mozart, and Pergolesi, Ilka retained a false memory of a vast space with dark reaches full of motes and mists.)

"You want to meet her?" Carter asked Ilka at the intermission.

"You know her, too?"

"I'm about to," said Carter. He walked Ilka through a door that led to the unornamented and deserted quarters back of the stage.

A young black man in a suit that looked too big for him blocked the stairs and said, "She's not seeing people."

"She'll see me," said Carter.

"Are you a friend?" asked the young man.

"Press," said Carter and showed the man a card.

"Let's go back," said Ilka.

The young man said, "She needs her break. She isn't feeling right. She's not seeing anybody."

"She will see the press," said Carter.

"Go on up," said the man.

"Don't let's go!" said Ilka, running up the stairs beside Carter.

At a long table, on the right, in a bare room like a room in a warehouse, sat the accompanist and an old woman, who looked around when Carter and Ilka entered. (Ilka subsequently doubted her recollection that they had been eating something out of a brown paper bag.)

Carter introduced himself and his friend, Ilka Weissnix from

Vienna. Ilka shook hands with the singer in the white, shining taffeta gown. She looked larger, up close, and also smaller.

"Fellow down on the bottom step didn't want to let us up," said Carter.

The singer smiled dimly. She said, "You came anyway."

"You are wonderful, wonderful," said Carter, "but you know that."

The singer smiled.

Ilka said, "Wonderful."

The singer's eyes looked hot. There were no whites showing. The brown skin had rough patches. Her forehead was pearled with sweat. The white gown was brown where it met the brown breasts. The edges of the gardenia were turning brown and curling inward.

"Well," said Carter. "You need your break." They shook hands with the singer.

"She may be singing Carnegie Hall," said Carter—angrily, thought Ilka—as they descended the stairs at a clip. "She's still the entertainer. I am the intelligentsia."

★   ★   ★

IT WAS a decade later that Ilka asked Ebony about the ball to which Carter had taken her.

"The annual Jet Fashion Ball," Ebony said promptly. "I remember when he took you. What was it like?"

"You never went?" asked Ilka.

"Never went to the Jet Fashion Ball," said Ebony.

"Versailles on the West Side—in the forties, I think it was, in some hotel. I can't remember the name."

Ebony supplied the name and location of the hotel where Carter had taken Ilka to the Jet Fashion Ball.

"I think Carter conjured it up. There are no such rooms,"

said Ilka. There opened up in the reaches of Ilka's memory floors, gilded columns supporting tiers upon tiers of galleries thronging with people in the act of going somewhere else. "There were long tables with white tablecloths," said Ilka. "The people sitting down kept calling Carter. Everybody knew him. Carter knew everybody."

"Everybody knew Carter," said Ebony. "And everybody who was anybody in the black world would be at the Jet Fashion Ball. Were there any white people?"

At all black functions to which Carter had taken Ilka, there had seldom been fewer than two, or more than three or four, other whites, who had walked, talked and sat with one another. Ilka had known their whereabouts in a room, at any moment, but had never attempted to speak with them or to catch their eye, and they never caught Ilka's eye. But looking back, around that long-past ballroom, Ilka saw no white people.

"No," said Ebony, "there wouldn't be—not at the Jet Fashion Ball."

"Except me tagging along behind Carter."

The women had worn gowns, the men dark suits. "I don't think the men wore tuxedos," said Ilka.

"They wouldn't wear tuxedos," said Ebony. "That'd be aping the white folks. Of course they *were* aping the white folks, but if they'd put on tuxedos they'd *know* they were aping them."

"People kept calling Carter to sit with them," said Ilka.

Carter had kept stopping to shake hands, reaching his right hand across his left, like a virtuoso piano player, to shake the hand of someone down the table, laughing his wide-open public laugh, calling people by their names in a high, gay, distraught voice.

"He kept introducing me. . . . Remembering is so interesting!" said Ilka. "I can see, now, what I didn't know when it was in front of my eyes: Carter was embarrassed because I was white and twenty-one."

"He was embarrassed," said Ebony.

"He sat me down at a table," said Ilka.

Carter had held the back of Ilka's chair but they were calling him from the next table. "Hey! Carter! When did you hit town?"

The woman on Ilka's right had spoken to Ilka.

"Excuse me?" Ilka had said. The woman repeated what she had said. She wore a feather in her hair, and a jewel at her throat. Ilka had answered her something. "Is that so!" the woman with the feather had said, and she had turned and said something to the man on her other side. Confused and oppressed by the motion of so many black heads, arms, shoulders, the glimmering of beads and pins and coronets, the commotion of feathers, flowers, streamers, the passing of glasses, the bursts of laughter, Ilka had turned to stone and the susurrus of massed conversation closed over her head.

"I remember the day," said Ebony, "that he took you to the Jet Fashion Ball."

Carter had put Ilka in a cab and raised his hand, absently, in a mock salute. There was such a bleakness in the view she had, through the rear window, of his back walking downtown, that Ilka did not look for the phone to ring when she got home. When he did not call the next day, Ilka called the hotel. He picked up.

"I thought you may be are ill," she said.

"I'm not ill," said Carter.

"Oh, good," said Ilka.

He said nothing more, and Ilka said, "What are you doing?"

"Sitting on the edge of my bed," said Carter.

Ilka thought he was going to ask her to come down and see him, but he did not. "So," she said, "I must go back to file."

"Carry on," said Carter.

★   ★   ★

CARTER CALLED on Sunday and asked Ilka to come down. He was wearing a clean pair of navy-blue pajamas with white piping. It seemed wonderful to Ilka that she had come all the way from Vienna, and was getting to know Carter Bayoux's several pajamas. There were some bottles on the floor around the bed. Carter had a Band-Aid across the bridge of his nose.

"I broke my glasses," said Carter. "Will you help me write my column?"

"Excuse me?"

"My weekly column for the *Harlem Herald* should have been in the mail yesterday."

"I don't write English so well," said Ilka.

"I will tell you what to write," said Carter. "There's paper in the top dresser drawer."

In Carter's top dresser drawer there were paper, envelopes, stamps, etc., and there were three nylon stockings. Ilka thought of the woman Ebony.

"Sit down," Carter said.

Ilka sat in the club chair. Carter sat on the edge of the bed and dictated: "As an American child comma the Negro internalizes a dream of freedom that is baffled . . ."

"How do you spell this?"

Carter spelled "baffled." ". . . baffled by daily comma small comma casual hurts and slights comma and by his lifelong experience of rejection and subordination period His energies are exhausted . . ."

"Slower," said Ilka.

"His energies . . . are exhausted . . . by the struggle to make . . . what Richard Wright has called . . . quote an honorable adjustment to the American scene quote semicolon his personality is eroded by learning merely to tolerate these earliest conflicts period I am not alone comma nor are you alone comma nor are we unusual in our hatred of white people period The next time we riot in Detroit . . ."

"Excuse me?"

Carter spelled "Detroit."

" 'Riot'?" asked Ilka.

Carter spelled "riot."

"You want to write 'riot'?" asked Ilka.

"Yes," said Carter.

Ilka wrote down, "The next time we riot in Detroit . . ."

". . . Detroit comma or burn down Chicago comma or blow up New York . . ."

Ilka put her pen down and said, "I think you cannot write this."

Carter took a cat sip of his bourbon and said, "Why cannot I write this?"

"I think the newspaper cannot print this."

"I'm not *inciting* to riot," Carter said. "I am stating the fact that there are going to *be* riots. Haven't you heard of the second amendment to the constitution?"

"Yes," said Ilka, "but one cannot write things like this."

"You think that I am drunk and don't know what one can and what one can't write."

That was what Ilka thought. They looked helplessly at each other. Carter took a sip of his bourbon and said, "If we can get somebody else, who is not drunk, to say that I can write it . . ."

"Who?" said Ilka.

"Ebony."

"Yes," said Ilka.

"Will you get me my address book, please?" Carter gave the switchboard Ebony's number and said, "This is Carter. My friend Ilka and I are having a problem we could use your help with. I will put her on."

Ilka blushed and said, "Hello. Carter is dictating and I think they cannot print in the newspaper what he is writing."

"Why don't you read it to me," said Ebony.

Carter on the bed listened as Ilka read, "As an American child, the Negro internalizes a dream of freedom that is baffled by daily, small, casual hurts and slights, and by his lifelong experience of rejection and subordination. His energies are exhausted by the struggle to make what Richard Wright has called 'an honorable adjustment to the American scene'; his personality is eroded by learning merely to tolerate these earliest conflicts. I am not alone, nor are you alone, nor are we unusual in our hatred of white people. . . ." Ilka paused.

"Go on," said Ebony.

"It is all right to say this?" asked Ilka.

"Amazing thing is we got to the fifties of the twentieth century without somebody saying it," said Ebony.

Ilka continued. " 'The next time we riot in Detroit, or burn down Chicago, or blow up New York' . . . You can you write this?"

"Yes," said Ebony.

"Then, thank you," said Ilka.

"You're welcome," said Ebony.

"Go on," Ilka said to Carter.

"Where was I?" asked Carter.

". . . 'blow up New York,' " said Ilka.

". . . 'blow up New York,' " Carter Bayoux dictated, " 'how will the president respond? Will he announce a Sunday of prayers, appoint a new commission to study race relations, or send out the national guard?"

Ilka had put her pen down. She said, "You cannot write this about the president."

"*You* cannot," said Carter. "I can write it. Would you help me find the other half of my glasses, which should be on the floor somewhere around here?"

Carter's glasses had snapped across the bridge. Ilka carried the two parts into the bathroom, and with no feeling of disgust, washed off the adhering blood and dried shreds of human flesh. After a couple of tries with several Band-Aids, Ilka had approximately fitted the two pieces. They sat askew across Carter's nose. He kept adjusting the angle and his distance from the paper until Ilka said, "I will write it!"

"It's against your thinking. I couldn't allow it. The last year of my mother's life she converted to Communism. A card-carrying mother. She was living with my wife and me," continued the half-blind, half-drunken Carter, able at one and the same time to write his newspaper column and tell stories. "Mother knew I was not a Communist so she wouldn't let me pay for her *Daily Worker*. An honorable woman, my mother: I gave her an allowance; she paid for it. Tell you a joke," said Carter. "Man and his wife are traveling in Paris. The wife keels over dead. Man doesn't have so much as a hat for the funeral, doesn't know, in his distress, what he's doing, walks into a pharmacy. Now the French word for a hat is the word they use for condom. Man says, 'A black one, please. My wife just died.' Pharmacist says, 'Ah! Monsieur!' "—and Carter touched his thumb to his forefinger and showed how the Parisian pharmacist had kissed his own fingers—" 'What delicacy!' Will you get me a stamp? Thank you. Now, if it's not against your thinking, will you drop this down the mail chute by the elevator?"

It was not against Ilka's thinking, but a programmed nerve, out of the reach of Ilka's reason, continued to expect that the police were going to come and take Carter Bayoux away.

When Ilka came back, Carter raised his great head and said, "So, are you and I going to be lovers?"

"You ask *me* that?" said Ilka.

Carter said, "Who should I ask, if not you? I can't make love to you tonight, but it would make me happy if you would lie beside me. If you lie beside me I think I can sleep." He stretched himself on the bed and turned on his side. He watched Ilka take her shoes off.

"Take your blouse off."

Ilka took her blouse off. "I have always wondered before how people come to have taken their blouses off," chattered Ilka. "I always wondered how the bed has become opened."

"Me too," said Carter. "Always, always wondered that."

"You!" said Ilka. "But you have been married!"

"Several times," said Carter.

Ilka thought of the nylon stockings and said, "And you had other women?"

"Dozens," said Carter Bayoux, "hundreds of women, and each time I wondered how to get the bed opened and their blouses taken off."

"I always thought you know how!" said Ilka.

"I know you think that," said Carter. "All of them always thought that."

Ilka went right on thinking that Carter Bayoux knew that and everything else. Ilka lay down beside him and he said, "I'll teach you how to sleep spoon-fashion."

Ilka marveled at the fit of the big man's bulk into her angles. She was moved by the delicacy of his enormous sleep. Her slightest motion—hardly more than an incipient impatience of the flesh—turned him around, and Ilka fitted herself against the radiant heat of the massive back.

"Seven-forty-five on the nose," said the midget voice on Carter Bayoux's bedside chair.

In the gray light that seeped between and around the curtains, Ilka studied the sleep-swollen lips and woolly hair of the sleeping head of—Ilka saw it for the first time—a Negro. The relaxed flesh of the cheek was folded upward by the gentle push of the pillow, inches from Ilka's face. Barry Johnson sang, "Happy in the morning, happy in the evening," and Carter opened his eyes. While Barry Johnson stepped on the scale and announced to the world that he had dropped six and a half ounces since the previous Monday's weigh-in, and passed on

Mrs. Shirley Feldman of Queens Boulevard's recipe for low-calorie pineapple pudding, Carter Bayoux made love to Ilka Weissnix from Vienna. At eight-thirty-five a car stalled in the Holland Tunnel, and Ilka said, "I must go!" and got out of the bed. "You don't have to take me down!" she said, but Carter was putting his socks on. He said, "I'm going to take you all the way home!"

"I'm not going home. I have to go to work."

"I'm going to take you all the way to work! First lessons the American boy learns is how the pilgrims came on the *Mayflower*, and that you take the girl you make love to all the way home. Second, third, and every grade through high school, the American boy learns about the pilgrims coming, and about taking a girl all the way and I took you all the way!" cried Carter, zipping up.

Ilka, buttoning her blouse, said, "You sound so triumphant."

"Triumphant!" said Carter and stopped to look at the word with displeasure. "Triumphant? I'm not triumphant!"

"I use the wrong word. I don't mean triumphant," Ilka said quickly.

"I don't enter you in triumph!" said Carter. "With happiness, with elation, with gratitude . . ."

"I don't mean that word," said Ilka.

"I don't triumph over the woman I love!" said Carter.

Carter held Ilka's hand behind the back of the tiny elevator woman. Ilka *wished* she would turn around. The switchboard girl was not visible behind her switchboard; the desk clerk was not behind his desk yet. The freckled elderly yellow bellboy stopped his broom to watch Mr. Bayoux and the blonde cross the lobby and walk out the door, behind the two ancient women from the second floor.

At the curb, Ilka and Carter waited behind their two moldering black furs. Their old women's mouths were smeared with the moon color that was fashionable in their twenties. "Who

who who who who who!" said the one who had a cane. "Who says?"

"Everybody!" said the other, who was crooked. "Everybody knows you are a witch."

"I notice you don't mind taking money from a witch!" the one with the cane said.

The crooked one said, "Mind! I don't mind taking anybody's money. Money don't smell. You need me, you pay me."

"I don't need you!" screeched the one with the cane. "Don't I manage Sundays? I cook my soup!"

"That I put in the skillet! Manage! Ha!" The crooked one performed an intricate hop and a step to avoid the cane, which the other stabbed in the direction of her ankles. The light changed. The crooked told the blind, "Cross now," and clutched her arm so spitefully she pushed her off the curb; the blind one with the cane shoved her back and grabbed her arm. Pushing, clutching, they hurried, arms intertwined, bodies bent toward the safety of the farther sidewalk, where our pair overtook them.

"What what what what what!" the one with the cane kept saying and turned her empty eyeballs that were the bluish color of skim milk. The crooked one had come to a dead stop. Her moon-purple mouth hung open, staring after Carter and Ilka holding hands down the subway steps.

"People are so stupid!" Ilka said hotly. "They have to look."

"Oh," said Carter, "I don't know. When I see white and colored walking, I always look, don't you? Always wonder if they make love. Don't you?"

On the sidewalk, outside the Council for Eretz Israel, Carter kissed Ilka and said, "Will you come down after work?"

While Ilka filed, her soul slipped away, back into Carter Bayoux's bed, committed to the reconstruction, in the correct sequence, of every particular that had taken place there. When she got to the part where Carter Bayoux's hand had lighted—so amazingly!—upon her left breast, Ilka's eyes happened to focus on six hundred dozen reverse bevels on the yellow card under her nose. Ilka filed the yellow card and went back to the beginning, where Carter Bayoux's eyes had opened inches from her own eyes, which she had closed, and picked up the next card. Once Ilka's eyes focused upon a curly black mustache and a set of teeth that were smiling at her in a most particular way from across the aisle, in a car, in the subway. Ilka became aware that she was smiling. She straightened the corners of her mouth, but they kept bending upward. Ilka let them bend. People entered, people exited. Ilka forgot the mustache.

The desk clerk was writing in his ledger. Ilka wished he would look up and see her waiting by the elevator going up to Carter Bayoux's room.

Ilka had a mind to drop her handbag and make the little elevator woman turn around. Even if she turned, Ilka couldn't tell her: "I have made love with Carter Bayoux."

Carter held the door with a small, formal courtesy. Ilka came inside and, overwhelmed with shyness, began helplessly to chatter in an English regressed to an earlier stage at which it was indistinguishable from German. Carter was so good as to lower his eyelids between his vision and her nonsense. By the time he raised them, their intimacy had been reestablished.

"I got some Scotch for you," said Carter. "I'm not drinking. I've been going through my mail: My ex-wife Georgia married the Bazwazi ambassador to the Court of St. James's! How about that! Everybody's getting married. I'm getting my pockets organized."

The mess of objects from Carter's dresser top lay in ten discrete piles on his plaid-covered bed. Carter said, "Two coat pockets, one breast pocket. Jacket breast pocket. Right and left jacket pockets. Right and left trouser pockets. Back trouser pockets. What do you know about Kabbala?"

"I know it's . . . I think . . . I have no idea," said Ilka.

"My first job, right out of college, I worked for a Jewish

man," said Carter. Ilka curled herself into the club chair in the confidence that she was about to hear something that would interest and amuse her. "We organized the first chapter of the Anti-Defamation League in New Haven! A sweet, good man. He liked me. He *looved* talking to me about Kabbala. In Kabbala everything is organized into ten—ten emanations of God, ten moral distinctions, ten intellectual distinctions, ten seasons, ten parts of the human anatomy. It stands to reason there are ten pockets in a man's clothing because everything is connected with everything else. Doesn't make a hell of a lot of common sense but it's beautiful the way every damn thing is either left or right or male or female or higher or lower. Everything has its protocol. When you booze a whole lot over a very long time," said Carter, "it damages the brain cells. Brain cells don't regenerate. Once they're damaged, that is it, so I figure if I get my pockets organized before I lose my marbles, I'll be in the habit of putting my hands into the right pockets. Drink your Scotch. That's good Scotch."

Ilka sipped. There was something she was wanting to talk about. Ilka wanted to understand why Carter liked her. She blushed and said, "I think I am not so good, making love?"

Carter stopped organizing, and gave Ilka his attention. It was true, said Carter, that Ilka's youth, so delicious in itself, precluded certain other goods. . . .

"What goods!" said Ilka.

The experience, Carter meant, that came with a great deal of very constant practice. Her potential, he gave Ilka to understand, was incalculable.

Ilka was relieved and gratified. She had not known, and would not have supposed, that she was incalculable. She blushed again and said, "I am not so beautiful."

Carter Bayoux gave this, too, its due attention. "Beauty is a funny thing." There was a line Carter recalled: Beauty is the promise of happiness, whereas Ilka's body had given him actual happiness. "Besides," said Carter, "you have terrific legs."

Here was another thing Ilka had not known. She let several minutes pass before she got up, walked into the bathroom and closed the door. She climbed onto the edge of Carter's tub and took a look at her legs, front, side and back, in the mirror of the medicine cabinet. She could not tell that they were terrific. Ilka supposed that she might not understand the points that made for a good, a bad, or an indifferent leg.

When Ilka came out of the bathroom, Carter was opening the bed. So much Ilka recollected perfectly when she tried, on the subway, going home, to reconstruct the event. It irked Ilka that her own clothes, and Carter's, seemed to have come off in the absence of the presence of her mind. Ilka tried to bring her mind back to the moment in which she had walked out of the bathroom: Carter was opening the bed. A sharp, rather sudden movement focused Ilka's eyes on what was immediately in front of them: the New York subway penis, erect and deeply purple. It touched itself lightly, rapidly to the back of Ilka's hand and disappeared into the navy darkness of the overcoat of the man whom Ilka now knew to have known to have been sitting on her left. He was plunging out the opening subway door.

All the way home and long after she had scrubbed the spot on the back of her hand, Ilka retained the feel of the exact temperature and the extraordinarily fine gauge of the skin of the alien phallus. Ilka wished it well.

★   ★   ★

Carter and ilka told each other things.

Carter said, "Mother was college educated, which was unheard of for her generation—a woman—a Negro woman. My dad was president of a small Negro college long since defunct."

Ilka loved to hear him say "mother" and "my dad."

"Mother was founder and president of the local Culture Uplift Society."

"This you are inventing!" Ilka said.

"The C.U.S. Mother was big on culture," Carter said. "Got us our library cards for our sixth birthdays. She took us to the opera when the opera came to town. Then my dad's college folded."

"Where was this? This was when?" Now it was Ilka's turn to try, as Carter had tried, and mainly failed—as one is bound to fail—to construct a biography out of a friend's stories.

"Nineteen-thirteen. Thereabouts. Mother picked up the pieces, went to work in the next town. My dad stayed home with the baby. My dad never got over it. Mother brought back washing to do nights. Man! did she ever do washing! My dad couldn't miss it."

"But it was necessary?"

"It was necessary. In the middle of the kitchen," said Carter, "singing Jesus songs, slowly, in time with her scrubbing. Couldn't *nobody* miss my mother doing washing, nights. Mornings she'd walk the forty minutes into town to save the five cents' bus fare, the way people used to do in the depression, worked all day in white people's houses, walked back, nights, with white people's washing. Then. One day!" said Carter. "My dad gave me a nickel, sent me to Groller's store. German fellow. Mr. Groller. He gave me twenty cents' change for a nickel. Guess he thought it was a quarter. Maybe he did it accidentally on purpose! Twenty cents! Four nickels! I took the bus to town and waited for my mother outside the white people's house. I must have waited a good hour."

"How old were you?"

"Nine. Maybe ten. My mother came out and she was so pleased! My mother wasn't much for hugging, but she put down her big old bundle of washing and she hugged me! I said, 'Ma, I come to take you on the bus.' I thought I was the cat's pajamas."

"Pajamas!" said Ilka. "A cat's?"

"Two-thirds of the way home mother says, 'Boy, where did you earn ten cents?' I said, 'Twenty cents!' and showed her the nickel I still had in my palm, and I told her about Mr. Groller. Well! Mother picks up that damn old bundle, says, 'Come, boy.' We walk to the front of the bus. She tells the driver, 'Stop the bus, please.' We get off. We start walking, my mother and the bundle that is the size of a goddamn calf. No scolding, never said one word to me the thirty minutes it took us to walk all the way back to town. She was a tall woman, my mother—a good-looking woman in her day. There's a photograph in the album."

"Yes!" said Ilka.

"Mother walked inside with me. I gave Mr. Groller the nickel out of my hand. Mother puts down her bundle. She gets out her change purse from the pocket in her dress, underneath her coat, opens the purse, looks inside, fishes around with her forefinger. She's found a dime. She gives Mr. Groller the dime, looks in her change purse, fishes with her finger for the other nickel. I want to die. So, for all I know, does Mr. Groller. We walk forty minutes home, mother singing Jesus songs, in time with our walking. She was a powerful bitch, my mother! I tell you the last year of her life she converted to Communism?"

Ilka asked Carter, "What will happen to us? Will we end up badly?"

"Of course," said Carter.

Ilka felt the thrill of it. "Of course!" she said.

★   ★   ★

SOVIETS IN BERLIN REFUSE . . ." said the black head-
line and underneath it said "U.S. DENIES . . ." Ilka raised her
face to the face of the man hanging on the same subway strap
and said, "Will it be war?"

The man said, *"Acabo de llegar y no entiendo ninguna cosa. "*
Ilka fell out onto the platform under the feet of the Russian
consulate. The small round women in their black coats
tut-tutted and picked Ilka up and dusted her off. They rubbed
her knee, they stroked her elbow. Their concerned faces ea-
gerly assured her that she was much hurt, though Ilka kept
shaking her head: she was fine; she was perfectly all right.
Their faces blossomed in relief. They chatted and seemed to
be telling each other that she was perfectly all right, but they
escorted her up the stairs, patting and murmuring.

Ilka ran the block to the agency, called the Bloomsbury
Arms, and asked Carter, "Will there be war?"

Carter said, "If it be not now, yet it will come."

"You sound happy!" said Ilka's paralyzed lips.

"Excited," said Carter. "Poor European Ilka! Let's go and
watch it happen. Do you know how to get to the United Nations?"

Ilka stood under the Olympian domino that looks to be perpetu-
ally falling. The sky was a freshly laundered, windy blue. Ilka,
who had continued all day at an untenable level of horror,
leaned over the parapet and watched the river move its lei-
surely traffic: A black coal barge. A sightseeing boat. The tour-
ists massed against the near railing. A man spoke into a horn.
". . . in place of the old, defunct League of Nations with a gift
of eight and a half million from John D. Rockefeller. The Secre-

tariat and General Assembly were officially opened in 'fifty-
two. . . ." The wind carried his voice away.

Ilka leaned her back against the parapet. On the expanse
of pink pavement milled a crowd of pigeons in a perpetual
exchange of place, dipping anxious, greedy heads with each
advance of each leg. Here and here, and over there, one or another raised and shook an agitated wing. Now one, now two,
now all rose off the ground and settled a few yards to the right:
it was Carter striding toward Ilka, large and laughing, raising
his arms: "Quick! The Russians are coming! You don't want
to miss the Russians coming!"

In a vast, bright, high glass-and-marble lobby, a handful of
people had collected at the foot of an upward-rolling escalator.
"Pierre was looking for you," one of the men said to Carter.

"Oh, okay. Thanks," said Carter. He laid his hand on Ilka's
shoulder and kept it there. He said, "Watch the very tall chap
with the briefcase. The British straggle in one by one." Ilka
fell in love with the thin, beautifully rumpled Englishman, who
stepped onto the escalator saying "How are you?" to the little
crowd of newsmen.

"How's it going, sir?" Carter asked him.

"And I thought you were going to tell me!" complained the
Englishman humorously and was carried upward.

"There. Now!" said Carter. "Watch."

Six, nine, eleven men, neither small nor large, dressed in
ordinary business suits, came at an ordinary pace and, looking
neither left nor right, addressing no word to the press or to
one another, walked not, of course, in step, but as a body, onto
the escalator and were carried up.

"That," said Carter, and he looked very excited, "is the way
power moves inside the enemy's territory!"

"Goddamn phalanx!" said the man who had told Carter that
Pierre was looking for him. "It's the Macedonians, and pow!"

"Come," Carter said to Ilka. He said, "Look in there."
Through a glass set into a sound-proof door Ilka saw the fa-

mous curving rows of seats of the General Assembly, empty except for two Negro women with dust cloths, chatting as they worked along adjacent rows, and a neatly dressed man bending over a microphone. He tapped the microphone, silently mouthed into it and raised an arm to a man in overalls, who was straightening coils of black cable. A woman in a sari was arranging sheaves of paper in the right upper corners of the desks on either side of the speaker's dais.

"Come." Carter walked Ilka into a square, well-lighted elevator and greeted another beautiful man. This one was brown with long white hair and the gaunt, spiritualized look of an old actor. Carter called him "sir," too and asked him if he thought the old bus was going to topple over this time around. The beautiful brown man smiled. He had long, yellow teeth.

"Krishna Menon," said Carter when they stepped out of the elevator.

"Who is he?" asked Ilka.

"My friend from Vienna," said Carter to a beautiful blond man, "just asked me who Krishna Menon is."

"Delighted," said the blond man, shaking Ilka's hand. "Pierre has been asking for you," he said to Carter.

"I'll just go check my desk," Carter said to Ilka.

The corridors of the news section of the United Nations looked like ordinary corridors. Inside the open doors were regular offices in which people sat or moved. Carter's desk was an actual desk in a large room with a large number of desks. On Carter's desk stood a small sign that said CARTER BAYOUX, HARLEM HERALD. Carter picked up a sheaf of papers that looked like the papers the woman in the sari had been arranging on the desks in the General Assembly. Carter put down the papers. He opened and closed drawers in a proprietary manner, waved at some people, who waved back, and said, "Let's go see what Pierre has got."

The four men inside the French newsroom stopped what they were doing to look up at Carter and the girl in the doorway. The middle-aged man in shirt sleeves beckoned them inside. He had a good, clever face with a long, humorous nose. Ilka really liked him. He gave her a brief, frankly curious, very friendly stare before returning his attention to the perpetual paper issuing out of a clatter of machinery. The paper glided over the man's left arm, which he held raised and bent as if around the back of a dance partner. Carter went and stood beside him. Carter and the Frenchman stood with their necks stretched for some minutes until Carter said in a high tone, "I guess we'll live, this time around."

"So it is over?" Ilka asked Carter, walking along the corridor beside him.

"No," said Carter. "First the General Assembly has to meet. The members have to identify the actions of the opposing governments as unwarranted aggression, and to explain the actions of their own governments as justifiable defense of their sovereignty, quoting the numbers of the rulings that support their arguments. *Then* it is over, this time around."

"So this is all nonsense!"

"No," said Carter, "it is protocol. Let's go see if there's something in the delegates' lounge I can get a column out of."

"Are newsmen allowed?"

"Try and keep us out."

The huge, bright chamber was furnished in extreme modern forms and textures. Pan Africa, in caucus on a flamingo-colored couch, rose to its feet at the approach of Carter Bayoux and a white girl. They shook Carter's hand; someone turned an enormous square chair around for Ilka; a space was made on the couch for Carter. A wrinkled black man in a white nightgown tapped a hairy fat black man on the wrist, and said, ". . . because of your run-in with the under secretary. Why don't you let Alex take it to Peking?"

"Run-in! Run-in? What run-in?" asked a black man with a long upper lip, who had vacated his seat on the couch for Carter, and perched on the arm of Ilka's chair.

"Let Alex take it to Peking," said the man in the nightgown.

"D'you want me to sound out the Israelis?" asked Carter. Everybody looked at Carter. "I got to know Peretz pretty well in London. I'll buy him lunch."

"Peretz is in Washington."

"I'll go to Washington," said Carter.

"And then Alex can take it up at Peking," said the man in the nightgown.

"And Quaitucan can get back to the under secretary," said a man who had been standing, with bowed head and one hand in his trouser pocket, behind the couch. Everybody turned. Everyone was silent a moment.

Carter said, "That's your procedure, then! What's wrong with that?"

Someone said, "He was in Accra, at the time. He was with Creasy."

Carter said, "He's your fellow." And the man in the nightgown said, "And Carter will sound out the Israelis in Washington, and Alex can take the whole package to Peking!"

Carter found a notebook in his breast pocket, unscrewed his fountain pen, and said, "Brief me."

It was at this juncture, when Ilka faced the immediate danger of learning the facts in this matter, that her spirit removed itself. Ilka dreamed herself a General Assembly in which she rose to address the curving rows upon rows upon rows of the heads of power. In round, emphatic syllables of perfect English Ilka's spirit spoke: "I have come before you, today, to discriminate between those of my government's actions that are justifiable in the defense of our sovereignty from those actions performed out of our greed, our anxiety, or because of misinformation or plain stupidity. Then it's your turn."

Carter had stood up. Everyone was standing up excitedly. Something had been achieved during the absence of Ilka's mind. A plan—a prosperous expectation—made them sweet and affectionate with one another: they embraced. They embraced Carter. Carter joyfully said, "We've got them by the balls! It's when *you* grab hold of your black power, and not a moment sooner, that we black Americans will be free! Come!" he said to Ilka and walked her rapidly across the room and said, "I need a drink!"

★   ★   ★

C ARTER TOOK Ilka to Washington. In the train he said, "My first wife, Jenny, was a white girl. We got married right out of high school and got cold feet and she went home to her house and I went home to mine." Ilka did not understand that Carter meant they would stay in different hotels.

Carter went off to meet the Israeli attaché. He had appointments all day. All day Ilka wandered in the clean, cold sun, alone and euphoric, along the dumb, grand, lovable vistas of Washington. On the return train an irate old woman with a pink hat walked down the aisle and told Carter to put out his cigarette. She pointed to the sign that said NO SMOKING. Carter looked straight before him. He sat excessively still except for his left arm, which continued to carry the cigarette to and from his mouth.

"Let's go to the smoking car," whispered Ilka. Her heart thumped unpleasantly. The woman in the hat addressed the other passengers, whose parts—legs, elbows, ears—protruded into the aisle. "Get the conductor. Somebody! Police!"

Carter's neck had thickened and shortened and streamlined his head and shoulders: he resembled a high-caliber torpedo. He continued to smoke. Two teenage boys got out of their seats and came down the aisle, passed, and walked out the door into the next car. The woman in the hat settled herself across the aisle in the direct path of the flag of smoke that might be imagined to be emanating from Carter's cigarette; she kept waving it away with her hand, muttering, "Pugh!" or it may have been "Pig!" Carter Bayoux smoked his cigarette down to the smallest possible stub, threw it on the floor and ground it out under his heel. This sent the woman into a transport of rage from which she seemed unable to recover. Her mouth kept working: "The dirty . . . dirty up the whole . . . ought to be . . . the whole pack of them . . ." She muttered the rest of the way to New York. Ilka, her heart in an uproar, kept glancing at the other's face distorted with hatred: the woman looked as if she were in pain.

★ ★ ★

C ARTER CALLED the day before Christmas to ask if Ilka knew how to cook a goose. Ilka didn't know how to cook much of anything. "Oh, well, then," said Carter, "we'll give tradition the go-by. I'll cook you a Christmas steak. Jonas and Ellen have dinner arrangements. We'll catch up with them later."

"Fishgoppel has just arrived," Ilka said.

"Bring Fishgoppel!" said Carter. "I want to meet a Fishgoppel. Bring her along."

The two shy young women flattened themselves against the wall of Carter's kitchen, the size of a closet, to let Carter get to the refrigerator no bigger than a breadbox. He took out an enormous slab of bloody meat. "Is that a steak or is that a steak! I'll teach you to make steak *au poivre*. A little French never hurt an American steak."

"Your name is French?" asked Fishgoppel.

"A corruption, presumably, of Bayeux. My father's owner was old Norman stock. Hold out your hands." He ground fresh pepper into their palms and said, "Smell!" Ilka and Fishgoppel bent obedient heads. "Spiced flowers! Better than flowers! Now we rub the pepper *into* the meat. Other side." Carter pounded, rubbed, stroked the raw muscle with the fingers, the palm and heel of his hand. "Ilka, would you wash the lettuce? Delicately! Don't bruise the leaves. My grandmother was from Benin, on the Gold Coast. My other grandmother was a Chihuahuan from Mexico, and *that* grandfather was half Liberian, half Scots."

Fishgoppel smiled and said, "Are you making this up?"

"Are you going to check me out?" Fishgoppel laughed. Her eyes had begun to shine. "Now," Carter said, "we let the steak marinate, and I will see if I can catch Jonas before they go out. . . . Jonas!" Carter said into the telephone. "What's the deal? Will you come here, or are we coming there? No, no, no. We will have eaten. Who do you think? I make a mean steak. . . ."

Ilka went and stood beside Fishgoppel, who was leaning over the severed hand on Carter's dresser. Ilka said, "Don't you think that's funny?"

"I *think,* " said Fishgoppel.

". . . Well, then, we will come there," Carter said into the telephone. "I'm bringing the best damn bottle of champagne, unless Ellen's church folks are going to be there. I'm not pouring vintage champagne down Cousin Ninny's throat. Oh. She is? They are?"

"Do you like this?" Ilka asked Fishgoppel, who was studying the etching of the howling Negro. Fishgoppel kept studying.

"Brooklyn!" cried Carter. "I'm not coming out to Brooklyn, for Chrissake, without a getaway car! So let Ellen's folks come into Manhattan and I'll take the whole crew out to dinner. So I'll eat a second dinner, what do you care? O.K., then, we'll *come* to Brooklyn. . . . Because I want to spend Christmas with my brother . . ."

"This looks like . . . it can't be a Rauschenquist!" said Fishgoppel in front of the brown paper bag.

"It is. He gave it to Carter in Paris, when they were young. We met him in a restaurant."

"Who? You met William Rauschenquist!" Fishgoppel said. Fishgoppel frowned over the slave ship. Fishgoppel frowned at the harvest of haloed heads growing from the branches of the saint tree.

Ilka said, "I think *that* is funny. I like that."

"That is the root of anti-Semitism," said Fishgoppel.

Ilka looked at the prone saint's two round eyes staring straight before him with no concern for the mystery growing from his belly. His two gothic feet pointed heavenward. "I like it," said Ilka.

Fishgoppel's forehead was criss-crossed as if she were in pain and she said, "So do I!"

". . . I see," Carter said into the telephone. "Yes, I see that. I see that also. That is perfectly fine. Let's get together at New Year's, then. Oh? Might you? I see. Sure. If you get back early give a call, or I'll call you. Very fine. A merry Christmas to you too, and to Ellen. Major mix-up," Carter reported to the girls. "So. The steak's the thing, and we get to drink all the champagne."

Carter instructed Ilka and Fishgoppel in the protocol of drinking vintage champagne.

Fishgoppel said, "You know William Rauschenquist!"

"Met him at Gertrude Stein's when we were *very* young men. Man, were we ever young! I dared him to ask Alice B. Toklas to luncheon and she was pleased as punch. He made me come along to do the talking. I was a glib bastard. Very brash. Very young."

Fishgoppel's eyes glowed. "Did you ever go to Shakespeare and Co.?"

Carter said, "All the time. Sylvia Beach liked me. Gave me stuff to read, till the day she introduced me to Joyce."

Fishgoppel's eyes looked polished to a high gloss as by an extra layer of tears.

"Sylvia said, 'This is Mr. Bayoux, I've been mentioning to you.' Joyce squeezes up his poor eyes, says, 'Ah, the blackamoor from San Francisco!' Me—I turned around and I went barreling out of there like the man out of the cannon. Didn't go back for a month."

Ilka, who had not got the full thrust of this story, sat and watched her two Americans, whom she loved, and marveled at having had it in her power to introduce them to each other.

At the door Carter kissed Ilka and said, "You must bring your cousin more often. It's a waste dropping names to a foreigner from Vienna," he told Fishgoppel, and he kissed Fishgoppel on the cheek.

Carter held the door until the young women had rounded the corner. Then he sat down on the edge of the bed and gave the switchboard a number in London and said, "Charge it to my room."

"Georgia?" he said across the Atlantic. "It's Carter. No, in New York. Sitting on my bed in the old Bloomsbury Arms! I had this yen to wish you a merry Christmas. Didn't wake you, did I? What the hell time is it over there? I can't do the arithmetic any more—I think I've pickled my brains in bourbon. I have your announcement! So! You got yourself an ambassador! I'm very happy for you! Everybody's getting married. Harris found himself a twenty-year-old. But you! You sound wonderful."

Georgia, it turned out, was going to be in New York the first week of the new year. Ferdinand was flying to the Peking summit, and Georgia was meeting him in New York.

"I'll throw you a party!" cried Carter gaily. "*You* know I know how to throw a party! God, it will be a treat to see you!" Carter put the receiver down, picked it up again and put a call through to Paris, but there was no one at home in Paris. He was luckier in Washington, where a crowd of his old friends had gathered for Christmas. Carter invited them all to the party he was throwing, the first week of the new year, for Georgia and her brand-new husband, the Bazwazi ambassador to London. Carter hung up and called Jonas and said, "You're back. So, how was it?"

"Irritating," said Jonas. "Ellen and I are in the middle of a monumental blow-up."

"I told you! Didn't I tell you to stay out of Brooklyn? When will you learn to mind your big brother?" Carter laughed long and heartily and said, "I'll get off the phone. Wouldn't want to come between a man and his wife and their blow-up."

"Ellen wants to—Ellen 'has' to—move back to L.A.," said Jonas. "Last year Ellen 'had' to move East."

"That was to get away from me," said Carter, "and now I've gone and turned up here. It really is too bad! Poor Ellen."

"Come on, Carter," said Jonas.

"That's a part of it. I know that," said Carter, "and you can't blame her."

"Carter . . ." said Jonas.

"Tell Ellen she doesn't have to move on my account. She doesn't have to have me over. I promise to stay out of her hair. And mind *you* stay the hell out of Brooklyn!"

"Carter . . ." said Jonas.

Carter said, "Georgia and her husband, the Bazwazi ambassador to London, will be in New York the first week of the new year and I'm throwing them a big bash. I'll have you and Ellen over. Tell Ellen whatever she may think, I love her!"

"Oh, O.K., Carter," Jonas said. "Listen, have a good Christmas."

"You bet," said Carter and put the receiver down, picked it up again, and gave the switchboard Ilka's number. There was nobody home.

Ilka and Fishgoppel were sitting in the subway going uptown. Fishgoppel said, "If I get us *milchig* and *fleischig* dishes would you like to keep kosher?"

"I! Why? I don't know how!" cried Ilka. "Do you mind if I don't?"

"No, no," said Fishgoppel. "No, of course. That is something I can do when I have my own household."

"But why would you want to!" cried Ilka.

Fishgoppel said, "You know the tree that grows out of a stomach—I'm trying to remember: there's a midrash . . ."

"Excuse me?" said Ilka.

"I think that tree is out of Talmud. I'm going to ask my Yiddish teacher from Vilna. He's teaching me Talmud. He and my landlady are getting married. He'll have a new American family," said Fishgoppel.

Ilka was wanting Fishgoppel to say that she liked Carter. Ilka said, "I like Carter so much because he tells me stories."

"That is very Jewish. That's what midrashim are. Stories. Carter has a Jewish mind," said Fishgoppel.

Ilka was disappointed. She didn't understand Fishgoppel had just told her that she liked Carter Bayoux.

★   ★   ★

Carter sat on the edge of the bed and gave the switchboard Dr. MacSamuels's number, but the doctor was not in the hotel. Carter turned the radio on and emptied his pockets onto the dresser top, then he closed the curtains, got out a fresh pair of pajamas and put them on and sat down on the edge of the bed, picked up the phone and said, "Send Wallace over for a fifth of house bourbon."

Ilka called Carter from the Council to tell him she had a letter from her mother. "My father was shot in the last week of the war when they were moving the camps. My mother writes *she*

left him on the road to Obernpest; that I don't understand. She
will be here in weeks!"

"That is news," said Carter. "And she is not ill?"

"She doesn't say she is ill," said Ilka. "How are you?"

"This way and that," said Carter.

"Ilka! Telephone!"

Carter said, "Can you come down?"

Ilka went down and Carter said, "I can't sleep."

"Should I make a little tidy?" asked Ilka.

"Please," said Carter. He said, "I can't eat." He watched
Ilka hang his pants in his closet and said, "When I snap out
of this, I'll get some saddle soap and do my luggage. I have
leather luggage. Sit beside me."

She must have left the closet door ajar, for in the angled
mirror Ilka saw the improbable pair sitting on the edge of the
bed. She saw the fresh-faced girl in the white blouse put her
arms around the shoulders of the large hunkered man like a
Roman senator in green-striped pajamas. The girl in the blouse
lifted her face and kissed the man on the cheek and kissed him
again and kissed him again and again and again and again and
again and again and again.

Carter said, "Thank you." Then he said, "This is no good
for you."

"It's good! *You* are good," said Ilka.

"I *am?*" said Carter in the voice of someone who has happened upon a subject of peculiar interest to him. "I always wondered about that!" he said with a slow tongue. "Jonas always
thought I was a bastard. I always got the girls."

Ilka could believe it. She said, "But that is to be attractive,
not a bastard!"

"I was a bastard, man!"

Ilka laughed.

Carter said, "What good do you know about me?"

"Are you interested in being good?" Ilka asked with interest.

"Oh! *yes!*" said Carter. "To be a just man in a just world . . ." He put his fingers over his eyes and wept and said, "If I die will you get my obituary in *The New York Times?* They ought to have me in their morgue. Or you can get the facts from *Who's Who in America.* I'm in *Who's Who in America.*" Carter raised his head to tell Ilka, " 'Report me and my cause aright,' " and wept, and said, "Holidays are a bitch."

★   ★   ★

I LKA CALLED Carter to ask how he was and he said, "Can you come *now?*"

Ilka hurried down the subway. At Times Square a small brown family got on the train. The hem of the little girl's pink dress hung several inches below her imitation tiger fur coat. She bagged an empty booth and urgently patted the seats: she wanted her mother and father and fat brother to come and sit down. A family booth. That was something Ilka could understand. The odds were against the child. People were crowding in both doors, and the fat brother sat down and yanked his father's arm. Ilka despaired for the little girl, but the father spoke peremptorily to the little boy; now the doors closed. The girl had got her way! She arranged her four people on facing seats—a marvel of coziness. The child knelt on the seat next to her mother and looked out at the passing blackness. The father laid his arm around the shoulders of the sulky little brother and rubbed the ball of his thumb up and down the fat, soft cheek and did not notice that the child was bending his thumb backward trying to yank the hand away. The father must be used to being yanked. He kept caressing the little boy while he leaned forward to say something to the harried-looking mother; she said something to him and removed the little girl's shoes off the seat with a sharp motion. The little brother's eyes became involved with an advertisement; he angled his head to read it. He kept hold of the father's thumb; the father kept stroking his cheek. Ilka watched the little girl grimace and converse with her image reflected in the window, until the train pulled into Carter's station.

Carter's door was opened by a middle-aged Negro woman, who already had one arm in the sleeve of an ankle-length fur; she was on the point of leaving.

"Come in. I'm on the phone," called Carter from the side of the open bed. "Jonas! Hi!" he said into the receiver, while he pointed his forefinger first at the woman, who had now got her coat on, then at Ilka, then back at the woman. He meant, "Introduce yourselves." They shook hands. "Guess who's here! Georgia hit town this morning!" said Carter gaily, excitedly, into the telephone. He flapped his hand at the woman in the fur; he pointed to the club chair. The woman perched herself on the arm, hooking her slender right foot behind her left calf, shaking her head and pointing at her watch.

"I told you Georgia's married Ferdinand Zambizi, the Bazwazi ambassador to London? He's flying in from the Peking summit. I promised Georgia a party and a party is what we're going to have." The woman on the arm of the chair shook her head. "Can you and Ellen come over?" Carter said into the telephone, staying the woman in the fur with his raised right palm. "Harris and his new bride are on their way over—you remember Harris—my friend, the doctor?—William and Kate Rauschenquist are stopping in. . . . So come for half an hour, I won't hold you. So come afterward. We will still be here. *I* will still be here. Whichever, but come! Jonas is coming," Carter told the woman in the fur coat. "I called William Rauschen-quist!" he said to Ilka.

"Carter, crazy as ever," said Georgia Zambizi. "I told you, I've got to meet Ferdinand at the UN."

"Call him and tell him to meet you here."

"Carter! He's in the air somewhere between Peking and New York."

"Call the delegation. Leave a message. Tell him to come to the party." Carter picked up the phone and put it into Georgia's hand.

"Why do I get involved in this?" said the elegant Georgia.

Carter then called down for more booze, and his ex-wife said, "You don't need any more booze."

"Ilka, get the door, would you? Introduce yourself to my brother Jonas."

But it was not Jonas. It was the bellboy. "Money's on the dresser," said Carter.

"You shouldn't leave your money around like that, Carter, Jesus!" said Georgia. "Every time I see you I want to marry you all over; ten minutes later I want to divorce you."

"It's mutual," said Carter and he took Georgia's hand and kissed it.

A knock at the door. "Ilka, please," said Carter.

It was William Rauschenquist and the thin woman, Kate. Kate wore a cowled, outsize, pewter-colored sweater and Ilka wanted it. Carter had risen from the bed and came and kissed Kate. William kissed Georgia, Kate and Georgia embraced and kissed, Carter and William embraced and patted each other on the arm. Ilka was jealous, so she turned to Kate and said, "That is the whole trouble with having been moving all my life to and fro Europe. I have not collected old friends."

Kate turned to Ilka with a surprised look—a look of dawning interest. Ilka was disappointed: her statement, though true, had been made in order to arouse Kate's interest, and she thought

Kate a fool and lost interest in her. (In the years to come Ilka learned which parts of her history affected her hearers and made good anecdotes; the rest remained untold.)

William was unwrapping what he had brought Carter: a small, furious canvas in voluptuous flesh tones not unlike the extreme female pink of Carter's severed rubber hand, shaded in green, spattered with yellow, and slashed with black lines that gathered into a set of upper teeth in rictus.

Into the noisy commotion of Carter's enthusiasm, pleasure, gratitude, erupted the next knocking. This, again, was not Jonas, but Harris and his bride, Nell, a classy, bespectacled woman in her late twenties. There was more embracing of old friends, another knock. Harris said, "Fanny and Philip wanted to see you, too."

"Fanny! Come come come come! Come in!" cried Carter. He kissed Fanny.

"I'm glad to see you again," said Philip, the bridegroom, to Carter.

"Indeed! Indeed!" Carter said and shook the big, smiling young man's hand, whereat the young man embraced him. Carter patted him on the arm.

Urbane in his navy pajamas, Carter effected introductions of those who were not acquainted, called down for extra chairs, accepted Philip's offer to go get a big bag of ice, and tried in vain to prevent Harris and Nell from leaving before Jonas came—before the arrival of Ferdinand Zambizi, straight from the summit in Peking! "At least stay and drink a toast to marriage, and to old men"—and he put out his arm and gathered Ilka to his side and drew her down onto the bed to sit beside him—"damned if we don't come up with a hard brick!" is what Ilka thought he said and she said, "Excuse me?" and looked around. The women stared into their glasses; Kate smiled. The men were looking in a very friendly way at Ilka. Carter laid his head awkwardly on Ilka's shoulder; Ilka was sorry to be glad when he removed it to rise and say good-bye to Harris

and Nell. They had wedding errands to run, for the better accomplishment of which Fanny was indispensable; Fanny was
leaving also. Philip asked if they needed him along and they
did not need him at all. Philip was staying.

"Will you mind seeing yourselves to the door? Nell, forgive
me. Welcome into the family. Fanny, good-bye." Carter sat
down on the edge of the bed, suddenly under the weather.

The Rauschenquists, too, had to be going—a prior
engagement.

"I'll see them to the door," offered Philip.

Carter lay down on the bed and covered himself with his
blanket. "Help yourselves to drinks," Carter said.

"Let me," said Philip.

Ilka said that she must leave but Carter held her by the hand.
"This is a party," he said.

"Fishgoppel is home for the holidays."

"Call her! Call Fishgoppel! Tell Fishgoppel to come to the
party!"

"She will not," said Ilka. "Fishgoppel now no longer travels
on Saturdays."

"Saturday!" cried Carter and called down for Wallace to
bring another bourbon.

"I'll go and get it!" said Philip.

"You don't need another bourbon," Carter's ex-wife told
him.

"I'll get the door," said Philip shortly before midnight, and
it was Georgia's husband, Ferdinand Zambizi. From his bed
Carter shook the hand of the small, dapper, smiling African,
whose clipped and charming English was the product of the
Bazwaziland government school, Cambridge University, and
Wayne State, in that order.

Carter asked Philip to pour the traveler a drink. "How about
you, Georgia? Ilka? No. No more for me, thank you," Carter
said.

Ferdinand sat down, smiled at his wife, and said, "Well! We're out!"

"Out?" said Georgia. "Out of what?"

"Bazwazi. Power," said Ferdinand.

"President Zamzi, you mean, is out!" said Carter and he sat up.

"What are you talking about?" said Georgia. "Why are you smiling?"

"Because I'm out of any alternative facial expression," said the little African.

Georgia said, "But that's awful!"

"Certainly is," said Ferdinand. "I'm out of a job."

"So why are you laughing?" shouted Georgia.

"Zamzi is out and our local military funny man is in. That must be why I'm laughing," said Ferdinand Zambizi.

"You've gone crazy," said Georgia, standing up and sitting down again.

"Where the hell is Zamzi?" asked Carter and put his feet on the floor.

"Good question," said Ferdinand. "We're out of communication."

Carter and Ferdinand laughed, and Georgia said, "Stop it. Both of you."

"The last thing we know is that his plane left Bazwazi airport at noon three days ago. It never arrived in Peking."

"Jesus!" Carter said. In his excitement he poured himself a water glass full of bourbon; he filled up the glass Ferdinand Zambizi held toward him.

Ferdinand said, "Was he *on* the plane, is the question. One rumor says he's in jail, another he's dead, or possibly he's fled to Ghana. There's been no word out of Accra since Monday. For all anybody knows, Nkrumah may be out too, in jail, dead, or fled . . ."

"To Bazwazi!" cried Carter and Ferdinand in a single voice, and they roared.

"What is the damn matter with you two?" shouted Georgia, "You're out of your minds!"

At this, too, Carter and Ferdinand laughed. "That's my gorgeous Georgia, whom I loved and left . . ."

"*You* left!" Georgia stood up. "Who left who? Ferdinand, I want to go."

"Where," asked Ferdinand, "are you going to go?"

"I thought we were staying with your UN ambassador."

"*What* ambassador?" said Ferdinand. "As of three days ago we do not *have* an ambassador at the UN!"

"Are we going back to London?"

"Where, in London, are we going? You and I are out of the embassy."

"What about my clothes!" said Georgia.

"You are out of your clothes," Carter and Ferdinand said in unison and doubled up.

"Have you seen your people at the UN?" Carter asked him, when they recovered.

"I went straight from Idlewild. Chaos meets doomsday! Nobody knows when the new boys are coming in; nobody knows who the new boys will be. Everybody is packing things, and shredding things, and crying, and drinking Coca-Cola."

"Won't you be recalled?" asked Carter.

"I have *been* recalled," said Ferdinand. "Everybody has been recalled. The question is, what have I been recalled to? Jail? To have my head cut off, or to a post in the new administration?"

"Could you get a job here?"

"That's another question," said Ferdinand. "I was going to call my old poli-sci professor at Wayne—to see if there might be a lectureship, but I'm out of a dime."

Philip, the bridegroom, put his hand into his pocket.

"Thank you, thank you," said Ferdinand. "Also I have a second cousin in Ohio . . ."

Georgia said, "One thing Ferdinand is never out of is second, third, fourth, and fifth African cousins, who come and squat at the embassy. Do you realize the Bazwazi language has a different word for each degree of cousinship from the first to the fourth four times removed?"

"Same beautiful bitch, Georgia!" said Carter. "So where are you people going to stay?"

"The Ohio cousins run a motel outside Columbus," said Ferdinand. "I was thinking of squatting with them."

The Zambizis, it turned out, had no roof over their heads. Carter called down to the desk. There were no rooms available at the Bloomsbury Arms, but Philip had a friend, who had a friend, who was out of town, who had an apartment. He did some phoning and shortly before one o'clock walked off with Ferdinand and Georgia.

Ilka went home and looked up "brick" in the dictionary. It said,

> brick (brik), *n.* 1. a block of clay . . . used for building, paving, etc. . . . 2. such blocks collectively. . . . 6. *Informal,* a good or generous person. —*v.t.* 8. to pave, line, wall, fill, or build with brick. . . . [late ME *brike* MD *bricke;* akin to BREAK].

Ilka further found "brick · bat," "brick · kiln," "brick · laying" and "brickle." Ilka looked up "hard."

> hard (härd), *adj.* 1. not soft; solid and firm to the touch. . . . 2. firmly formed; tight: *a hard knot.* 3. difficult to do or accomplish; fatiguing; troublesome: *a hard task.* . . . 6. involving a great deal of effort, energy, or persistence: *hard labor* etc.

but no brick that old men do or do not come up with.

★   ★   ★

CARTER CALLED Ilka at the Council and said, "I have to eat."

"I wish I could cook!" cried Ilka. She bought him a sandwich. Standing by the elevator, she observed the back of a large man in a Chesterfield, waiting to talk to the desk clerk. The desk clerk was on the telephone, saying, "This *is* Mr. Boyd, and I can*not* talk to you any longer, I have a gentleman here. . . . No, sir. No. What's Wallace going to use for money? No, I cannot. I have your account in front of me, Mr. Bayoux, and I cannot."

"Let me," said the gentleman in the Chesterfield and took out his wallet. It was Philip, the bridegroom.

Ilka and the bridegroom went up in the elevator together. Carter opened the door.

"I've come back," said the bridegroom.

"So you have, haven't you?" said Carter and went and sat back down on the edge of his bed. He looked at Ilka's sandwich in distress. "Would you put this in the icebox? I will eat later."

"You must eat," said Philip.

Carter raised his head. "Keep my strength up, eh?"

"*Yes!*" said Philip.

Carter lowered his head into his hand.

"We didn't get a chance, yesterday," said Philip. "I want to make up, about that business at the wedding . . ."

"Christ!" Carter said very slowly. "Prince Mishkin in person! Don't you understand anything, you silly man!" He fortified himself with a cat sip of his bourbon. *I,*" he said and pointed to himself, "injured *you*"—he pointed to the bridegroom. "*You*'re supposed to be angry! You're supposed to be mad at me!"

Philip smiled and said, "I'm not mad at you. I can't stand being mad at people or having people mad at me."

"No stamina, eh?" said Carter.

The bridegroom smiled. "I can't stand things unresolved."

"You must have a hard life, then," said Carter.

The bridegroom did not look like someone who had a hard life. He looked big and friendly and had a large, round, smooth face with something, still, of a boy's fineness of skin, pink, at the moment, with his excited embarrassment, which he carried as loosely and easily as his excellent suit: Philip looked fortunate.

Carter Bayoux said, *"How* am I going to hate you! Have a drink. You do drink, don't you?"

"Oh, yes," said Philip.

"Thank goodness for small mercies."

"I think you're terrific," said Philip. "Fanny thinks you're terrific."

"Ah, yes," said Carter and took another sip of bourbon and said, "And how is little Fanny."

"Terrible," said the bridegroom. "We're having a terrible time. . . ."

"Would you do something for me?" Carter said slowly.

"Of course!" Philip said.

"Don't tell me about it."

Philip laughed. He said, "It started before the wedding. . . ." Carter lay down on his side with his eyes open and stared at the young man, who sat on the carpet in front of him and recounted, not without some wit, the cumulative disasters of his young marriage.

Jonas called to say they were going back to the West Coast.

Carter said, "Come and say good-bye. We have to talk."

Jonas said, "I'm going to try."

Philip called and asked if there was something he could do.

"Must be *something* a big, good-looking chap like you should be able to do," Carter said.

"Can I do something for *you?*"

Carter said, "Can you cook a steak? I need a rare steak to sop up the booze."

When Ilka came, Philip was sitting on the carpet. Carter was sitting on the edge of the bed. He raised his head and said, "We are discussing Philip's alternatives," and with excruciating slowness added, "We are deciding which, of a number of available options, or combination of options, will maximize Philip's opportunities."

"And Fanny's opportunities," said Philip.

"And Fanny's opportunities," said Carter and put his chin back into his hand.

Philip summed up, to bring Ilka into the picture, the advantages of A: getting a political science Ph.D. at Berkeley, where they could stay at Philip's people's place; or B: doing political science *or* history, at Columbia, so that Fanny could keep her job, which she liked but was willing to give up; or, which was what Fanny wanted, C: doing law at Harvard; or D: doing a year in Washington.

"Tell you a Jewish joke," Carter said slowly. "Young fellow comes to the rabbi, says, 'Rabbi, I want to go to the university.' Rabbi says, 'What d'you want to go to the university for?' Young fellow says, 'Rabbi, if I go to the university, I'll get a good job!' Rabbi says, 'So, you'll get a good job, so what?' Young fellow says, 'But, rabbi, if I get a good job, I'll become a rich man!' Rabbi says, 'So, you'll become a rich man, so what?' Says, 'Rabbi, if I'm a rich man I'll get a beautiful wife!' 'So, you'll get a beautiful wife, so what?' 'Rabbi, if I have a beautiful wife, I'll be happy!' 'So, you'll be happy, so what?' "

It took a second before Philip laughed. He blushed and continued, "What Harris wants us to do is for both of us . . ."

A knock at the door.

"Jonas!" said Carter, but it was Bones.

"They left this for you," said Bones.

Carter sat up. He took a quart bottle of bourbon out of its long paper bag. There was a note. "My glasses . . ." said Carter. He read the note and his eyes opened with a jolt of emotion which Ilka, who was watching him, mistook for pleasure. Carter said, "My brother and his wife are on their way to Idlewild. They dropped this off. I tell my brother I need to talk and he drops off a quart of bourbon. My brother is telling me, 'Drink yourself into the grave.' "

"They were catching a plane!" "They didn't have time!" Ilka and Philip said.

"My brother has given up on me," said Carter, and lay down and turned himself to the wall.

Philip and Ilka were much impressed and moved, and Ilka said, "If we leave, do you think you might sleep?"

"Maybe," said Carter with his face to the wall.

Philip and Ilka tiptoed out. Philip asked her if she had had dinner. They ate in the hotel dining room. "He's so terrific!" said Philip.

Ilka agreed. "He can't eat," Ilka said. "He can't sleep!"

The call woke Ilka up. Carter's thick voice said, "You shouldn't see me any more. This is no good for you. Don't see me any more."

Ilka said, "You don't want me to see you!"

After a pause Carter said, "I don't want you to see me."

"All right," said Ilka. She heard the phone replaced at the other end and hung up and doubled over with black pain.

Carter sat on the edge of the bed.

"Bucky?" said a young male voice. "Can I speak with Bucky Bailey?"

"This is Bucky Bailey. What can I do for you?"

"Oh, Bucky! Oh, boy! I been trying to reach you for two months! I been calling every day!"

"Getting to be a habit, eh?"

"Yeah! And today! Right off, first try! I picked up and . . ."

"Must be your lucky day. What's on your mind?"

"About Washington's birthday," the young man said. "I read someplace the queen's birthday is not on her birthday."

"You mean the queen of England?"

"Yes," said the young man.

"You mean that the queen's *official* birthday is not on the date that commemorates the day of her natural birth? Is that what you mean?"

"Yes," said the young man.

"Are you British?" asked Bucky Bailey.

"No," said the young man.

"Oh, O.K. . . . All right?" said Bucky Bailey.

"O.K. Thanks, Bucky. Bye now."

"The program," said Bucky Bailey, "is *Your Time to Talk.* Our number is WX 9-1100."

Carter picked up and said, "Give me WX 9-1100."

"Hello, hello," said the voice of Bucky Bailey in Carter's ear a split second before the voice of Bucky Bailey in Carter's radio. "This is Bucky Bailey. What can I do for you?"

"I have a birthday, too," Carter on the edge of the bed said a split second before his voice on the radio.

"O.K.," said both Bucky Baileys uncertainly.

"I have my birthday April twenty-two," said both Carters very, very slowly.

"Is there something you want to talk about?"

"There is something I want to talk about," said Carter.

Bucky Bailey said, "Sir, please, say what you have called to say; I don't want to have to cut you off altogether."

"Don't cut me off altogether," said Carter.

The phone clicked off in Carter's ear. "Bucky Bailey here,"

Bucky Bailey on the radio said. "The program is *Your Time to Talk*, where we get all sorts and all kinds. Our number is WX 9-1100. . . ."

Carter, leaning forward to replace the receiver, pitched into the bedside chair, which fell backward dragging everything with it. Carter lay on the floor. The receiver lay beside him. Carter gave Ilka's number and said, "Come quick."

Ilka said, "Are you ill? Carter?" There was no sound at the other end. "Coming!" said Ilka.

In the station a ragged, drunken black man stuck his face into Ilka's face, studied it and said, "Man, are you ugly!"

There was no one in the car except a man stretched at his full length on the seat across the aisle. He seemed unhinged by sleep. The motion of the train tossed him as a wave might toss a drowned man, but this one wasn't dead. His blood was slowly seeping into an unspeakable handkerchief loosely and ineptly tied around the knuckles of his hand. Ilka watched the supine body teeter on the edge of the seat. It was flung against the seat back, and back to the edge. What if he rolled onto the floor? Would Ilka have to pick him up? Ilka wanted to get up and walk into the next car but did not dare to look away, as if it were her looking that kept him aloft. Ilka kept her eyes on the sleeping man except to look through the window to see that it was Carter's station in which the train had lurched to a halt, and heard the thump, like no other of the world's sounds, of a human body hitting the ground. Ilka fled through the opening doors and never looked around. She walked the half block to the hotel with a sensation that she was running. She ran along the thirteenth floor and knocked on Carter's door, and called his name and was about to hurry down to the desk when she heard a sound inside she could not interpret: an elaborate fumbling—a fumbling on a large scale—as of a soft mass colliding with a variety of surfaces; there was a small crash.

"Carter?"

"Coming."

Ilka listened, it seemed for a very long time, to the soft sliding and thudding that seemed to be approaching.

"Are you all right?"

"Coming," said Carter's voice, surprisingly, from just the other side of the door. Ilka watched the handle of the door slowly turn, then nothing.

"Carter!"

After moments, the door cracked. Ilka saw why it did not open: Carter's bulk occupied the space into which the door would have opened. He was on his hands and knees, attempting to maneuver himself backward. "Coming," he said.

Ilka squeezed through. "Can I help you?"

"No, thank you." Carter crawled on his hands and knees in the direction of his bed, turned himself slowly into a sitting position. He said, "I broke my radio." He leaned his back against the foot of the bed. He heaved his breath as if from an insufficient supply. Ilka sat down on the carpet beside him. "I'm going to snap out of this," said Carter. "Reestablish protocol."

★　　　★　　　★

CARL CALLED and said, "This is Carl from Philip and Fanny's wedding. How are you doing?"

Ilka asked Carl what he had said about Jews not drinking, and other people—about Negroes drinking.

Carl explained to Ilka that Negroes drink because they live in an oppressive society.

Carter called Ilka to meet him for lunch. He looked gray and ill and his arm trembled violently. Ilka took his arm. They walked to Madison Avenue and Ilka explained to Carter why he drank. "People are so stupid!" she said ardently. "People think you drink because you *like* to drink. They don't understand it is because you live in an oppressive society."

" 'And that's true, too.' Also," Carter said, "I like it. I like the taste."

Ilka laughed and said, "I love you."

Carter said, "I wondered about that. Why do you?"

Ilka said, "Because you won't let me be stupid. And because you tell me stories."

Carter said, " 'She loved me for the dangers I had passed, and I loved her that she did pity them.' "

"Excuse me?" said Ilka.

They sat at their corner table and Carter ordered milk from a buxom dark young Spanish-speaking waitress, who had replaced the angry elderly German one.

"Is she a Negro?" Ilka asked Carter.

"Puerto Rican," said Carter, thereby giving a name to the category into which Ilka was now able to file the woman in the early-morning subway who had sighed for her mother; the skimpy brown man with the antique smile and no overcoat; the little brown girl who settled her father, mother and fat brother into the subway booth; the man who had hung on Ilka's strap, whom she had asked if there was going to be war; the one with the extravagant mustache whose teeth had smiled at her across the aisle; and the old woman who brought her parcel into the corner post office on Broadway and had not understood what the clerk said to her, and carried the parcel away again. Ilka had acquired the word by which to distinguish this group of people from other groups of people, with the concomitant loss of the likelihood that she would henceforward distinguish any member within the group from any other.

"So," Carter said, "are you and I going to be married?"

Ilka said, "Yes," there being no way she could think of, quickly, to say "No." Ilka was appalled at the glad emotion in Carter's face. "You'll see," he said, "I won't drink if I'm not sitting alone in that bloody hotel room! Do you want to move in with me, or would you rather we have an apartment? We'll pick up a *Times*."

They picked up a *Times* and went and sat in the park with their backs against the stone back of the Forty-second Street library. Carter put on his glasses and got out his fountain pen. "Amsterdam and Hundred-twenty. I can't go back Uptown. Trouble is I'm scared of Downtown. Downtown is scared of me. There are parts of the Village we can live in. Are we looking for two bedrooms? Your mother will live with us? It'll be murder, but we can hack it."

"Who are all these people?" Ilka was looking round the square little park. The mildness of the day had brought out the city's strays. They sat on benches, on the stairs, raising their poor faces to the surprising sun. "How many years must it take to collect so much dirt into the cracks of the skin. Look, Carter, at that man." Ilka meant a man in cardboard shoes, picking a butt off the ground.

Carter said, "I don't want to look. How far, do you think, am I from that man? 'Morton Street. Two bedrooms, living room, breakfast nook!' Breakfast *nook!* We don't need—we don't *want* a nook. 'Kitchen.' We want a kitchen. Let's go take a look at this."

But at the corner of Fifth Avenue and Fortieth Street Ilka threw up. The lunch-hour secretaries walked around her at the edge of the sidewalk, but Carter stood by and held Ilka's handbag and held Ilka's forehead. "Thanks," Ilka kept saying.

Carter said, "I'm an expert at throwing up."

"Sorry. Yeach. Thanks. I'm sorry," Ilka kept saying. Today was not the day for apartment hunting.

"Sunday is the best day for apartment hunting," said Carter. But the next Sunday Carter was sick.

Then Ilka called him to say, "On Monday comes my mother!"

* * *

FISHGOPPEL ARRIVED in the morning. They went to the wharf and stood in the cold drizzle watching the people walk down the gangplank. Ilka was afraid of not recognizing her mother. She kept saying, "I haven't seen her in eleven years. I was ten years old," and saw her mother in a wheelchair being wheeled down the gangplank, but it was not her mother. Ilka ran forward, and it was her mother.

In the taxi Ilka looked sideways at the woman who sat next to her, who was her mother. It wasn't the added years only: events accrued to her that Ilka did not know anything about that made her a stranger. And it wasn't only that. Her actual person coincided with Ilka's memory of her person; the memory hung about like a ghost, competing for the space filled by its incarnation. Ilka looked out the car window and Riverside Drive was real and her mother returned into that transparent, unstable stuff our memories of the dead are made of. Ilka looked at her mother. Here she was.

"This is our street, Muttilein."

Ilka's mother stood in the New York street. Ilka did not think she looked.

They showed her her bed and stowed her things and explained the apartment to her. She was gray with emotion and fatigue, but did not want to lie down. Fishgoppel asked her in Yiddish if she thought she ought to see a doctor.

"What does she want from me?" Ilka's mother, who thought Fishgoppel was speaking English, asked Ilka in German.

"I don't know," said Ilka.

They made coffee. They sat at the kitchen table and Ilka's mother told how she had left Ilka's father sitting on the side of the road just outside the little town of Obernpest, "near Lake

Bautzen, where we spent the summer—I think it was in
'thirty-five. Ilka, you were too young to remember. Vati kept
thinking he recognized the names of the villages. The Nazis
thought they were moving the camps back from the front; even
the soldiers couldn't tell which were their guns, or if the front
was in front or behind, so they turned us around, and marched
us the other way. Vati thought he recognized the name Obernpest. Ilka, you wouldn't remember—you were a baby—the ri-
diculous parrot-colored guesthouse that we stayed in on Lake
Bautzen. Mauve with green shutters! Tell her," said Ilka's
mother. Fishgoppel was leaning forward, looking from one to
the other. Ilka translated, "The allied planes were flying over.
They dropped—I don't know what you call those little papers.
They said the Red Cross was sending a small number of ambu-
lances, only for those too sick to keep walking." Ilka's mother
said, "Vati sat down on a spot on the side of the road and told
me to keep going. Never never never have I understood how
I went on and left him sitting on the road! There was a man,
afterward, on the boat. He saw a soldier shoot a man with spectacles, who was making a pipi behind a bush."

"Vati didn't wear spectacles!" shouted Ilka. "It wasn't
Vati!"

"How how how how how how did I go on and leave him sitting on the side of the road!" Ilka's mother did not want to
walk up to Broadway, or to go down to see the Hudson River.
Maybe she would go and lie down.

"Ikh will sein tsurik in tsvey weeks!" Fishgoppel told them and
ran to catch her train back to New Haven.

"What did she say?" Ilka's mother asked Ilka.

Ilka said, "I keep telling her we don't speak Yiddish."

That was the night Ilka's mother first dreamed about the burglars, "who are really ants," she told Ilka coming into Fishgoppel's little sausage-shaped kitchen in her tasseled jacquard
dressing gown—a survivor, too, from pre-Hitler mornings of

Viennese coffee and buttered rolls. "Who rang on the telephone already before breakfast?" she asked Ilka.

"A friend," said Ilka. Ilka was sitting at the table fully dressed with her coat on her lap. Carter had sounded ill and had said, "I don't want to start drinking!" and Ilka had promised to come down for half an hour before work.

"So peculiar!" her mother said. "Have you ever dreamed that you were dreaming something you have dreamed before?"

"*Lots* of times. That's not so peculiar!" said Ilka. She bent over her mother's hand, which lay so amazingly here, in Manhattan, on Fishgoppel's kitchen table. The skin, spotted with the pale beginnings of age, was so finely grained it felt fragrant under Ilka's lips. "So what did you dream," she asked her mother and laid her right palm over the face of her wristwatch.

Her mother poured herself a cup of American coffee, tasted it and grimaced. She settled herself in her chair. "I dreamed that the door opens—or Vati opens the door, or it already *is* open and Vati is holding it . . ."

"And . . ." Ilka said.

"And," said her mother, "these three ants walk in. Vati is holding the door open for them. No, he is the one who opens it. I *think.*"

"*And* . . ." Ilka said.

"And they walk inside and start to grow, and they grow and grow and stand upright, and they are really men only they are ants, with sections, a head, a middle and a tail end, like three black beads, shiny like patent leather only not like patent leather . . ." While Ilka's mother sat staring into last night's dream to see what it is, exactly, that ants are black and shiny like, Ilka noticed the churning inside her chest. She imagined Carter waiting on the edge of his bed. Ilka still thought if she got there in time everything might be all right. She wound her watch under the table.

"The biggest ant must be the father," said her mother, "because he makes them wash their hands. He asks Vati where they can wash, please—perfectly polite. Vati, very polite too, with his little bow, shows them behind a sort of—you know the kind of folding screens they put up between beds in hospital? I'm surprised—this is so peculiar—*in the dream* I am surprised that there is a row of bowls in the kitchen, and they wash and the father makes them dry very thoroughly . . ."

Here Ilka looked openly at her watch.

"Then the father leaves," said Ilka's mother. "At any rate, he is gone, and the two who stay behind have a black bag like a doctor, but they are burglars. Ilka, you remember Dr. Shey always let you shut his black bag if you opened your mouth like a good girl, because you liked the way it snapped. Remember?"

"I remember," Ilka said, "that I thought I liked the way it snapped because Dr. Shey let me snap it shut when I opened my mouth like a good girl. It never occurred to me until this moment that I never cared whether it snapped or not."

"You *loved* it!" her mother said. "You always *loved* to snap it shut."

Ilka had got up. She put her coat on. Her mother followed her into the narrow little foyer and said, *"In my dream* I'm wondering how I know that they are burglars, and I turn to ask Vati, but he is gone—you know how that is in dreams—someone is there, then they are not?"

"Not in dreams only," Ilka said. "Muttilein, I get back from work around five. You should go out a little?"

"Go out? Where?"

"To the corner. Walk to Broadway. The butcher is from Vienna, called Herschel."

"A *Polischer!*" said Ilka's mother. "What will I do if the phone rings and it's for Fishgoppel?" she asked Ilka.

"You say, 'I do not speak English.' Say it after me."

"That I know how to say," said Ilka's mother.

. . .

Carter was all right. He was fine. Ilka told him how her father
had been left behind on the road. "I have to stay with her tonight," she said.

"You have to stay with her," said Carter.

"You go already again out?" is—word for word—what
Ilka's mother said, which released in Ilka a perfect thrill of
exasperation.

"Again! What do you mean 'again'!" she shouted. Whereas
Ilka's mother counted the times Ilka went out, Ilka counted
every time she stayed at home, and every time she went out
she felt that she *ought* to have stayed. She said, "Again *what?*"

"Again you go out," Ilka's mother said bravely, it seemed
to Ilka, because Ilka had the impression that her own, too-wide-
open eyes were yelling at her mother. She normalized them.

"You go again out," said her mother.

"Yes, I go out!" yelled Ilka. "And you sit in Fishgoppel's
apartment! Mutti, this is in New York!"

"I dreamed about the burglars again," said her mother.

"What did you dream?" asked Ilka with a palpable reluctance.

"That they have a black bag."

"So you told me."

"They keep behind my back, and I can't see what they are
doing, but I can hear everything. They knocked over the
kitchen stool. I think maybe they are looking for the electric
outlet."

"In your dream," said Ilka.

"Yes," Ilka's mother said. "I dream I'm thinking one of
them must be quite a young boy, because the other says—you
know how hard it is to remember what people say when you
don't understand what is going on—something like 'Hold this
here, idiot!' or 'Hold it by this, *here*, idiot!' very impatient,

which is why I think he's talking to a boy. When will you be back?" she asked Ilka.

"It's Wednesday. I have my English class. Muttilein, if I register you for Beginners' English, will you go?"

"Go where?"

"Just three stops on the subway."

Ilka's mother came into the foyer and asked Ilka, "What do I do if the telephone rings and it's for Fishgoppel?"

Ilka's mother slept and dreamed that the burglars moved around the kitchen behind her. She listened to the small clanking of metal, and tried to understand what kind of instrument it was that they seemed to have trouble knowing how to assemble. She kept meaning to turn around to take a look; however, she did not turn. It seemed to her that they were bungling whatever it was they were trying to do, and she wished the father would come back and stop them; she kept looking toward the door and heard the key and awoke. It was Ilka in the foyer.

Ilka's mother said, "There was a phone call for you."

"Who was it?"

"I don't remember the name."

"Man or woman?"

"It was a man."

"Was the name Carter? Carter Bayoux?"

"Nothing like that."

"Carl?"

"No."

"Harvey?"

"It wasn't Harvey."

Ilka instituted a pencil and pad next to the telephone and said, "Next time somebody calls put it down right away, before you can forget it."

. . .

"She *will* not go out," Ilka said to Carter.

"A drink?" Carter asked Ilka.

"Thank you, no. All she does is sit in Fishgoppel's apartment and have bad dreams."

Carter brought Ilka a glass and one for himself and said, "Good whiskey. Taste."

Ilka sipped and said, "She won't even go to Broadway unless I go with her."

"She's scared," said Carter.

"Excuse me?"

"She's frightened," said Carter.

"This is New York," said Ilka.

"I'm frightened in New York," said Carter.

Ilka often had a sensation of falling in love with Carter all over again. Wanting to diminish the distance between them, she came and sat on the carpet by his feet and rubbed her cheek against his knee.

"Drink your drink," said Carter.

Ilka sipped.

Carter said, "I'm going to come and see your mother."

★   ★   ★

W HAT DO WE offer?" her mother asked.

"Nothing, Mutti. He's just coming in for a few minutes to meet you."

"You have to offer something when somebody comes," said her mother.

"Muttilein," said Ilka loudly and too suddenly because she had been practicing in her head all day how to say what she had to say without offending her mother, "don't tell Carter about your burglars."

"Me! I tell him?" Her mother was offended.

"People don't want to hear other people's nightmares."

"Whom do I tell anything? How am I supposed to tell? He understands German?"

"Fishgoppel doesn't understand German either and you've told her your Obernpest story three times."

"Because you would not help me properly to say 'leaflets' in English."

"I didn't *know* how to say 'leaflets' in English. All I'm saying, Mutti, is everybody already knows all these stories. They have been in the papers, they've been on the news at the movies, and on the radio. . . ."

"It's been on the radio that I left your father sitting ill on the spot on the side of the road before Obernpest? Did Fishgoppel know the Red Cross dropped leaflets?"

"Fishgoppel is different. Fishgoppel *longs* to hear everything. Carter is not Jewish."

"You told me Negro."

"They have their own stories, Mutti. They don't need our nightmares."

"I will not tell him anything. I won't even speak to him," her mother said, and the doorbell rang.

Ilka's father had been a small portly man. Carter Bayoux was an unusually large portly man. Ilka's mother began to speak in English.

"Ilka, take the mister the coat away, isn't it?"

"Mutti, we're leaving in a minute."

Carter took off his coat.

"Coffee for the mister, Ilka."

"You want to stay for coffee?" Ilka asked Carter.

"Please," said Carter.

"Ilka has told, isn't it, that that here are not our furnitures?"

"Mutti," Ilka whispered in order not to shout.

"That all here is belonging to a cousin which has not—how says one *auf Englisch 'Geschmack,'* Ilka?"

"I don't *know,*" said Ilka.

Carter said, "I have met Fishgoppel, and I'd guess her mind works at such a white heat it would shrivel any thoughts of furniture."

Flora Weissnix did not know what Carter Bayoux was saying but she understood that he was talking to her. His face, his shoulders, his chair were turned toward her, and she said, "We have everything lost and not only furnitures. I have Ilka's father left on the street before Obernpest. How says one in English, Ilka, the *'Nazis'?*"

But Ilka had left the room. Unwilling, however, to abandon Carter to a lengthy English conversation with her mother, Ilka threw water into a kettle and ran back into the room, where Carter was sitting quietly, his hands folded on his considerable stomach, his face serious, without that gravity of a listener anxious to be perceived to be listening.

Ilka's mother was saying, "How names one in English such many little papers falling?"

"Leaflets," said Carter.

"On where written stood, 'It comes only few *Ambulanzen* for the which cannot further go.' Funny is," she said, "other times were it always I which have not well gone. Every Sunday, when we have gone out where, was something with my foots, my shoes, never the daddy, Ilka, isn't it? But in the camp has he already fevered. How comes it I have left him on the road before Obernpest? How comes that I have further gone!"

Carter offered his handkerchief. Not only were her eyes red and streaming, her nose ran; her face was a devastation. "We have nothing to offer, not cake, not fruit!" howled Ilka's mother. "Ilka, the coffee—which is not as by us in Vienna," she told Carter.

Ilka ran out into the kitchen and threw cups onto a tray and ran back in, and her mother was doing charades, telling Carter about the burglars. She avoided Ilka's eye.

"It is a . . ." She made a slicing motion.

"A knife?" asked Carter.

"Yes. In the begin, I have thought is how you say . . ." she pointed to the outlet.

"An *electric* knife!" said Carter.

"Yes, but that it is not. I hear no . . ." Ilka's mother whirred. "But I know is made out from—how you say *'Metall'?*"

"Metal," said Carter.

"It is out from metal, because it feels itself cold on the skin exact here," and Ilka's mother pointed to a place on her back a little right of center and out of the reach of her hand.

"You come again, isn't it?" Ilka's mother said to Carter when she saw them off in the foyer. "I will make you a goulash, but not like by us in Vienna, because in America knows nobody how cuts one properly up a chicken."

"How do *you* know what one does and does not know in America!" shouted Ilka.

"You will come to my hotel," Carter said to Ilka's mother. "I will cook you an American steak."

"My mother didn't have a choice, except to leave my father on the road, and go on," Ilka said as they walked to the subway. "But she loves to convict herself. She *wants* to tell that story over and over, only I don't want to hear it over and over. Fishgoppel can't get enough of my mother's Hitler stories."

Carter said, "I ever tell you about my first wife?"

"Jenny. After the wedding you went home to your home and she went to her home."

"Jenny liked my dad. I told you my dad was born a slave?"

"Ah!" said Ilka with a solemn thrill.

"Jenny used to *love* my dad's slave stories. *I* used to walk out of there, putter around, and I'd walk back in an hour later, and there was Jenny sitting, and my dad telling slave stories."

"You had *three* wives?" asked Ilka.

Carter walked on. "More than three," he said.

"Did you have four wives!"

Carter walked on.

"Did you have more than four wives! Did you have five wives! Carter, how many wives did you have?"

Carter would not say.

"Why won't you tell me how many wives you had?"

"Because I'm ashamed," said Carter.

"But that is so *interesting!*" Ilka said and found herself impaled on Carter's wide-open and angry stare.

"Don't," Carter said. "Don't, don't, don't, don't."

"Did you invite him for dinner?" Ilka's mother asked her when she came home.

"Did you wait up for me! Don't wait up for me!" shouted Ilka. "Go to bed!"

"I'm afraid to sleep," said her mother. "I don't want to dream. It's horrible."

"*What* is!" said Ilka. "How horrible can something be if you *know* it is a dream? It's not so horrible!"

"Because they are behind my back. I can't see what they are doing, so I never know when they are going to start again."

"Start *what!*" shouted Ilka.

"That's what I don't *know*. It wouldn't be so horrible if I knew what they are going to do, or if I knew when. I sit there, thinking, *Now* they are going to do it? Now? And *always* on the same exact spot that hurts from last time."

"In your *dream*, you mean, it hurts," said Ilka.

"Right here." Her mother pointed to the place on her back. "That's why I don't want to sleep."

"You don't want to sleep because you're not tired, because you don't go out! Mutti, let me register you for Beginners' English."

"Tomorrow," Ilka's mother said, "I'll go to Broadway. I'll explain to the *Polischen* how one cuts a chicken for a proper goulash. Will you come with me?"

. . .

Ilka's mother said, "That man called again, on the telephone. I wrote down his name. He is a mumbler. He does not pronounce properly."

Ilka said, "Mr. Wunsch? I don't know any Wunsch."

"Maybe Winsch," said Ilka's mother. Ilka was putting her coat on, and Ilka's mother came out into the foyer and said, "Aren't I going with you? He invited me for dinner."

"Not today, Mutti. He has to buy the steak first, and prepare it."

"Invite him here, and I will cook a goulash."

Fishgoppel arrived for the weekend. She inclined her neck and back tenderly toward Aunt Flora and told her she was looking wonderful. "Whatever made you ill is quite gone. Tell her," said Fishgoppel.

"I have dreams," said Ilka's mother. "What I can't understand is why burglars have to wash their hands so thoroughly."

Ilka experienced the release, not into her mouth but into the cavity below her chest, of a taste like bile. She looked in horror at Fishgoppel, who sat leaning forward. Poor Fishgoppel kept thinking if she listened harder she would understand what Aunt Flora was saying.

Before she caught her train back to New Haven, Fishgoppel ran down and bought her aunt the *Aufbau*, a Jewish German-language weekly. Henceforward Ilka's mother could document her New York fears. "Did you see in the *Aufbau* where they held a girl at knife point from the Bronx to the Battery? Where is the Bronx? What is Battery? A nice-looking girl. There is a picture of her. Look. You are going out again?"

"Yes," Ilka said.

"I wish you would stay at home."

"I can't stay at home!" shouted Ilka. "I have to find a proper job. I have to meet people. All *you* want is to sit in Fishgoppel's apartment!"

"I don't want to dream," Ilka's mother said. "Did you see where they pushed a man onto the subway tracks?"

"I think they have moved in," said Ilka's mother.

"Who has moved in where?"

"The burglars live in our kitchen. I've been wondering if maybe they have always been living here, except then they would have known where the bowls were. They wouldn't have had to ask Vati."

"In your dream, you mean," said Ilka and had the impression that some little self inside her was looking rapidly to the right, the left, the right.

Her mother said, "I don't remember if anything was ever said about the father coming back. My needing him to come does not, unfortunately, mean that he will come." She picked her cup of coffee up, sipped, grimaced and said, "Good it isn't." The little self inside Ilka's head not only looked, but ran frantically from one side to the other, but there was no exit.

Ilka's mother said, "The father doesn't know what is going on here, so why should it occur to him to come back? Are you going out?"

"Into the foyer." Ilka put a call through to New Haven. She was going to ask Fishgoppel, "Did you notice anything wrong with my mother?" Fishgoppel was out. Ilka called Carter. There was no answer. She took the Manhattan telephone directory and riffled through the A's with a hectic hand.

"Whom do you call?" her mother asked.

"Nobody. I don't know anybody *to* call," said Ilka.

All next day and the next Carter did not answer his phone.

Ilka's mother said, "What I'm going to do is ask them what they are going to do to me. I keep meaning, I keep thinking I am about to turn around, and look them in the eyes, and I'm going to ask them, 'Why do you hate me?' " Ilka's mother said,

"I keep wondering if there is a way I could get word to the police to let them know what is going on here."

Ilka yearned to lay her head down on her mother's lap and say, "Help me. If you are going mad I won't know what to do." But her mother's lap was out of sight, under Fishgoppel's kitchen table. Ilka's mother sipped her coffee with an air of reluctance and said, "I have no way of knowing when either or both of them are looking at me. They are behind my back. I wouldn't know when to make my move. You are going out?" she asked Ilka.

"Just to see if Carter is all right."

"Ask him to dinner."

"Mutti," Ilka said, "I think Carter may be really ill."

Ilka's mother came out into the foyer and said, "Why don't you marry him?"

"What are you talking about!" shouted Ilka. "You don't understand anything about it!"

"I understand that you like him," said her mother. "I understand that it is not good for a man to be alone."

Ilka went up in the elevator with two large overalled men delivering an oversize carton. They got out on Carter's floor. Ilka followed them to Carter's door, which stood open.

"Come in, come in!" Carter called from the edge of his bed. He had his green pajamas on.

"You want to sign here?" one of the overalled men said, pointing to the place on a paper clipped to a clipboard.

"I want to sign," Carter said.

"What *is* it?" Ilka asked.

"A home entertainment center," Carter said. He took a sip from the glass.

A man on a stepladder was stringing wire along the top molding. He asked Carter where he wanted the second speaker.

"Yes," Carter said. The two overalled men and a boy who

was stringing wire along the baseboard stopped and looked at Carter.

"You want it here or you want it over there?" the man on the ladder asked.

"Both," Carter said.

"You want three speakers?" the man asked.

"Four," Carter said. He closed his thumb and forefinger with difficulty around the pen which the overalled man kept holding toward him and, raising his head to Ilka, said, "We may have no home, but we'll have entertainment."

"You want four speakers?" the man on the ladder asked.

"Five," Carter said. He lowered his head, aligned the point of the pen with the place on the paper on the clipboard and, raising his head once again, said, "Though the center will not hold. And you don't even know what that is!"

"What is it?" Ilka asked.

"She's a foreigner," Carter slowly turned his head to tell the man with the clipboard, lowered his head and slowly signed.

"Use your phone?" the man who had stepped off the ladder asked Carter.

"Help yourself," said Carter.

"Says he wants three more speakers," the man said into the telephone. "That's what he says. What kind of antenna did you want for the TV?" he asked Carter.

"Both," said Carter. "Would you and your friend," Carter asked the overalled man to whom he was handing back the pen, "oblige me by unpacking that?"

"We're delivery," the man said and caught his partner's eye.

"I appreciate that," Carter said, getting his tongue with difficulty around the word inside his mouth. "As you see"—he took a sip of bourbon—"I am under the weather. I would naturally expect you to compensate yourselves." Ilka had the impression of a measurable passage of time elapsing between Carter's intention to raise and the raising of his right arm in the direction of the bills and coins lying on the dresser top.

"You got a screwdriver and a hammer or a knife will do it," the overalled man said.

"A knife," Carter said, and raised his slow-motion arm in the direction of the kitchen, while his left hand picked the phone up. "Have Wallace bring a screwdriver," he said into it.

"This is O.K." The overall man had found the bread knife.

"Come in," Carter called to a man in a peaked cap in the doorway.

"You the party for the shortwave?" the peaked man asked.

"I am the party," Carter said.

"You want all this paper out?" asked the overalled man. They had exposed the huge black cube of the television.

"Please. Wallace, come in," called Carter to the boy, who came with a set of yellow-handled screwdrivers. "Help yourself." Carter raised and held his hand toward the dresser, which immobilized the embarrassed bellboy.

"You got a record to try this?" asked the man who had got back on the ladder.

"Give me the record shop," Carter said into the telephone in his left hand. "You the record shop? Send a record. Send a box of records. I don't know what records. What do *you* like? Start with the A's. B's are better? So start with the B's. Bach is good. Beethoven, he's good. Come in!" he called to two men with boxes of speakers and rabbit ears. "Send Bird. How many Birds are there? Send Charlie Parker. Send B-y-r-d. Both," Carter said. "Not later. Send them *now*. So find another boy. There are a lot of boys. Or come yourself and I'll give you a drink. Don't go!" he said to the man with the peaked cap. The phone rang. "They want you at the desk," he told the bellboy, who left. The peaked man had other deliveries and left. The man came with the records but would not stay for a drink, and when the two overalled men had taken out the last armload of wrapping, they went away. The man collapsed his ladder, the boy rolled up the remaining wire, and when they had gone Carter said to Ilka, "Don't leave me."

"My mother sits alone in Fishgoppel's apartment."

"It is terrible to be alone," Carter said, and put his thumb on one eye and his forefinger on the other. Ilka saw tears seeping through and embraced Carter, who fell back on the bed, drawing her down with him. Ilka said, passionately, "Don't be unhappy!"

"*Am* I unhappy?" Carter stopped weeping to ask in an interested voice. "Don't let me snow you."

"Excuse me?" Ilka said.

"I'm a terrible ham."

"Pardon me?"

"I can't tell any more where the whiskey stops and the tears start," Carter said, weeping.

"You are—you are very unhappy!" cried Ilka.

"Well well well well well," Carter said. He allowed Ilka to help him sit up and sat very still until she relaxed her embrace. Then he reached for his glass, sipped, and said, "Friend of mine—" and named a famous name, and looked at Ilka, and said, "and you don't know who that is!" Ilka smiled. She rubbed her cheek against the back of his hand. "This friend," said Carter, "used to say he had the 'Negro Problem' licked. Said, 'Get it disseminated to the white folk we don't fuck so good either.' "

"You fuck very good," said Ilka.

"When did I last fuck you?"

"You did! You do!"

Carter raised his immensely slow head till he was looking Ilka full in the face and said, "You love me."

"I told you," said Ilka.

"You're crazy." He looked into Ilka's face. "Women in love are crazy people. They don't even notice they're not getting fucked. You think this is all terrific," he said and covered his eyes with his thumb and forefinger.

Ilka's mother listened to them quarreling behind her.
"Let me," the boy said.
The other one said, "You hold it and I will. Hold it here, by this."
"*I* will! I can!" the boy kept saying. "Why can't *I* do it?"
The cold metal was introduced at a shallow angle with a slicing motion. She imagined a knife with teeth—a saw—for which the boy must be grappling, because it was violently agitated in her flesh. She screamed.

"My mistake," she told Ilka, "has been to keep hoping that the father was coming back to stop them. In other words, I've been wishing not to have the pain. That is not one of my choices. What I *can* choose is *how* to have it and what I'm going to do is to concentrate on having pain. Perhaps that is a way to bear it. I am going to fix exactly what pain *is.*"
"You do that," said Ilka. She was getting used to knowing that her mother was unbalanced, and not doing anything about it, there being nothing, it turned out, *to* do. Ilka had called Fishgoppel. Fishgoppel had not understood what it was Ilka was telling her. Ilka felt relieved.
Ilka went down to tell Carter. Carter's door stood ajar. Carter slept with his face to the wall. Ilka made a pass at cleaning up, but there was something ferocious about the mess of soiled clothing, bottles, papers, wires. It came to Ilka—and not for the first time—that she must disengage herself, and the prospect produced a familiar blackness of pain, as if a hand had thrust into her gut and emptied her out. Ilka took the subway home and called Carter but there was no answer. She went down after work next day and Carter's door was locked and taped with a police seal.
The desk clerk wore a white carnation in his lapel. He lev-

eled his eyes at Ilka's collarbone. Ilka saw the switchboard
blonde's listening left ear. It was that older, yellow bellboy who
leaned, one elbow akimbo in the stance of the *boulevardier.* The
desk clerk said, "We don't like that kind of thing in this hotel."
Each round little word popped out through a round little hole
formed by the lifting of the left portion of the desk clerk's
upper lip. "It got so the maid won't go in there."

"Where is he?" asked Ilka.

"Back in the bughouse," said the desk clerk.

The facility was overcrowded. Newcomers had beds put up for
them in the corridors. Carter sat on the edge of the bed. His
face, all jaw and jowl, discouraged chatter. Ilka studied his
fiercely crumpled pajamas and did not ask him why the pajama
jacket was fastened with pink Band-Aids instead of buttons.
Carter smoked. He said, "Patients who don't get out the first
week are sent up to the state hospital." He brought the cigarette to his lips, took it away and said, "You can sign me out
if you say I live with you."

"But you don't live with me," said Ilka.

"You can say I'm your cousin."

After a moment Ilka said, "But you're not my cousin." She
touched Carter on the arm and was shocked by the unyielding
surface that held him together.

Carter never afterward asked Ilka to sign him out.

Ilka was surprised that, between the two abysses in her life,
life continued—had eased up some. Ilka's mother learned to
go to the corner to get her German paper. She quarreled with
the Polish butcher. She sat on a bench in the sun. Spring had
come. A strong white sun sparkled the garbage of upper Broadway, where Ilka waited for the upstate bus.

The bus stopped inside the hospital gates. They were large
grounds, and green. Ilka had a sense of walking in a well-kept
park except for the complex of buildings of a uniform orange

brick with no grace note of decoration to relieve their size and squareness.

Carter said, "I'm first floor. Mild cases." In a large room furnished with steel folding chairs with plastic seats in primary colors, the inmates and their Sunday visitors sat in little groups. The inmates without visitors watched a ball game on a television mounted on three crates draped with a purple chenille throw.

Carter was quieter, looked better; he seemed optimistic. "I can turn this thing around if we can find a summer house in the country."

"Without me," said Ilka.

Carter looked frightened.

"Carter, this isn't useful, do you think? I must get on with my life. I've got to find a proper job, where I can meet people. . . ."

Carter walked Ilka to the door and said, "Next Sunday bring me something salty, something that has taste."

Fishgoppel's term was over. She slept on the couch in the room with Ilka. Ilka's mother talked German to Fishgoppel. She said, "Today I turned around and asked them. I said, 'Why are you doing this to me?' What I had forgotten is, you can't *look* ants in the face. They don't have faces—I mean not what *we* mean by face. It's possible they don't know that I have a face—that my face *is* a face. They may not *know* that my flesh feels like flesh, because they are made out of different material—nothing like black beads or patent leather. More like the parts of a black motorcycle."

"I don't understand a word she is saying," Fishgoppel said sadly.

One day Ilka came home and her mother said, "Your friend called."

"Mr. Wish in person," said Ilka.

"No, your friend," said her mother.

"Carter? Impossible!" said Ilka. She rang the hotel, and Carter picked up. He sounded hilarious. He had pulled a cousin from Chicago out of his hat, and she had signed him out. A summer house had materialized in Connecticut. "We're going in with Ebony and Stanley and some friends."

"But I have a job," said Ilka.

"You'll come out weekends!" said Carter.

"I can't leave my mother with Fishgoppel," said Ilka.

"Bring your mother! Bring Fishgoppel. It's a big place! Ebony and Stanley have gone ahead. I'm going out tomorrow. Can you come Friday?"

"I don't think I should," said Ilka. "I'm going to look for a real job."

On Thursday Ilka called Connecticut and asked, "How is it?"

"Come and see."

"Just tell me if you like it."

"I'm not saying a word," said Carter. "Come."

SUMMER

CARTER WAS waiting on the platform. The little station-house was made of brick, the color of raw sausage with bottle-green trim. Carter wore shorts.

"Whose car?" asked Ilka.

"Ebony's. Come, get in."

Ilka said, "I must go back Monday."

"When is your vacation?"

"*This* is my vacation," said Ilka. "I must go back and look for a proper job, Carter." Ilka saw his shirt sleeve at close quarters and kissed it and said, "I must get on with my life, mustn't I? Carter?"

Carter said nothing. Ilka stared out of the car window. "It looks green! Carter, look at that big, lovely house, there, on top! *This* is it?" cried Ilka. Carter had turned up the hill. He drove around the big white house and stopped in back, at the door of a little house.

"This is silly!" Ilka meant that this was the little house with fence, window with curtain, roof with chimney, sky with cloud that Ilka used to crayon on pieces of paper on the dining-room table, in Vienna. "I don't believe this!" As Ilka stepped from the car, the curve and dip of fields turned to gold.

"Come inside," said Carter.

Inside it was raw wood. The floor was a collage of odds and ends of faded antique rugs—oriental reds and blues and dim and dark cloths, patterned with cerulean lozenges like crescents of sky. "I don't believe it." Ilka meant the condition of happiness. "This is silly."

They got into the bed like a cave hewn out of some aboriginal wood, immovable as ships' furniture, and when they heard Ebony hallooing across the grass there was no way to stop her short of shouting, "We're in here, naked, making love!" Already her cheerful knock was pushing the door open. She said, "I beg your pardon," stepped backward and closed the door.

"Am I wanted at the house?" Carter called out.

"No hurry," Ebony called in. "Just walked over to tell Ilka hello."

"Hello," said Ilka and kept her head flat on the mattress. She looked at the ceiling. It was wood.

"What time is dinner?" Carter called out.

"Seven, if that's all right with Ilka and you. Stanley can start the fire," Ebony called in.

"Is seven all right with you?" Carter looked down to ask Ilka.

"Yes," said Ilka.

"Seven's fine for Ilka and me. I'll be over to make the drinks in fifteen—make that twenty—twenty-five—minutes."

"Wonderful!" called Ebony and went away.

Ilka wanted to laugh, but Carter had resumed his interrupted motion.

Carter said, "I *make* the drinks; I don't drink them. Come over when you're ready."

Ilka made her solo way across the darkening grass. The big house had turned a magical blue. Ilka stopped to listen to the voices of many strangers speaking English and wished herself back in New York. That was Carter saying, "Whatnoswizzle-stick?" Ilka listened harder. A male voice said, "Shake it," and Carter's voice said, "Andbruisethegin?" Ilka's understanding sharpened with the sounding of her own name. "So, where is your Ilka?"

Ilka stepped around the corner. On a great slope, beneath a high lemon sky, milled an undeterminable number of persons like black paper cutouts. They would not stay put and would not stay attached to the names Carter kept telling Ilka. She walked behind Carter. Carter carried a tray. He said, "Ilka Stanley Stanley Ilka Stanley your bourbon Percy bourbon Percival where the hell are you Percival Ilka Sarah Sarah your martini Victor martini wasn't it Ilka Victor Doris Mae Ilka Doris Mae where the hell is Percival?"

"Hello," the people said to Ilka.

"Hello," said Ilka, keeping her eye on a naked child with short, fiercely flying hair, who ran in narrowing circles around and around a central vessel of live coals that flared as darkness fell from the air.

Indoors and in place around the long dining table they turned into a finite number of partially clothed and undistinguished-looking individuals. Ilka was disappointed. She let the talk flow around her while she organized them into those first categories by which we fix strangers: four males and four females created he them, five whites—not counting the baby—and three Negroes, nine souls in all including herself. Carter had said Stanley, Ebony's husband, was a Jew, so which one was he? The pink, smiling, wizened little man, like a stick figure, who sat at the foot of the table, could not be the husband of the ample Ebony. . . .

Ebony stood up at the head of the table to address the rare steak of beef. She speared the first cut and walked it to the other end, put it on the plate in front of the little stick man and said, "Everybody will excuse us if we serve Stanley's plate first. Stanley gets upset when he is hungry and what we want to avoid at all costs is Stanley getting upset, baby, don't we!"

The creased little pink man grinned at the beauty on his plate and gave the woman's bottom a pat, so he was her husband.

Ilka tried to understand how the rest of the people around

the table were connected with one another, and what promise
they might hold for herself: there was one other white man.
He sat across from Ilka, was young and bare-chested and had
blue eyes. He kept smiling at Ilka in a particular way; Ilka
could tell that he was wanting to say something to her, but the
baby, whose naked stomach and back were welted with red
mosquito bites and mottled blue in the chilly evening air, stood
up on her chair trying to stuff a macaroni up the young man's
left nostril, so he must be the father. "Annie, sit down. Annie!
Annie, don't!" the young man kept saying and arched himself
away from the invading pasta. "Sarah! Do something!" he said
to the plain young woman who sat on the baby's other side and
must be his wife. She had the nice sort of face that eschews
vanity—the face of one who means well and tries hard. Ilka
liked her face.

"Annie, don't," the young woman said without conviction.

"I have here," said Ebony, "a piece of meat that looks exactly the right size for Annie, if Annie will come and sit on
this chair, next to me. We'll put the *Britannica* A to AUS on
top of the Connecticut telephone directory so you can reach
the table, and we'll tie the dish towel around your neck, like
this, like a napkin which is traditionally worn under the chin
to keep crumbs off the shirt front, but you don't have a shirt
front so you can wear it like a cloak to keep the draft off your
back, like this. Now, if you will pass this plate to Aunt Ilka.
No, that is Aunt Doris Mae. *That's* Aunt Ilka. . . ."

"Why do we have to have her at dinner?" the baby's father
complained to his young wife. "Why can't she be put away?"

"The peas, please," said the prettyish blond young woman
with wire-rim spectacles who sat on Ilka's left side. Ilka passed
her the peas. The young woman heaped peas onto the plate
of a bespectacled and perfectly black—a blue-black—man with
a silly mustache, who sat on *her* left. He was the blackest man
Ilka had ever seen. "Bread, please. The butter, please," said

the bespectacled blond woman. She buttered a piece of bread for the black man and put it on his plate.

Carter said, "No starch for me, thank you. Ebony, a small piece of meat, please. This is my summer for shaping up. Neat soda!" He lofted the seltzer bottle he kept close by his plate.

"Annie, will you pass this small piece of meat to Uncle Carter, please?"

Ilka sat and smiled her self-conscious, gap-toothed smile, hoping for a pause in the conversation to coincide with something interesting it might occur to her to say. Ilka's English tended to regress when she was excited or nervous or tired, and she was all of these. The prospect of sending her voice out among so many strangers made her heart beat and strangled her breath. Later, under cover of conversation grown general, Ilka turned to the blond young woman, who seemed least formidable, and said, "Tell me one more time what your name is."

The young woman turned serene wire-rimmed eyes to Ilka and said, "Doris Mae."

"It is interesting," said Ilka, "how always, after I have sat beside a new person ten minutes, I think I have known them from childhood. You are not by chance born in Vienna?"

"Oklahoma," said Doris Mae.

"I don't believe Oklahoma!" Ilka smiled. "There is not such a place."

"What do you mean?" asked Doris Mae.

"So," said Ebony. "And how does Ilka like our Connecticut."

Ilka was grateful for the opening and said, "I always have a difficulty. I *see* that the American landscape is green and beautiful, but I have a difficulty to *feel* that it is."

"You and me both," said Ebony, using her bread to backstop the piece of meat little Annie was trying to spear onto her fork. "Always have difficulty with the American landscape."

"It always looks to me as if something is wrong."

"Always, always something wrong with the darn thing!" said Ebony, nodding her profound agreement.

"But what is wrong, I think, is my way to look," said Ilka.

"We'll teach you the right way to look at the American landscape," said Ebony.

"That is what I would like!" cried Ilka. "I want to see everything!"

"There are some lovely walks," said Sarah, the baby's mother. "There's a swimming hole we kids used to go to when we stayed with Aunt Abigail. I'll show you the rock we used to jump off. We called it Elephant Rock!" she told Annie.

"Abigail," Carter turned to explain to Ilka, "is Sarah's aunt. This is Abigail's house. She's lent it to us for the summer while she goes around the country organizing the revolution. Which revolution is Abigail organizing these days?" he asked Sarah.

"She's in Washington working for school desegregation," replied Sarah. "There is a nice old place, where she used to take us to lunch, called the White Fence Inn."

"I've never been to an American inn," said Ilka.

"There!" said Ebony. "We'll swim in Aunt Abigail's hole and have our lunch at the Black Fence Out, genuine Wasp cooking. Oops," said Ebony and gave her pink husband down-table an extravagant version of the classic look of the child caught with the forbidden cookie. "Stanley don't like me beating the boy—not while he's having his dinner, baby, do you! And I was doing so good!"

" 'Beating the boy,' " Carter explained to Ilka, "is a Negro phrase. It means sitting around comparing our bitty triumphs and monumental defeats in the white world."

"And I was going to like everything and everybody," said Ebony. "Going to make a project out of it! First week," she said, "I was going to like the slope, just in front of our house. Second week I was going to like Thomastown, third week Connecticut. . . ." Ilka looked and saw Ebony's little nubbin of a husband sitting with a sweet smile of enjoyment, his hands locked behind his head, watching his wife talking. Ilka began to like him. "Fourth week I was going to like the whole of New England. God only knows," said Ebony, "what all I might have ended liking!"

"Where are you going?" Carter asked her.

"Going to clean up the kitchen," said Ebony.

"Can we all sit a moment?"

Ebony sat down again and so did Sarah, Doris Mae and Ilka, who had risen with her.

Carter said, "I propose that we constitute ourselves a forum for this little polis." Everybody looked at Carter.

Carter said, "Has anybody policy to propose, questions to ask, gripes to air? Speak now or forever after hold your peace."

"I have a question," said Ebony. "Does everybody have the room they want? Stanley is supposed to sleep on a hard mattress, so we took the hardest. I mean because we came ahead . . ."

"And put in a lot of work," said Sarah. "I can tell. I know Aunt Abigail's housekeeping."

"I will entertain a motion for a vote of thanks to Ebony for all the work she put in," said Carter. The motion was unanimously seconded.

Ebony compressed her lips and dipped her head in something between a profound nod and a shallow bow and said, "Thank you, thank you. There's nothing sacred about these arrangements. Carter, would you and Ilka prefer to be in the big house? There's a perfectly good spare room. We just thought you might enjoy having the cottage to yourselves."

"We do," said Carter.

"We do," said Ilka.

Ebony said, "I know the bed is O.K., because I tried it. First night out I couldn't sleep, what with Stanley snoring and the old New England moon standing right outside the window, glaring at me. I woke poor Stanley, didn't I, baby? and made him switch sides. Stanley went on snoring. Damned if that old moon didn't switch sides! Right in my face! So the next night I tried the bed in the cottage."

"Well, *we* tried the bed," reported Carter, "and it's first-rate."

"Third night, I tried your mommy and daddy's bed, in your room," Ebony said to little Annie. Annie sat on her father's lap and pressed herself into his chest and watched Ebony's face. "There's another terrific bed for lying awake all night and not being able to fall asleep in!"

"Insomnia is *a* bitch," said Carter. "I happen to hold the North American indoor record for insomnia! Anybody else want the cottage? Anybody want the cottage any part of the summer? Does anybody want anything that they do not have, or want not to have anything they do have? Amazing!" said Carter.

A honeymoon of mutual accommodation carried them through the division of labor, which, in the fifties, was a comparatively simple matter: The men constituted themselves into a lawn-mowing, garbage-disposing detail. Ebony volunteered Stanley as a maker of superior fires.

"Bags the cocktails. Making, not drinking," Carter said.

"About the cooking," said Sarah, the baby's mother. "Everybody has to get their own breakfast and lunch and we take turns making dinner."

"If nobody minds," said Ebony, "I'll get Stanley's lunch. Stanley loves to be waited on, baby, don't you?"

Ilka was appalled into speech. "I don't think I can cook dinner for so many! I am not a good cook."

"Well, I am," said Ebony. "I am such a good cook I'm terrible at eating anything anybody else cooks. I'm real mean that way, so I'll be glad—I'd prefer, if it's all right with everybody—to just be let to do the cooking."

Well, it was not all right. "That wouldn't be fair to you," said Sarah. "Why don't we all do it together?"

"Fine!" cried Ilka. "Then I can help and I can learn how!"

"It'll be fun!" Sarah said.

"Fun, fun, fun," said Ebony, nodding and nodding her head.

"We'll play it by ear. See how it works." And so that was settled as well.

"Any other business?" Carter asked.

"About the damn agency woman . . ." Victor, little Annie's father, said to his wife, Sarah.

"I was telling Ebony," Sarah said, "Victor and I have decided to adopt. There are thousands upon thousands of babies in institutions, so Victor and I decided instead of having another of our own we're going to adopt a little brother for Annie."

Victor said, "And the stupid agency woman wants to come to look at us."

"What they really want," Sarah said, "is to tell us their idiotic reasons for quote matching us unquote with the quote unquote right baby, when there are literally thousands upon thousands of nonwhite babies sitting in institutions." Sarah was breathing hard. She said, "Victor and I feel they're giving us the runaround."

Ebony said, "Could I have a drop of your seltzer, Carter, or will you run out?"

"I bought a whole case," said Carter. "Do you want a little ice in it?"

"I'll take it neat, please. Thank you," said Ebony.

"Anyway," said Sarah.

"The question on the floor, as I understand it," said Carter, "is policy in regard to having friends up."

"Not friends," Sarah said. "The agency woman is not a friend."

"In regard to guests in general, then."

"We have the spare room," said Ebony.

Guests in general were voted in, Carter stepping down from the chair to offer an amendment that prior notice be required for sleepovers to avoid the coincidence of potentially hostile elements, and stepping back, passed the matter with every parliamentary minutia of procedure. He was having a lovely time. "Any other business? Do I have a motion to adjourn? A second? A show of unanimous hands. We are adjourned. I am very happy to be here."

Ilka's happiness brought her to the edge of tears. She had it in her heart to envy herself for being alive, here, in this beautiful house on an American hill carrying dirty dishes into the kitchen with these variegated Americans. She crossed paths with Victor, the child's father, coming in with a tray. He said, *"Also du bist aus Wien. Ich bin ein Berliner."* Ilka kept walking and knew that she had known it all along—had known by the blueness of his eye and his naked chest at table—it was just that it happened not to have occurred to her to say to herself that Victor was German. "I put these down here?" Ilka asked Ebony.

"Wonderful!" said Ebony. "Except I just swabbed it off for the clean dishes."

"Sorry," said Ilka.

Sarah said, "Victor, get Annie off to bed, will you?"

"Where are her pajamas?"

"In the car."

"Where in the car, Sarah?" Victor presently hollered from outside.

"In the trunk, in the back, Victor!" Sarah shouted back.

Upstairs the sleepy baby began to wail and Sarah said, "I'm sorry, I better go up and give him a hand."

"Oh, do do do do do," said Ebony.

Ilka heard the imminent shriek in the woman's voice and said, "Sometimes help is more a trouble, no?"

"You can say that again," said Ebony. "Why don't you go in the living room? Go and sit by Stanley's fire."

"Come, sit by the fire," said Carter.

Ilka dropped into the surprise depth of an upholstered chair, its springs relaxed, its stuffing broken and molded by decades of American backsides that had rubbed the cretonne primroses, tulips, lilacs to a gentle monotone. The eyes of generations of beholders had connected the heads of the bluebirds in the vines on the wallpaper into blue stripes. Sofas, chairs, the standing lamp had put down roots into the carpet, which might have been gold once, or rose. A small table sprouted by Carter's elbow to hold his seltzer bottle.

In his chair Carter laughed. The blue-black man with the mustache sat on the other side of the mild summer fire and said, "Mother used to tell us boys, said, 'Why you got to always hang around those black next-door children I never will know, you black enough yourself, Lord *knows* you don't get it from my side of the family. Why can't you play with those light-skin Jones boys can make something out of themselves one of these days?' A good woman, my mother, wanted the best for her children." Underneath the outsize mustache his long yellow teeth smiled subtly, and Ilka's heart gasped with the little pain of falling a little in love.

Carter laughed and laughed and rose, picked up his glass, and said, "Ice anybody?" He walked out of the room.

Ilka ignored her racing heart and the absence of her breath and spoke: "I like it so much to see old friends talking together."

The mustachioed blue-black man looked at Ilka with surprise and stopped smiling.

Ilka persevered: "I traveled so much to and fro Europe I have always lost all my friends again." The black man said nothing. Ilka asked, "Where did you all meet each other?"

The man stared into the fire. He was thinking. He said,

"Stanley I know I know from the CP, but Carter was never CP. . . . Carter was a Wobbly and Abigail was into everything. She was CP treasurer—that's how I know Abigail, and I met Carter with Abigail—that was it." He mused into the fire.

Ilka was glad when Carter came back. Ilka wished they would all come in and sit down. Where was everybody?

The German walked in and said, "So!"

"Yes, indeed," said Carter.

The German's wife, Sarah, came in and said, "Darn, darn, darn, Victor! You know what we forgot!"

"To call the agency!" Victor actually slapped himself on the forehead. "Tomorrow in the morning!"

Ebony came from the kitchen with the bespectacled blonde with the two names, who wiped her hands on the seat of her neat short shorts and went and sat down on a low stool next to the mustachioed man—what *was* his name?

Ebony sat on the ottoman in front of the fire and asked, "Did Stanley go up?"

"Is Stanley all right?" asked Sarah.

"Stanley hasn't been right all spring—all year."

"Maybe he should see Dr. Hunter," said Sarah. She looked so concerned Ilka really liked her. "He's a good doctor and a dear man. Aunt Abigail used to take us when we smashed ourselves up. His office is right on Main."

"Maybe *I'll* go see the dear man, get myself a pill or *something*," said Ebony.

"Pills! What pill?" asked Carter.

"Something to make me sleep."

Sarah said, "Victor and I were saying, before you came in, we have to call the damn agency in the morning. Did I tell you we think they're giving us the runaround?"

"You did, you did." Ebony picked up the poker and worried the little fire.

"We think it's not the fault so much of the woman," Sarah said. "It's the idiot agency."

"Sarah refuses to understand," said Victor, "that the idiot agency may have the idiot law on its side."

"Idiot, idiot, idiot law," said Ebony, poking and poking and poking the fire.

"We intend to go through the courts if that's what it takes," said Sarah. "Meanwhile thousands and thousands of little non-white babies are sitting in institutions."

"Only thing under the circumstances," Ebony said, "is to go to bed," and she planted her feet wide, placed her hands upon her thighs and pushed herself up. "Are you O.K. for blankets?" she asked Sarah.

"I'll come with you and see," said Sarah. The two women went out.

After a small silence, the Berliner said, "So. I know who does not need a pill to sleep after so much driving." He stood up, said, "Good night," and went out.

"Well," Carter said, "what do you think?" and he grinned.

The mustachioed man said, "I think exactly what you think," and looked so charming and malicious Ilka *really* liked him.

Carter laughed. "Are we going to make it through the summer, do you think?"

"*I* will make it." The mustachioed blue-black man stood up. The bespectacled blonde stood up with him. "About anything or anybody else," said the mustachioed man, "I would not wish to speculate. Good night."

"Good night, Percy!" Carter roared. "Good night, Doris Mae," and he kept laughing. It did not seem to Ilka that there could be, in the world, anything funny enough for such enormous and protracted hilarity.

In the cottage Carter put on his green-striped pajamas and said, "You don't happen to have such a thing as an old nylon stocking, do you?" Ilka happened to have such a thing. Carter tied a knot six inches from the top, wet his head, and drew on the stocking cap, flattening the hair against his skull. Then he got into bed and said, "Come," and raised the layers and layers of threadbare blankets; they warmed by the pound.

Ilka said, "I have questions."

"Shoot," said Carter.

"The railway stationhouse—it is made out of what?"

Carter said, "Brick."

"That is what I thought," said Ilka. "What is the name of the man with the mustache?"

"Percival Jones. He is a writer. He is famous."

"The woman with the two names is his wife?"

"Very much so. Doris Mae."

"You know Aunt Abigail?"

"Very, very, very well," said Carter.

"What is CP?"

Carter explained.

"What is Wobblies?"

"Oh, Jesus!" said Carter. He explained.

"What is Wasp?"

Carter explained. Ilka thought it was the wittiest thing she had ever heard.

Ilka said, "Ebony is wonderful."

"Ebony," said Carter, "is a hostile bitch."

"You don't think that she is beautiful!" cried Ilka.

"She's a beautiful hostile bitch," said Carter.

"I like her so much!" said Ilka.

"I love Ebony," said Carter.

"I don't believe this!" Ilka said, next morning, when she opened the door and saw a bush arched to the ground with the weight of blossoms. "This was not here last night. Did you do this?"

"Yes," Carter said.

"There is a bird on top of the top branch."

"I did it," said Carter.

Ilka walked across the grass toward the big house. Stanley, in a deck chair in the sun, waved his *New York Times.*

The Berliner stood smiling in the doorway. Ilka pressed past, avoiding contact.

At the table in the sun-filled kitchen, Sarah was feeding little Annie breakfast. Annie was crying and saying, "I want to stay with Aunt Ebony."

Ebony brought Ilka coffee and said, "Coffee, Doris Mae?"

The bespectacled blonde was standing with her back to the room, absorbed in the arrangement, on a four-legged wicker tray, of a plate, a knife and fork, a cup and saucer. She aligned the napkin with the spiritual precision of a Mondrian. "I'll take him his juice and come back." She went out the door.

"Is Percy sick?" asked Sarah with a frown of concern.

"Nope," said Ebony.

"I want to stay with Aunt Ebony," wept Annie.

"Don't you want to come with mommy and daddy and see the Elephant Rock? Anybody want to come swimming?" Sarah asked.

"Can we have lunch in that inn?" asked Ilka.

"Sure can," said Ebony. "Ain't a damn thing we cain't do."

"Why can't I stay with Aunt Ebony?" screamed Annie.

"I've got an idea for Annie," said Ebony. "Annie, you and I will go to town and do the marketing, if that's O.K. with your mommy, if your mommy will get you a pair of pants, because this is Connecticut, where they're sticklers."

"It *would* help," said Sarah, "to have some quiet to phone the idiot agency, but I don't want her bothering you. Did you get any sleep?"

"Not any," said Ebony.

Ebony and a blissful Annie in a clean seersucker playsuit drove off.

The German stood in Ilka's path. He said, "Sarah and I go for a walk. Would you like to come with us?"

"No," said Ilka and said, "thanks." Because he continued to stand smiling at her, Ilka said, "I have to find Carter."

Ilka found Carter lying mother-naked in the grass behind the cottage. The sky was perfectly blue. Carter said, "I turn copper-colored in the sun."

"We go swimming and to lunch at the inn," reported Ilka.

"Who goes?" asked Carter without opening his eyes.

"You don't want to go?"

"At this moment," said Carter, "my head is not reeling, my stomach is not pitching. I'm not moving."

Ilka found the blonde with the two names in back of the house hanging a shirt on the line. "Your husband is sleeping?"

"He's writing."

Ilka said, "You look so familiar! You're sure you were not born in Vienna? Prague? Paris? Grenoble? Constantsa? Lisbon?"

"I was never out of the States except for our senior high school trip we went to Quebec," said Doris Mae.

"Very sensible of you to get born right away in America."

"How do you mean?" said Doris Mae.

"Think of all the time you saved not queueing in consulates, waiting for quota numbers, alien cards, affidavits, sponsors, visas, permits! What are you doing?"

"Hanging Percival's shirt to dry," said Doris Mae.

"I mean what do you work?"

"Before I married Percival I was a gym teacher," said Doris Mae.

"Aha!" said Ilka and walked away.

In the kitchen Ebony was holding the refrigerator door for Annie and saying, "*Wonderful!* Now the milk, which will and will not fit on that shelf. Try the top shelf. *Terrific!*"

Sarah walked in and said, "God, I didn't mean you to baby-sit! Annie, come with me!"

"No problem," said Ebony. "Annie and I bought some mushrooms for an omelet, and a beautiful salad. I'll fix a bit of lunch."

"Can I help?" asked Ilka.

"I believe everything is under control," said Ebony. She ran water through every convolution of every leaf of lettuce, patted, dried and tied the lettuce in a towel and said, "If you would like to put this on a shelf in the fridge, that would be terrific."

"I can cut the onion," offered Ilka.

"Wonderful," said Ebony.

"How small?"

"Don't matter a hoot," said Ebony.

"How's this?"

"Terrific," said Ebony.

"You want still smaller?"

"Maybe just a smidgen."

"How is this now?"

"Wonderful. I'll just give it a couple more chop chop chop chops. . . . *There* we are!"

"Where shall I put the onion?"

"Why don't you just leave it?"

"I want to wash up the board."

"Except the sink is full of lettuce. I'll clear it later."

"I can clear," said Ilka, and picking up the board, set the knife sliding, and bending to catch it, dropped the board on Ebony's foot. Ebony screamed briefly.

"Sorry!" Ilka knelt to wipe the onion off the pink-rimmed brown foot.

"Not with the dish towel!"

"Sorry," said Ilka. "Shall I cut more onion?"

"You do that," said Ebony. "I'll go up and catch me a little nap, maybe, now there's no moon to spook me."

. . .

Outside, Victor stood in wait for Ilka. "Jews in Connecticut!" he said in German and smiled and shook his head.

Ilka said, "I have a headache."

"You should lie down," the young German said.

Ilka began to walk very fast in the direction of the cottage. He kept beside her. "When did you come to America?" he asked her.

"Last year," Ilka said and walked faster.

"You went through the whole war! Are your parents alive?" he dared, intolerably, to want to know.

"My mother lives in New York." Ilka lifted her eyes to his round and friendly face. "The Nazis shot my father on the road, the last week of the war," she said and bolted into the cottage and closed the door and found she really did have a headache. At least a pulse beat so furiously behind her eyes she felt her head jerked forward and backward in space.

★　　　★　　　★

M Y D E A H!' " said Ebony, when she had finished serving dinner and had tied the dish towel around Annie, who insisted on wearing it backward, like a cloak. " 'You'll never *guess* what I saw this *morning!* In the supermarket!' " Ilka looked up in surprise at the stranger's conspiratorial and salacious voice emanating from Ebony's thinned and pursed lips. Ebony leaned intimately toward no one sitting on her left and, cupping her hand to prevent the nonexistent crowd on her right from overhearing, said, "A colored! Right down the center aisle! My deah! Without shoes! Could I ask a favor?" she said in her normal voice. "I don't only like fixing food, I like serving it, I like buying it, I even like cleaning it up, so could I be let to do the kitchen by myself, just for tonight, so tomorrow I'll know where everything is?"

"Can you *believe* we still have not got through to the idiotic agency?" Sarah said to the group around the fire. Stanley lay stretched at his full length, asleep on the sofa. Carter and Percival sat where they had sat the first night, one on each side of the fire. Ilka looked around for Doris Mae. Ilka wanted Ebony to come in and sit down and complete the circle. What Ilka wanted was to be happy.

"We called first thing in the morning," Sarah said, "and got the cleaning woman. She said they didn't come in till nine-thirty. At nine-thirty they said our woman wasn't expected until ten, so we went for a walk and gave her till ten-twenty and she had *just* walked out and wasn't expected back till around four, four-thirty. We called back four-thirty and she had left for the day. By this time you begin to smell a rat. So tomorrow we start all over."

"Monday, you mean," Victor said.

"I mean Monday."

In the ensuing silence Ilka heard the murmur of a distant conversation. She got up and went and looked in the kitchen door: Doris Mae was cleaning out the sink; Ebony was swabbing down the table. Ilka was jealous.

"I have a question," said Ilka when she lay in bed beside Carter. "Percival is very clever, no?"

"Very," said Carter.

"Why did he marry what is her name again?"

"Doris Mae," said Carter. "I guess he likes her."

"She is not interesting." Ilka felt a personal affront when interesting men liked dull women. "She doesn't talk," said Ilka.

"She talks to me. I like Doris Mae."

"And why would Doris Mae marry. . . ." Ilka became puzzled and stopped.

"A Negro twice her age?"

"*You* think *I* mean *that?*" cried Ilka.

"What *did* you mean?"

"*That!*" said Ilka with the thrill of revelation. "I'm a racist!"

"Not to worry," Carter said. "Some of my best friends are racists."

★   ★   ★

A N O T H E R   B R I L L I A N T   morning. "Was that our bird, do you think, from our bush?" said Ilka. It had left its three-pronged claw print across the silver-wet grass. The air was perfectly white. The big white house stood in modest dignity upon its eminence; another hour, and the gold impurities of day would compromise its sharp new outlines.

"Morning!" Ebony said. "Hot biscuits! It's Sunday!"

"Once, can we go to the church in the village?" said Ilka.

"*No!*" Carter and Ebony said in one voice.

Ebony was looking into the oven. "Not *quite* done," she told Doris Mae.

Doris Mae was setting out Percival's tray and said, "I'll take him his juice."

"Anybody brought me my food in bed," said Ebony, after a silence which could be trusted to allow Doris Mae to have reached the top of the stairs, "I swear I would eat *them!*"

"He does," said Carter.

"He does, he does, he has! Eaten her right up!" Ebony said, nodding her head.

"That's not food," said Carter in the same low voice, "it's a ritual."

"Right! Right! You're right! And I thought it was breakfast! A ritual is what that is."

"You saw the reverence, the piety," said Carter.

"Certainly did. I saw it." Ebony nodded and nodded. "Poor Stanley! All he ever gets is food."

"Good, good, good food," Carter said.

"Poor, poor, poor Stanley! *Good* morning," Ebony said to the sleep-heated, tousle-headed Annie in the doorway. "You are just in time to see if these biscuits are ready to come out of the oven. If you will stand over there, we're going to take a look. How many more minutes would you say?"

"Ten," said Annie.

"Right!" said Ebony and nodded her head. "Me too. I like my biscuits burnt good and black, so we'll leave one for you and one for me another ten minutes, but in case some of these other people might prefer theirs this uninteresting golden color, would you bring me Aunt Abigail's ironstone platter from the table over there. *Wonderful.* Hold it very steady, just like that. *Marvelous!* Now you come and sit here. Here is the clock. When this hand comes around to there, you sing out and that's when ours will be done. Meanwhile you could start on one of these dumb white ones," she said and buttered a beautiful hot biscuit and poured a glass of milk for Annie. "Doris Mae, I got some biscuits wrapped in a napkin keeping warm for Percy."

"Thank you," said Doris Mae, who lofted the tray and bore it out the door.

"Poor, poor Stanley!" said Ebony. "You ever hear Stanley snore? He doesn't snore, he snorts, he grunts, he gasps—you wouldn't think a little skin-and-bone man like that could perform such a racket! He's got to dip so far down to get his breath up I think he's never going to make it back, and I lie and I wait. I'm thinking this is the middle of the night in the middle of Connecticut! Do I call the doctor and say, 'Dr. Hunter, get out of your bed, my husband stopped breathing'? I wait another second. One more second. I'm going to count to ten. Are you watching the clock?" she asked Annie, who chewed slowly, watching the drama of Ebony's face. "Now I panic. I sit up. I lean down. I listen for Stanley's heart. . . . Damned if he doesn't snort—right in my ear! Gasp, gurgle, as if somebody's trying to strangle him. So I turn over. I'm going to sleep, no matter what. I'm just about to drop off when, rattle and snort, Stanley throws his arm around, slap in my face! Wakes me right up! I was never so mad!"

"Ten," yelled Annie.

"Come," said Ebony. "There, you see! Two charcoaled biscuits which are great for writing one's name on a paper napkin. A N N I E."

"Here you are," shouted Sarah in the kitchen door. "Didn't I tell you not to bother Aunt Ebony!"

"We're just fine and dandy. No problem," said Ebony, but Sarah hauled the shrieking Annie up the stairs.

"Have we got in touch with the agency yet?" Carter asked Ebony in a low voice.

"We have not got in touch," Ebony said, "yet."

"Man," said Carter, "that is *the* slowest damn pregnancy, black *or* white, that I have ever had the misfortune to be obliged to listen to a blow-by-blow account *of.*"

"Not a blow spared," said Ebony. "Good morning, Stanley. Did you know you slapped my face for me in bed last night!"

"Bastard," said the smiling Stanley.

"I got so mad," said Ebony, "I wrapped up in my blanket and came downstairs and tried the living-room couch, and nothing."

"Anybody go for my *Times?*"

"I did," said Ebony. "Baby, you think that little village store would order me the *Harlem Herald?* Carter, don't you get the *Harlem Herald?*"

"Heck, no! I write for the *Harlem Herald.* I don't read it!

That's what you need," Carter said to Ebony. "The *Harlem Herald!* Put you right to sleep! I know a joke. Two colored meet on Good Friday. One says, 'Say, Jack, I see you got the mark on your forehead, Lord be praised, you seen the light at last.' Jack says, 'Lord showed me the way, after all these years, hallelujah!' Says, 'Hallelujah. So, what you goin' give up for Lent this year?' 'Man,' says Jack, 'goin' give up the Negro press, after all these years, Lord be praised!' "

Stanley grinned affectionately at Carter. Carter laughed and laughed and laughed. "Goin' give up the Negro press, Lord be *praised!*" hollered Carter.

"The Negro press!" Ebony nodded and nodded her head without the hint of a smile, "That is a fun-ny sto-ry!" she said. Her eyes were very brilliant and her voice was very harsh.

"Today can we go to that inn?" said Ilka in order not to be saying nothing.

"Absolutely." And Ebony nodded her head up and down.

*　　　*　　　*

T H E　C A R S began to arrive in the late morning. They parked in the shade under the trees. The doors opened and out stepped two, three, five, ten, a dozen black people. Black people covered the slope. "Jack!" said Carter to the man in the brown three-piece suit. "You remember my friend Ilka. Jack," Carter explained to Ilka, "is the principal of Ebony's school. Ginny!" He embraced the brown, red-haired woman, who said, "Brought you my homemade piccalilli that you like." A bare-backed black woman in high heels unwrapped a roast chicken; others were taking casseroles out of baskets, and salads, pickles, cheeses, loaves of presliced bread and rolls and buns and cakes and bags of fruit. The men set up the tables and brought out chairs.

"Annie, come and get your juice," said Sarah. Annie sat on Ebony's lap and pressed herself voluptuously into Ebony's bosom and shook her head.

Sarah said, "Annie! I told you I don't want you bothering Aunt Ebony."

"We're just fine. We're O.K.," Ebony said.

"Well, send her over here when you've had enough," said Sarah.

"Will do," said Ebony. "Carter, tell how you lost your head in Syracuse, New York. That is a fun-ny sto-*ry.*"

"Not in Syracuse, New York; *Knossos,* New York," said Carter, "is where I lost my head. That was the time I still went all over and lectured on race relations in clubs and organizations and churches and universities. That was O.K. What I couldn't take was afterwards, when I was exhausted from the trip and the talk and wanted to hole up in some little black hotel with a bottle of booze and pass out, there was the dinner at some white faculty's house, and the reception to meet students, and all those questions and all that good will! Got so I didn't mind talking to white folks," said Carter, "so they didn't talk to me about race relations."

"All that good *will,*" said Ebony.

"So I'm at the University of Knossos, New York, and the dean comes up, says, 'Mr. Bayoux, I know that I am talking on behalf of all my faculty and students and everyone who has heard your eloquent and moving address here tonight'—everyone stops talking; everyone is listening—'when I say that this has been a memorable occasion for us. You have given us food for thought, Mr. Bayoux. You have made us aware of situations and conditions that do not ordinarily come our way, I am ashamed to say, and, Mr. Bayoux, we owe you a debt of gratitude. And I will speak to my faculty, and I will speak to our student body, and to our civic leaders, and the leaders in the private sector, who, I am certain, will wish to join me in turning this feeling into something tangible. We want, Mr.

Bayoux, to do something not only for your people, but to express our gratitude to you personally in any way or form you may wish to suggest to us. Mr. Bayoux, is there something, sir, that we can do for *you?* '

"Well, I was moved! All those good white faces, so pleased and so eager, I lost my head!"

"Lost—your—head!" said Ebony.

"I told him, I said, 'Well, yes, as a matter of fact something does come to mind. I'm two-thirds into my book about the effect of an emerging Africa on the American Negro that I've been working on for the last couple of years. Now, if I could take the spring off and work through the summer in some quiet place' "—Percival smiled—" 'just outside of town' "—people began to laugh—" 'on one of your beautiful lakefronts, perhaps some little cottage. . . .' "

"Sure lost your head." Ebony nodded so profoundly she sandwiched little Annie between her breasts and her lap. Annie giggled. "Just a little old cottage!" cried Ebony.

"On the lakefront," shouted Carter. "Dean said, 'We will certainly look into that little matter for you, keep our eyes skinned, see what we can come up with,' " hollered Carter. " 'We want you to believe—I know everyone here agrees with me one hundred percent—what a truly, truly memorable occasion this has been for every single one of us here. . . .' "

"Sure was one me-mo-rable occasion!" yelled Ebony. "Just a little cottage, just right on the lakefront . . ."

Ilka held her smile through the protracted storm of black laughter.

Ebony said, "Carter, d'you dare tell the story about Oink. That's another funny story."

"You tell it," said Carter. "You tell it good."

"There's two colored," Ebony said, "live up North, going home for a visit, and come through this little spot on the road, and, man, is it hot! They want water so bad they drive round the back of this old ramshackle farm, and the one calls out,

'Lady, can we get a glass o' cold water?' Ol' white woman, she sticks her head out the upstairs window, sees two colored, she up and starts hollering, 'Help! Police! Murder! Rape!' Well, two fellers, they think 'Uh-huh. Time to skedaddle.' One says, 'Listen, they goin' string us up for sure, may as well be for something,' so they pick up this little black pig is running around and put it in the front seat between the two of them and head out of town. Sure as hell fire, there's the old siren, right behind, so they pull over and the one, he puts his hat on the little pig's head. Sure enough, the uniform gets out, walks over, says, 'O.K., you boys, they's a fine white lady been raped and beaten, left for half dead. You seen two evil-looking black bucks pass this way in a old jalopy?' One feller, he says, 'No, *sir*, I ain't seen nobody, not of that there description like you said there, and we done come right through there, no siree. You seen anybody fitten that description there at all?' he says to his buddy. Buddy says, 'I ain't see nobody a-tall. You seen anybody a-tall?' 'Uh-*huh*, I didn't see nobody.' 'All right all right all righty,' says the trooper. 'If you boys see anybody that's fitten that description, you-all tell them to get their black asses right on back here and see me at the stationhouse, you hear? What's your name there?' Feller says, 'My name is Wadsworth.' Trooper, he writes down, 'Name is Wadsworth, and your buddy there. What is your name?' Buddy says, 'Name Jesse.' Trooper writes it down. 'Name Jesse. And you there, in the middle. What is your name?' Wadsworth, he pokes the little black pig. Pig squeals, 'Oink.' Trooper writes down, 'Name is Oink. O.K., you Wadsworth, Jesse, and Oink, I want you boys to haul outen this town and don't come back in a month o' Sundays.' Say, 'Yessir, officer,' and they start up and hit the road. Trooper he walks back to his partner, says, 'That ain't them. Lady said two, and them there's three boys in that old jalopy. Man, I seen ugly in my life. That Wadsworth—he is ugly; that Jesse, *he* is ugly; but that Oink, man! That is *the* ugliest nigger I ever *see!*'"

"That," said the man in the brown suit, and he stood up, and he was not laughing, "is a word I don't permit to be used in my hearing." He wished everyone a good day and strode away in the direction of the parked cars. Ebony stood up, setting Annie, who had fallen asleep, onto her feet. Sarah picked up the shrieking child and carried her into the house. The red-haired woman was gathering jars into a basket and walked after the man in the brown suit. Ebony walked after them. The red-haired woman stopped. The two women embraced before the red-haired woman got in the car with the man in the suit. They drove away.

"Stanley!" said Ebony. "Baby, make us a fire in the living room. It got chilly. Stanley? Did Stanley go up? We'll go inside," said Ebony. Everyone was rising. Everyone had to get back to town. Tomorrow was Monday. There was no holding up the desultory but unmistakable trek, amidst thanks and congratulations on the fabulous house, the fabulous afternoon, in fives, in threes, in twos back into the cars.

Carter, Ilka and Doris Mae walked into the house after Ebony. Carter sat in his chair and said, "Well well well well well well."

Ebony poked at the dead fireplace. Carter said, "Getting so I can't talk to middle-class black folk."

Ebony said, "When did Stanley go up? Where's Percy?"

"Percival went on up," said Doris Mae.

Ebony said, "I'm going up—see what happened to Stanley."

Doris Mae opened her mouth and said, "First Negro man I ever saw, when I was nine years." Doris Mae said there were no Negroes in Oklahoma, where she came from, and the first she ever saw was on her aunt Martha's farm. Doris Mae said Aunt Martha sent her to get Bowser's dish, and washed it and she put ham on it and bread. Doris Mae asked her aunt why she was putting bread on the dog's dish and Aunt Martha said, "You take this out back," and Doris Mae took it and there was an old, dusty man, sitting on Aunt Martha's back stoop. His shirt was the same color as his face, the brim of his hat was turned all the way up around his head, and he wore glasses.

Ilka said there were no Negroes in Vienna and the first she saw stood at the entrance of a circus tent. He had on red harem pants and a turban like a purple doughnut so high up it was almost out of sight in the sky. Ilka asked her father if he was real, and her father had said, "Pssst." The huge Negro in the sky had frowned thunderously and said, "What do you mean am I real?" and reached down his immense hand and patted Ilka's hair.

Carter said he and the other boys used to hide around the corner from the little sooty synagogue that was three blocks from school. They wanted to see what a Jew looked like. They used to dare each other to scoot past the door and scoot back to make a Jew come out and do whatever Jews did to little black Christian boys—cut off their balls at the very least. There were people all the time going in and out of the synagogue. Saturdays a whole lot of people went in and came back out lunch time, but they never ever got to see a Jew.

"I should go back tomorrow," said Ilka, as they undressed for bed.

"And come back out on Friday," said Carter.

"Carter!" said Ilka, "I should not go on like this, should I? I must find myself a proper job and meet new people. Mustn't I, Carter, get on with my life, don't *you* think?" Ilka was shocked to be facing Carter's outraged and unhappy face.

He said, "What you must not do is to keep threatening me, because I cannot bear it."

"I threaten you!" said Ilka.

Carter said, "I will be grateful, no, joyful—I will be joyful—if you stay with me, as long as you can stay with me. I will be unhappy indeed if you find you have to leave me, but this cannot be a decision in which I should be made to participate."

"You are right," said the girl, immensely struck. It thrilled Ilka to be correctly corrected and made her fall in love with Carter all over again. They lay together and it was settled between them that Ilka, who had recently turned twenty-two, could afford to make over another year to Carter, and that until that time the question of their parting should be held in abeyance. Ilka agreed to stay the rest of her vacation, and they made love.

★ ★ ★

And so it was Monday morning. Ilka jumped when the quiet sunny kitchen asked her if she wanted coffee. She had not seen Ebony hunkered at the table with her hands wrapped around her cup as if it were the source of warmth, and looking, in her cotton housedress and rusty black kerchief wound round and round her head, like Ilka's notion of somebody's black cook.

"You didn't sleep again!" said Ilka.

"Didn't sleep," said Ebony. "Dr. Hunter can see me this afternoon, if somebody will do my cooking for me?"

"I *can* not!" cried Ilka.

And neither could Doris Mae. She was going to Boston. Percy was driving her to the station. "I should have told you!" said Doris Mae. "I thought I did say I was going into town Monday and get my hair done."

"You very likely did. You did tell me, I'm sure. I remember you told me," said Ebony.

"It's just these little salons out here won't know what I want done. Sarah can do the cooking. She really wants to share the cooking."

"Sarah can do the cooking," Ebony said. "No problem."

But there turned out to *be* a problem. Sarah was distressed.

They had just this morning—not ten minutes ago—finally managed to get through to the stupid agency! "We're going to New York."

"I don't want to go to New York," said Annie.

"Annie, don't you want to see the dear little babies?"

"I want to stay with Aunt Ebony," wailed Annie.

"Annie, don't! Annie's bowels are loose today of all days," said the distraught Sarah. "Victor, call them back and see if we can come tomorrow."

"Don't you remember, the idiot woman was on her way going out?"

"I don't want to see the idiot woman!" howled Annie. "I want to stay with Aunt Ebony."

"Poor Aunt Ebony has a headache. She has to go and see Dr. Hunter. Maybe I could cook when we get back, except Annie will have a hunger tantrum."

"So will Stanley. No problem. We've got a capon in the icebox. I'll make a nice liver stuffing, pop it in the oven, no fuss, no problem."

"I will help," said Ilka.

"There, you see," said Ebony. "There is no problem."

"*I* want to help!" shrieked Annie.

"I've got an idea for Annie, if Annie will stop crying and start chewing!" said Ebony. The little girl turned her tear-glistening face to the source of interest and satisfaction, and closed her mouth over the mess of cereal, milk, sugar, and salt tears and heroically masticated. Ebony said, "Do you think you could put up with those babies today, and tomorrow we'll all go swimming in Aunt Abigail's swimming hole?"

"And lunch at the White Fence Inn!" said Ilka.

"You're not just whistling Dixie," said Ebony.

*   *   *

I T EXCITED Ilka and made her nervous to be left alone with Ebony. She said, "There are people natural in a kitchen, no? Doris Mae, I think, doesn't have to ask all the time where things are and what to do next."

Ebony nodded her head and said, "Doris Mae doesn't have to talk all the time."

Ilka blushed and said, "I know how I can help and learn and not be a nuisance!"

"How is that?" asked Ebony.

"*You* will tell *me* when I can help you something. I will stand here and I will watch you, and you explain what you are doing."

"Okey-dokey," said Ebony. "I'm taking the capon out of the icebox."

Ilka stood at Ebony's elbow. Ebony said, "In New York I buy kosher hens and draw them myself. I'd never get my liver like this raggedy thing." She cupped the gross matter tenderly in the palm of her hand. Ilka watched the deft, cleanly motion with which Ebony flipped the fowl and intertwined its wings as if the naked bird had casually crossed its arms. Under Ebony's palpation the bluish, pimpled flesh plumped and glowed.

Ilka asked Ebony if she had read Karel Čapek.

"No," said Ebony. "I'm putting the capon back in the icebox. I'm taking out the onion."

Ilka said, "Čapek has an essay. The title translates 'Make a Ring Around the One Who Is Doing Her Work.' "

Ebony's knife continued to chop with the rapidity of a hummingbird's wings. Ilka's eyes must have registered the infinitesimal spasm that dilated the black woman's eyes, and tightened her shoulders and neck with the dead stillness of a wild thing alerted to the imminence of an attack. Ilka heard Ebony say, "And cooking is doing my work, is it?" Ilka's penetration of spoken English was still comparatively gross, or perhaps she lacked the feel of certain hard American facts; certainly it was the flow, not of Ebony's mind, but of her own thought that carried her forward. Ilka said, "Yes. Čapek means how beautiful is work when done beautifully."

"Oh, brother," said Ebony.

"You don't believe work can be beautiful?"

"Where have I heard that idea before?"

"Now what are you doing?" asked Ilka.

"Tossing the liver with a little butter and the minced onion, scraping up every last little delicious bit. This is going in the stuffing, which is going into the capon, but only just before the capon goes in the oven, or the whole thing will go bad."

"That I did not know!" said Ilka, quite elated. "I am learning something!"

It was at this juncture that Sarah reentered the kitchen. She said, "Would you mind cooking up some rice for Annie—I hate to ask you . . ." Sarah held a box with a grinning Uncle Ben toward Ebony, whose right hand held the spoon with which she was scraping the skillet, the handle of which she held with her left hand. Ilka, whose hands were unoccupied, took the box out of Sarah's hand and said, "Where shall I put this?"

"Any damn where," said Ebony.

Ilka set Uncle Ben on the table among the soiled breakfast dishes.

"I mean it's for Annie," Sarah said in her despair. They could hear Annie wailing outside, in the car. "To bind her," Sarah said, "because of her bowels." Victor tooted the car horn. Still Sarah stood in the door waiting for mercy. Ebony ran water into the skillet. "So," said poor Sarah, "listen, thanks, I mean really. You don't mind?"

"You bet," said Ebony. "Have a nice trip."

"Thanks. We should be back six-thirty—seven at the latest. I'm sorry. O.K.?" and she went.

"Now," Ebony said to Ilka, "if you would wash up the breakfast dishes that would be terrific. I'm going up and find where to lay my aching head."

This was the juncture at which Ilka discovered something she had not known about herself: she could not bear Ebony telling her what to do, and when to do it, and she said, "Does it make a difference if I will do it later?"

"It makes no nevermind," said Ebony.

"I have to look for Carter. I will do it, definitely, later."

"Okey-dokey."

Carter was lying in the grass behind the cottage, and Ilka said, "I have an idea. Let's go for a walk."

"Don't have ideas," said Carter. "Sit down. Lie down and tranquilize."

Ilka lay down. She shaded her eyes against the sun. She slapped at a feathery head of grass crawling up her leg.

"Lie still," said Carter.

Ilka turned onto her side. The two grasses growing closest to her eye were the size of two tree trunks. Ilka sighted along the curving horizon—the noble rise, it seemed to Ilka—of Carter's stomach against the bluest sky. Ilka laughed. Carter did not ask her why and Ilka said, "Your stomach does not know yet that you are shaping up."

"Never you mind my stomach," said Carter equably. "There's many a woman been known to grow fond of my stomach."

"I have grown fond," said Ilka. She sat up.

"Lie down," said Carter. "I never met a Jew yet knew how to tranquilize."

"I have to go and wash up the dishes," said Ilka.

Carter did not open his eyes.

When Ilka returned to the kitchen, Uncle Ben stood laugh-

ing on his box, on his spot on the table. The table, the sink
had been cleared. The whole kitchen was silent, sunny, cleaned
within an inch of its life.

I *said* I would do it. She didn't have to! Ilka argued, but
she felt horribly uncomfortable.

★   ★   ★

A NNIE'S WAILING, like an attribute of the Connecticut
summer carried temporarily out of earshot, had returned. Its
volume increased sharply with the opening of the car doors.
Sarah lifted the weeping child out on the left, while Victor, on
the other side, fussed over a small pale lady in a lilac summer
dress with a Peter Pan collar and buttons down the front: the
idiotic agency woman in actual person!

Ilka made her way over to the big house in the spirit of sheerest nosiness. She was a good-hearted girl, who did not want
people to get hurt, but she liked the excitement of a row. Ilka
entered the kitchen by the back door at the instant in which
Sarah walked in the other door and took in that tidy perfection.
"She hasn't started dinner!" Sarah dumped Annie into a chair.
Annie howled. The narrow lilac lady made a little *moue* and
rolled her eyes and said, "Poor little dear, feeling so poorly!"
in a thin voice like a voice at the other end of a telephone. She
put out a sympathetic forefinger toward Annie's tear-smudged,
suffering face. Annie drew back her head, squinting at the pink
hand coming at her, and continued, exhaustedly, to cry as if
she would have liked, but could not remember how, to stop.

"Why can't you feed her and get her to bed," Victor said
through smiling teeth.

"Because there is nothing *to* feed her," snarled Sarah under
her breath. She stood looking into the refrigerator. "Our

friend, who was supposed to cook, had to go to the doctor,"
Sarah told the agency lady.

"She didn't go to the doctor," said Ilka.

Now Victor introduced Ilka and Mrs. Daniels. Mrs. Daniels
made her little smiling *moue*, like a comical disclaimer of some
long-ago attempt at wit, when this little humor had been appro-
priate but unsuccessful, so that its small ghost was compelled
to repeat itself forever in search of the laughter that had never
come.

Sarah took Ebony's careful bowl of sautéed liver out of the
icebox.

Ilka said, "That's the stuffing for the capon!" but Sarah had
begun, with a trembling hand, to stuff the brown matter into
Annie's mouth, opened in a helpless howl of panic.

Now Ebony entered, was introduced to the agency lady, and
said, "You'll be staying for dinner, of course!"

"We tried to call—we tried a couple of times. The phone
was always busy. Annie, chew!"

"My fault," Ebony promptly said. "I took the darn thing
off the hook. That was bad of me!"

"How's the headache? ANNIE, STOP!"

"Headache is terrific. I better get that bird in the oven!"

"I gave Annie the liver," said Sarah.

"Ah, yes?" said Ebony.

"There was nothing else," said Sarah.

"No problem," said Ebony. "What's wrong with a nice
bread-and-herb stuffing? We got parsley, we got chives. . . ."

"I'm sorry, Ebony. Annie! SHUT UP!"

Now there entered Carter ex machina, large and urbane, to
be introduced. The little lilac lady rolled her eyes and made
a *moue* and said that she was pleased to meet him, from which
Carter deduced that she came from London, where, he said,
he and his ex-wife had spent two years on dear old Finchley
Road. Mrs. Daniels absolutely flushed with the pleasure of the

coincidence: she had been born quite near, on Primrose Hill! Carter's smile suggested it was not coincidence, it was not intuition, but a certain expertise, he happened to have, in placing a person's birth within a two-mile radius anywhere in the United Kingdom, from the way they pronounced "Pleased to meet you." He poured her a glass of predinner wine, and one for himself, and walked Mrs. Daniels out onto the mellow evening slope, not two moments before Sarah laid her head on the table and sobbed.

"Oh, come. Don't." Victor caressed her back. "She is human, and she is not stupid. She will understand."

"No, she's not stupid! She'll understand we are a mess."

Ebony sent both of them upstairs to get Annie to bed and to freshen themselves up.

"Can I help?" asked Ilka.

"Yes," said Ebony. "You can set the table. Here are Aunt Abigail's linen napkins. Get some blossoms from that bush outside your cottage. We're going to put on the dog for the agency lady."

The enormous chicken didn't make it to the table till well past ten o'clock. It was a magnificent, a baroque bird, copper-colored, glistening; it sizzled. The men, as by unspoken agreement, had put their jackets on, and with shirts opened at the throat looked decorous and at ease. Ebony in a white cotton dress wore her hair, as she had worn it at the benefit, pulled into a cap that fit close to her excellent small skull. Ilka kept staring at Ebony. It was a gay and gala meal. The spirited talk, pitched at a decent volume, flowed naturally around the petrified Sarah and Victor and buoyed their guest. Mrs. Daniels looked pink with pleasure. She told them something: when she was a girl she had loved learning Shakespeare speeches by heart.

"Would you have liked to be an actress?" Ebony asked her.

No. No, it wasn't that Mrs. Daniels had wanted to act, or

to be onstage, no, really, not at all. She had been *such* a shy, tongue-tied girl! It had been a relief to talk in Viola's or Portia's voice.

Did she remember any of her speeches? Could she say one? Mrs. Daniels could, and did, and did not roll her eyes or make a single *moue*, though it was a very long speech. Ilka sneaked a look and saw Ebony listening with none of the embarrassment that kept Ilka staring into her plate.

Mrs. Daniels acknowledged the applause with a pleased flush. Well, she said, but you couldn't go through life speaking Shakespeare. It wasn't that it got at all easier as one got older; one never really grew any less shy or stopped feeling embarrassed all the time. It's just one learned to just *be* shy and *feel* embarrassed and to take no notice and get on and do what needed doing, wasn't that right?

That was quite right. "Now!" Ebony said. "Victor, Sarah!" They jumped.

"Take Mrs. Daniels into the living room. You must have so much to talk about."

Mrs. Daniels demurred. First, they must all help wash up this wonderful, wonderful meal.

"Heavens to Betsy! No!" cried Ebony. "That is my department! Baby, you make one of your beautiful living-room fires."

"Oh, but we mustn't, you know, keep you out of your own living room!" Mrs. Daniels made a *moue* and rolled her eyes.

"*No* problem!" said Ebony. "We're ever so much happier in the kitchen. . . . Just the bittiest little swipe!" Ebony said to Carter after the small commotion that had convulsed Victor and Sarah into action and gentled their guest out of the room. "Didn't beat that boy but just this once, all evening long! I was good! Wasn't I good?"

"You were wonderful," said Carter. "We were all wonderful."

"Man, didn't we rally!" Percy said.

"We rallied," Carter said.

"Rallied right around!" said Ebony.

"Man!" said Percy. "When we rally, we surely do rally!"

They laughed *sotto voce*, but they laughed and laughed with the relief—Ilka understood that—of being three Negroes among themselves, except for herself, who did not count, and it was to insist on her existence that Ilka opened her mouth and said, "Now your hair looks nice."

"Why, thank you kindly," Ebony said and nodded, and said, "That's what my mother used to say when I got home from the barbershop Saturdays, with my scalp on fire from conking the wrong kind of curl out of my hair."

Carter explained, "Conking is a chemical process that relaxes Negro hair."

"Aha!" said Ilka.

"Nine to twelve every Saturday morning. Every Sunday morning, before church, my mother yanked the comb through every last strand, heated up the curling iron, and ironed in the right kind of curl, then she'd say, '*Now* your hair looks nice.' Somebody, some one of these days, is going to do a book about our hair, and when they do they better know what they are talking *about*. Anybody talks to me about my hair is walking into a buzz saw."

"I got me a notion," said Carter, "one of these days our hair is going to stand up and start the revolution." Ilka looked to see if he was laughing. Carter was not laughing.

Ilka lay in bed with Carter and said, "About Ebony. You think to *me* she is hostile?"

"*Yes!*" said Carter.

★   ★   ★

THERE HAD BEEN two occurrences in the night for Ebony
to report to Carter and Ilka, when she filled their cups at the
kitchen table. "Doris Mae is back," she said.

"And how is Doris Mae?" asked Carter.

"Doris Mae is *just* fine," said Ebony with a nodding action
that engaged her upper body to the waist. "You'll see just as
soon as she comes down from carrying Percy his juice, and,"
said Ebony, "I got into bed with the agency lady."

"Tell the whole story," said Carter.

"Well, you just know I will!" said Ebony. "Don't nothing
stop me telling the *whole* story. If there's a story, you just know
I'm going to tell the whole of it."

"You don't hear me complaining." Stanley put down *The
New York Times* and interlocked his hands behind his head.

Ilka, who was jealous, said, *"Today* can we have lunch at
that inn?," depressed by her skimpy voice compared with the
range of Ebony's brass-and-velvet tones.

"I'm lying in my bed," said Ebony, "wondering what is
going to happen to me if I don't get some sleep sometime
soon. . . ."

"Oh, man!" said Carter.

"Stanley is snorting to beat the band, so I wrap up in my
blanket, take my pillow under my arm and walk into the spare
room, and I'm lifting my knee, hoisting myself onto the bed
when the agency lady sits up and says, 'Eeeps!' "

Carter roared. Stanley grinned. Ilka kept smiling.

Ebony said, "So I come on downstairs. I'm going to give the
porch swing a try. Going to face that old New England
moon—I'm going to spit in his eye—and I walk out the front
door and there *is* no moon? What have they done with the Con-

necticut moon? What have they done with Connecticut? Where
did they put Thomastown! Did you ever look out the front door
around midnight? There—is—nothing—out—there! Did you
know the abyss starts right where our front porch stops—right
where there's that nice slope in the daytime.

"Man, it is black, but I mean pitch out there, and something
is throbbing—something is chugging louder, louder, LOUDER,
and it's Doris Mae's taxi from the station, so we went in and
had a nice long cup of tea, Doris Mae, didn't we? Carter, don't
you just love the way they did Doris Mae's hair for her in Boston?"

"They certainly did," said Carter.

"It's just it's cool for the summer," said Doris Mae. "Off
my neck."

"Well, *I* think it's darling! I think it suits the bones of your
face. Carter, don't you think it suits Doris Mae's bones?"

"It's easy to keep," said Doris Mae.

"I think it's darling," Ebony said.

"Percival likes it," said Doris Mae and picked up her tray.

Carter, his eyes round with delight, waited till she was safely
up the stairs, then he said, "She goddamn Afroed it!" claiming
ever after, to his own entire satisfaction, at the very least, that
it was he, on that occasion, who coined the word for the use
of decades to come.

"I must have scared you half to death," said Ebony when Sarah
and Victor brought their guest to say good-bye. "Me in a white
blanket, pillow under my arm, like the headless ghost! I didn't
know that anyone was sleeping over."

"I didn't know I was sleeping in your bed! I am so sorry!"
The agency lady made a *moue* and rolled her eyes.

"Not my bed," said Ebony. "Not at all. I'm sorry I woke
you. I keep haunting from one bed to the next, looking for the
one that I can close an eye in."

"Once," said Annie with a look of bliss, "you slept in my mommy and daddy's bed."

"I did! I did! I did indeed."

"I'm really sorry," said Sarah, her forehead desperately furrowed. "I thought you knew that Mrs. Daniels was sleeping over, because dinner got so late."

"Nope," Ebony said. "I guess I didn't know, did I!"

It was lunchtime before Doris Mae came downstairs. Ilka followed her out back to the clothesline. It occurred to Ilka that she never hung Carter's shirts out.

Ilka said, "You slept late today?"

"When one of us has been away for the day," said Doris Mae, "we just like to lie, and we talk."

Ilka asked, "You tell each other what you did?" She meant, "What can anybody talk to *you* about?"

"Oh!" said Doris Mae and lifted up her head. The soft pallor of her skin absorbed light. It showed the creeping at the throat and around the eyes. She looked older than Ilka had noticed before, and lovelier. "Oh!" Doris Mae said, and her frizzled shafts of hair, like so many spirals of the finest gauge of brass wire, caught the sun. They held the sun: "We just don't ever get enough of talking."

★   ★   ★

SARAH CAME to the dinner table flushed and feverish with hope. "She says not to give up! She's willing to stick her neck out for what she thinks is right."

"And what is that?" asked Ebony.

"You explain it," Sarah said and hid her face, racked with emotion, against Victor's arm.

"She says the agency processes two to three hundred babies . . ."

"A year," said Sarah.

"Mrs. Daniels says a typical breakdown would be eighty-five percent nonwhite babies—that is to say Negro, Latino, a few Orientals—almost no Jewish babies!" Victor said to Ilka. "And fifteen percent others. Now you break down the families that want to adopt a baby . . ."

"Who are able," Sarah said, "who can afford to adopt . . ."

"And you get less than thirty percent nonwhites. She says if they persist in the idiocy of 'matching' babies with adoptive families, you can 'match' thirty out of every hundred nonwhite babies with the thirty available nonwhite families, the fifteen available other babies with fifteen of the other families and there are fifty-five other families with no other babies to adopt and fifty-five non-other babies still sitting in institutions!"

"Did Mrs. Daniels say 'fifty-five *non-other* babies'?" asked Carter, his eyes perfectly round.

"Yes, and that's just one of goodness knows how many agencies around the country!"

"And that's talking percentages!" said Sarah. Her tears rolled down her cheeks. "We're talking about babies! Thousands—hundreds of thousands of little non-other babies!"

"Amazing!" said Carter.

When they lay in bed, Ilka asked Carter why he and Ebony and Percy kept laughing at Sarah and Victor's wanting to adopt a Negro baby. "Why is this not a good thing they are doing?"

"Tell you a story," said Carter. "White fellow visits with this poor old niggerman, says, 'It's a living shame, you living in this lean-to, wind blowing, snow coming in your chinks, while me and my family is all snug in our town house and I come out all the way here to tell you: I told my wife, "So long as that nigger is freezing his butt, don't nobody light a fire in my house." And I want you to know my wife, she's walking with the chilblains on her feet, my baby got his nose frostbit and my mother-in-law is like to die with the pneumonia.' Old nig-german, he listening. Says, 'Your wife walking with the chil-blains, your baby got his nose frostbit, your mother-in-law like to die of the pneumonia, you don't get no brownie points from me.' What are brownie points?" Carter quizzed Ilka.

"I don't know," said Ilka, and Carter began to laugh. Ilka considered taking offense, but the jiggle of his belly felt so per-fectly friendly that she lay and waited till he had finished laugh-ing and then she said, "I don't think Ebony is a hostile bitch. It's that she can't sleep."

"Oh, I see," said Carter.

★   ★   ★

WHO'S GOING to come swimming?" asked Ebony the next morning.

"We're going swimming?"

"Yes," said Ebony. "What's going to happen to my hair doesn't bear thinking of. Baby, are you coming?"

"I am going back to bed," said Stanley.

"You'll have to get your own lunch, then," said Ebony, "be-cause we are having ours at the White Fence Inn."

"We are!" cried Ilka.

"I can get my own lunch!" said Stanley. "Why do you think I can't get lunch?"

"Why indeed! Percival? Doris Mae?"

"I, if everybody will excuse me," Percy said, "will borrow Stanley's New York Times and go sit in the sun."

"And I will sit beside you," Carter said.

"Bunch of sissies," Ebony said to Annie.

· · ·

So it was only Ilka, Ebony, and the three Hamburgers who walked onto the plush little grassy beach, shaded and sun-flecked, with such fine, high arborage as Fragonard painted around his naughty courtiers to give them privacy. On a gray prominence, like the insulating back of a submerged elephant, a squirm of shivering, dripping little boys queued up for always one more splash into the clear brown water.

"Everybody has to turn around," said Ebony. "Everybody, have a good old look."

Ilka too had trouble keeping her gaze from Ebony's astonishing breasts and hips and improbably narrow waist skinned over with what looked like elasticized metal. Ebony glimmered and blazed with leaping silver lights that made her legs, arms, shoulders and small, handsome head look the sheerest black.

A family of decorous picnickers, who had turned their heads toward the newcomers, turned back to their picnic.

"Take a good look and get it over with," said Ebony.

But their party was destined to retain a high visibility. It was the size that makes decision difficult: one wanted shade, one wanted to tan, one wished to sit near the water, another wanted privacy. None wanted to impose, or to relinquish, a preference, until Victor sat down where he stood, on the only bald patch of ground that had no advantage of any kind. Annie wanted to go into the water and cried.

Ebony produced an outsize bottle of candy-pink shampoo out of a plastic shopping bag and took Annie's hand. A sunbather rolled onto his side and watched the voluptuous black-and-silver woman, sitting in the shallow edge of water, washing the hair of the skinny, sandy-haired child. Then the child washed the black woman's hair and the water bore the film of soap downstream. The next boy in line drew up his knees, embraced air, and a voice in Ilka's hair said, "Jews not permitted here." She looked around. Victor's smiling moon face eclipsed the world.

.   .   .

Annie was sleepy and wailed. The vertical sun had turned nasty. They collected their things and nothing more was said about any lunch at any inn. They piled silently into the car. Ebony wanted to get home and see Stanley getting his own lunch! "That is going to be some*thing!*"

When they walked into the kitchen Percival's raised voice was saying, "What do you *mean* 'Sammy Davis is not an artist'?"

Ebony said, "Uh-huh!"

"I mean," replied Stanley, "that Sammy Davis Junior is a successful entertainer, loaded with talent. He is not an artist."

"How about 'artiste,' " offered Ebony.

"He is an entertainer," said Stanley.

"That depends," said Percival, "on your definition of 'artist,' doesn't it?"

"No, it does not," said Stanley, "depend on your, my or anybody's definition, but on what does and what does not constitute art."

"In your racist definition," said Percival.

"How is it racist? I own one of the best private jazz collections in the goddamn country! Louis Armstrong and Charlie Parker are artists. Sammy Davis Junior is an entertainer," Stanley said to Percival's back walking out the door. "Shit," said Stanley.

It was mid-afternoon. Ilka stopped to hear a whisper—a faint aroma of music. She looked into the living room. The gentle flowered curtains had been drawn against the heat. Stanley beckoned. "Psst! Here. Listen." A scratchy record turned on the handcranked gramophone. "Schumann. Fischer-Dieskau. Artists! Goddamn Germans!"

Five o'clock and Percy poked his head out and looked around the lawn. There were no hostile elements. Ilka did not count. He came and sat by Carter and said, "Anybody's going to say anything to me about my boy is going to have his head handed to him. We're not having any of that, not here, not with me around." He was very ruffled and did not smile.

"Who is Sammy Davis Junior?" Ilka asked in bed.
"A successful Negro entertainer."
"So you agree with Stanley he is not an artist."
"No," said Carter, "I agree with Percy that he is a successful Negro."
"The discussion was, is he an artist."
"Stanley's discussion."
"But you agree that Stanley was right."
"I know Stanley is right, but I agree with Percy."
Ilka lay awhile. She said, "She wears a silver bathing suit. Then she's surprised people are looking."
"She's not surprised. Tell you a story," Carter said. "First black soldier is getting his medal for bravery. Whole black regiment is standing to attention on the White House lawn. President, he puts the ribbon round his neck, says, 'There is just one thing, my fine fellow: What the hell were you doing gallivanting above and beyond the call of duty where they shooting to beat the band?' Soldier says, 'Well, sir, Mr. President, I'll tell you. See now, ever since the first day I ever was born I been waiting somebody going to shoot my ass. That day I says to myself, says, "Two things I know to do: I can take my ass AWOL or I can take it where I *know* they going to shoot it. Onliest thing I cannot is wait one other minute." ' "

★   ★   ★

B ABY, " Stanley asked his wife at dinner the next day, "why are we eating late again?"
"Because I was down the village," replied Ebony. "John sends his best," she said to Sarah.

"John?" asked Sarah. "Which John is that?"

"Hunter. On Main Street."

"Dr. Hunter? You went to see Dr. Hunter?"

"Went to see John."

"He must be close on eighty, isn't he? How is Dr. Hunter?"

"John is just fine. John couldn't be better. You know how I know his name is John? I'm going to do it!" she said, looking with mock alarm at Stanley down the table. "I've been good, baby, haven't I? Didn't beat that boy but twice all week. If I have one more go at him I figure I'll get through this summer real good! Nobody going to ask me how come I know his name is John?"

"It says on his shingle, doesn't it? Dr. John Hunter."

"Probably does," said Ebony, "but that's not how *I* know. *I* know because I asked him what his name was. I walk in. I say, 'I'm Ebony Baumgarden, doctor. I spoke with you on the phone.' 'Oh! yes?' he says. 'Ah!' he says. 'You did say you were up in the old Highel house. So, Ebony, sit down. What can I do for you?' I said, 'Well, first thing you can do is tell me what your name is.' 'Dr. Hunter,' he says, a bit puzzled—not nervous. What's John got to be nervous about? I said, 'I know it's Dr. Hunter, but I didn't catch your Christian name.' 'My name is John,' says John, looking a liiitle bit peculiar, the way people look when they know something is going on but they don't see it. They don't know what it is. 'Well,' I said, 'John, ever since I came out here to your beautiful Connecticut, I haven't slept one wink.' "

"I think," Sarah said, "doctors just always call everybody by their first name. Of course he called us kids by our first names, but he calls Abigail Abigail. They are old friends."

"That's right. He does," Ebony said and nodded. "Said, 'I heard Abigail's niece was back at the Highel house.' "

"I'm surprised he remembers me," said Sarah.

"Oh, he remembers. He said, 'She broke her little finger jumping off Elephant Rock. I set it for her.' "

"That's right! He remembers. He did!"

"So then John says, 'I heard that little Sarah Highel married a Hamburger. Oh, those Highels! Always have to do everything different!' He says, 'My wife told me she saw you walking down the aisle, in the supermarket, with a little girl! So that was little Sarah's girl, was it! How long have you been working for the Hamburgers?' "

"Did you get your pills?" Carter asked her.

"Got my pills."

Next afternoon Carter said, "We're going for a walk."

"We are! Where are we walking?" cried Ilka.

"It do not matter," said Carter.

Carter walked beside Ilka. Ilka had the impression that they were walking the wrong way up the backside of the hill and said, "Let's walk the other way."

They turned around and this was another backside of the same wrong landscape. "Are you all right?" Ilka asked Carter, who was tacking like a sailboat going upwind. He fell over. Ilka helped the big man stand up. He leaned his dead weight on Ilka's shoulder, walking with a wide, slap-footed gait, and fell over. Ilka helped him get up. His temple was bleeding.

Carter took a nap and was in time to make drinks for everybody except himself.

"I want a drink," said Ilka.

"Very fine," said Carter.

"You can sit on our blanket," Victor said to Ilka but Ilka went and sat on the grass. She leaned her back against Carter's legs. The sky was green and copper. Everybody was here. Ilka rubbed her cheek against Carter's knee. He said, "Finish up your drink, I'll get you another." But the first half of Ilka's first was turning her chest liquid with warmth for Stanley lying way down in his deck chair; for Doris Mae on her low stool, like the effigy of an Egyptian wife who knows her proper size in relation to her husband, her straight back at right angles with her lap at right angles with her parallel shins. Her face, parallel with her husband's face, looked out unsmiling and serene. Annie sat on Ebony's lap. Ebony interlocked her fingers on the child's bare belly; Annie untwined the thumbs and forefingers and got to work on Ebony's middle fingers; the thumbs and forefingers relocked. Annie laughed. On their blanket Sarah leaned against Victor's chest.

Carter was saying, "Beautiful goddamn bitch! Fouled me up at twenty, fouls me up at fifty. God*damn* New York!"

The absence of reference to herself struck Ilka and made her eyes water.

Carter said, "What the hell am I doing here, when I might have stood in California, drunk year-round in the goddamn sun!"

Ilka said, "I want another drink."

"Right you are," said Carter.

The warmth in Ilka's chest turned to lava. Ilka knew the elegant thing was to walk to the cottage and do her crying privately, but what was the fun of that? She leaned against Carter's knees and silently cried. Carter patted her head. All through dinner Ilka let the strange tears flow down her face. Victor looked sympathetically at her and passed her potatoes; he passed her the peas. Ebony speared a handsome hunk of lamb and walked it personally around the table to put on Ilka's plate. Carter sipped his soda. Doris Mae piled food on Percy's plate. Annie kept putting her fork in her mother's plate, and Sarah told her to stop it.

Ilka said, "Excuse me," rose from the table and lay down on the faded sofa in the living room and cried and cried.

When dinner was over, Carter came and sat beside Ilka and stroked her back and said, "If you don't stop I'm going to feed you some of Dr. John's pills."

Ilka laughed, which brought on a new paroxysm. She wanted to say, "You never even mention about being married any more!" but did not wish to remind him of a subject that had made her throw up. She said, "What am I crying *for?*"

"You're having a crying jag," said Carter. After a bit he went away.

Victor came and said, "Sarah and I are sorry you are feeling sad," and he went away and came back with one of Aunt Abigail's afghans and put it over Ilka. Ilka cried and cried and cried.

The phone rang while they sat at dinner Thursday. Sarah went to answer, came back, sat down and with great emotion said, "She thinks they may have a baby for us."

"Now, this is a non-other baby?" asked Carter.

Percival said, "You know the joke about the white lady takes her darky to carry soup down to this poor, sick family. Little pickaninnies running all over. Lady says, 'The Lord works in a mysterious way! How anything so cute can turn into a big ugly black buck like you!' "

Sarah said, "You *will* not take an interest."

Imagine the rush of air that would occur if the world reversed direction. There was no such rush.

Ebony said, "Baby, I got a nice piece of crackling skin for you. Stanley loooves skin."

Doris Mae said, "Pass the potatoes."

Ilka saw Sarah was about to cry. She said, "You have refused, from the first night, to have any sympathy about this adoption."

Stanley said, "I'm going to bed."

"Don't!" Sarah said. "Please . . ."

"I'll take Annie up," said Victor.

"No!" cried Sarah. "Stay, please, everybody. I want to talk this out."

"Everybody stay," Carter said. "The forum is in session. Sarah, what do you want to talk about?"

"Everything!" said Sarah. "The bedrooms . . ."

"Your aunt's house," said Ebony. "You should have had the master bedroom."

"Not," cried Sarah, "because it is my aunt's house, but to each according to his need! There are three of us, with the baby's crib, in the smaller room!"

"I explained," said Ebony. "Stanley has to sleep on a hard mattress. However, mattresses can be moved. You should have had the master bedroom." She nodded.

"It's not the room!" Sarah sobbed, recovered herself, and said, *"You* know I don't care anything about the room."

"Would you hold it there, before we move on," said Carter. "The business of rooms, beds, et cetera, was opened for discussion at our first forum. Ebony brought it up. Why didn't you say your piece then?"

"Because . . . that was my fault. It just seemed such a chintzy thing . . . and I didn't even know I minded. I didn't mind. I *don't* mind. I don't even know what's the matter. It's just I wanted to talk things out before the whole summer goes all wrong. . . . I wanted this summer so much! I want these friendships, your friendship," Sarah said to Ebony, "as much as I ever wanted anything."

Ebony nodded profoundly, as if she were bowing, and that seemed to be the end of the revolution, but Sarah said, "That is why I couldn't bear your not being sympathetic about the adoption."

Ebony nodded as if she were making an obeisance to her right toe and said, "We thought we rallied. We thought we behaved rather well to your Mrs. Daniels."

"Why *my* Mrs. Daniels?" cried Sarah.

"By the by," said Carter, "didn't we vote to announce guests ahead of time?"

"We did!" said Victor. "We asked the first night about having her up."

"And we tried to phone ahead. I thought we told you," said Sarah. "The phone was off the hook."

"My fault," said Ebony.

"You didn't announce your Sunday guests!" said Sarah.

"They weren't sleeping over," said Carter.

"Mrs. Daniels wasn't going to sleep over, except dinner got so late," said Sarah.

"My fault again," said Ebony.

"It was *not* your fault at all!" shouted Sarah. "You were not well. It was my fault for leaving you with all the cooking—except I couldn't help it."

"No problem," said Ebony.

"Don't say that!" shouted Sarah.

"Oh, all righty," said Ebony.

"It is *not* all right! That's what I mean! That's what I want to talk about," said poor Sarah.

Ebony nodded with compressed lips.

"I believe," said Ilka, and everybody looked at her, "Ebony has been so generous doing all the whole cooking."

Ebony made her obeisance and said, "Thank you, thank you."

But Sarah cried, "I don't think it's generous!" and bolted out of her chair and walked to the wall and leaned her forehead against it and wept. They waited. When she turned around she said, "I don't want her to do my work for me! It makes me very uncomfortable not to do my share. I don't want to be cooked for and I *don't* want to be served by Ebony. And I don't know why Ebony and Stanley always sit at the head and foot of the table! Why not Percy and Doris Mae, or Victor and I, if this is a democracy?"

"Forgive me for bringing this up once again," said Carter, "but shouldn't this have come under the headings of policy, grievance or gripe? That was the purpose of our first forum."

"Of which," cried Sarah, with her hands on the table, leaning her face toward him, "you appointed yourself president!"

"President? Oh, please! Chairman. Tyrannous."

"Whichever," said Sarah.

"No no. Not the same thing."

"The point is, I didn't vote for you!"

"That is a point," said Carter.

"And I would have! I would have nominated you and voted for you, but you didn't give me the chance! You play at democracy and deny me my vote!" she cried and, in her passion, approached her face, over which the tears were freely running, close to Carter's face. And this was the first time, since she had known him, that Carter's face did not please Ilka. It was tilted to offer its great, flat surfaces to the young white woman's anger. His mouth was shut in a determinedly neutral line, the eyes were open and unblinking, as if to demonstrate the wish not to miss whatever more she might have to lay against him—the arrogant look of one impenetrable to anything that any Sarah might have it in her power to say.

Sarah sat down and reached for Annie and pulled the little girl onto her lap and held her and pressed her wet cheek against Annie's head. The child was frightened and howled.

Exhausted and forlorn, Sarah said, "Maybe we should just pack up and go home."

"Not tonight, heavens to Betsy! I mean, look at the time," said Ebony. "Why don't you wait till morning?"

"Any other business?" asked Carter.

"About Victor," Ilka said into the general commotion. Everybody was rising. Stanley sneaked off to bed. Sarah, bitterly weeping, carried the screeching Annie up the stairs. Ebony and Doris Mae took dishes into the kitchen.

"About me?" Victor asked Ilka across the table at which they found themselves face to face, alone.

"You make anti-Semitic remarks!" Ilka said in German.

"I? How anti-Semitic? I speak as a Jew to another Jew."

"You are Jewish!" said Ilka.

"But I told you, the first night. Don't you remember, I told you, I'm from Berlin!"

. . .

"What did Sarah do so wrong?" Ilka said in bed to Carter.

"The lamb lay down with the lion to induce the coming of the Peaceable Kingdom. The kingdom didn't come. The lamb got eaten up."

"But why eat up your friends?" cried Ilka.

"Friends the only ones get close enough to get your teeth *into*. I ever tell you the story about the indignation meeting? Niggers in this two-bit Alabama town are holding an indignation meeting out in the back barn. Young buck name of Roy, he sees the old drunken white lawyer, only friend the Negroes got in town, coming in the door, says, 'You, Dave Dougherty, get out of here. Don't you know this is a indignation meeting?' Everybody says, 'Roy, you shut your mouth. Dave, sit down.' So they commence indignating, just beating that boy. Fellow name of Joe says, 'Sheriff put me in the slammer all of Saturday night. Said I was falling down drunk! He is one mean white bastard.' Dave he listens, says, 'Now you hold on there one little old minute.' Says, 'You right, sheriff always was a real stinker and getting worse, but you sure were drunk Saturday night, and you know it and I know it 'cause you and I, we tied one on together.' Roy stands up, says, 'I tell you whitey going stick up for whitey?' and they get ahold of old Dave Dougherty, is already out of his seat and halfways through the door, and they beat him up but good."

"But that's not fair!" cried Ilka.

"Damn unfair!" said Carter and he laughed and he laughed.

* * *

CARTER REFUSED to wake up next morning. Ilka, who wanted to see what was going to happen, made her way across the grass to the big house. Stanley, collapsed down into his deck chair, looked asleep. Under the trees Victor was fitting the folded crib into the trunk of the car. Ilka, who was embarrassed to have mistaken him for a Nazi, slipped into the house.

"D'you have time for a cup of coffee?" Ebony called to Sarah, who was bumping the last suitcase down the stairs.

Sarah came into the kitchen. Her face looked raw.

"I'll take a cup for Percival," said Doris Mae.

"Say good-bye to Percy," Sarah said and wept and embraced Doris Mae.

"Good-bye," said Doris Mae.

"I made you a chocolate pie to take along," Ebony said to Annie.

"Where are we going?" asked Annie.

"You shouldn't have done that! When did you do that?" Sarah asked. She had begun to cry again.

"Made the crust last night. I *knew* I was never going to shut an eye."

"Neither did I," sobbed Sarah.

"My mother always used to say, 'Ebony gets upset she starts baking.' "

"I want to stay here," said Annie.

Sarah said, "Call me, Ebony, when you get back in September. We'll have lunch and we will talk."

"Ab-so-lutely," Ebony said, and nodded and kept nodding. "I don't know what I'm going to be doing this fall—see how Stanley is doing. I just might take off from teaching so I don't get so rattled. I do get rattled, don't I? Coffee, Victor?"

"I thought we'd get an early start," said Victor and picked up Sarah's suitcase.

"Come." Sarah took Annie's hand.

"I want to stay with Aunt Ebony," said Annie. Ebony took Annie's other hand. They followed Victor out onto the shining morning slope.

"Why can't we stay here?" asked Annie.

Sarah wept and said, "I don't remember."

"I know what you mean!" said Ebony. "Day my first husband moved out we could neither of us remember why."

"Don't wake Stanley. Just tell him good-bye for us," said Sarah.

"Surely will," said Ebony.

Stanley lay so very still Ilka stared and her blood curdled: Stanley's right arm was unnaturally angled.

"Tell Carter we're sorry we missed him," said weeping Sarah. She embraced Ilka.

"I want to stay with Aunt Ebony," screamed Annie.

"Annie, get in," said Victor. He shut the trunk.

Stanley raised a skeletal right hand at a pesky fly: Stanley was not dead yet.

Victor came around, embraced Ebony. He shook his head at Ilka. Ilka blushed and Victor hugged her, and it seemed to Ilka she had always known that he was Jewish. One could tell from the very temperature of his embrace.

Sarah got in the car. Victor got in. "Annie, you will please sit down."

But Annie howled and had, at last, something to howl about, for the friend for whom she stretched her arms through the car window was walking back toward the house, entered it and shut the door.

★   ★   ★

EBONY CAME hallooing across the grass. "Ilka, telephone for you!"

Fishgoppel said there was no need for Ilka to come rushing home. Aunt Flora seemed to be quite all right again.

"What is it?" Ilka's gut somersaulted and short-circuited the common light.

"She isn't in pain now. She seems fine. She says she doesn't want to see a doctor."

The two hours on the train so harrowed Ilka that she was surprised to find her mother looking exactly like her mother.

"I must have lain badly." Her mother pointed to the place on her back. "I'm fine now."

"Of course, you're going to be fine. We're both of us coming to the doctor with you."

Ilka's mother lay on the doctor's table and said, "Why don't you sit in the waiting room with Fishgoppel?"

"Don't be silly. I'm staying with you."

"Don't look at me," said Ilka's mother.

"Why shouldn't I look at you!"

"Don't shout." Ilka's mother folded her arms over her thin breasts. Her legs were very thin.

"What is wrong with being naked!" shouted Ilka.

"Go and wait with Fishgoppel."

"You're afraid to be naked!" shouted Ilka. "You're afraid to go out! You won't learn English. . . ."

"Ilka, not now."

"You're not an old woman! You were born the same year as Carter, did you know that?"

"The father has come back," said Ilka's mother.

"Terrific," said Ilka, breathing hard, and grateful to have her tirade halted.

"It is horrible," her mother said.

"What is horrible now?"

"The father is not going to stop them," said Ilka's mother. He has known all along what they were doing. He *is* the police, Ilka. The black is their uniform. They are, all three of them, policemen! That is the horror."

"Why is that the horror?"

"Because they are *supposed* to do it. It is the law."

"What is the law?"

"That they must cut me," said her mother. "Here comes the doctor."

Afterward the doctor talked to the three women in his office. He said, "Why don't we keep her here and do a couple of tests?"

"Now?" said Ilka.

"What does he say?" asked Ilka's mother.

"Why not now? We have her here, we happen to have a bed. . . ."

"Is there something wrong?" Fishgoppel asked.

"That's what we're going to find out, isn't it?"

"I don't understand what he says," Ilka's mother kept saying in German. "What are they going to do to me? *Now* are they going to do it? I don't understand what is happening."

PART TWO

CARTER WAS back in town. Ilka went down to see him. The yellow bellboy was operating the elevator. "What happened to the tiny old woman?" asked Ilka.

"What tiny old woman?" Carter sat on the edge of the bed watching his television: a very tall, beautiful young man was talking to a lot of fat, close-mouthed old men. You could tell they were greedy and mean-spirited old men. The young man was so honest his mouth hung open.

"Gary Cooper. Sit down here and watch," said Carter.

Ilka watched a pretty girl with a wide, lipsticked mouth rooting for Gary Cooper.

Ilka said, "I have to go to the hospital to see my mother."

"How is your mother?" asked Carter.

"You look quite beautiful," Ilka said to her mother.

"I know," said her mother. "Dr. Shey used to say I was a bed beauty. When I get well I want to go to Obernpest."

"What for? Mutti!"

"I wish you would come with me," said Ilka's mother. "I told you we spent a summer on Lake Bautzen in 'thirty-five—maybe it was 'thirty-six—Vati would remember—you were just a baby—maybe not half an hour from Obernpest."

Ilka said, "Mutti, and when you get to Obernpest, what are you going to *do* there?"

"Find the spot on the road where I left your father. There was a mountain in the back, to the left, with a very characteristic shape." Ilka's mother drew a rather steep line in the air.

"It dipped like this, and flattened. There's no mistaking it."

"Why don't you just hurry up and get well," said Ilka.

Next time Ilka went to see Carter they sat on the edge of the bed and watched the girl with the lipsticked mouth, in a uniform, walking on the deck of a ship. The tall man, dressed up as a girl, walked behind her.

"Gary Cooper!" said Ilka, but it was not.

"Cary Grant," said Carter.

Cary Grant was walking on high heels with his knees bent outward and kept stumbling. Carter laughed. "How is your mother?" he asked Ilka.

"She wants to go back to Obernpest!" said Ilka.

Next time the tall man was wearing an old-fashioned uniform, kissing the lipsticked mouth of the pretty girl in a long gown, and he was Farley Granger.

Next time he was *Stewart* Granger.

Ilka said, "We're bringing my mother home tomorrow."

"That's good news," said Carter.

They brought Ilka's mother home. She was very weak.

When Ilka was able to go down to see Carter the bed was open, the curtains drawn, and he had his green pajamas on. The contents of his pockets lay on the dresser top. On the bedside chair stood a full glass of bourbon. Carter said, "I can't sleep."

Ilka said, "You're not going to start drinking again!"

"I'm going to have a bourbon," said Carter. He lit a cigarette.

"But if you start drinking again," said Ilka, "you will get sick again!"

"Probably, but not a certainty," said Carter.

Ilka leaned toward him and said, "If you know what is going to happen again, why do you start again?"

Carter said, "It's a mystery."

"You haven't started yet!"

"I haven't started," said Carter.

"Don't, oh!" cried Ilka, "don't start! Carter, call Dr. Wharton."

"No!" said Carter.

"Yes! Carter! Call him! I'll call him for you!"

Carter said, "No!"

"Carter! I'm going to call him!"

Carter set his chin into the cup of his hand and watched Ilka.

Ilka called Dr. Wharton and said, "This is Ilka. We are frightened that Carter is starting drinking again. Are there some pills you can give him?"

"No," said Dr. Wharton.

"There is nothing to prescribe him?"

"There are many things," said Dr. Wharton.

"Can you prescribe him something?"

"No," said Dr. Wharton.

"Is there another doctor who can prescribe something?"

"There are many doctors," said Dr. Wharton.

"Will you give me the name of another doctor?"

"You can find a listing of doctors in the telephone directory."

Ilka listened, but Dr. Wharton had stopped talking. "So," Ilka said, "good-bye."

"Good-bye," said Dr. Wharton.

Carter brought the cigarette to his mouth and said, "Harris has given up on me."

Ilka said, "I can't and can't believe if one *knows* ahead what is going to happen, one couldn't find *some* way to stop it!"

Carter said, "Can't you?"

"Let me call your brother, Carter!"

"Call my brother," said Carter. He set his chin in his hands. Ilka called California but Carter's brother was not at home. His sister-in-law was at home but did not know where his brother was nor did she know when he was coming back.

Carter said, "Ellen can't stand me." He said, "There's a play by Giraudoux called *Tiger at the Gates.* When the play opens the Trojans are returning home from a terrible battle with the Greeks. All through the play the Trojans and the Greeks are trying to prevent the Trojan war. When the play ends the Trojan war has already started. What are you looking for?"

"There must be some agency," said Ilka, riffling through the telephone directory: "Alcohol Advisory, Alcoholism Advisory Center, Alcoholism Advisory Services, Alcoholics Anonymous Central Office for Groups of Greater New York. Carter, Alcoholics Central Agencies . . ."

"I used to run agencies," said Carter. "I ran an agency in San Francisco. . . ."

Ilka said, "I'm going to call Ebony!"

"Call Ebony," said Carter.

Ilka called Ebony and said, "Carter is about to start drinking again!"

"Is he?" said Ebony.

"What can I do!" cried Ilka.

"You can make him a cup of coffee," said Ebony, "if he wants coffee. If he wants to go out you can hold his coat for him to put his arms into."

"Can you come over!"

"Does Carter want me to come over?"

"Do you want Ebony to come over!" Ilka asked Carter.

Carter raised his head out of his hand and said, "I'm always happy to see Ebony."

"He wants you to come over!"

Ilka said, "Promise not to start till Ebony gets here!"

"O.K.," said Carter.

"I brought you some soup I was making for Stanley," said Ebony. "You want me to warm this up for you?"

"Please," said Carter.

"I *wish* I could cook!" said Ilka.

"And I brought you some nylons I've been saving for you."

"Thank you. Would you throw them in that top drawer, please?"

Ebony stopped and looked at the pink rubber hand on the top of Carter's dresser.

Carter said, "Saw that in a store window on Fourteenth Street when I first hit town. Their glove display. They didn't want to sell it—didn't know what to charge. I told them, I said, 'Name your price.' "

"It's ugly," said Ilka.

"Sure is ugly!" said Ebony.

"Ugliest damn thing I ever saw!" said Carter. "Old pink fingers reaching to grab your balls and squeeze. Soup is delicious! Are you teaching this fall, Ebony?"

"Teaching fifth-grade American history," said Ebony.

Ilka said, "I wish I knew American history!"

"The only American history is fifth grade," said Ebony. "What are the three problems—not two problems, not four or six problems—what are the *three* problems that faced the white settlers on the Great Plains?"

"Were there three problems that faced the white settlers?" asked Carter.

"There were three problems. The three problems," said Ebony, "that faced the white settlers on the Great Plains were, one, how to keep the cattle from getting out, two, how to keep the Indians from getting in, three, how to get the Indians. What two new discoveries—not old discoveries, what two *new* discoveries—helped the white settlers on the Great Plains solve their three problems?"

"What were the two new discoveries?" asked Carter.

"Barbed wire and six-shooters. Better get back and give Stanley his dinner," said Ebony.

Carter rose to see her to the door and said, "Give Stanley my best."

"Thank you," said Ebony.

"Carry on," said Carter.

When Carter had shut the door behind Ebony, Ilka said, smiling, "Do I grab your balls and squeeze?"

"Never," said Carter.

Ilka's smile impaled Carter. Carter said, "So when did you ever know anybody to give up a prejudice because of experience to the contrary?"

Ilka laughed. She said, "You are going to drink, aren't you?"

"Oh, yes," said Carter. "Didn't you know that?"

"Oh, yes," said Ilka.

"Are you going home?" asked Carter.

"I've got to get back to my mother," said Ilka.

Carter said, "When you take another lover promise not to tell me!"

★   ★   ★

NEXT TIME Ilka asked Carter, "Now which one is this?"

"Jimmy Stewart," said Carter.

Chaos was threatening, once again, to overwhelm Carter's room. Ilka tried to tidy it, but Carter said, "I wish you would sit down."

Ilka took her shoes off and climbed onto the bed. She leaned her back against the wall and put her stocking feet on Carter's back.

"Watch the movie," said Carter.

Jimmy Stewart's mouth was hanging open in the excess of the honesty with which he was talking to some more of these close-mouthed, fat old men; there was another pretty girl with a wide lipsticked mouth. Ilka said, "American movies are stupid."

"I like them," said Carter. "I like American movies."

Ilka rubbed her feet on Carter's back, and after a moment Carter said, "Don't. One doesn't play with a sick man."

"If I bother you," said Ilka, "why don't I go home?"

"Stay with me," said Carter.

Ilka said, "You can always tell which pretty girl is the good girl: her eyes are open. The bad girl's eyes are half closed and she looks sideways."

"Don't," said Carter.

"At the end of the film, the bad girl puts on a blouse with a bow at the throat, opens her eyes, and turns out to have been really a good girl all the time!"

Carter said, "Ilka, don't. I'm trying to keep my mind on this movie. I'm trying not to throw up."

Ilka sat awhile, then she climbed off Carter's bed and got her coat.

Carter said, "Stay."

Ilka said, "This is not a good visit."

Carter said, "Will you come back?"

"Oh, *yes!*" said Ilka.

★   ★   ★

CARTER'S DOOR was open. Carter, in his green-striped pajamas, sat on the edge of his bed and said, "You remember Mrs. Daniels, of course."

The narrow little agency lady wore a mauve blouse with a bow at the throat. She sat in Carter's club chair on top of several of Carter's dirty socks. She gave Ilka her pink hand to shake and smiled and made an apologetic *moue.*

Carter said, "Mrs. Daniels found her London pictures."

Mrs. Daniels said, "I promised to show Mr. Carter my pictures. This one was taken the other side of Primrose Hill, which, as you know, is just this side of Regent's Park. This is the Embankment. In my big album I have a better one taken from the South Bank, showing the Houses of Parliament in the background, which I'm rather proud of." She rolled her eyes.

Carter said, "Mrs. Daniels has written to her mother for her big album."

"I wrote in July, so it should come any day. Well." She smiled. She rose. She rolled her eyes. "I must be getting along. If you would like to keep these to look at, you can ring me when you're finished. You have my office number?"

"I have," said Carter.

"I'll write it down here just in case. This is my extension; I'll put it down though the girl will put you through, except I do a lot of my work in the field. You can always reach me at home, after six—I'll write my home telephone here—any day except the first Friday every month, because I have a subscription to the opera."

Carter took the card out of her hand. He said, "Thank you."

Mrs. Daniels said, "Saturday, Sunday, you can always get me at home. Don't get up!"

"Maybe Ilka will see you to the door."

In the doorway Mrs. Daniels stood and said, "I'll ring you when the big album comes."

"The big album," said Carter.

"From my mother." Still Mrs. Daniels stood. "And you get better."

"Carry on," said Carter.

Ilka closed the door behind her and laughed.

Carter said, "She was married for three months. Her husband fell in the first week of the First World War." Carter put his forefinger and thumb over his eyes. In a moment he said, "How is your mother?"

"Today was her first time out since she came from the hospital. I took her to Broadway," said Ilka. "She makes little, little steps."

★   ★   ★

C ARTER CALLED Ilka in the evening and said, "Could you come and see me?"

Carter's door was opened by a tall old man. His more than ordinarily white teeth glared at Ilka. "What do *you* want?"

"I'm a friend," said Ilka.

"She is my friend," said Carter from the edge of the bed. "Ilka Weissnix, from Vienna." He extended his slow arm from Ilka to the tall old man: "Dr. MacSamuels. From the sixteenth floor." He bent his elbow and replaced it on his thigh; it slipped off. He raised, centered and replaced it with careful delibera- tion and lowered his head into the cup of his hand.

"Ghrwettts!" said the doctor. "The hotel is not going to put up with your friend very much longer. Let me send you to the hospital, eh?" he said to Carter.

"No hospital!" Carter's head came up with surprising vigor. "No hospital. I've *been* to the hospital."

"I don't know how a man like you, with so much going for you, can get yourself in such a pickle! *Be* a man! Pull yourself together."

"Holler!" Carter said. "Lecture me, and prescribe me some medicine. That will pull me together."

"Grnkt," said the doctor. He sat down in Carter's club chair after scooping its contents onto the floor. He uncapped his pen and said, "Gts!" when the instrument spluttered and raked the surface of the paper. "One every four hours, as needed. Two in a crisis. Next time don't call me because I don't know what to do with you, you hear me?"

"Loud and clear," Carter said very, very slowly.

"Here," the doctor said to Ilka. "Go get this made up for your friend here. Then *you* go *home!*"

"She hears you loud and clear, too," said Carter, and when Ilka had left with Carter's prescription, Carter raised his head to say, "You will forgive me if I don't see you to the door."

"I'm not *going!*" shouted the doctor. "I'm going to stay here till your 'friend' gets back, though I don't know *why* I bother with you!"

"Because you are a good man. You are a good, sweet man," said Carter and put his hand over his eyes.

"Grwhthths!" said the doctor.

Ilka sat on the bed next to Carter and they watched a ballet of mayhem on the television screen: a man on a stepladder whacked his thumb with a hammer, dropped the hammer on his foot and fell off the ladder.

Ilka said, "That's horrible. Why are we watching this?"

The stepladder collapsed on the man's head. Carter laughed.

"American movies are sadistic," said Ilka.

"Why are you always knocking American movies?" said Carter.

"You don't think this is stupid?"

"It's not stupid," said Carter. "The Three Stooges disseminate a deep truth: Calamity is the mother of calamity. Where's my medicine?"

Ilka said, "The doctor said *one* every four hours!"

"Two in a crisis," said Carter, throwing three pills into his mouth. "Would you get me a glass of water?" He drank, lay down, flung himself into a sitting position and said, "One more. As needed," and reached for the vial, which was not there. "Where is my medicine?"

"I have hidden it," said Ilka.

"One more will put me to sleep," said Carter.

"In four hours," said Ilka.

"Don't play games," said Carter. "Medicine acts in ratio to body weight. Any doctor will tell you that, and I'm big. I'm a big man. Give me my medicine."

"It's a quarter to eight. At quarter to twelve you can have another pill. Two in a crisis."

"This is the crisis," said Carter. "Where is my medicine?" He reached for Ilka; Ilka backed off.

Ilka stood in the middle of the carpet. Carter got to his feet. He stood, sad and huge, and said, "Give me my medicine."

Ilka said, "At quarter to twelve." She had a sensation of, spiritually, broadening her stance. She checked her heart and felt no alteration in the rate or volume of its beat at the approach of the enormous man. Ilka watched the beat of his pulse at the base of his throat inches from her eyes. He said, "Give me my medicine."

Carter's two huge hands easily encircled Ilka's two arms above the elbows, in order to exert pressure, or in order, perhaps, to preserve her from the pressure he might have exerted. They stood a measurable moment. Then Ilka leaned her cheek against the green pajamas and said, "I can't stay and watch you do this."

"I understand that," said Carter.

"I'll stay, or I'll give you the pills and go home. Which do you want?"

"At this moment," said Carter, "I want my medicine."

Ilka put her hand into the pocket of her skirt and brought out the vial of pills. "Do you want some water?"

"*I* will get it," said Carter, "since it is against your thinking."

Ilka laughed.

When Carter returned from the kitchen, Ilka was putting her coat on.

"Are you angry with me?"

Ilka said, "I think, helpless."

"Ah, yes! Me too," said Carter. He lifted his head and said, "Harris Wharton has given up on me. My brother, Jonas, has given up on me."

Ilka said, "Philip thinks you are terrific."

Carter said, "Philip will give up on me. One day you will give up on me."

"I don't think," said Ilka.

"You will be the last, but you will give up on me," said Carter.

★   ★   ★

THE NEXT TIME Ilka went down, Carter's door was locked and sealed with a police seal. Ilka went to see him at the over-crowded facility. He said, "I want out."

"What does Dr. MacSamuels say?" asked Ilka.

"Dr. MacSamuels," said Carter in a voice Ilka had not heard before, "is a racist pig."

"I mean Dr. MacSamuels, from the hotel."

"Dr. MacSamuels cannot conceive that a Negro may know his constitutional rights. You can't put a man away without his consent and against his expressed wish. When I get out I'm going to get Dr. MacSamuels. Dr. MacSamuels doesn't know I know the governor. Go to the hotel and get me my address book out of my room."

Ilka went to the Bloomsbury Arms and asked Mr. Boyd to let her go up for some things Mr. Bayoux wanted from his room.

"No way," said Mr. Boyd.

"He sent me to get him his address book."

"Sent you, did he? And whom does he think is going to have the time to go up there and stand around while you go poking in his things that the hotel is responsible for his things so he'll come back and sue the heck out of the hotel, no sir, not while I'm responsible to the hotel and the hotel is responsible to Mr. Bayoux even if Mr. Bayoux doesn't even care *who* goes poking up there *the hotel* is going to care and so you can tell him from me." Ilka had been watching the left side of Mr. Boyd's mouth work the round hole out of which his words popped like so many hard, round little turds. It came to Ilka that she was prejudiced against Mr. Boyd. She did not believe him capable of anything good or clever; she did not believe he was made out of the same intellectual material, did not believe he was human in the sense that she was human: she wished him ill. This frightened the girl, for if she hated Mr. Boyd, she imagined how Mr. Boyd—how a world full of Boyds, must hate her. The little desk clerk picked up the phone, dialed, and leaning his elbow on the desk, thrust his shoulder in the direction of Ilka's eye.

Ilka went home and called Ebony. "Carter is back in the hospital."

"Is he?" said Ebony.

"How is Stanley?"

"In the hospital," said Ebony.

"I am sorry," said Ilka.

"You bet." Ebony said, "You and I will keep in touch," and Ilka was gratified.

Ilka called Philip. Philip and Fanny were leaving for Boston.

Carter said, "Philip has given up on me. What's that young fellow's name—with the nose—from the wedding—you said he works for the ACLU. . . ."

Ilka called Carl. He went to the hospital with Ilka.

Carter said, "Take a pencil. Call the governor's mansion. I wish I had my damn address book! Ask for Dave Clybourne. Dave and I were on the same blue-ribbon jury. And you might try Bob Burnside at the Pentagon. If he's out of the country, talk to Nelly—on Burnside's staff, what *was* her name . . . I used to sleep with her . . . O'Keeney. Ask for Nelly O'Keeney. She'll get you Burnside's whereabouts. Here are some names you can look up at the UN. . . ."

Carl called Ilka and said, "I got the Clybourne fellow on the phone and damned if the governor hasn't got Carter out!"

"Carter is out?"

"He's back in his hotel."

Ilka called, but Carter's line was busy.

Ilka called Ebony and Ebony said, "Well I'll be! Carter! He is something *else!* You think he's down and out, he pulls a rabbit out of his hat."

"He knows the governor!" said Ilka.

"Pulled the governor right out of his hat!" said Ebony. "God *damn!*"

Carter's line was still busy, so Ilka got on the subway and went down. Ilka waited by the elevator and listened to the switchboard saying, "He is not *in* his office. He is not in the hotel. His office does not know where he is or when he will be back in his office. All you'll be doing is tying up your own line."

Carter opened the door to Ilka. He was wearing his black trenchcoat unbuttoned and said, "Come in. I'm on the phone," and sat back down on his bed and said into the receiver, "Tell him that I will keep calling as often as it takes to get him to come to the phone, so he might as well come to the phone. Yes. I will hold on."

Ilka took her coat off and went and sat on the bed and put her arms around Carter and kissed the cold, taut flesh of his cheek. It had the feel of a paralyzed limb.

Carter was saying, "I will outwait him. Tell him if he takes his phone off the hook I will come up in person, to the sixteenth floor, and stand in his office and make a stink that will be highly undesirable. Tell him I will wait until he is finished with the patient he is with." Ilka could count the fingers Carter counted inside his pocket. "Dr. MacSamuels. I am obliged to you for coming to the phone. What I have to tell you is brief indeed: I have lodged a complaint with . . . No, sir, I do not want to hear what you have to say. You will say whatever it is you have to say to the governor, with whom I have lodged a complaint. I am about to initiate an inquiry, with the

ACLU, into the legality of committing a man without his consent. You will be hearing from their attorneys in due course. That is all, sir, that *I* have any intention of saying to you at this or any other time."

He hung up, stood up and took his coat off.

"When did you get back? Have you eaten?" asked Ilka.

"I don't think so," said Carter.

"Do you want to go out?"

"In a moment." Carter sat down on the bed, picked the phone up and said, "Get me the Civil Liberties Union." He gave the number and said, "I will wait."

Ilka was frightened and said, "You don't believe Dr. Mac-Samuels meant you any harm."

"Then I will try again," Carter said into the phone, replaced the receiver, picked it up and said, "The governor's mansion," and gave the number and said, "Haven't you figured yet that I'm going to keep calling until you get me whatever number I ask you to get me, and I've asked you to get me the governor's mansion," and he gave the number again and said, "How often? As often as I bloody ask you to get it for me!" He hung up, picked up and said, "Get me the bloody governor's mansion," and he gave the number.

Ilka stood up and put her coat back on and said, "I'll call you tomorrow, or call me when you're done."

Carter had hung up the receiver, picked it up again, gave the number and said, "You bloody *know* I will wait." He did not notice when Ilka went out the door and closed it behind her.

★   ★   ★

C ARTER CALLED Ilka. He asked her if she had come across the concept "flight into health." "I can't go back to that bloody hospital. I'll go to Alcoholics Anonymous. Will you come with me?"

Ilka thought it was going to be terrifically interesting. The meeting was held in the basement of a church on the West Side. The light looked dirty. Folding chairs stood stacked against the wall. Around a long steel trestle table sat some twenty more or less regular-looking persons. Ilka liked the pale man in shirt sleeves at the head. He looked gentle. He said, "My name is Mike. I'm an alcoholic."

Everybody said, "Hello, Mike."

Mike said, "I see a few new faces. We are glad you've come. Why don't we go around the table and introduce ourselves, tell something about ourselves—everybody. . . ."

"Oh, Christ," said Carter.

"Bert, you want to start the ball rolling?"

An unsmiling man on Mike's left said, "My name is Bert. I'm an alcoholic."

"Hello, Bert," the people around the table said.

Bert said nothing more and Mike at the head of the table said, "We're glad you've come. D'you want to pass the cookies down this way? There's coffee over there. Dave," Mike said to the man who sat at Bert's left, and Dave said,

"My name is Dave. I'm an alcoholic."

Everybody said, "Hello, Dave."

Dave said that when he was quite a young fellow, in Vermont, he took the bus down to Bennington about a job as janitor there, at the college. Bus took five hours. Dave said when he got off the bus he was so scared he got back on the bus and went the five hours home and went in a bar and knocked himself out. "That was thirty-odd years back," said Dave. "I been scared ever since."

"Well, you're not so scared you don't come to AA, and we're glad you're here and we're proud of you," said Mike. "Herb?"

"It's the Liquor Store Christian!" whispered Carter.

"Who?"

Carter was looking suddenly cheerful. He was looking hilarious.

"My name is Herb. I'm an alcoholic," said the Liquor Store Christian.

"Hello, Herb," said everybody.

Herb said his father's father and mother had been alcoholics. His father and two brothers were alcoholics. He couldn't remember a time when he wasn't an alcoholic. Then his father got a cancer. Doctors gave him six months and Herb made a pact with God: if God would let his father live, Herb would let the liquor be. Next day he joined Alcoholics Anonymous and never touched a drop since, and his father was alive and this was twelve years ago come September.

A round of applause. Mike at the head of the table said, "We're real proud of you. May?" he said and the woman on Herb's left said,

"My name is May. I'm an alcoholic."

"Hello, May."

"I'm proud I learned to say I'm an alcoholic though actually I'm not an alcoholic really, except AA says I've got to learn to say I'm an alcoholic, so I'm proud I learned."

"We're proud of you. We're glad you came," Mike said.

"I'm not an alcoholic," said a young boy who sat out of the light, a little back from the table.

Mike said, "What's your name?"

"Bill," said the boy.

"Hello, Bill," everybody said.

"We're glad you came," said Mike.

"Parole officer said I got to come."

"Anything you want to tell us?"

"No," the boy said.

"O.K., Bill, you want to pass the cookies? Steve?"

"My name is Steve."

"Hello, Steve."

"I'm an alcoholic," said Steve.

"We're glad you're here," Mike said.

Steve said the time he knew he was an alcoholic he was really hitting that bottle. He wanted to quit so bad he thought he'd get away from everything, so he took this job as watchman on the mothball fleet they use for storing grain in those old rusty World War I ships they got tied up in the Hudson upriver. Living right on the boat, by himself, seemed like a good way to keep out of trouble. Launch took him over. They showed him how to dip this long old pole to check for damp. All he ever had to do was keep checking the grain from one boat to the next. First day he made himself up a berth in the old captain's quarters—why not? He was poking around, and what do you know! There's three cases of booze, never been opened. "With my luck I thought this'll be wood alcohol, so I took this real little sip, I didn't wake up dead or blind. Thirty-six bottles of Laphroig! Listen, you don't quarrel with fate when you just hit the jackpot!"

A motion on her right made Ilka look around. Carter was ecstatic.

"Next day I went back on shore, laid in supplies. Stayed under till the next inspector came around—must have been three weeks. . . ."

"Well, we're glad you're here," Mike said.

It was Ilka's turn and she said, "My name is Ilka. I'm just a visitor."

"Hello, Ilka," everybody said.

"We're glad you came," Mike said.

Carter said, "Carter Bayoux."

"Hello, Carter," everybody said.

"Anything you like to tell us? How did *you* first know you were an alcoholic?"

"First time? Oh," said Carter, "probably the time in London at a diplomatic dinner, they were serving champagne. I called the waiter over, slipped him a couple pounds, said, 'I want you to make it your business to keep my glass filled to the brim.'

Said, 'You keep your eye on my glass. When you see the champagne getting down near halfway, you keep filling it up!' Said, 'Yes, sir.' Don't think I remember how I got back to my place."

"Well, we're glad you came. Let us pray."

"Damn skim-milk religion," commented Carter when they were walking along.

"You didn't like it!" cried poor Ilka, seeing the prospect of a miracle bite the dust.

"I liked the part where that poor son of a gun puts himself away on the goddamn mothball fleet and finds three cases of Laphroig!" shouted Carter.

"I thought they were nice. They are gentle people, Carter, didn't you think?"

"Bunch of bores is what they are. If I'm going to be prayed at I'll go to a goddamn *church*. Come with me?"

★　　　　★　　　　★

SUNDAY AFTERNOON they went to St. Egbert's. "Episcopal," said Carter. "Ah, the British! The agency lady is going to take us."

They met Mrs. Daniels inside the gate of a tiny, elegant graveyard between two skyscrapers. She rolled her eyes and made her *moue* and said, "We're invited to the vicarage for tea. I've told him all about you."

"Have you?" said Carter.

Fewer than a dozen people sat in the polished wooden pews. They stood up and sang "And did those feet in ancient times." They sat down. They stood up and sang "For those in trouble on the sea." Ilka and Carter remained sitting when the others knelt to pray the "Our Father." Everybody sat. The vicar, a noble-looking man with good pink skin and a ridge of a nose, read a scholarly sermon on the Hebrew sources of the concept of "conscience" unknown to the Hellenes. That was interesting! Ilka glanced sideways at Mrs. Daniels's dainty profile, the purity of her aging skin, and she liked Mrs. Daniels. Ilka glanced to her right, at the weight and hopelessness of Carter's huge countenance, and she loved him.

It seemed that the entire congregation was invited to move across the windy little graveyard, through the gate between privet hedges, up the path into the stone vicarage. In the formal, pleasantly worn sitting room, a table had been laid with a white cloth. Mrs. Daniels introduced Carter and Ilka to the vicar's wife, who must have hurried ahead to put on the kettle. She had a pretty face; her smile stuck to the top of her teeth. While she asked them if they took milk and sugar her eyes kept moving. "Laura, Mr. Wentworth's cane. A chair," she said to one of the two decorous little girls, in dresses and white socks, who carried platters of thin-sliced plain cake.

And now, with a commotion of cold, fresh male air, entered the vicar. In his loose, threadbare black jacket, without his surplice, one saw he was missing an arm. Ilka supposed it might be the vicar's beautiful silver hair, his clever eyes and kind manner that had, long ago, faded his pretty wife.

Carter was counting his fingers. He said, "Let's get out of here."

The vicar's wife shook their hands and invited them to come again next Sunday. She sent one of the little girls to show them their coats. The vicar walked them to the door and kept Carter chatting. Ilka saw Mrs. Daniels looking after them and waved to her.

The wind had risen into a little gale. Carter pulled on his French beret. They walked around the corner with heads lowered against the assault of the uncivil cold. Carter looked behind him. "Where the hell are we?"

"East Side," said Ilka. "D'you want to go home? It's cold, Carter."

Carter said, "I know a trick: you walk and you walk and you watch out for the next wave of sleepiness and grab a cab and ride it right to bed." A cab passed. "But you have to be sleepy enough, or you wake right up again and sit a thousand years in that old hotel room."

They walked. At the corner Carter looked up. The little rain spat in his eye. He looked around. "Where are the damn street signs?" The light changed; they crossed. Carter said, "Is this up or downtown we're walking?"

"We're walking east," said Ilka.

"I don't know what they do with their street signs on the East Side! You either know where you are or the heck with you." They crossed the street. Carter said, "Did you know, during the war the British took down all road signs. Confuse the invader. What street is this?"

Ilka said, "Avenue C. There's the bridge. Let's go in somewhere, Carter. It's cold."

There were no people about except for a young woman at the foot of the ramp. She wore a belted coat and was trying to draw her wind-whitened face into the upturned collar. She handed them a cheaply printed pamphlet. She said, "Christ will be. Christ is. Christ has been."

"You're from Australia, by the sound of you," said Carter.

"Yes, we are," said the young woman.

Ilka said, "Do you know, is there a place around here where we can have something warm?"

The young woman said, "There's a little Arab restaurant a block that way. They have hot soup."

"Hot soup!" said Ilka.

"I believe I'll go in with you for ten minutes—just warm up a bit."

It was a family restaurant, dark, warm, poky. A baby walked

around with the nipple of his milk bottle depending from his teeth. Everywhere hung cloths of many colors and pattern upon pattern, each so different from every other they had no business all being beautiful together.

Ilka ordered hot soup from a low-breasted, dark woman in a black cardigan.

"Tea, please," said the young woman and undid her coat but did not take it off. She was recovering from her crisis of cold and misery and shook out her hair and could be perceived to be a personable, ladylike girl. Carter asked her how long she had been standing there.

"Nine o'clock. Weekdays we start at seven to catch the people leaving the city. My sister is on the Queens side to catch the incoming crowd."

"Do people stop their cars, then?"

"Well, no. Really they don't."

"Maybe you haven't hit a good bridge?"

The girl said, "Well, we don't know the city very well yet."

"How long have you been here?"

"Today is Sunday . . . we came ten days ago. My brother-in-law thinks New York is the place for my sister and me to start the East Coast. He is starting in Hollywood."

"A pincer movement," Carter said. "How many of you are there?"

"My brother-in-law, my sister and I. We're quite a young denomination."

"What do you call yourselves?"

"The Christ Has Beens. Sundays," the girl said, "on a bitter day like this, there's really little we can do."

"You can work on us, in here, in the warmth." Carter was looking cheerful. "What are the tenets of your denomination?"

The girl took a sip of tea and said, "We believe Christ has already come and gone the second time."

"That's the saddest thing I ever heard," said Carter. "Can I buy you a sandwich?"

"Oh, no, thank you. My brother-in-law says it's not so sad if you look at it the right way. I think he means it's bracing, once you get used to the idea there's no use hoping for anything. I should go back out there. We only have a month in America. Then we'll do Europe. I wish I could exactly explain it as well as my brother-in-law says it in this pamphlet. My brother-in-law says hope is the enemy. People think hope is the only good thing that came after all the terrible things that came out of Pandora's box, but my brother-in-law thinks hope *is* the bad thing that came out. He says hope is the root of all evil—like the hope for power, the hope for money, for happiness. . . ."

"For sleep," said Carter.

"For love," said the young woman, "though I don't really understand why that is a bad thing. You can read the pamphlet. Hope is the devil's instrument. My brother-in-law says it wasn't the knowledge of good and evil, it was hope the serpent gave Eve to eat in the middle of the garden. He says every hope is really a stand-in for the hope for the Messiah to make everything be all right, but He has already been. And gone. So. And it's a good thing. I always understand it perfectly while he's explaining it, but when *I* explain it I get really more muddled."

"Do they need you over in Europe? Does your brother-in-law think they're having too much hope over there?"

"The big cities, I suppose. In a way. We're going to start in London. Paris. I better get back out." She reached for her handbag.

"Will you allow me the pleasure of treating you to tea? What about Asia? And does your brother think they're having much hope in Africa?"

"We may leave Asia and Africa to our next generation. Thank you very much for the tea. Good-bye."

Carter and Ilka sat and Carter said, "I goofed. Now I'm wide awake again. I should have grabbed the cab back there! I see what happened: It wasn't that I wasn't sleepy *enough!* It was the wave already passing over! Now I'm not sleepy any more. I've got to keep walking. Oh, Christ," said Carter.

"I should go home to my mother," said Ilka.

"When I snap out of this I'm going to come and see your mother," said Carter.

"The stronger she gets the less she wants to go out. She won't even go to the corner of Broadway."

Soon Ilka's mother was strong enough to refuse to walk out of the front door. Then she would not leave her room. Presently she would not get up or get dressed. She sat on the edge of her bed and said, "The burglars are back."

In the night Ilka's mother screamed. Ilka ran in. Her mother was sitting up, shaking violently. Ilka spoke to her: "What, Mutti? Mutti? What is it? Mutti!" Her mother's eyes were open but she was caught inside her nightmare. Ilka went to embrace her; but she screamed again and shrank from Ilka in horror. "Mutti. Tell me! What is it?" Ilka's mother sat on the bed. Ilka could sit beside her and put a blanket about her shoulders, but could not enter the horror inside which her mother was alone, shivering uncontrollably.

Carter said, "I've got the name of a drug therapist. Something new. I'm going, and I'm taking your mother. This man is very big on the West Coast. He commutes to Hollywood. He'll be in New York on the fifteenth and sixteenth."

When Carter brought Ilka's mother home, she was laughing.

Carter said, "It turns out all our problems are chemical, after all! Unless the chemicals are moral, after all."

Ilka's mother stood in the middle of the carpet shivering; her eyes were abysmal. She kept laughing.

★   ★   ★

MRS. APFEL came into the room at the Council saying,
"This is one for the books. There's a *Schwartzer* wants to go
to Israel! Harvey from Youth Aliyah is down in reception trying
to get him to go home."

"He wants to go to Israel! What for?"

"Wants to emigrate to Israel."

"What for!"

"He wants to help build the new Jerusalem. He *says* he
knows Peretz. Something about the Kabbala in ten pockets..."

Ilka got up and said, "I know who it is."

"Then would you go down and give Harvey a hand with
him?"

Ilka took the elevator to the ground floor. Golda, the recep-
tionist, caught Ilka's eye and, tucking back the right corner
of her lips, shook her head. Harvey with a callow new beard
sat on the bench against the wall next to Carter, saying, "Well,
we really don't have that kind of an opening."

Carter said, "What kind of opening don't you have? How
do you know what kind of opening I have in mind? Why don't
you let me fill out an application?"

"We don't have applications, really," said Harvey.

"I want to help you build Israel without the old mistakes.
Israel hasn't made the old mistakes yet. Probably will, but
hasn't had the time to make them yet. I want to fill out an application."

Harvey asked him, "If you're looking for a job, maybe we
can help find you something. . . ."

"I have a job, thank you. What makes you think I'm in need
of help? Why are you so sure I can't be of help to you, eh?

Don't sell me cheap. I'm a seasoned journalist and an experienced negotiator. Why won't you make use of me?"

"Hi," said Ilka, "Carter."

"You know this fellow?" said Harvey. *"You* talk to him." And he rose gratefully and was going to walk out the door when Carter called after him, "Stay! Wait a moment! I know a little poem I want to say to you. It goes like this:

> *A little murder now and then,*
> *A little bit of burglarizing,*
> *Won't earn the hate of fellow-men*
> *As much as being patronizing."*

"Ha ha ha, all right," said Harvey and walked out.

Carter said to Ilka, "Come to Israel with me! I can't sleep in America!"

Ilka said, "Fishgoppel wants you to come to a seder with us."

"I'll come to a seder with you," said Carter.

★   ★   ★

A MAN WITH a yarmulke opened the door. A woman came out of the kitchen wiping her hands, made much of Ilka's mother and talked Yiddish to her.

"My mother doesn't know Yiddish," Ilka told her.

Women kept coming out of, and going back into, the kitchen—a sister, an aunt, two grandmothers, two daughters and a daughter-in-law. They all talked Yiddish to Ilka's mother. Ilka's mother kept saying, "Can I help you something?" The bell rang and it was a family of cousins with twin boys. More cousins came. Ilka said to Fishgoppel, "They should not wait for Carter. He may be ill again," and Ilka hoped Carter would not come.

Ilka's mother sat on one side of Ilka, saying, "By us in Vienna, we did that before this, Ilka, you remember?" Ilka remembered the mystery of the plate with the bone and the egg and the several little bowls of things; the blind Hebrew script, and someone pointing a finger to a spot on a page, saying, "Here's where we are"; and the mild activities: dipping the finger into the glass of wine; raising the glass and not drinking, raising it and drinking; passing around the table, on pieces of matzoh, the bitter herbs of affliction, which tasted delicious. Ilka didn't remember that she remembered these things.

Ilka followed the story in English and complained in a whisper to Fishgoppel, who sat on her other side: "If God *hardened* the Egyptians' hearts, was it fair to punish them for the hardness of their hearts?"

Fishgoppel said, "He knew the Egyptians would not let Israel go. Do *you* doubt the hardness of the hearts of the enemies of Israel?"

Ilka said, "It says *God* hardened their hearts."

The story unfolds in its own time, and in its time the meal was served by the women of the house. Fishgoppel opened Ilka's question to the table. They pounced gleefully and gave Ilka several answers, some beautiful, some silly, several mutually exclusive, leaving the original question unresolved and opening several new questions.

Ilka said, "What sort of God decrees the death of anybody's first-born children?"

One said, "The Egyptians decreed the death of every male child born to Israel."

One said, "He did it for the Jews."

One said, "They enslaved the Jews!"

"And God killed even the first-born of the slave girl!" cried Ilka. "What did she ever do to the Jews?"

"She was Egyptian. The Egyptians were the enemies of the God of Israel."

"Because *He* hardened their hearts!" cried Ilka.

Well, they said, that's how the story goes.

The leader of the seder at the head of the table said, "It was the time of the creation of Israel as a people. It was the time to show the might of His arm in the defense of Israel."

"He did it for the Jews."

Fishgoppel said: "You remember God's answer when Job questioned Him? 'Where wast thou when I laid the foundation of the earth. . . . Canst thou draw out leviathan with a hook? . . . Shall he that contendeth with the Almighty instruct him?' "

Someone said, "Job isn't even really Jewish."

Ilka said, "What about God telling the Jews to steal the Egyptians' gold and silver! I thought we were not supposed to steal?"

One said, "That was the legal compensation owed to slaves."

One said, "That was before the ten commandments."

The leader said, "It was a different time. Later the Talmud refined the moral issues."

Someone said, "What does she want all the time with the Egyptians? They were against the Jews."

Ilka shouted, "And that makes it all right to kill their first-born and steal their silver and drown them?"

Fishgoppel said, "Ilka! An army sent out against the Jews!"

The leader of the seder said, "There is a midrash. The angels are singing hosannas to God for the rescue of Israel from the Egyptians and God chides them. He says, 'How can you rejoice while my Egyptian children are weeping?' "

Someone said, "When we dip our fingers in the wine it represents the tears shed by our enemies."

"But nobody," cried Ilka, "grieves over the death of the first-born of the slave girl!"

"Yes, they do. You do. You are a Jew and you are doing

it!" It struck Ilka that all the time they were arguing with her, they kept looking sweetly and happily at her. They began to question her about this or that member of the Council for Eretz Israel Ilka had never heard of, whom they seemed to know all about. Soon they slipped into the coziness of a habitual conversation about the expressed public friendliness, but probable private hostility, toward the Jews of this or that political figure. Ilka wished Carter were here so that she might have caught his eye, or turned to him and whispered: "They are beating the boy!"

The phone rang. Nobody answered it because it was a holy day.

Ilka said to Fishgoppel, "I gave Carter the number."

Fishgoppel said to the leader of the seder, "It may be Ilka's friend and he may be ill." The leader of the seder said, "If he is ill it is not only allowed to answer, it is not allowed not to answer."

Carter said, "Can you call the hospital to come and get me?"

"You want to go back in the hospital?"

"I want to go in," said Carter.

"Let me come down," said Ilka.

"I don't know where I am," said Carter.

"You're not in the hotel?"

"I'm in a phone booth," said Carter.

"Where in a phone booth are you?"

"I don't know," said Carter.

"What street, Carter?"

"I don't know. They've taken down the street signs."

"You're on the East Side," said Ilka.

Carter said, "I'm trying to remember a trick. . . . When we used to lose our things mother made us remember everywhere that we had been. I can't remember where I've been! There is no picture in my mind. It's the booze has destroyed my brain cells." Ilka could hear him weeping.

Ilka said, "Ask somebody where you are, Carter, and I'll come down. Carter?"

Carter said, "That's how the British were going to catch the invaders . . . they were going to have to ask somebody."

"Carter, look outside. What's the building across the street from you? What's on the right? What's on your side of the street? On the left?"

Ilka said, "You're on Madison and Thirty-sixth. Stay in the booth and I'll come down."

"Call the hospital to come and get me," said Carter. "Tell Fishgoppel I'm sorry I missed the seder. How is your mother?" and Carter wept.

Ilka arrived before the hospital people and Carter was sitting on the little triangular seat inside the phone booth like a ship inside a bottle. He looked too large to have got in and unlikely to be able to get out. Ilka was pulling his hands when the minibus with the hospital logo drew up, the uniformed guard leaped out with his night stick raised, crying, "Watch out, lady."

"Don't, don't, don't!" Ilka shouted. "Don't hit him! He's perfectly gentle! He's signing *himself* in!"

Carter came out with his arm covering his head and was hoisted into the bus with his arm still up. He looked around and said, "Come with me!"

"Can I come?" said Ilka.

"*If* you sit *way* in the back and don't give me any trouble," said the guard. Ilka could tell he was embarrassed that he had mistaken the situation.

From where she sat Ilka could see Carter's arm still covering his head—perhaps he was confused; perhaps the buckle on the sleeve of his trenchcoat had got caught. Ilka watched the arm descend, little by little, as the bus shot north on Madison.

★ ★ ★

C ARL CALLED Ilka to tell her that the Union was interested in the civil-rights aspect of the review procedures. The strategy would be to haul out the whole vexed question of the definition of insanity: was there a clear distinction between the sane and the insane, between those inside and those outside institutions?

Ilka went up on Sunday. Strolling about the autumnal grounds, they passed two young people so intertwined they had slowed to a standstill. Ilka tried to figure out a decorous, middle-aged group consisting of a man and three women, one of them elderly. How were they related? Which was the inmate? "Well, but not if you're taking the train. I thought you were going to take the train," one woman said to the elderly woman. They stepped off the path, and moved up the grassy slope toward a bench under a golden tree.

Ilka said, "You can't tell which are the inmates, which are the visitors. There's no clear distinction between people inside and people outside the institution."

"There's a distinction," said Carter. "The people on the outside can hack it, the people inside cannot. That's a clear distinction."

Ilka came early the next Sunday and stood in the door of the large room with the primary-color chairs. She observed Carter standing, like an urbane headmaster on parents' day, chatting, over the head of a great fat boy on a chair, with an anxious, flustered and flirtatious mother. Carter's back was to Ilka but Ilka knew he had seen her: his foot was already turned. He was making a last remark and one more and yet one more last remark to deny to the other woman that he was about to walk away from her.

Carter came walking toward Ilka. He said, "Boy's been here since his twelfth birthday. He stabbed his mother with her sewing scissors. I want you to meet my friends." He walked Ilka across the room to where a man in a good white shirt sat watching television, but rose civilly and shook Ilka's hand. "Ilka, this is Francis Rhinelander. Francis signed himself in; he was hearing music."

"In toilets, elevators, out in the street!" said the man in the shirt.

Carter said, "You went to a restaurant. . . ."

"I went to the restaurant around from my office. Everybody's eating lunch. *I'm* hearing music! I ask the waitress, 'Could you do me a favor and turn off this inane music?' She says, 'What?' I go to the men's room and the toilets are playing violins. Monday I walk into the lobby of my building. The lobby is playing the 'Indian Love Call'! This is eight-thirty in the morning! I go into my office. I put through a call. The operator says, 'Hold on.' The telephone is playing 'A Tisket a Tasket,' in my ear! That's when I got my coat and got back on the elevator playing a whole orchestra! The cab is playing pop guitar! Signed myself into the nuthouse! I think, now, I got me a handle on this, Carter, look at this TV, will you? Now. Are *you* seeing a pretty girl brushing her teeth?"

"Very pretty," said Carter.

"Is she smiling?" asked Francis Rhinelander.

"Smiling to beat the band," said Carter.

"Now: I tried this out in front of my mirror: you can brush your teeth and be simultaneously smiling. In a sense you can't brush your teeth and *not* be simultaneously smiling. Is she *still* smiling?"

"Yes," said Carter.

"There you are then! *I*"— cried Mr. Rhinelander, with the look of acutest penetration of a man about to outwit himself— "*I'm* hearing her singing, 'Brush your teeth with Physolile and smile smile smile smile,' which is not in the realm of the possible. I've tried it in front of my mirror. It is a physiological impossibility to be simultaneously smiling and singing! *I'm hearing things,* " said Francis Rhinelander triumphantly. "So, Carter! When's the next forum?"

"Seven-thirty in the dining room," said Carter.

"You cleared it with King Kong?" asked Mr. Rhinelander.

"Cleared it with Kong."

"That's the big black bruiser over there—our guard," Mr. Rhinelander told Ilka.

"He's all right if you handle him," said Carter. "See you at seven-thirty?"

"Wouldn't miss it."

"Carry on," said Carter. With his hand on Ilka's shoulder, he steered her across the room, saying, "Clark? Will we see you at the forum in the dining room, seven-thirty?"

"You bet," said the bespectacled black young man in a wheelchair. He shook Ilka's hand with his left hand. His right arm and both legs were in casts.

"He thinks he is Clark Kent," Carter said, walking Ilka away.

"Who is Clark Kent?" asked Ilka.

"Oh, good grief!" said Carter. "Foreigners! Wolff, we're coming to sit with you." He turned around a green chair for Ilka and a yellow for himself and said, "Ilka, this is Wolff Samovicz, from Poland."

The man smiled mildly, sweetly, thought Ilka. He had no lower front teeth, and his neck and chest, where the collarless shirt missed a button, looked inflamed. Ilka stared in horror at the soft, swollen old man's hands lying in his lap, palms curled upward, crossed and tied at the wrists with a twisted thong. Carter said, "I told you about my friend Ilka from Vienna."

Wolff Samovicz said, "My first wife was from Vienna. I went to the Vienna *Handelsakademie,* nineteen-eighteen to -twenty-four." He lifted and offered Ilka his right hand and returned it, palm up, to his lap, where he laid it across his left hand. Ilka stared, for there was no thong. Ilka's imagination had tied and twisted the old man's helpless hands. Why?

Carter said, "Wolff lost his family, his wife."

"She was expecting our child," said Wolff Samovicz and nodded and seemed to be faintly smiling, and rocked with a little rocking movement at the waist.

Carter said, "Ilka lost her father."

Wolff Samovicz nodded and rocked.

Carter said, "I hope you have no plans for tonight. The forum meets in the dining room at seven-thirty."

"I will check my schedule," said Wolff Samovicz. "Carter is organizing," he told Ilka. He pointed all around the room, at Mr. Francis Rhinelander, leaning intently toward the television screen; at Clark Kent, who waved his remaining hand— Carter and Wolff Samovicz waved back; at the back of the fat boy sitting with his mother.

Carter said, "I'm an old organizer from way back. I tell you the first thing I ever organized was the New Haven chapter of the Anti-Defamation League, when I was just out of school?"

"And you were working for that little Jew," said Ilka, and found herself impaled on Carter's eye and blushed with the familiar and not unpleasurable expectation of learning something about herself that was at once true and not to her credit.

"What 'little' Jew?" asked Carter.

"Who told you about Kabbala."

"Gershom Hirsch was a six-footer. Now, why do you think you imagined him as a 'little' Jew?"

"Miss Weissnix was thinking about me," said Mr. Samovicz with his sweet smile.

Ilka laughed. She asked, "What forum are you organizing?"

"Wolff?" Carter gave him the floor.

Wolff Samovicz said, "Before has everybody been queuing for our pills an hour every morning, an hour every evening. Now we stand by alphabet, A's to H's, then I's to N's and so forth: twenty minutes. We elected Carter our chairman," said Mr. Samovicz. "He carries our resolutions . . ."

"Duly proposed, seconded and voted . . ." said Carter.

"To Mr. King Kong," said Wolff Samovicz. "Carter teaches us parliamentary procedure."

"The protocol of protocols," said Carter. "Wolff, I'm going to walk Ilka to the bus. Will you join us?"

Wolff Samovicz shook his head sadly and said, "I have not yet ground privilege."

"Why doesn't he have ground privileges?" asked the outraged Ilka as they walked down the corridor. "There's nothing wrong with him! Why is he even here?"

"He's depressed," said Carter. He opened the door to the excessively bright outdoors.

"He lost his wife, he lost his child. He lost! He lost! Why would he not be depressed!"

"Clinically depressed," Carter said. He held Ilka's elbow down the steps. "He had a new American family. He turned on the gas." Ilka had stopped walking. "It did him no good. He survived all over again. Life, she is a bitch. How is your mother?" asked Carter.

"She is talking about going back to the spot on the road before Obernpest!"

★   ★   ★

CARL ASKED Ilka to dinner to explain the game plan to her. Carter was to keep a log of the events in his review process, thereby earning a byline in the eventual report. The fact *of* such employment *by* the ACLU would in turn expedite the review process, and his release.

Ilka reported to Carter on Sunday. "So when are you going to get started?"

"Started?" said Carter.

"On the log. Of the review process."

"When the review process gets started," said Carter.

They passed the great fat boy and his mother sitting on chairs on the grass. The mother had taken off the boy's shoes and socks and exposed the bloated, mushroom-white calves to the thin new sun. She gave him a sock to hold. He held the sock by its two ends and looked at it and pulled it: it had the minimal elasticity of knitting; he pulled it again, and looked at it and pulled it. The mother detected a black speck or mote—or was that a little bug?—on the boy's instep. She leaned down to inspect it. She flicked it away. It was still there. She flicked again. She picked at it with the nail of her thumb.

Ilka said, "Could you meanwhile be writing up your experiences of past reviews?"

"Don't," said Carter.

"What?" said Ilka.

Carter said, "I may do it and then again I may not. I will probably do it. I will do it, but your wishing can have no bearing on the matter except to hassle me. I am unable to support your wishing."

"But you could be getting started!" said Ilka.

Carter said, "Dr. MacSamuels is dead."

"The hotel doctor! You mean dead?" Ilka stopped in the path.

"Heart attack," said Carter. "How is your mother?"

Winter came suddenly and harshly. Ilka and Carter sat in the large room with Wolff Samovicz. Carter said, "Wolff is teaching me Talmud."

"For instance," said Ilka.

"Carter?" Wolff gave Carter the floor.

Carter said, "Talmud teaches that it is a greater sin to shame your neighbor with words than to defraud him of his property."

Wolff said, "And why is this the greater?"

"Because property can be restored by the action of the court, but to cause another to blanch with shame is like drawing off his life's blood and is tantamount to murder. When a people—a whole race—is systematically humiliated, it is tantamount to genocide. Talmud says only he who is guilty of shaming his neighbor must abandon hope of ever getting out of Gehenna. Talmud is right: the loss of face is the only misfortune of which we can make no use at all. I can learn from pain, poverty, unhappy love, because I can get over them; I hardly know how to wish away past sufferings, which have made me what I have become; it would be like wishing my own face away. But there is no use to which I can put my humiliations. They don't strengthen my muscle for suffering. They erode me. They don't dissipate. The one thing from which one does not recover is the loss of face."

Wolff Samovicz, who had been looking affectionately at Carter, said, "There are losses one does not recover. There are other losses." He had begun to rock.

"I know, I know there are. I know there are," said Carter. "I know there are."

Ilka's mother cooked Carl a Thanksgiving goulash.

Ilka reported to Carter. She said, "Carl says the Negro and the Jew have a parallel experience."

Carter said, "Yes, indeedy: parallels are two lines that run side by side and never meet except in infinity."

Carter said, "Will you come and see me Christmas Day? Holidays are a bitch."

Spring, and Ilka told Carter, "Carl has got me an interesting job at the ACLU."

It was June. The crowns of the trees on the far side of the hill showed in their lush fullness before so much as a leaf had turned dusty or dog-eared. Ilka said, "I won't be coming out next Sunday."

Carter's eyes snapped open.

Ilka said, "It's my vacation. I'm taking my mother to Austria. Fishgoppel and I are thinking if she sees that road and sees the spot where she left my father maybe she might put it behind her."

"Will you come and see me the Sunday after you get back?"

"I'll come and report." Ilka glanced sideways at Carter's heavy, unsmiling face. She asked, "Is the forum still meeting?"

"Yes."

"Does Wolff Samovicz have his ground privilege yet?"

"No." Carter remained depressed and Ilka found in herself a lethargy—an absence of whatever it would have taken to give him comfort. Her mind was on her own backward journey.

★   ★   ★

THE MAN in the passport office told them where to go to get their passport photos: it would take a good twenty minutes—it might take half an hour. He was sending down for coffee and Danish and asked them if they would like anything.

The stewardess spoke German with an Austrian voice and Ilka's childhood address came intact into her head. "Mutti, hey listen: "AchterBezirkJosephstädterStrasse81ZweiterStock-Tür9."

They burst into the streets of Vienna. "The J *Wagen!*" cried her mother. "It goes—it used to go to Vati's shop. You were too small to remember. . . ."

But it turned out that Ilka remembered what she did not remember, as if she had reentered a childhood tale: she might not recall how it came out but knew what the next sentence was going to say. "JosephstädterStrasse will be the next left. It is! Cobbles! And nothing over four stories! There was a bank that had a door that cut the corner off the building that was closed when I went down with Vati, the morning after Hitler. Here it is! Mutti! You see! The corner door!" To be proved correct had that odd little importance one feels in presenting certification—a driver's license, a library card: this proves that this is me. The person standing before you is the person standing before you. It is I who lived here. "Mutti! Schmutzki's sweet shop. They had a mongoloid son. He used to peck his head forward like a pigeon, with every step. Like this."

"Oh, Ilka!" Ilka's mother laughed.

"I used to practice walking like that."

"Ilka!"

Remembering is a complicated act. The often-documented alteration of the size of the object, because of the viewer's altered size, is its simplest aspect. There is, besides, that coincidence of the ghostly, transparent, unstable stuff memory is made of, with the hard-edged material object, which, as often as not, is, in fact, altered: "The Schmutzki's sweet shop selling shoes!" Ilka's mother peered through the display window and said, "The counter is the same counter but they have it on the other side. The cash register is in the same place but this is a modern cash register." And there is the degree of history the viewer shares with the view, whether it's the fact, merely, of having passed, or of having been at home here, where his neighbor had hated him to death.

Ilka said, "The Schmutzkis 'put their head in the gas oven,' as the grownups put it."

"Frau Schmutzki said to me, 'What country is going to give us a visa, with the boy?' Walter was his name. They put their heads in the gas oven, the father, mother, and the boy."

"I used to lie in bed trying to picture them kneeling side by side. I'd fall asleep trying to imagine three heads into one oven."

Ilka's mother said, "The next time, I can see that one might rather put one's head in the gas oven."

"One might survive again," said Ilka.

"One might survive all over again," said her mother. "I can see how one might rather put one's head in the gas oven. Here it is. Number eighty-one. The court has got shabby."

"AchterBezirkJosephstädterStrasse81*ZweiterStock*... that's the second floor. Those are our windows. Let's go up and ring the bell!"

"What are we going to say?" asked Ilka's mother.

Ilka remembered the speckled marble stairs and how they curled around the central elevator no one ever used. "Achter-BezirkJosephstädterStrasse81ZweiterStock*Tür9*—door number 9."

"What are we going to say?"

Ilka rang and listened. She said, "The kitchen is immediately on the left, with the maid's room behind. The foyer goes to the right, past the dining room, past the bathroom, and makes an ell to your and Vati's bedroom. There's nobody home. What happened, Mutti, to the little green marble boy on the tree stump taking a splinter out of his foot on a little round doily on the console next to the bathroom?"

"I don't know. It must be somewhere."

"There they are." The slurp of slippers approached from the left. The kitchen.

"What are we going to say?"

An eye in the peephole. A woman's voice—not a young voice—said, *"Ja?"* and Ilka asked for her father: "Please I want to speak with Herrn Max Weissnix?"

"There is no Weissnix. Here lives Hohenzoll. You can enquire from the superintendent on the first floor."

Ilka said, *"Danke schön,"* which means "Thank you beautifully."

The woman said, *"Bitte schön,"* which means "Beautifully please," and clicked the peephole shut and slurped to the right around the ell into Ilka's parents' bedroom.

★   ★   ★

Out the train window Ilka watched the summer meadows
turn into foothills, which raised themselves up and became
Alps. "Are you all right?" she kept asking her mother. Ilka's
mother said she was all right, but when they stood, with their
bags, on the platform of the Obernpest railway station she said,
"I have to sit. There's a porter." Ilka saw the porter. He looked
to be a man of fifty. Where had he been standing—or lying
or sitting—when the columns marched through here? Inside
his house? Eating his supper? Had he looked out of the window? Ilka waved to a young porter, her own age. He had been
a little boy when the columns marched. Ilka asked him for the
nearest hotel.

"We'll have supper and go to bed. After breakfast, tomorrow, we'll do whatever it is you want to do."

Ilka's mother was too tired to want supper, and the next
morning she did not want breakfast. She did not want anyone
to drive them. "It's out in that direction, just outside of town.
Not far."

Early morning and nobody about—a pretty town by MGM,
waiting for winter and Sonya Henie. Ilka's mother said, "They
marched us *toward* Obernpest, so the mountain will be on this
side." She drew its profile in the air. "Not far. What I don't
understand is this lake all of a sudden. There was no lake. I
would have remembered a lake."

"You said there was a lake!" shouted Ilka.

"Ilka, Lake Bautzen, where you and Vati and I stayed when
you were a baby! Let's walk in that direction."

They turned their backs on the silver morning lake and
walked, and Ilka said, "Are you all right?"

The light was so pure it picked out the stems of the individual firs up the mountain wall like the hairs of a new crewcut. Ilka's mother said, "There was a path just like that path that forks off to the left, there, except it was on the right, and the mountain was on the left." Ilka's eye traced the path, like a zigzag parting, to where it lost itself in the rock face above the treeline. Out of the menagerie of English phrases stored in the back of Ilka's mind one separated itself. She said, "Like the monstrous beauty of an elephant's behind. Who said that?" Ilka yearned—and found she was not at liberty—to love these Austrian wonders all above and around.

"I know there was no lake," said her mother. Soon a six-lane *Autobahn* lay across their path. "This is new, of course. We have to get over there."

They watched the cars sizzling past and Ilka said, "How are we going to get across there?"

"So let's walk along it on this side. Unless. I was thinking: they turned us around. It's in the other direction!"

"Mutti! What direction?"

"The other direction."

They turned around. "I remember that mountain that looks like a man with one shoulder higher was on our right. The one I'm looking for, behind, a little to the left of the spot on the road was lower—really one of the foothills."

"Mutti!" said Ilka. They walked awhile and Ilka said, "You're tired?"

"I'm tired."

"Sit, Mutti, here's a rock on the side of the road."

"Where are you going to sit?"

"Here is a tree stump."

Ilka's mother said, "There was a bush—like that bush—near the spot where Vati sat down."

Ilka saw a bush, a lot of bushes. She saw a dirt road fork off to the right. Ilka saw the hairy mountain wall, the sheer rock, the sheer blue sky, a lot of stones, clumps of grass, a mass

of blue harebells. What a lot of flowers there were everywhere!
A little wind fingered Ilka's hair, now her bare arm. She
slapped at her ankle, but the ant's small poison had already
raised a red welt. Ilka's eyes followed a column of ants, their
hectic portage up the slope of the ant heap that looked to be
in a state of healthy and industrious economy.

Ilka's mother said, "It could be the *other* side of Obernpest.
I think we must have approached Obernpest from the side, because there was no lake."

"Mutti, breakfast."

It was midmorning. The pretty thoroughfares were asquirm
with sunburned young and sunburned middle-aged German
flesh.

"Not even good coffee," said Ilka's mother. She said, "Vati
was sure there was a place called Obernpest or something like
that not ten minutes by car from Lake Bautzen. Maybe it wasn't
Bautzen. I remember, the year before you were born, we stayed
in Mallnitz. I can't remember if there was a lake in Mallnitz."

In the plane home Ilka's mother said, "That was not our doorbell we rang."

"Yes it was. Door nine, first stairway, second floor."

"Aha!" said Ilka's mother. "In Vienna the second floor is
the mezzanine and the third floor is the second floor. The door
we rang was mezzanine door nine."

They hit Idlewild late on a dog day. Ilka kept a nervous eye
on her mother; she looked exhausted. "Are you free?" Ilka
asked a black porter, who replied, "Today I'm not. Tomorrow
I will be."

"What?" The hot and irritable Ilka, suspecting a proposi-
tion, scowled at the laughing Negro.

On Sunday Ilka went to see Carter. She told him about the
laughing Negro porter who was not free but would be free tomorrow.

Ilka told Carter about the search for the spot on the side of the Obernpest road. She said, "Of course, there is no spot on the road."

Ilka told Carter about the German girl in the subway who had hung from Ilka's strap and studied her German guide book. Ilka did arithmetic: the girl had been an infant in the Hitler years. She smiled at the girl. The girl asked in a strong Berlin accent, "This is correct going uptown to Harlem?"

Ilka had said, "No. For Harlem you change trains where I get off."

The girl from Berlin checked the station passing outside the window and said, "This train is going uptown."

Ilka said, "There is uptown and Uptown."

The girl from Berlin consulted her guide and said, "Uptown is going correct." Ilka got off the train that would carry the girl from Berlin to the Bronx.

And now the time had come for Ilka's naturalization. "I will sign a piece of paper and be an instant American. I will be 'naturalized'! Until today I have been unnatural. I've asked Ebony and Fishgoppel to be my witnesses."

Ilka looked up "naturalize" in her dictionary:

> naturalize 1. (botanical) to introduce into a region and cause to flourish as if native. 2. to bring into conformity with nature. 3. to invest with the rights and privileges of a citizen.

★　　　★　　　★

I N A S M A L L courtroom cleared for the purpose, the prospective American was tested and found competent to name her district's senator and congressman, and to recite the terms of the office of each. Ilka promised that she would not violently overthrow the government of the United States, would commit no moral turpitude, and thought that she would, if required, take up arms for America.

Thought? Ilka's examiner looked at Ilka over the rims of her half eyes. She was a soft-fleshed elderly woman with short battleship-gray hair. A very large purple orchid was pinned to the bosom of her flowered dress. She asked what Ilka meant by "thought."

Ilka meant she thought she would take up arms.

"You 'think' you would take them up?"

"I just mean I would have to think before taking up arms," said Ilka. She looked the other woman in the eye because she did not believe the other did not, in her heart, believe what Ilka believed: "To take up arms against living people is something one would have to think a lot about, I mean, wouldn't you?"

"Certainly not," said Ilka's examiner. "If every American was going to think if they would or would not take up arms we'd never get to fight any war at all. No," said the examiner, "if my country required me to take up arms I would take them up as my father and his father and his father's father did before him, and I can't put my signature to this paper until you can assure me that you would take up arms for America and for the things that have made America the greatest nation upon this earth. If required, would you take up arms for America?"

"Yes," said Ilka. "I think."

The examiner straightened the edges of the papers on her desk and said, "Go and think outside, and when you are ready tell the guard and I'll recall you. Next!"

Ilka went outside. Fishgoppel and Ebony were talking together. Ilka discussed her problem with her two witnesses. Ebony said, "I saw her go in—the old Southern biddy. She's just going to hassle you." Fishgoppel said, "She's an anti-Semite. There'll never be conscription for women! She's raising a problem that will never come up."

Ilka said, "It's not 'will I' but 'would I' take up arms and maybe I would. Against the next Hitler I would!" And so Ilka was able to resolve her problem: "I'll say I 'would' and the problem will never come up."

The examiner watched Ilka's approach over the rims of her half eyes. Ilka stood before her. "Have you finished thinking?"

"Yes."

The examiner bent her battleship-gray head over Ilka's naturalization papers, poised her pen and asked, "If required, would you take up arms for America?"

"Yes, I would," said Ilka, "I think," and the examiner, completing the signature on which she was already embarked, handed Ilka the paper without looking up and said, "Go on, get out of here. Next."

★   ★   ★

I N A W O O D - P A N E L E D room, Ilonka Weissnix and some couple of dozen brand-new Americans of many shades and accents took their communal oath. The flag hung peacefully. A small, bald judge with a remarkably fine voice invited them to repeat the words after him. When Ilka found herself swearing that she swore "without reservation of mind" she felt a thrill of love for a law so subtle it could be trusted to find out the secretly crossed fingers within her own heart.

Ilka invited her witnesses to lunch in a little restaurant across from the courthouse.

"Are you still teaching fifth-grade history?" Ilka asked Ebony.

"Nope," said Ebony. "I got my certificate to teach the children whom the public school system will not accommodate. I'd like to see a Hispanic heading up the New York system. Show me a Hispanic child and I'll show you a child that is loved."

Fishgoppel stared at her. She said, "Everybody knows Jewish children are loved."

Ebony nodded her head profoundly and said, "You need to see a Puerto Rican father deliver a daughter to a friend's house and pick her up again—like a little ingénue."

Fishgoppel said, "Jews care enough about their children to give them an education."

Ebony said, "Negroes were lynched if they learned the alphabet."

"We had pogroms," said Fishgoppel.

"Slavery," said Ebony.

"Holocaust!" cried Fishgoppel.

"Are there no griefs that aren't racist or anti-Semitic!" shouted Ilka.

"Like what?" said Fishgoppel and Ebony, turning their agitated faces against Ilka.

"Old age," Ilka said.

"In Israel," said Fishgoppel, "they have hardly any nursing homes. Jews love their parents."

"The Egyptian language," said Ebony, "doesn't have the word 'nursing home' because they don't have the concept, nor 'racism' nor 'slavery.' "

"They enslaved Israel four hundred years!" Fishgoppel shouted.

Ebony said, "There is not an iota of evidence that there was slavery in Egypt," and she got up.

"What about the Bible!" shouted Fishgoppel, and she got up.

"Except the Bible," said Ebony and they put on their coats and walked out the door in different directions.

All these things Ilka reported to Carter as they walked about the hospital grounds on a Sunday afternoon. It was August. Ilka could not help the sense that this was a Grande Jatte, where she strolled with her lover.

"Where are we going!" asked Carter. Ilka was moving him off the path, up the grassy slope and over the hill.

"Are you fond of nature?" Carter asked Ilka.

Ilka laughed. His backward glance toward the safety of the complex of orange brick buildings apprised Ilka of her own intention. She kept walking. In the dense little copse out of sight behind the hill, Ilka pulled Carter onto the grass.

Carter said, "This is insane."

Ilka lay on her back on the unaccommodating ground among last year's dead sticks and papery foliage. Through the low-growing vines she could see, at a considerable distance, the hospital gates, the waiting bus. Ilka looked up at the large face laboring above her, the eyes closed. Ilka kept her eyes open and kept her attention on the gorgeous commotion in her parts.

"My, you've learned," said Carter.

It was September. They stood by the bus. Ilka said, "Fishgoppel is leaving for Israel. I can't come next Sunday. I'm making Fishgoppel a good-bye party."

"You could come," said Carter. "Make the party Saturday. Come and see me on Sunday."

"Carter, I can't. Fishgoppel observes the Jewish Saturday."

Carter said, "You could come up Sunday."

"Maybe I should just come up every other Sunday. There are so many things I have to do."

Carter said, "Come every Sunday, or don't come at all."

Ilka said, "Maybe I shouldn't come for a while."

Carter said, "All right, come every other Sunday."

But Ilka said, "I think maybe I better not come."

"Come up with the William Rauschenquists. I'm going to write to William," said Carter.

Ilka found it was not hard to say "I can't."

Carter said, "The Sunday *after* Fishgoppel's party. You could come up."

Ilka said, "I think not."

Carter said, "I'm going to start writing up my log for the review process."

Ilka shook her head. Ilka walked beside Carter and tried to think what Carter might say to her that would change her mind, and there was nothing he could say. Carter Bayoux had, so far as Ilka was concerned, run out of rabbits to pull out of his hat. At the bus stop he said, "I'm going to write to the governor."

Ilka raised her face and touched her lips to the paralyzed flesh of Carter Bayoux's cheek. Ilka saw his despair and it tempted her compliance as little as someone who has overeaten is tempted by the offer of another helping.

Ilka sat on the bus and mourned her absence of sorrow: She understood that if Carter could wear out his power to move her, then Ilka would wear out her power to move the loves that had not yet so much as begun.

END

STILL ILKA and Carter were not finished with each other. One Monday the hospital sent Carter home. Ilka took the subway down to the Bloomsbury Arms. They talked, and they made love. They sat on the edge of the bed and watched movies, but their story has come to the part where an invisible forefinger and thumb take hold of the left bottom corner of the leaf of a calendar and tear it off, and tear off the next, and the next, speeding the passage of a time in which nothing happens. Ilka's mother cooked Carter Thanksgiving goulash. In the week between Christmas and the New Year Carter told Ilka that he was leaving New York. The *Herald* liked the idea of a West Coast column. Stanford had offered him a series of lectures that might be parlayed into a course—into a book. He might raise a grant someplace to do a book. *The Third World and the World Press.* One could always raise a grant. "Poor old Ellen! Here I come again! And you will visit," Carter said to Ilka. "Now you're a proficient New Yorker, I'll teach you San Francisco."

Ilka didn't know if she would come to San Francisco, but she knew it was Carter whom she loved.

Carter said, "Love somebody else; just don't tell me about it." Ilka liked to think that Carter was leaving with the generous intention of freeing her; it was a notion Ilka was fond of.

Ilka took Carter to Idlewild and returned to the empty city, freshly washed by a winter squall and glittering in its own reflection. Carl took her to dinner; they talked about Carter. Ilka marveled at the unreasonable difference it made to have him suffering in San Francisco instead of the Bloomsbury Arms downtown, or the upstate hospital. She wrote Carter that they had both been right: she *had* made love with Carl and it *was* Carter she loved. Carter sent the letter back with a note: "Don't lay that on me ever again." It was not the note, it was her own handwriting, which had come home to her and lay on the foyer table, that was peculiarly unpleasant. Ilka walked close to the opposite wall for several days before she could bear to pick the thing up and drop it in a drawer.

The calendar leaves detach themselves at an increasing speed. The old calendar is replaced with the new. Carl is gone. Stanley has died. Ebony was moving to Toronto.

"You can't do that!" cried Ilka. "Don't everybody leave me!"

"I can't work in a New York school system run by all these Jewish Shankers." Ebony had a friend in Toronto. The friend's daughter had just married. The friend had a big old apartment.

Ilka called Carter in San Francisco. "Wasn't that an anti-Semitic remark to make to me?"

"Of course," said Carter.

"And I didn't say anything! How can you argue with an anti-Semitic friend who has just lost her husband! The fact is I never argue with Ebony, even when I disagree with everything she says."

"*I* never argue with Ebony," said Carter. "You don't disagree with a tiger you got by the tail. Have you been seeing Ebony?"

"We have lunch," said Ilka. "I always need a month to recover. Then I want to have lunch again." But the Shanker remark persisted in Ilka's mind like a small stone inside a shoe with which one continues to walk. Ilka's affection for Ebony was larger than the size of the stone. Before Ebony left for Toronto the two women made a sentimental trip to Connecticut.

Ilka said, "Let's have dinner at the damn White Fence Inn!"

"You bet!" said Ebony. "There's our hill. That's the house. This is the driveway!"

"Ebony, shall we ring the bell? We can ask to use the bathroom."

"We don't know who's living in there now. They may not
want *me* in their bathroom. That's why I travel with my own
equipment." Ebony carried an empty can inside the glove com-
partment.

They passed Dr. John's shingle. They walked into a dear little yellow stone museum. Ilka was reading the names of the
patterns of American pressed glass: Snake Drape, Hooks and
Eyes, Hooks and Darts, Stippled Double Loop with Moose
Eyes, Beaded Moose Eyes in Sand, Inverted Baby's Thumb-
print, Oswego Waffle with Banded Spear Point, when Ebony,
in the doorway, said, "Psst! Show you something!" Ilka followed her past fans, needle-cushions, samplers, faceless wigs
and headless bridal outfits, to a vast canvas, heroically framed
in gilded scrollwork: *Battle of Thomastown.* The upper left corner showed two sunlit clouds symbolically fleeting. Below was
a panorama of smoke and gloom, with cannon, boots, peaked
caps, opposing flags on the move. Right of center, a conference
of generals unfurled a map.

Ebony was pointing to the group commanding the lower left
half of the composition: On a huge stomping horse, which he
controlled with the reins in his left hand, sat a young Negro
soldier in a cocked tricorn; his braided coat flared behind him
like a wing. In his raised right fist he grasped the rope that
bound a crumple of broken Red Coats, bandaged legs and
heads, and arms in slings. The soldier's face, sketched in agitated strokes of lampblack, had its mouth wide in a crisis of
exhaustion—or was it the horror, or the exhilaration, of war?

"A lot of Negro soldiers fought for America!" said Ebony.
"Didn't you know that!"

All these years Ilka had imagined a cottage White Fence Inn,
but it was a rather large, rather grand place. Elegant pilasters
connected the verandas surrounding each of the four stories.

The dining room was a high, immense, crimson room with a crimson carpet. Gilt ropes caught back the velvet curtains. It was off season. There was nobody except Ebony and Ilka and a very old black waiter.

Ebony said, "There's a luncheonette on the next block. Are you very hungry?"

"Yes. I'm very hungry," said Ilka.

The old black waiter, inclining his head solemnly, led them to a table by a window that gave onto a lawn bounded by a white fence. The waiter held the back of Ebony's chair for her and came around and held Ilka's chair. He poured them water. He brought hot rolls wrapped in a white serviette. He recommended the soup, the freshest fish. They might want to wait till later to decide on their dessert. The black old man and the black woman and the young white woman did not catch one another's eyes, but played out a courteous and delicious game of protocol.

Ilka had a new Carl. He belonged to the species of man who brings a chair and you discover you are tired. He brought Ilka her coat. It was winter.

Ilka tended, in those years, and for years to come, to drop Carter Bayoux's name to black people, who knew who Carter was. To white people, who knew nothing about him, Ilka was driven to say, "I have a friend who thinks . . ." "A friend of mine used to say. . . ." She told Carl about Carter. Carl said "He sounds fascinating!" too rapidly, but not rapidly enough to hide the involuntary widening of his eyes.

Carter was under the weather again. He called by day and he called several times at night. "What is the time?" he asked. "Is this Tuesday?" Ilka wanted to take the phone off the hook, but Carl said, "You can't cut him off! Suppose he's seriously ill?" Ilka and Carl discussed Carl's excessive interest in Carter Bayoux. Ilka said, "Carter used to say, 'Whatever it is, race and sex will bring it out.' "

"Bring out what?"

Ilka told Carl how his eyes had widened when she told him about Carter and Carl was struck: "How observant you are!" he cried, passionately embracing Ilka.

Carter sent a bad piece of African sculpture as a wedding present. The baby was born next fall. Ilka was nursing the child when the phone rang and Carl said, "A friend of Carter's from California wants to come and see you."

"Invite him over!"

"Her," said Carl.

Carter's friend was a large, high-pink and golden child, who looked seventeen but was probably twenty-four or -five. Carl stared. Afterward Carl and Ilka referred to her as the Californian Specimen. The Specimen filled the room the way young people fill a room, in the sense in which light fills a room. There was a glow of skin if not of eye. If she was no more than ordinarily pretty, she was more than ordinarily long and straight of leg, and squarer of jaw, and blond. Ilka invited her to sit. The girl sat down and put her golden head into her hands and wept. Ilka sat beside her; Carl brought her a tissue. She wiped her eyes and said, "He's back in the hospital. They didn't give him the grant! Did you know when he needed his brother just to come and talk, his brother left a bottle of bourbon at the hotel desk?" She wiped her nose and raised her face to Ilka's face. "He wanted me to come and see you. He thinks you are terrific!" Carl took Ilka aside and asked her if it would be suitable to send Carter a check.

Ilka called Ebony. Ebony had moved to St. Louis. Toronto had not worked out. Ilka told her about the Californian Specimen.

"Well, I'll be!" said Ebony. "Another hat! Another rabbit!"

"So blond," said Ilka, "so young, so healthy, so good-hearted. One day she will give up on him. She will step right over him and walk right on. But she'll have learned something, Ebony, don't you think? She will be the better for it."

"Sure will have learned something!" said Ebony.

The Specimen called from California and wept and said, "He's starting to drink again! You know what's going to happen if he starts again!"

"Sure," said Ilka.

"What can I do!" cried the girl.

"You could ask him if he would like a cup of coffee," said Ilka.

Ilka heard the girl in California ask Carter if he wanted coffee. "He doesn't want coffee. He's going down to get a bottle of bourbon!"

"You can hold his coat," said Ilka, "for him to put his arms into."

Carter called, and said, "Guess who's turned up on the West Coast. Ebony! I found her a little apartment round the corner. Poor Ebony! Still looking for a bed to sleep in! She says she can't sleep."

"How are you sleeping these days?"

"This way and that," said Carter. "How is Fishgoppel?"

"Settled in Israel."

"Has she? How is your mother?"

"Good. All right. She takes my beautiful little girl to the sandbox. The burglars are letting her alone, for the time being."

"Well, that's good," said Carter. "For the time being is good."

Carter's Californian friend called, weeping. Carter was dead. He had been in a really bad way. . . . It took Ilka's mind many hours to turn Carter into a dead person. She called Ebony. Ebony was back in New York. Ilka and Ebony talked and talked. They talked of the part of their lives that they had lived together in a world where women lose their men, a world without Stanley in it, without Carter.

Carter's friends at the United Nations held a memorial service. Ilka met Jonas, who looked bottomlessly sad. And Ilka met his wife, Ellen, who seemed an intelligent, perfectly nice woman. Ilka was surprised. They returned to the West Coast immediately after the service, not staying for the "read-in" planned for the late evening.

"When is it?" Ilka asked Ebony.

"Just his students are arranging it," said Ebony.

"Where?" asked Ilka.

"I think," said Ebony, "they'd just as soon other people didn't come."

"They don't want you to come!" said Ilka.

"They don't want *you* to come," said Ebony.

Ilka said, "Don't they know that . . . ?"

"They know that."

"I'm not the enemy!" said Ilka.

Ebony said, "They think you will exploit Carter."

"Do *you* think I exploited Carter?"

"No. I think the other way around."

"He did not!" cried Ilka. If it was disagreeable to be thought exploitative it was more unpleasant to be thought to have been exploited.

"I exploited him too," said Ilka. "When I'd learned all the American he could teach me, didn't I move on? Didn't I step right over him and move on? No, but Fishgoppel sent me Blake for my birthday, and, Ebony, you know that poem 'Mercy has a human heart, Pity a human face'?"

"I don't know that poem," said Ebony.

"I have thought that Carter and I were merciful to each other."

Ebony said, "I think that you were."

Ilka couldn't leave it alone. "How do they think that I exploited Carter?"

"That you *will* exploit him."

"How will I exploit Carter?"

"They think you will write a book about him. *They* want to write the book about Carter. They want the book about Carter to be a black book. I think what they really want is to have a love fest and they'll be more comfortable just among themselves."

"Well, that's just too bad," said Ilka, "because if there's going to be a love fest, I'm coming too."

"Okey-dokey," said Ebony.

Ebony sat with Ilka, a little back of the small circle of Carter Bayoux's graduate students. They had come all the way from Stanford. The Carter Bayoux, in their reminiscent stories, was a recognizable but different man from Ilka's tragic, cosmopolite lover. This was a black man among blacks, a man among men.

A bespectacled student read an interview he'd done with Carter for the student paper—a young Turk come to beard the old lion, being bearded and bested by Carter's mischievousness.

A tall elegant student told the story Carter had told about losing his head in—the student couldn't remember where in upstate New York.

Ilka wanted to say, "It was in Knossos, New York."

A bearded student read a paper on Carter Bayoux's theory of the American Negro's fear-hate-fear complex in relation to the white man. A stout and beautiful student read a paper on the psychological damage of bearing one's slave name. Ilka unlocked her teeth and opened her mouth and in an English congested with accent said, "Carter has asked me once to ask my cousin Fishgoppel how she got such a name." Carter's black graduate students turned their heads reluctantly in Ilka's direction. Ilka said, "It means 'Fishfork.' My cousin thinks it was given to her grandfather by a Polish commissar trying to be a comedian." The dozen young black faces might not choose, but neither could they help, the degree of kindness with which they were regarding Ilka. Ilka's tongue loosened. Ilka said,

"Carter said my name was a joke also. I told Carter Weissnix means 'Knownothing,' but Carter said it meant 'Notwhite,' because I am a Jew."

The young black men continued to look sympathetically at Ilka until they understood that she had finished speaking. Then they turned back into their circle and went on with what they had been going to say before Ilka interrupted.